# "You don't want me to stay away."

Brice's stubbled chin grazed the underside of her jaw, making it impossible to refute his accusation.

How could she even speak when the ethereal vibrations of his hot breath skimming her skin paralyzed her vocal cords?

All that escaped was a small mewling sound from the back of Cassie's throat. It didn't sound like the protest she meant to project and Brice didn't take it as discouragement.

Delicate kisses replaced his breath along her jaw. The feathery sensation penetrated her senses, muting the wisdom to push away and run. What was the point? She'd already learned the futility of trying to outrun a wolf.

Cassie tipped her head, exposing her neck. He could rip out her throat if he wanted, but he seemed content to nip and lick and suck every inch. Trembling, she felt no less devoured as her strength failed from the hum of sheer pleasure.

Dangerous, oh, so dangerous.

# AWAKENED BY THE WOLF

## KRISTAL HOLLIS

First Published in Great Britain 2016
By Mills & Boon, an imprint of HarperCollins*Publishers*
1 London Bridge Street, London, SE1 9GF

© 2016 Kristal Hollis

ISBN: 978-0-263-92175-5

89-0616

Our policy is to use papers that are natural, renewable and recyclable products and made from wood grown in sustainable forests. The logging and manufacturing processes conform to the legal environmental regulations of the country of origin.

Printed and bound in Spain
by CPI, Barcelona

Southern born and bred, **Kristal Hollis** holds a psychology degree and has spent her adulthood helping people and animals. When a family medical situation resulted in a work sabbatical, she began penning deliciously dark paranormal romances as an escape from the real-life drama. But when the crisis passed, her passion for writing love stories continued. A 2015 Golden Heart® Award finalist, Kristal lives with her husband and two rescued dogs at the edge of the enchanted forest that inspires her stories.

To Sylvia Plumey, my 9th grade English teacher—a promise kept.

Sincere thanks to Brenda McLaughlin, Candace Colt, Joanne Calub and Raven Winter— my awesome critique partners. To my first fans, Angela Jarvis, Michelle Ochoa and LuAnn Nemeth, much love for your unwavering encouragement and support. Mom, thank you for the gift of reading. An extra special thanks to Keith, the hero of my heart. And to my editor, Ann Leslie Tuttle— thank you for believing.

# Chapter 1

Naked and wet, Brice Walker crouched on the back porch of his grandmother's log cabin. The splintered grooves of the weathered boards bit sharply into his sore hands and feet, intensifying the throb in his right leg.

He focused his better-than-human night vision and tuned his ears to any movement along the forest's dark tree line. Every muscle clenched in fight-or-flight readiness, though he was too tired for either. The three-day trek in wolf form and subsequent swim up the Chatuge River had overstretched his endurance.

If things were different, he would've driven from Atlanta to his grandmother's home. His present situation being what it was, he no longer enjoyed that freedom.

He'd fucked up. Colossally.

One careless mistake and he'd lost his family, his friends, his home.

Regret flared inside him like a backdraft. He tried to swallow the burning ache, but its fiery fingers fastened around his throat and squeezed until his mouth prickled from the embers.

His banishment was well deserved and if he got caught slinking into the territory, the sentinels would waste no time hauling his bare ass in front of the Alpha.

All things considered, Brice would've preferred catching rabies to facing his father. Distance didn't always make the heart grow fonder. Sometimes it fostered bitterness.

A faint August breeze stroked his skin like a lover grown cold and distant. Out of habit, he sniffed the night air. The familiar scents of pine and honeysuckle eluded him. Once his nose had been his pride. Now he depended on his eyes, ears and gut instinct to compensate for his lost sense of smell.

The evening symphony of crickets calling their mates

salted the wound of his loss. Scent triggered a Wahya's mating urge. Despite the heightened acuity of his other senses, only his nose could lead him to his true mate.

With a heavy humph, he shook. The water droplets that had pebbled on his heated body thwacked against the deck. A silver-coated house key fastened around his biceps with corded silver—the only substance that wouldn't disintegrate during a shift—slapped against his arm. Each time it struck, electric shocks pinched his skin.

He untied the key and rubbed it between his fingers to dispel the residual shift energy, wondering if he wasn't about to make the second biggest mistake of his life.

When his uncle, Adam Foster, had whisked Brice to Atlanta after his first epic fail, he didn't have time to say goodbye to his beloved grandmother. Of course, he hadn't known that his uncle's offer of respite disguised a permanent relocation.

Brice unlocked the back door. His heart paused at the click. For the past five years, the Walker's Run pack had considered him wolfan non grata.

Trusting that Margaret Walker wouldn't disown her only surviving grandson, Brice clamped down on his nerves and limped into the kitchen. The dim light above the stove softly illuminated the pie on the counter.

First his heart swelled. During his college days, Granny always had a fresh-baked pie for him on his weekend visits.

Next Brice's gut clenched, his stomach bellowed and his mouth watered, putting him in serious danger of drooling. Despite the ample game he'd encountered on his journey, he hadn't eaten in days. The thought of killing again triggered nauseating sweats—if he was lucky. God-awful flashbacks if he wasn't.

Silently he snagged a small saucer from the cabinet, a spoon from the drawer, a knife from the wood block. Then he cut a large wedge out of the pie. The first bite of sweet-tart deliciousness slid down his throat, slow and easy.

*Mmm, cherry!* His entire body sighed.

One piece wasn't enough. He had to have two. A chug of milk washed down the third. Abandoning all etiquette, he scarfed down the rest and licked the pie pan clean. At long last, a warm, cozy satisfaction ebbed from his belly.

*God, it's good to be home.*

The snazzy penthouse apartment above his uncle's law offices served as a place to eat and sleep. Brice felt no more connection to the space than he would a hotel room. His heart and soul resided here, in this simple cabin. Always would.

He hobbled through the dark house. Each right step shot pain through his calf.

"Granny?" He rapped a soft knock against the bedroom door. A few seconds later, Brice slipped into her unlit room.

Nothing seemed amiss or out of place, so he assumed she'd spent the night with his parents. She often stayed in the family's private quarters adjacent to the Walker's Run Resort whenever they hosted a social event. Granny never missed a good party.

Vacillating between disappointment and relief, he wanted his grandmother's welcoming embrace and assurance that all would be well between them again, but he was too weary to face the alternative. He headed down the narrow hallway to his old room, each gimping footstep heavier than the last. At the door, his senses tingled even before he set eyes on the small lump in his bed.

The mixed feelings Brice had about his homecoming knotted into concern. Granny knew wolfan law forbade adult males and females of blood relation to share bedding, so why had she fallen asleep in his room?

"Granny?" He eased onto the edge of the mattress and touched her leg.

An unfamiliar feminine gasp prickled the skin along his spine.

"Who the hell are you?" Brice didn't mean to sound so rough and angry, but pain and exhaustion made him edgy and terse.

"Stay away from me!" The woman kicked out of bed and grappled with the bedside lamp.

*"Fuck!"* The sudden brightness stung like a fistful of sand slung in his face. Shielding his light-sensitive eyes behind his arm, Brice tuned into his other senses. The air thickened. He could almost taste the sharp tang of her fear. Her breaths came hard and fast.

"Get out before I call the cops," she demanded.

"With what? Telepathy?" To his knowledge, Granny had one telephone. A landline in the kitchen.

"I have a cell phone." The uncertainty in the woman's voice said she didn't.

"Nice try." Swiping his eyes, Brice sensed a change in the air pressure, heard a hitch in her breathing. His instinct warned that she had inched to her right.

"I don't need my eyes to track you." He pointed to where he knew she stood.

The woman stopped moving and quite possibly stopped breathing. Nothing but howling silence filled the space between them. Any second she would hit the floor in a dead faint. Brice forced his eyes to open.

Not that he had any doubts, but the fragile-looking young woman pressed against the wall was definitely not his grandmother. Wild spirals of red hair gave her a sexy bed-head look regardless of the cornered animal glint in her cinnamon eyes.

She wore an old Maico High baseball jersey. Wait. That was *his* old baseball jersey.

His bed, his clothes. What else had she claimed that belonged to him?

And why?

She was human and likely unaware of the implications of marking a male Wahya's belongings with her scent.

As if he could smell her anyway.

Still, that this small slip of a woman had claimed his discarded clothes and his abandoned bed sparked a possessive thump in his chest. His gaze prowled the small swell of her breasts and the narrow curve of her hips cloaked beneath his shirt.

She sported the longest legs he'd ever seen on someone so petite. Soft, toned legs that inspired steamy visions of them tangled around his hips as he moved inside her until she shattered in ecstasy, breaking him with her.

The full moon had passed, so his attraction was real. Not something prompted by primitive hormones riddling him to fuck the nearest willing female.

That this one didn't look so willing was like an ice dump on his stiffening cock.

"You need to leave." A pink flush rose from her slender throat to color her face. She anchored her arms over her chest, her fingers tightening around her flesh in a vise grip that would leave marks on her porcelain skin if she didn't relax.

"What I need is a good night's sleep." Brice watched her cute little toes curl in the shag of the small white rug in front of his dresser.

The rug was definitely not his. Neither were the feminine touches on the dresser.

A tightness squeezed Brice's chest. His grandmother had been forced to take in a boarder because he wasn't around to help out.

"Are you drunk?" Condescension hardened the woman's delicate features.

"No. Why?" He flexed his foot. The pain stabbing his leg would scale his entire body if he didn't lie down soon.

"Because you're in the wrong cabin and you're *naked*." Her voice thinned on the last word.

"You're only half-right. I am naked." Although nudity was second nature to Wahyas, Brice pulled the rumpled bed covers over his lap. The tattered comforter's hideous color scheme caused an unpleasant twitch to crinkle his nose.

*Whack!*

"What the hell was that for?" He rubbed the sore spot where the can of hair mousse smacked his head. "I covered up."

"This is a private residence. The resort's rentals are down the road." Her voice sounded tight and her words were clipped. "Now, get out, frat boy."

*Boy? She thinks I'm a boy?*

"Wait—" He barely had time to block the candle she lobbed at his face. "Hey! Take it easy, lady."

She stood battle-ready, shoulders squared, feet spread apart, a hardcover book gripped in each hand.

"I'm not going to hurt you. I'm Brice Walker, for chrissakes!"

Okay, maybe his tone was a little too patronizing, but he didn't deserve the wallop to the chest from the book she flung at him like a ninja star.

"Freaking perv, *get out*." The woman wasn't simply frightened. She was downright mad.

"I'm not—" he dodged the second book "—a pervert."

Projectiles of various sizes targeted him with the precision of heat-seeking missiles. Who knew a woman's hair and beauty products did double duty as a weapons arsenal?

He slid to the floor, using the bed as a shield. "I can explain."

"Not interested."

A wolf doll dressed in a tiny Maico High jersey bounced on the floor next to him. Either the woman had been an athlete in school or she had dated one. Since she looked too small and fragile to have played sports, Brice assumed the latter.

"I'm not going anywhere," he grumbled, holding the stuffed animal to his nose. After a few futile sniffs, he tossed the toy aside and peeked over the mattress.

Her impromptu armament depleted, the woman's gaze ricocheted around the room. "Just leave and I'll forget you were here."

Guilt plagued Brice's conscience. He knew from experience how helpless she felt being trapped. Tomorrow, after he and Granny talked, Brice would issue the frightened woman profuse apologies for what he was about to do.

In the territory without permission, sleep-deprived and beyond exhaustion, he couldn't risk anyone else discovering his presence. Tying her to the bed so he could get some sleep seemed like his best option.

An unexpected thrill electrified his body, temporarily numbing Brice's pain. Another time, another place, he would have had an entirely different motivation for tying her up. He almost smiled.

"Easy, sweetheart." He stood, hands lifted in mock surrender.

"I am not your sweetheart."

For some illogical reason, Brice felt the distinct need to disagree. However, the critical way she assessed him down to his bare toes made him think that she found him lacking.

Or not.

Before he could cover himself again, she jerked the ugly comforter off the bed and stashed it behind her.

"Like what you see?" He straightened to his full six-foot-four height.

"Hardly." She swept a mass of curls from her heart-shaped face. "What I'd like to see is your ass walking out the front door."

"Not going to happen." Brice smirked. He liked that the woman had spunk in spades. "Look, darlin'. All I want is a good night's sleep. Preferably with you next to me, all sweet and cuddly."

"Yeah, that's not going to happen, either." She stuffed her small feet into a pair of worn sneakers. Her gaze teetered between him and the bedroom door.

His predatory senses sparked. "I wouldn't try it if I were you."

"It's a good thing you aren't me." Her chin tilted and one eyebrow arched as if upping his challenge. She snatched the lamp from the nightstand and yanked the plug from the outlet.

If the little spitfire thought dousing the light gave her the advantage, she was oh-so-wrong. In milliseconds, Brice's eyes adapted to the darkness.

The lamp shattered near his unprotected feet. Shards of glass skittered across the wood floor. She dashed past him and he couldn't intercept. Not without slicing his soles.

*Damn.*

The woman was smart. Cunning. Fast.

And the chase was on.

# *Chapter 2*

Adrenaline shot through Brice's body like rocket fuel burning through his veins. His heart pounded to near rupture. Using the bed as a springboard, he leaped over the broken lamp pieces and landed solidly on his good leg.

"You can't outrun me." Even with his handicap, in his wolf form Brice could outpace a human.

"Watch me." The lithe woman dodged him around the living room furniture.

His mouth did not have permission to spread into a ridiculous smile. It did anyway. Growing broader and more outrageous by the second.

She sprinted to the front door. He heard the lock click and the door swung open. He lunged to capture her. His chest slammed into her shoulder, forcing his breath out with a harsh *oomph!*

Brice turned her during the tackle so that he took the brunt of their fall. God, it was good to feel playful again. And she was the best kind of playmate. Soft and warm, with just the right amount of pluck.

"Let. Me. Go." She shoved him with more strength than he expected. He struggled to maintain his hold.

"Take it easy," he grunted. "I won't hurt you."

She head-butted his shoulder. Every time her hair swept his skin, desire—hot and demanding—tore through him. Totally inappropriate and ill-timed considering the circumstances.

His wolf nature didn't care. This woman wore his clothes, slept in his bed and wrestled him with the strength of a she-wolf in heat. To a Wahya male, her behavior was an open invitation.

However, fear marked her scent, not desire. Brice needed to tamp down the carnal thoughts before his primal instinct overruled his intellect and he gave her a real reason to be frightened.

Finally he flipped her onto her back.

"Get off me!" She landed a solid punch against his nose. Brice's head jerked.

"Damn, that hurt." Hurt like hell.

Before she could do further damage, he latched onto her hands, pinning them over her head. She kicked his shin. Thankfully it wasn't his bad leg or his instinct would have been to retaliate rather than to restrain.

"Calm down before you get hurt," he snarled, using his body to flatten her to the porch.

He gave in to the instinct to snuffle her hair. In one long, indulgent breath, he inhaled without expectation, though he desperately wanted to smell something. Anything. Even dirty dandruff was preferable to nothing.

To his utter disbelief, a soft, feminine fragrance teased his nose. Convinced he imagined the scent, he sniffed a second time to be sure, moving from her provocative red curls to the dimpled spot just behind her ear. As he breathed in, her sweet, luscious musk filtered through his body, warming him like beams of sunshine.

"God, you smell good," he gushed like an eager pubescent boy trying to get to second base.

"Get away from me." The woman bucked, and the rub of her pelvis against his crotch ignited a craving that would culminate in an all-out home run if she didn't stop.

"Be still," he rasped. "I only want to smell you. But if you continue thrusting your hips at me, I'll lose what control I have and do more than scent you."

She went limp, although the daggers in her eyes remained unsheathed.

Tired, horny and more than a little confused, Brice appreciated the reprieve. He wanted to gorge on her intoxicating scent without battling her and his super-charged libido. "Don't be frightened, Sunshine. I won't hurt you."

He rubbed against her. She was soft, spirited, with a mouth-watering scent—a combo like that could bring a wolfan to his knees. "You have no idea how happy I am to smell you."

A droning thud in his head joined the possessive thump in his chest. Resonating one beat, one word. Over and over and over again. Mine. Mine. Mine.

*Oh, no. No, no, no. Fuck no.*

"This isn't happening," he mumbled.

"You got that right." She jammed her knee against his crotch.

Excruciating pain screamed through Brice's groin. The air swooshed out of his lungs. His body curled into a fetal ball.

The house was dark. His vision grew darker. Still, he saw the triumphant gleam in her eyes a second before she escaped.

*Brice Walker, my ass!*

Cassidy Albright jumped down the front porch steps. She had no idea who that dirt-streaked hobo was, but he certainly wasn't the Brice Walker she knew.

Well, had known from a distance.

She sailed past her car. The old clunker wouldn't have started on the first crank anyway, and she'd have been a sitting duck if the naked imposter turned out to be a dangerous intruder instead of a drunken resort guest.

Shoes crunching the gravel driveway, she sprinted toward the Walker's Run Resort a mile and a half down the mountain. An easy stretch for Cassie, who'd earned medals in track. Each time she ran, she simply imagined herself running until the layers of her mother's bad luck and bad reputation peeled away, leaving Cassie free and clear.

She had a way to go before that happened. Only one more semester of college and Cassie could start over. In a town where Imogene Struthers's past wouldn't wreck her daughter's future.

She rounded the first curve of a hairpin turn. A creepy vibe spiderwebbed across Cassie's skin. She glanced back at where she'd been. The waning three-quarter moon provided enough light to see a man wasn't behind her, but a very large, very hungry-looking wolf.

Cassie's heart slammed against her chest before spiraling to her feet. She could outrun a man on a dirt road. Outrunning an animal presented an entirely different race.

She veered into the woods. Zigzagged through the trees. Zipped around bushes. Leaped over a fallen pine. Sweat coated her skin. Her breaths grew hard, laborious. A stitch gnawed at her side. Her leg muscles began to burn.

Another downed tree lay ahead. Slightly larger than the last, though not so big that Cassie couldn't clear it. She sailed over it with ease.

The landing was harder.

Her foot slipped on a patch of moss. The belly flop to the ground unleashed an explosion of pain in her chest. Her lungs, shriveling into two tight balls, squeezed out every molecule of air and then some. She couldn't catch her breath, cough or even wheeze.

Cassie didn't want to die, not with a new life finally within her meager grasp. She forced her chest to expand. The muscle beneath her breastbone gave one final spasm and relaxed. Whereas she'd had no breaths before, they now came in rapid-fire succession. In zero to five, she went from starving for oxygen to drowning in it.

Wolf drool on the back of her neck was imminent if she didn't get moving. She swallowed two giant mouthfuls of air, the way she did when plagued by hiccups, and locked her elbows to push up. All the adrenaline that helped her run had tanked.

"No, no, no." Frantic, she patted the ground, searching for a rock, a branch. Anything.

Out of luck and out of time, Cassie faced the wolf with the only weapons she had. Her hands and sheer grit.

He approached, head hunched lower than his shoulders. His thin black lips mocked her with a menacing grin.

"Nice wolfy," Cassie panted over her heart's rampant beat.

His ears perked up and he tilted his head, taking his sweet-ass time to assess the most delectable spot to munch first.

A low rumble rolled through the woods. His hungry gaze lifted and a snarl drew back his snout, revealing very large, very pointy teeth.

Cassie had no hope of winning an outright wrestling match with an animal of his size and bulk. Gouging his eyes might give her a slim chance of survival, and slim was much preferable to none.

Before his nerve-numbing growl chased all her bravado into the pit of her stomach, Cassie steeled her thumbs.

The wolf sprang.

Cassie screamed. She didn't mean to, but some invisible force seized her vocal cords and wrenched loose the armor-piercing shriek. Apparently the same malevolent force also screwed her eyes shut, because she had to pry them open to see.

The wolf now paced behind her. Ears flat against his head, he snapped at the woods. A strip of fur bristled along his spine, and the fluff of his tail stretched behind him, arrow-straight.

With his attention diverted, Cassie scooted backward to get away from the wolf. Her heart pounded so hard and loud that she feared the drum would draw the wolf's attention from the rustle in the woods.

The wolf hunched forward, ready to pounce at whatever emerged from the forest.

It was now or never. As she labored to stand, an ear-shattering squeal sliced through the night.

She jerked toward the commotion. A huge blur barreled past the snarling wolf and skidded to a halt at her feet. Hot breath steamed her bare legs.

Cassie didn't move.

Neither did the angry sow.

The wolf, however, plopped on his haunches, and the tips of his fur shimmered with silvery light.

*Poof!*

Just that quick, the wolf vanished. Hunched in his place appeared a fully-grown naked man.

Not just any naked man.

The naked man whose balls she'd coldcocked.

*This isn't happening.*

Obviously she'd whacked her head and was suffering from a massive delusion. That was good news, right? Delusions couldn't hurt her. They weren't real. Just figments of her imagination.

Well, um, her naked delusion stood. Displaying all his glory.

Cassie squinched her eyelids shut. *He isn't real. He isn't real. He isn't real.*

Satisfied her temporary insanity had passed, she drew in a calming breath and opened her eyes.

The naked delusion limped toward her.

Whether he was real no longer mattered. Cassie sprang to her feet. The startled sow danced around her legs. The lack of traction on the soft, damp earth caused Cassie to lose her balance. She landed on her hands and knees, face to snout with the hog.

Cassie sucked in deep, measured breaths to slow her erratic pulse. Unfortunately, her heart and lungs were running a marathon. She swayed from a wave of lightheadedness.

"Leave her alone, Cybil." The soft, tantalizing command of the wolfman's Southern baritone hummed through Cassie's body with the hypnotic power of the Pied Piper. That fairy tale hadn't ended so well. Cassie didn't want to share a similar fate.

The hog pivoted toward the wolfman. A twitch of her curly tail, a determined squeal, and she charged with the gusto of a matador's bull.

Wolfy wasn't as quick on two legs as he had been on four furry ones. He thudded to the ground.

"Dammit, Cybil. How long are you going to hold a

grudge?" Shoving the sow aside, he lumbered to his feet. Undeterred, she circled around and plowed into him again.

Transfixed, Cassie watched them tussle. Crazy as it seemed, she found herself rooting for the wolfman, who was trying not to hurt the disgruntled pig. Cybil wasn't as careful.

In the scuffle, she stomped his leg. A silent scream of pain twisted the wolfman's face. Cassie's chest tightened in sympathy, though she couldn't fathom why.

Cybil backed away, allowing him to sit up and rub his calf. After a few long-drawn breaths, he opened his palm. The sow shuffled close enough for him to scratch beneath her chin. Then he murmured in her ear.

Cassie wasn't one to ascribe human attributes to animals, but the hog's expression appeared contrite. Cybil snorted, flicked her tail and trotted back into the woods.

*A werewolf pig-whisperer. Imagine that.*

Cassie rubbed her temples. She didn't want to imagine anything of the sort. She wanted her sanity to return.

The wolfman peered at her with the same stark expression the wolf had given her. He—whatever *he* was—crawled toward her, his movements smooth, stealthy. Deadly.

Cassie jumped up and ran. For all of ten feet before she was falling.

*Oh, no. Not again!*

The wolfman cradled her as they hit the ground.

"Damn, you're fast." Rolling Cassie onto her stomach, he immobilized her with the full length of his hot, hard body.

"Get off me." The more she squirmed, the more a wicked heat licked her skin. Fear was supposed to be cold and clammy, so what the heck had ignited those fiery flashes?

"Easy there, Sunshine." His deep, rich voice dripped like sickly sweet sorghum.

Suddenly Cassie remembered a spilled bottle of syrup. Tasted the sticky sweetness on her fingers. Smelled the gingerbread cookies baking in the oven. Heard her mother's tinkling laughter in the sunny kitchen of the run-down apartment where they had lived when Cassie was seven.

*Is this what it means to have your life flash before your eyes when you're about to die?*

"Are you listening?" The wolfman's insistent growl dispelled the memory. "I don't want a repeat of what happened on the porch."

Cassie's survival skills abandoned her. She tried to buck him off, but her body was too busy mooning over his mesmerizing accent to respond.

"I'll release you on two conditions. First, don't run. The woods are too dangerous for you. Second, keep your knees away from my groin. They're too dangerous for me. Agreed?"

Considering her position, did she have a choice?

Though she couldn't bring herself to verbalize consent, Cassie nodded. His weight lifted, yet the heat from the intimate contact remained. She sat up, rubbing her arms.

He squatted just beyond her reach, yet close enough to catch her before she could make it to her feet if she tried to run. Twice he'd caught her and not harmed her. Three times might break her luck.

Moonbeams filtered through the trees, giving just enough soft light to make out the concern etched in his features.

"Are you hurt?" His polished tone contradicted his appearance. Bits of leaves and pine needles stuck out of the waves of his thick black hair. A scruff of dark whiskers framed his determined jaw. Dirt smudges accented the sharp angle of his cheeks. A smear of blood crusted beneath his nose.

"No." Cassie struggled to remain calm, rational. "Well, maybe."

Nothing ached, yet something unbalanced her mind. Had she imagined the wolf or the transformation? Because the man invading her personal space was no delusion.

The hard, sleek build of his scarred, muscled body pulsated with a raw, masculine strength and a primal vitality that made her shudder despite the heat flashing through her body.

"Either you're hurt or you aren't." Even though his expression remained neutral, she heard the frown in his voice. "Which is it?"

"I might've hit my head when I fell. I'm seeing things."

The wolfman was on her in an instant. Hands in her hair, fingers caressing her scalp. His urgent yet gentle touch sparked an odd tingle that seeped into dark places no man had touched. Unsure of how to handle the startling titillation, she ducked out of his reach.

"No bumps or cuts on your head." Sitting back on his knees, he continued the inspection without the use of his hands. Inch by inch, his squinted gaze stroked her skin. Lingering here, then there as if memorizing the details of her body he couldn't possibly see with clarity due to the filtered moonlight.

The air between them became charged. Her muscles clenched to resist the palpable energy. The tension only magnified his phantom touch.

It wasn't the first time a man had looked at her with carnal interest. It was, however, the first time Cassie didn't feel threatened.

His scrutiny complete, his focus flashed to her face and fell to her breasts. The longer he stared, the more her budded nipples strained against the sweat-dampened baseball shirt clinging to her chest.

Heat rushed to her face; pride kept her from turning away flustered. Instead, she returned the same intense inspection. Where her attention landed made her body burn as though she'd fallen into an inferno.

In the bedroom, she'd intentionally looked everywhere but there. Now she couldn't drag her eyes away from the long, meaty shaft arrowed toward his flat abdomen rippled with hard, sleek muscle. The temptation to reach out and touch *it* just to see how one felt in her hand was dangerous. And stupid.

"Why do you think you're hallucinating?" the wolfman asked, yanking her attention to his masculine mouth and the full, strong lips pulled taut in thought or pain or simple contemplation.

"One second I saw a wolf. The next you were squatting in his place." Pushing aside distraction, Cassie's mind grappled for a logical explanation of his transformation. "Either I'm seeing things or you pulled a whammy of a magic trick on me."

"I'm neither a hallucination nor a magician. I'm Wahya," he said as if that should explain everything.

"Please tell me that's a society of illusionists." *Please, oh, please. Oh, please.*

"Wahyas are wolfan shape-shifters. We can change forms at will."

Cassie's heartbeat failed, yet the rush of blood rumbled in her head, and she wondered if the noise was the sound of madness.

# Chapter 3

"Are you going to kill me?" Cassie lifted her chin, set her jaw and forced every bit of self-control to diffuse her panic.

"If I wanted you dead, you would be." At the wolfman's bone-chilling matter-of-factness, fear slithered down her spine and along her nerves until she shivered.

"What do you want with me?" She hugged her chest. "To turn me into a werewolf like you?"

The whip of his narrowed gaze lashed her skin as he slowly counted to twenty beneath his breath. "The term *werewolf* is offensive, and I'd appreciate it if you wouldn't use it to reference me."

"Give me a break," she snapped as hysterical aggravation eked out over apprehension. If he wanted to hurt her, he wouldn't take the time to point out the political incorrectness of her word choice. "Don't get all snarky with me, buster. This is all new to me." Cassie shoved back the curls that fell across her face. "Who the heck are you, anyway?"

"I told you." He inched forward, his mesmeric gaze lasering straight into her soul. "I'm Brice Walker."

Cassie's breath caught in her chest, and her heart missed a beat. The only times she'd seen Brice Walker up close and personal, he'd been mummy-wrapped and hooked up to a life-support machine. Each time she'd snuck into his hospital room, she'd had the same reaction of excitement and dread. Excitement that it might be the day he woke up for more than two seconds, dread for how he'd look at her when he did.

Brice came from a respectable, well-to-do family, she from the likes of Imogene Struthers. Cassie couldn't help her origins, but she would be forever grateful to Margaret Walker for helping her start down a different path when no one else would give her a chance.

*Oh, no.* Did Margaret know what her grandson had become?

Knowing Margaret, it wouldn't matter. She loved Brice unconditionally. Nothing would ever change how she felt about him.

"This is unreal." Cassie swallowed the lump her heart had caused when it jumped into her throat. This wasn't how she'd pictured their first actual meeting. Fully clothed at his parents' resort, the hospital or even Margaret's cabin at a reasonable hour was what Cassie had expected of him. Brice naked and wolfy had never crossed her mind.

"I assure you, I'm very real." Brice snuffed the space between them.

Her breath evaporated. Yes, yes. He was very real. No denying that. Nope, no sirree.

He gently dusted his thumb over her cheek and electrified every cell in Cassie's body. Her skin warmed, and a ticklish sensation swirled in her belly.

*Run!*

She'd already tried, only to be captured. Twice. A third attempt would turn out no differently. She couldn't outrun a wolf or match the man's brute strength. All she could do was steel herself against his very presence, which seemed to undermine her sensible self effortlessly.

For her future's sake, Cassie had to ignore her body's irrational reactions to Brice the man and force her mind to compartmentalize his animal side. "I'm sorry about what happened on the porch. I didn't expect you to show up at your grandmother's house. In the middle of the night. Naked."

*So very naked.*

"I hope I didn't do permanent damage to your, um…" Her gaze tumbled down his chest to his erect penis.

*It* didn't look damaged, but what did she know?

Brice's laugh rang hollow. "Nothing's broken. Of course, if you want to check, I won't object."

"No, no." Cassie curled her fingers into the soft dirt.

"Too bad." Ever so slowly, he reached for her hair. Rubbed

the strands between his fingers. Pulled a curl straight. Released it. As it sprang back into shape, his mouth carved a lethal smile into his granite face.

Cassie might've managed to stomp out the silly excitement polluting her brain if he hadn't lifted her hand and inched his nose up her arm. The soft scratchiness of his whiskers wiped out her common sense. Her body throbbed, and not just where he grazed her skin, but in places deep inside.

No man had touched her with such reverence and delight. Actually, no man had touched her at all. Still, she didn't think just any man's touch would make her feel this cherished, which was why he had to stop.

"Brice—"

"God, you smell good." His nose teased the curve of her jaw and traced the column of her neck. Cassie couldn't help but inhale his scent. Salty, earthy and something distinctively male that made her quiver. The alien sensations almost made her forget who he was. And who she wasn't.

"Stop!" Wanting to push him away, she meant to place her hand on his chest. Where it landed was somewhere lower, maybe a smidgen higher than his groin. Hard and warm, the skin beneath her fingers trembled.

Brice's throaty rumble rendered Cassie senseless. Her body remembered his heat and strength pressed against her when he'd trapped her on the porch and again when he'd immobilized her on the ground. Each time, he'd taken care not to hurt her. Just as he did now. Holding her firmly to prevent escape but not forcefully enough to arouse alarm. Instead, his possessive hold caused her to snuggle against him. His strong arms made her feel sheltered and safe.

"Who are you?" Brice's hot, heavy breath fanned her ear. "What are you doing here?"

"Cassidy Albright," she answered. "I work for your parents."

Brice roughly pushed away from her as if the mere act of touching the daughter of Imogene Struthers would infect him with Ebola.

The wispy, feel-good high Cassie was flying on took a nose-dive. Apparently Brice—along with a multitude of others—judged Cassie for her mother's sins.

So much for being the perfect gentleman Margaret had painted him to be. He wasn't a gentleman at all. He was a freaking werewolf.

She should've known better than to let hormones cloud her good sense. No man was worth risking her future.

Not even the wolfy one standing with his back turned so that she had to look straight at his tight, nicely shaped ass. Thank goodness it wasn't his crotch. If she saw that thing again, she'd never get the blasted image out of her head.

Rational mind rebooted, she stood and brushed the dirt from her arms and legs.

"What did my parents hire you to do, Miss Albright?" Brice's long fingers raked the turbulent waves of his hair.

"I'm a guest services clerk at the resort." For the past four years, though her history with Brice's parents and grand-mother went back much further. Not that he had ever noticed.

"Tell no one that I'm here." His tone implied *or else*.

Cassie thought the request odd since everyone expected him to come home, but his personal affairs weren't her business. "Whatever you wish, *Mr. Walker*."

"Come with me." He turned, offering his hand in a way that made Cassie feel as if she had the cooties.

"I'd rather not." She didn't need his feigned chivalry.

"It wasn't a request." Brice's steel fingers cuffed her wrist. Tiny bolts of electricity scuttled up her arm.

"Don't touch me." She slapped his hand and jerked free before the shock wave pulverized her resolve.

Brice had the audacity to look stricken. "I won't hurt you. I promise."

The words rolled off his tongue, soft and gentle, and landed on her heart like glops of acid—searing and scarring on impact. From the first syllable, his assurance was a lie. Though

Brice wouldn't physically harm her, his reaction to her identity gouged deeper than a wolf's teeth ever could.

"Did you hear me?" As he loomed over her, he bore most of his weight on his left leg.

"I'm not deaf or stupid. I don't care if you are Brice Walker. I'm not going anywhere with a freaking *werewolf*." She rushed to leave the woods, alone.

At the spot where she had fallen, Cassie kicked the log. A black racer slithered from underneath, lifted its rounded head and stuck out its forked tongue in silent laughter. Even nature mocked her foolishness.

Brice snatched the snake and slung it out of her way.

"Would you please cover up?" Cassie gritted her teeth and continued toward the road.

"With what?" Brice limped beside her.

"Can't you conjure something?" Walking next to a naked man in the middle of the night was unnerving enough. Walking next to a naked werewolf in the middle of the night was pushing her hold-it-together abilities beyond capacity.

"I told you, I'm not a magician. I can't do magic." He hedged in front of Cassie and forced her to stop. "I don't understand why you're upset with me. I can't help what I am."

"Neither can I." She matched his defensive tone.

"Okay." Brice's dark brows drew together. He clasped her hand and stroked his thumb against her dirt-smudged knuckles. "Let's go back to being friends."

*Can't do magic. Ha!*

Even now his charm-the-panties-off-a-nun grin wove a spell through Cassie's spirit, lifting her to lofty places that she knew better than to perch. Friendship was too much of a liability. However, for his grandmother's sake, Cassie would be civil. "Casual acquaintance is the most I can offer."

"You've claimed my bed and my clothes. I'd say we're beyond the casual stage."

"Borrowed," she corrected. "I don't *claim* things that aren't mine. You can have your shirt back when we get home. And for the record, the sheets on the bed are mine. Yours are in the closet." Cassie stepped around him.

Brice's firm fingers squeezed her shoulder. "Sleep in my shirt. Hell, roll around naked on my bed. I don't care. Just explain why you are living with my grandmother."

The tops of Cassie's ears heated more from irritation than embarrassment. Three days ago, she'd awoken in her trailer to the sound of bulldozers. The scuzzy landlord had failed to inform his tenants that the county had declared eminent domain over the mobile home park. The residents had fifteen minutes to pack and vacate the premises or face arrest for trespassing. "I lost my home, and your grandmother invited me to live with her."

Cassie bristled at Brice's impassive expression. "I'm not taking advantage of her. I cook, clean and run errands in lieu of rent. Your parents are aware of the arrangement. I guess they forgot to mention it when they called you."

"I haven't spoken to my parents in five years." The cold, hard edge in his voice caught her off guard.

"Seriously?"

"Disownment isn't something I joke about." Hurt shimmered beneath his grim expression.

Something wasn't right. Gavin and Abigail Walker were proud of their son, but had they been unable to accept what he'd become? Was that why he'd moved away?

Cassie's stomach worked itself into knots. "So, you don't know what happened last night?"

"No. Enlighten me." His dramatic splay of hands irked her.

"It's not my place to discuss your family's matters. Talk to your parents."

"Cassidy, what the hell is going on?" Worry threaded through the irritation in his voice.

Cassie decided if she said the words superfast, the effect would be like ripping off a Band-Aid. A sting at first, and then the worst would be over.

For her, anyway.

She drew two steady breaths and blurted, "Yourgrand-motherhadaheartattacklastnight."

Brice simply stared, squinty-eyed and pensive as if he hadn't heard her at all. Cassie huffed, gathering the gumption to say it again. This time, a little more slowly.

"Your grandmother had a heart attack last night."

# *Chapter 4*

Brice slumped, his mouth fell open and he appeared to have stopped breathing. He was a tall, tall man, and from the way he swayed, he looked ready to topple.

"I'm too late?" His words were barely audible in the silent woods.

"No." Afraid he would drop from shock, Cassie stood on her toes and tapped his face. "She isn't dead. Okay?"

Though he stared at her through large, unblinking eyes, his trembling hand found hers. He held her palm to his cheek, pressed his nose against her wrist and inhaled shallow breaths until his composure returned.

She ignored the ridiculous notion that he drew comfort from her touch. Maybe the cherry-scented body wash she used smelled like his girlfriend's fragrance. Although Cassie imagined the women Brice dated would be able to afford a more luxurious and expensive brand than the dollar store variety she used.

"How is she?" Brice's jagged voice squeezed her heart. His distress over his grandmother's health sounded as genuine as Cassie's concern.

A kind, decent woman, Margaret Walker had hired Cassie to clean her house before Cassie was old enough to apply for a real job. And when family services threatened to put her in foster care after Imogene got sick, Margaret helped Cassie file emancipated minor papers. She'd also encouraged Cassie not to give up on her education no matter how bad things got—and for a while, things got pretty darn bad.

"She's in serious condition, as far as I know. The nurses wouldn't tell me anything else or let me visit her." Cassie swallowed the residual sting of being turned away because she wasn't family.

"I need to see her. Now." Brice squatted at Cassie's feet and went wolf.

The transformation took less than a second, which didn't give Cassie enough time not to look. Her brain did a mental loop-the-loop. "Don't do that in front of me." She held her head to stop the spinning. "It's freaky."

The wolf's ears flattened. Although Brice's au naturel appearance unnerved her, Cassie preferred his nudity to this scowling, four-footed fur ball.

"Well, what are you waiting for?" She pointed up the road. "Go."

Crinkling his nose, the wolf pulled his thin lips back in a peevish snort.

"Good boy?" She thumped his head. "Don't roll your eyes at me. How am I supposed to know what you want? I've never owned a dog. Hey, stop that!" She swatted his cold nose away from the back of her knee.

His yips grew impatient. After a few nudges and some wolf drool from Brice tugging on the hem of her nightshirt, Cassie understood he wouldn't run ahead and leave her behind.

She jogged toward the cabin. Brice loped beside her without touching his right hind leg to the ground.

Surreal didn't begin to describe the situation. Of all the things she might have expected of Margaret Walker's grandson, being a wolfman wasn't one of them.

*A very sexy wolfman, sans the wolfy part.*

A girlish giddiness bubbled through her body and caused complete loss of coordination in her limbs. She tripped on the porch steps.

Brice, the man, curled strong fingers around her arm.

"I can manage." Cassie shook him off and scurried into the cabin to turn on the lights.

"Fine." Brice shaded his eyes behind his hand. "I need a shower." He brushed past her.

"Fine." Cassie locked the door, then spun around and knocked full frontal into him. After the way he'd cast her aside in the woods, she should have been disgusted by the contact. Instead, her nerve endings jumped with excitement, and her body begged and screamed to cozy into him.

Ignoring her sensible brain's command to move away, Cassie steadfastly stared straight into his eyes. From across the bedroom, Brice's irises had appeared almost teal. Had she been close enough to realize that his left eye was a vivid shade of dark blue and his right one was a bright green, she would've recognized him by his reputation of mismatched eyes.

*And missed all that delicious touching and tackling and more touching.*

She couldn't wait to do it again.

"Stop!" Oops, she hadn't meant to say that aloud.

"I can't show up at the hospital naked." He dipped his stern face within inches of hers. His mismatched gaze bore into her as if willing Cassie to say something, but her mind filled with two thoughts: how striking his eyes were and how much she wanted to rub her body against him like a frisky cat.

Being a wolf, he probably didn't like cats. Except maybe to eat them.

Cassie's sex clenched and her thoughts ran amok with visions of his soft whiskers against her inner thighs and the pressure of his masculine lips against her folds, sliding his moist, firm tongue along her slit, sucking her nub and thrusting into her wet heat until she came undone.

Just because she didn't have actual sexual experience with a man didn't mean she hadn't fantasized, and she'd have been a liar to say she didn't want fantasy to turn into reality. Right here, right now.

He wanted it, too, if the mammoth size of his erection heating her stomach was any indication.

*He doesn't want you, specifically. Like all men, he just wants sex. Doesn't matter with whom.*

"Clothes," Brice growled.

"I, um." The swirls of hairs on his chest teased the palm Cassie pressed against his torso. Her hand itched to stroke every inch of his body, and she wondered if his penis would feel as velvety as it looked.

*Focus!*

"Your grandmother never wanted to throw out your stuff. Everything is where you left it." Cassie tugged down the dirty hem of the baseball shirt. "Mostly."

"Grab me a pair of jeans and a shirt." Brice left her standing, breathless and out of sorts, in the middle of the foyer.

Cassie resisted a retort about not being his maid. By the time she thought of it, the shower was running. Barging into the bathroom to make the grand announcement was probably a bad idea.

She headed into the kitchen for a broom. A bloodied nose and bruised balls were bad enough. She didn't want Brice to cut his feet on broken glass.

She flipped on the kitchen light and stared, slack-jawed.

*Oh, no.*

"He didn't."

Oh, yeah. He did.

The fog numbing her senses evaporated. In its place came the startling reality that although Brice Walker was a wolf-man, he was also a pig.

Cassie no longer felt sorry about the pain she'd inflicted. If he'd been standing in the kitchen at that moment, she would've beat him with the broomstick. He could've eaten anything else in the whole darn kitchen, but no. He had to eat her pie.

The freshly baked, made-from-scratch cherry pie promised to Rafe Wyatt in lieu of a cash payment for her clunker's scheduled oil change. Now she'd have to cancel the car service. Again!

She glared at the white dribbles of milk and red splatters of pie filling on the counter. In the sink sat a dirty plate. A sticky spoon. A suspiciously spotless pie pan.

*Gross!*

Brice had licked it clean. Cassie knew he had. Probably drank straight from the milk carton, too.

"Men!" It seemed some male traits were shared between species.

Grumbling, she grabbed a cloth and scrubbed the dishes and countertop clean before hurrying to the bedroom with a death grip on the broom. By the time she dumped the last of the broken glass into the trash, her irritation had mellowed. To be fair, Brice hadn't known she bartered pies for services when he ate it.

Cassie tossed her dirty nightshirt into the laundry basket. She had found the worn baseball jersey on the closet floor when she moved in and couldn't resist wearing it to bed. She should've known borrowing something without permission would bring bad luck.

She knelt beside her battered suitcases and sorted through her clothes until she found a comfortable pair of shorts and a thin, long-sleeved T-shirt. The shower shut off, so she dressed quickly and straightened the bed. By the time she'd finished, Brice had yet to emerge from the bathroom. Suspicion made her glare down the hallway.

Brice had commandeered her new razor to shave that scruff from his face. The certainty of it threatened to rekindle her temper. Good sense snuffed it out. No matter the history between her and Margaret, Cassie was the hired help. She shouldn't make too many waves.

Massaging the muscles in her neck, she dutifully pulled his clothes from the closet and laid them on the bed. She'd play butler to a grown wolfman if it meant she would continue to have a place to live.

After rummaging through the dresser drawers, she called out, "I can't find your underwear."

"I don't own any," he answered from the hall.

A zip of excitement swirled in her lower belly. She slammed the drawer shut. "I didn't need to know that."

Clean-shaven, with his damp hair slicked back but for one rebellious wave, so black it almost looked blue, tumbling over his formidable brow, Brice leaned against the door frame, naked. Of course.

She tried not to look at his penis, but there it was again. A massive rod of rigid flesh, jutting proudly from a nest of dark hair. Human or not, Brice Walker was definitely all male.

An arid wind whipped through her being. On its wings rode the devil himself. With a stern mental shove, she shooed him away.

Circumstances being what they were, Cassie couldn't afford to give in to temptations that she had no experience managing. She'd focused on work and school. Allowed no time for boys, or men. No distractions, no detours. Nothing could get in the way of finishing her business degree—her golden ticket to a better future.

"Didn't I tell you to cover that thing?" Proud that her voice didn't squeak, she tossed him the jeans and shirt.

Humor crinkled his eyes, and seemed to simmer with a mischievous desire she would do well not to encourage. "Most women can't wait to get me out of my clothes."

Cassie understood why.

Made for the cover of *GQ*, his face had the most perfectly balanced features she'd ever seen on a man. Slightly swollen from her ramming palm maneuver, his straight nose rested between sharp chiseled cheeks arrowed toward his generous, masculine mouth, the corners turned up in taunting tease.

"I'm not most women," she said, watching him dress.

The dark hairs that dusted his limbs and swathed the broad expanse of his chest did little to disguise the angry, dark slashes running up his sinewy arms and across his strapping shoulders. More streaks scored his left hip bone down to his knee. He favored the right leg, which bore deep, saw-toothed indentions around his entire calf.

Her gaze lifted to the jagged, purplish-red half-moon marks on his neck. Proof something had tried to rip out his throat. She touched hers in sympathy.

When Cassie had stumbled upon Brice's room during one

of her mother's multitude of hospitalizations, he'd lain still as death, covered in layers of bandages. On a ventilator, he opened his eyes for a few mere seconds and locked onto her heart.

The front page of the *Maico Monitor* had heralded Walker Boys Mauled by Feral Boar.

"You weren't attacked by wild hogs, were you?" Cassie's throat burned at the savagery he'd endured.

Brice zipped his jeans and slid his arms into his shirt-sleeves. His long, nimble fingers fastened the small, flat buttons with a fluid grace. "No," he answered, his voice a soft caress.

Chill bumps puckered on her skin, though Cassie was far from cold. She rubbed them off. "Was it another Wahima?"

*"Wa-hi-ya."* Exasperation lit his eyes, though none was reflected in his tone. "Four *Wahyas* attacked while my brother and I were hunting."

"Is that how you became one of them?" Cassie sat on the bed and tucked her hands beneath her thighs to resist the urge to offer physical comfort. She needed to keep a tight rein on the feelings Brice awakened. Nothing good would come from setting them loose.

Brice's sigh sounded weary, or maybe frustrated, considering his mouth's downward turn. "Wahyas are born, not made."

"Wait. You were born that way?"

Brice's shoulders bowed like a cobra ready to strike. "Stop looking at me like I'm some sort of freak."

*Touchy. Touchy.*

"Sorry." Cassie hugged her knees to her chest. "I'm trying to understand."

Brice's nostrils flared, sucking in a long, deep breath that expanded his chest. He appeared to be counting again. She could almost hear the numbers tick one by one until he reached thirty.

"It's probable humans and Wahyas share a common ancestor. Somewhere along the evolutionary trail, our DNA metamorphosed, and we developed the ability to shape-shift into wolves. We aren't mutants, we aren't diseased and we aren't monsters." His emphasis reeked of sarcasm. "We're civilized."

"Then why were you attacked?"

"They were rogues." Brice sat next to her. Not so close they touched. Not so far as to leave a space.

Cassie's body hummed from the energy passing between them. The tiny vibrations sharpened her awareness of her own femininity in stark contrast with Brice's overwhelming masculinity.

"Rogues?" She coughed to disguise the breathiness in her voice. Seriously, she needed to figure out how to moderate her body's responses to him. Quickly. Before she became the rabbit trapped in a foxhole alongside the big bad wolf.

"Rogues are Wahyas who have no loyalty to a pack," Brice said. "Most are curs who prey on the weak."

"You don't strike me as weak." Defying the scars and pronounced limp, Brice projected a will of steel and the muscle to enforce it. Someone would have to be insane to believe him weak.

"I stepped in a steel trap." Brice lifted his right leg, though his jeans hid the old injury. "The rouges saw an opportunity and took it. Mason died protecting me."

Cassie's heart swelled in her throat. Brice had nearly died, too.

While everyone else inundated him with their sobs and wails, waiting for the inevitable, she had read to him, shared the little gossip she knew, held his hand when tremors of pain had wracked his body, willed him to breathe when his lungs failed. Kissed his tightly bandaged head, begging him to live.

The day she saw him awake, she left the hospital and never visited him again. What was the point? On the road to recovery, he didn't need the likes of her mooning over him any more than he did now. "I'm very sorry for the terrible ordeal you went through."

# *Chapter 5*

Bitterness fisted in Brice's throat. What he had suffered was insignificant considering his brother died because of him and his damn nosy nose.

Cassidy mysteriously revitalizing his scent receptors couldn't be a good thing. Neither were the gentleness in her voice, the genuineness in her eyes or the mess of curls cascading over one shoulder.

Brice twirled a red ringlet around his finger. A man might promise foolish things to feel those silky strands sweep his stomach or tickle his inner thighs. He rubbed the curl against his cheek. The feminine softness eased the ever-present knot in his chest.

No woman had affected him to such a degree, and it was a damn shame Cassidy did. He had time only for a passionate night or two, and she didn't seem the type for a brief, inconsequential fling.

He dropped the curl. "Shoes?"

She retrieved a pair of loafers, but he needed more support for his leg.

"Not those. I left a pair of Timberlands somewhere."

"They aren't here," she said, rooting around the closet.

"Check under the bed." He tilted his head as she hunkered down, shoulders touching the floor, hips high in the air.

"I can't see anything," she grunted. "Wait, I feel something."

Brice felt something, too. It grew more demanding each time she rocked forward to reach beneath the bed. Oh, the things he could do to her.

"Ah-ha." She surfaced, his shoes in tow, and promptly dumped them in his lap. "Anything else?"

His gaze rested on her chest, so close and damn near eye

level. The way her nipples puckered against the fabric of her T-shirt when she breathed soothed his residual annoyance from walking into the room to discover she had discarded his jersey.

The urgency to feel her touch again threatened to overpower his restraint. Wahyan females had sleek, sinewy bodies. Cassidy's skin had a suppler texture. Her muscles, although strong, were more pliable. He'd enjoyed how she pillowed him when he'd pinned her to the porch and wondered how gratifying it would be if she pulled him into her softness rather than fought him off.

Brice massaged the bunched spot between his eyebrows. The handful of aspirin he'd taken after his shower hadn't kicked in. His entire body throbbed. Overworked muscles teetered on the verge of spasm, his leg hurt more than it had in a long time, the bridge of his nose pinched every time his nostrils flared to catch Cassidy's scent, and his groin, for chrissakes, was sore from a solid kneeing and tight from on-and-off-again erection.

After he visited Granny at the hospital, he might crawl into an empty room and ask Doc Habersham for a morphine drip. Banishment be damned. Brice needed some relief.

"Grab me a pair of socks." Most of the time Brice recognized the general look of an irritated woman. The sharply arched eyebrow, the tightly pursed lips, a hand resting on a hip, fingers tapping out a count. Any man, human or wolfan, should have enough sense to placate that look.

Apparently, tonight he didn't. When Cassidy didn't respond, he nodded toward the dresser. "Bottom left."

She gave an exaggerated "Ugh."

"What?" Brice opened his palms in a halfhearted shrug, intrigued by her vacillation from sweet and doe-eyed to pissed and prickly in a matter of seconds.

She snatched open the drawer, threw him a pair of white socks and stomped out of the room. "Would it hurt you to say please and thank you?" echoed down the hall.

Wahyas had little need for those particular *human* social graces. While living with Granny, he'd been more conscious of the etiquette. She would expect him to treat Cassie with the utmost Southern charm. However, if he did, the effect might backfire. Cassie's annoyance provided a safety barrier. A breach could lead to a world of trouble he had no time to mediate.

Tying his shoes, he stared at the two ragged suitcases in the corner and the sparse belongings that only an hour ago had been angry missiles. He didn't know why she had so little, but when he left he would make sure Cassidy Albright had everything she needed.

His stomach lurched, preparing an imminent launch into his throat.

*Oh, God. Not this again.*

When he'd awakened in the hospital after the attack, the scent of blood and bowel and death had imprinted in his nose, blocking all other smells. He seldom ate because of the debilitating nausea. Nothing cleared the stench and the relentless ordeal pushed him to the feral edge until one morning, after a brutal night of vomiting, he woke up and couldn't smell a damn thing. No one could explain why.

With his stomach settled, he ate solid food again, and he could relax around people because their scent no longer slapped him in the face like decomp. Being scentless was a godsend.

For about six weeks. Then he realized the downside.

No earthy musk before the rains. No whiffs of smoke from campfires in the fall. No more sweet-smelling flowers or fresh-cut grass. No comforting scents of family, or friends, or the enticing fragrance of females.

Yeah, he could survive without ever smelling anything again, but his experiences were muted and dulled. Much like watching a Technicolor 3-D blockbuster on a twelve-inch black-and-white television. A lot was lost in the downgrade.

Over the years, the devastating loss became a penance.

A constant reminder that if he hadn't been so curious about tracking a strange scent, he wouldn't have stepped in a trap, the rogues wouldn't have found them and Mason would still be alive.

God-awful nausea reeled in his stomach with a vengeance. Hands balled into her comforter, Brice pressed the shabby material to his face, grateful and relieved her scent lingered in the threads. Sucking in a deep, exaggerated breath, he held her unique fragrance in his lungs, counting the seconds. Her residual essence filtered through not only his body but also his soul, warming every nook and cranny of his being. Stirred by the phantom familiarity, Brice's wolf instinct prowled his conscience.

*Mine!*

No, she wasn't. He had only a few days to settle matters with his grandmother. Then he had to leave. For good. His future lay outside Walker's Run, and he intended to embrace it alone. He had best keep his cock in his pants and his hands off Little Miss Albright's feisty body, except to smell her. Luckily for them, it would take time for his errant mating urge to reach the fucking point of no return. He could handle a few days of temptation.

Meeting him in the hallway, his temptress chucked him a set of keys. "My car will get you to the hospital and back. It just needs a few cranks to start."

"Oh, no." Brice caught her arm before she locked him out of the bedroom. "You're coming with me, Cassidy."

"It's almost midnight, and I have to be at work at six." She twisted out of his grip. "And call me Cassie. Cassidy is too formal considering—" her eyes took all of him in "—well, everything."

Brice stood straighter. Plenty of women had stared, ogled and gawked at him. None had blushed so prettily or affected him the way she did.

He wanted to tease her. Test her boundaries. And conquer them.

*No, no, no!*

No conquering allowed.

"All right, Cassie, you have two options."

"Oh, really?" She cocked her hip and folded her arms across her waist. Such a cute little protest.

"Put on your shoes and come with me like a good little girl." He stepped close enough that she had to tilt her head to keep eye contact.

She didn't balk. "Yeah, that doesn't work for me. What's the second?"

"Barefoot and braless, hog-tied in the backseat." He made a point to stare at her chest until her nipples pebbled against her thin T-shirt.

"What kind of choice is that?" Her skin colored to the exact shade he wanted to see.

"The kind where you get to choose the *manner* in which you'll accompany me, Sunshine." He jingled the keys. "Don't take too long, or I'll think you're into kinky."

# Chapter 6

"Why are we crawling through the bushes?" Aggravation weighted Cassie's whisper.

Brice grinned because she continued to follow him, creeping along the outside of the hospital in search of the window to his grandmother's room. "I'm banished," he answered in a hushed tone.

When he'd tried to explain his situation on the trip into Maico, Cassie had held up her hand and refused to look at him while she drove. Her silent irritation had pounded him until they reached the hospital parking lot. In an attempt to smooth things over, he'd thanked her for coming and added how much it meant to him to see his grandmother again.

Cassie's defenses faltered, and the hardness she projected dissolved. Compassion filled her eyes, and the more amicable side to her personality emerged.

The transformation made him forget that he didn't deserve her sympathy, because when the tension dropped between them, the thoughts that filled Brice's mind were not his past failures but a new hope. He didn't understand it. Didn't expect it to last. However, he sure as hell would make the most of it while he had it.

"What do you mean, banished?" Her gentle probe held no judgment.

"My pack turned me out because I'm the reason Mason is dead." Resentment leached into his words, followed by shame. "He would've been our next leader."

Behind him, Cassie stopped, so Brice didn't continue forward. She missed a breath, and the back of his head burned, possibly from the heat of her gaze.

"Anyone who blames you is an idiot," she announced. "Sometimes bad things happen and it's nobody's fault. What happened to you and Mason was one of those times. You know that, right?" The warmth of Cassie's small hand against his arm urged Brice to believe.

His heart wouldn't allow it.

At the next window, Brice peeked inside. His grandmother's old flowered housecoat hung across a chair.

"This one." Brice's excitement turned to dread. He dropped into a squat. What if seeing him became too much for Granny?

An icy chill caused him to shudder although a light sheen of sweat coated his skin. His head pounded the same rhythm as his heart. Both felt ready to explode.

He tipped his nose toward Cassie less than a foot away. The balm of her sweet scent infiltrated his senses.

Her head swept side to side. "All clear."

Brice appreciated her watchfulness, though his wolfan senses gave him a more accurate account of their surroundings.

They faced the visitor parking lot, deserted this time of night except for Cassie's old car parked in the shadows. A mildly curious grackle watched them from its perch on the nearby telephone lines. A car on the highway a block away sounded a faint hum in the stillness of the night.

A roach inched toward Cassie, twitching its divining rod antennae. Brice chucked a piece of mulch at the insect and sent it scurrying away before she noticed.

"You should hurry." She motioned for him to get moving.

Brice peeked in the window again. The monitors and IV pole partially blocked the view, so he couldn't see if someone sat in the other chair near the bed. He dropped down again.

"Please tell me you aren't going to Tom-peep the window all night." Cassie's no-nonsense tone matched the exasperation on her face.

"I can't tell if someone is in the room."

"Knock on the window. Maybe they'll let us inside before someone calls the cops." Cassie moved from a crouch to a sitting position and leaned against the brick wall. "I don't want to spend the night in jail."

"Neither do I." Brice released a nervous breath.

"I doubt you would get arrested. Me, on the other hand..." Cassie's voice trailed off. She picked at a blade of grass that had wormed its way through the mulch.

"They'd haul me in the same as you. Then they'd call the pack liaison, and he'd call my dad."

"The sheriff's office knows about your wolfy people?"

Brice shook his head. "To them, and everyone else, we're the Walker's Run Cooperative. Tristan Durrance is our law enforcement liaison. He's a pack sentinel and a sworn deputy. Trust me, I'll get the worst of this if we're caught. My dad doesn't want me in the territory."

Cassie tugged the grass blade free and peeled it into symmetric strips. "He's expecting you. He told the resort staff that when you arrive, we are to give you any room you want and anything else you request. Without question. Why would he want us to accommodate you if he doesn't want you here?"

"I don't know." The tightness in Brice's gut reached into his chest. His father was planning something, and whatever it was, Brice would certainly suffer the consequences.

He stared at the black sky, devoid of stars due to the glow of civilization. The woods around his grandmother's cabin protected the small homestead from the incandescence of modernization. Stretched on the grass on the slope of the backyard, he could watch the twinkling skyline for hours. He'd missed that peace and comfort in Atlanta, where he'd found only a few places a wolf could run and even fewer to stargaze.

Brice rubbed his palm along the denim covering his sore calf. The aspirin hadn't worked as well as he'd expected. He needed to do something or go home before the pain flared to unbearable again.

He eased to the window and tried to push up the pane. "The lock is jammed. I can't pop it."

"Nice to know breaking and entering isn't your thing." Cassie brushed past with a follow-me wave. The innocent contact triggered a rush of moony feelings that Brice vigorously shook off.

Sneaking through the hedges, she led him within a few yards of an emergency exit. The door stood ajar, and a hospital employee lingered on the stoop. The orange glow from a cigarette sharpened his blocky facial features. He took a long drag and exhaled a plume of white smoke.

Brice didn't understand the human fascination with smoking. Wahyas avoided it like the mange because it skunked their sense of smell.

Cassie's shoulder rustled the bushes. She froze. Brice did the same. The orderly leaned against the rail and squinted in their direction without any apparent concern.

Since the hospital worker seemed in no hurry to rush back to his duties, Brice crouched in a position that relieved the pressure on his bad leg. Beneath his jeans, his calf grew itchy and tight. If the inflammation moved into his foot and up to his hip, the pain would cripple him.

Hoping Cassie's scent would relax him, Brice closed his eyes and inhaled slowly. Although she crouched less than two yards away, her magic failed, or at least malfunctioned, because his nose caught wind of a faint, nasty odor.

He blew quick puffs of air through his nostrils to clear the smell. Instead of this ridding him of the stink, a putrid pungency assaulted his senses. The sensation of scurrying spiders rose in Brice's chest, and he slapped both hands over his mouth to keep from chucking up cherry pie.

"Stop making that noise," Cassie hissed. "He'll hear you."

If the severe nausea that plagued him after the attack returned, he'd go stark, raving rabid. Nothing—not Dramamine or Compazine or Phenergan or Antivert or a whole slew of other drugs—had controlled the queasiness.

"He's going inside." Cassie rose to her feet.

Brice grabbed her around the middle, and they toppled into the mulch.

"What the heck are you doing?" She elbowed his chest.

Dizzy and sweaty, Brice buried his face in her hair. "I need to smell you before I puke."

The argument he expected never came. She allowed him to smell at will.

"That's the weirdest thing anyone's ever said to me. Does that line work on wolfy women?" Cassie wiggled beneath his weight.

"I don't know. I've never said it to a she-wolf." Brice relaxed in the comfort of Cassie's scent.

"Jeez, aren't I special."

"Yeah, you are. Before I met you, I couldn't smell a damn thing. Now I smell you and that Dumpster over there." He eased away from Cassie before her essence lulled him into believing the mating urge wasn't a fluke after all.

"How flattering." Her soft-looking lips curling into an unpleasant frown, Cassie dusted wood chips from her clothes.

"Cas, your scent reminds me of a beautiful meadow of wildflowers." And he loved her scent as much as he loved the rich, buttery flora that bloomed midspring beneath the full sun at a hollow within the wolf sanctuary.

After a few tense moments, Cassie's mouth softened into a timid smile. "Thank you."

Oh, no. She gave him the look. The one that hooked him with her modesty and reeled him in with her sincerity. His insides went all gooey, and that had never happened. If they'd met before his life had spiraled into chaos, maybe... just maybe.

Brice cleared the frustration from his craw. He had only one path now. A path a mate couldn't follow.

Cassie raced up the steps and jerked the emergency door handle. "Hurry up. I don't have all night."

"Is the alarm busted?" Brice slipped past her.

"I think someone disabled it a long time ago."

"You think?"

Ignoring what he believed must be his most incredulous look, Cassie shoved him into the laundry room, where ample uniforms stocked the shelves.

Owned and operated by the Walker's Run Cooperative, Maico General not only provided state-of-the-art medical services to the town's human residents but also maintained a private ward for sick or injured pack members. If uniforms or linens stained with wolfan DNA ended up in the wrong hands, well, the fallout would be disastrous.

The Woelfesenat, the international wolf council governing the Wahya populace, had made significant political strides in recent years. Although some governments had acknowledged the wolfan population in secret negotiations, Brice knew revelations to the public-at-large would be a long time coming.

"Put that on." Cassie pointed at a white lab coat.

"Something tells me that you've done this before." He shoved his arms into the sleeves.

"When my mom got sick, I had to work after school to help pay the bills. Visiting hours were over before I could get here, so I'd sneak in." Cassie yanked a pair of yellow scrubs over her clothes.

"Did she get better?"

"Nope." Cassie handed him a green surgical cap.

"I'm sorry, Cas." Brice wanted to pause a moment to let her know his sympathies were sincere, and it tweaked him that Cassie seemed indifferent to them.

"Act normal and don't make eye contact." She cracked open the door. "Most people will only see the uniform unless you give them a reason to notice. Count to thirty before you follow me."

Brice's stomach lunged. "Wait!" Pinning Cassie against the industrial dryer, he nuzzled her with abandon. His entire body sparked from her tantalizing scent and the soft suppleness of her skin.

"Hey, what happened outside was sweet, if not a little awkward," she said. "But this is getting creepy."

"You'll get used to it." Brice couldn't stop his grin.

"Holster your nose, *Benji*, before someone catches us." The fire in Cassie's cinnamon eyes counteracted her unamused frown.

"Oh, that hurts, Cas. Calling me a scruffy little dog when you've seen how big my wolf is."

She flicked him a *whatever* wave and left. Brice counted to eight before the impulse to follow her won out. He stayed far enough behind so it didn't appear they were together.

Cassie confidently navigated the corridors. The determination in her steps, the no-nonsense sway of her hips, the steel in her spine—all of it was a pretense to conceal her tender heart. Beneath the bravado, this woman was far more delicate than she looked, and she looked fragile enough that a gust of wind might blow her to smithereens.

The human ward clerk looked up from her computer. Brice slowed his pace, lowered his head and sharpened his senses.

The woman squinted her eyes and lips at Cassie. "Are you the loaner from Chatuge Regional filling in for Rita?"

Cassie veered toward the station. "Is she the ER nurse who broke her ankle?"

The ward clerk's broad, snaggletoothed grin plumped her cheeks. "Yeah, the old biddy should've had more sense than to skateboard at her age."

Brice shook his head. One of the blessings and pains of small-town living was that everyone knew everybody's business to some degree. Miracles or pure luck had helped the Wahyas of Walker's Run avoid discovery.

Then again, Brice suspected some of the pack's longtime neighbors knew of their duality and kept their secret out of loyalty and respect. Such as Cybil's owner, Mary-Jane McAllister.

She lived on the fringe of the co-op's wolf sanctuary, a large area of protected forest where the pack roamed. High electric fences ensured human interlopers with cameras and shotguns stayed out, while sentinels patrolled the territory to ward off rogues.

Unfortunately, even the best security measures sometimes failed.

# Chapter 7

Brice hurried down the hall and slipped inside his grandmother's room. A woman lay motionless on the bed. Wires peeked out from the neckline of her gown, and IV tubes sprouted from her arms. The faint line of an oxygen tube rested beneath her nose. The old lady appeared so feeble that she couldn't possibly be his grandmother. He backed up, hoping not to disturb her.

"Is someone there?" The woman's weak voice stopped him.

Brice's mouth went dry, and his body felt as if it had been packed with sand. "It's me, Granny." He scratched his throat, though the itch seemed to spring from his voice rather than his skin.

"Oh, my boy." She lifted her tethered arms. "Come give me a hug."

Obediently Brice trudged to her bedside, bowed over her and offered a timid embrace.

"You call that a hug?" Granny squeezed his neck, then rubbed and patted his back. When he eased away, her celestial-blue eyes scrutinized his hospital garb. "Changed professions, did you?"

Brice snatched the flimsy green cap from his head and sifted his fingers through his hair. "I don't want Dad to know I'm home. I came to see you, not him."

Granny tsked. "You have to face him sometime."

Brice doubted that he did.

"End the quarrel, Brice. If not for your sake, do it for mine." Granny's plea tightened around his heart until he struggled to breathe.

"Dad has to make an effort, too." Brice limped to the window. "I'm not a priority for him."

Never had been.

All Gavin Walker's love and attention had gone to his first-born, the Alpha-in-Waiting. Brice learned at a young age that his father held little regard for him, treating his second son as if he was lower than a pack Omega. Ironic, considering the Walker's Run pack didn't subscribe to the ancient social order for its members. Everyone had their place and purpose, but no hierarchy existed aside from the succession of the Alpha family, which the pack continued to endorse.

"Talk to him," Granny urged. "You'll be surprised at what he has to say."

Nothing Gavin Walker said interested Brice. Too many hurts had hardened Brice's heart and mind to listen.

He wiggled the locking mechanism on the window until it loosened. After hoisting the pane up and down several times, Brice returned to Granny's bedside.

Ignoring her one raised eyebrow and one-sided frown, he pulled the chair closer to the bed and sat down. The heat of her silent chastisement forced him out of the lab coat. Guilt ate at him for not giving her what she wanted. Still, Brice wouldn't agree to something that he had no intention of doing. "Tell me what happened last night."

"The pain started after supper. I told Cassie that I had indigestion." A mischievous sparkle lit Granny's tired eyes. "She's such a sweet girl. I think you'll like her."

Oh, he liked her, all right.

"About last night?" Brice fidgeted to find a comfortable position for his leg.

"Cassie dialed 911, gave me an aspirin and then called Gavin. If she hadn't been there, I probably would've gone to bed."

Brice's heart registered another tally in Cassie's favor. Casually he rubbed his shirtsleeve across his face. A hint of her scent lingered in the fabric. Anticipation tickled his nose and spread to his groin. He couldn't wait to snuffle her sweet spot again.

"I worried that Adam wouldn't tell you." Granny held out

her knobby hand, and Brice gently sandwiched her fingers between his palms.

"He didn't have a chance. I left Atlanta on Thursday as a wolf. He has no idea where I am. No one knows."

One of the monitors beeped louder, faster. "Brice Walker! What if something had happened to you?"

"Easy, Granny." He stroked her arm. "I can take care of myself."

"Doesn't give you the right to be reckless. For goodness sakes, you are the Alpha-in-Waiting."

"No, I'm the fucking screwup who got the real one killed."

Granny's dry lips puckered. "I'm not too sick to scrub your tongue with soap, young man, so watch your language."

"Yes, ma'am." Brice dropped his gaze and bowed his head.

"You must let go of the past. Grief is eating your soul. Death is a part of life. Whether peaceful or violent, how we die is less important than how we live." Granny's fingers scrunched the hair at the back of his neck. "You aren't the only one who suffered loss, my boy. Neither is your sorrow any greater than ours. You lost your brother, but the rest of us lost you both." She lifted his chin until their eyes met. "Mason can't come back, but you can."

"Dad won't allow it." Brice said the words as if he didn't care.

"Is that what you believe?" Granny's penetrating stare splintered his thin veil of indifference. Shame, humiliation and a deep-seated hurt forced Brice to turn away.

"Good heavens, it is," Granny gasped. "What has Adam done to you?"

"He gave me a place to belong." Brice squeezed the bridge of his nose to curtail the migraine building behind his eyes. He didn't want to waste their time arguing.

"Where you belong is in Walker's Run." Granny's words held the conviction of a red-faced minister preaching hellfire and brimstone at a camp meeting revival. Brice wanted to believe. He truly did. Walker's Run was his home.

*Had* been his home, a lifetime ago. Soon the path he chose would ensure he never called Walker's Run home again.

The door swooshed open and closed. "The nurses are starting rounds."

"Who's that?" Granny turned her head toward the woman in the shadows.

"Cassie." Brice noticed how her presence de-escalated his tension.

"So you've met." A curious smile lifted Granny's voice.

"I found her asleep in my bed." The possessive thump in his chest wanted to erase the drop-dead smirk on Cassie's face. Resisting her would be quite a challenge.

He couldn't wait.

"Oh, dear." Granny's grin ruined any worry her tone might have carried.

"We had a rough introduction, but I think she likes me." Brice winked at Cassie. "Especially naked."

"Don't bet on that, *Benji*," she countered, though her eyes held an unmistakable spark.

Brice chuckled, and the mirthful sound surprised him.

"Oh, this does my heart good." Granny rubbed her chest. "Cassie, my girl, come give Granny a hug."

Cassie's stone face said that she didn't want a hug. So did her ramrod-straight back.

"Come, come. Don't be shy. I don't bite." Granny smiled. Without her dentures, she looked as harmless as a toothless infant.

"Don't worry, Cas." Brice walked her to his grandmother's bedside. "Granny is human."

Careful to avoid the IV lines and monitor wires, Cassie leaned in for one of Margaret Walker's famous hugs. A hard tremble rocked Cassie's body.

"It's all right." Margaret rubbed Cassie's back. "Granny's just a plain old granny. No need to be frightened."

Cassie had no fear of Margaret, though learning the woman didn't sprout fur and bay at the moon came as a relief.

Pure and simple, Cassie hated hospitals. They were cold and impersonal and rank. No amount of disinfectant or deodorizers could expunge the smell of suffering.

Her mother had spent years in and out of hospital rooms. It had been horrible. The false hope. The rally, the decline. The numbing acceptance that while miracles did happen, they didn't happen for everyone.

"How are you feeling, Mrs. Walker?" Cassie crossed her arms to hold on to the warmth of Margaret's hug.

"Fit as a Hardanger fiddle now that my two favorite people are here." Margaret poked Cassie's elbow with an arthritic finger. "And I've told you to call me Granny."

The simple term of endearment struck a raw nerve. Cassie wanted to say it, but she couldn't push the word from her lips. She couldn't risk bonding with Margaret, or anyone else, if she expected to leave Maico with no regrets.

"Yes, ma'am" was the most Cassie could offer.

Margaret rested her eyes. A sweet sigh quivered her lips, and her features no longer held the harried look Cassie had seen so often in recent years. Now the old woman looked peaceful, content. Not what Cassie expected from someone who'd suffered a heart attack.

Brice palmed Cassie's back, and she leaned into him for support. Yes, it was a moment of weakness. The stress of the past few days had left her bone-tired. What harm could come from siphoning a little of Brice's strength?

"Granny, what did Doc say about your condition?" Brice's somber voice clashed with Margaret's serene expression.

"Oh, there's nothing to worry about," Margaret said. "I'll be good as new in no time."

A brittle smile formed on Cassie's lips. Imogene had said that, too.

# Chapter 8

"I am not sleeping with you." Pillow and comforter in hand, Cassie attempted to navigate the formidable obstacle blocking the door.

Although they were both adults, as Brice readily pointed out, sharing the bed was an unreasonable demand. Hadn't she done enough for him already?

"This isn't a negotiation." From the strong set of Brice's jaw, she could tell he meant it.

"Glad you agree. Now move."

Brice waved toward the mattress. "This is a perfectly good bed."

"And you're the one sleeping in it, unless you changed your mind about your grandmother's room." Cassie hugged her bedding to her chest.

"A Wahya male doesn't sleep in a female relative's bed. It's just wrong."

"Well, I'm not sleeping in Margaret's room, either." Heaven forbid if something went missing. People would blame Cassie even if Margaret didn't.

"Then it's settled." Brice's hard expression softened.

Cassie stood tall. Well, as tall as her five-foot-two figure could against a mountain. "I'll take the couch."

"You aren't sleeping anywhere except next to me." Brice snatched the pillow and comforter from her clutches. "Got it?"

"If I had known that you were so bossy, I would've run faster." She grabbed the bedding he'd confiscated. "I'll sleep on the floor."

"Cassidy Albright, get your ass in that bed before I pick you up and drop you in it." Brice delivered a growl so low and menacing that chills bungeed down Cassie's spine.

She jumped into bed. "You've had your shots, right? Distemper, parvo." She paused to fluff her pillow and straighten the comforter over the sheet. "Rabies?"

Brice snickered. He probably thought she was kidding.

The lights went out. Followed by a rustle of clothes. A second later, the mattress moved beneath his weight.

"Stay on your side of the bed." Turning her back to him, Cassie scooted toward the edge of the mattress. She tucked her hand beneath her pillow and tried to ignore the jitters of sleeping next to a man—a naked man, at that—for the first time. "And don't hog the covers. I hate waking up cold."

Brice shoved his side of the comforter at her.

She tensed, waiting for him to move closer to sniff her. He lay so still, so quiet, Cassie decided he'd fallen asleep until she heard the soft catch in his breathing.

"What's wrong?"

"My leg hurts," he snapped, and then groaned. "It's nothing. Go to sleep."

She reached to turn on the nightstand lamp and remembered that she had smashed it on the floor.

"Where are you going?" The brush of Brice's fingers down her back caused an electric current to course through her body. Cassie wished she wouldn't react to him the way she did. She prided herself on keeping her emotions in check, particularly around men.

Then again, Brice was a different breed altogether.

"Don't worry. I'm not running away." She flipped on the overhead light.

Brice's right leg stuck out from beneath the sheet. The calf had swollen to almost twice the normal size, the skin a reddish-purple, the scar almost black. He crooked an arm over his eyes.

"How did it get this bad?" she shrieked.

"Well, let's see." He ticked the count on his fingers as he recapped the night's adventures. "Now that I think about it, the last half hour standing and debating you is what did me in." The acerbic bite in his voice bounced off Cassie's thick skin.

"Don't blame me for your pigheadedness. If you had let me sleep in the living room, you'd be fast asleep by now."

"I doubt it." He moved his arm away from his face. Pain, sadness and a certain wistfulness that Cassie recognized as loneliness churned in his gaze.

Alienated from his family and his pack, and worried about his grandmother, Brice sought companionship. That's why he'd forced her to go to the hospital. Why he insisted they share a bed. He didn't want to be alone.

Cassie empathized, though sleeping together was going a bit overboard.

"Come back to bed." Brice started to get up. "I'll watch TV in the living room."

"Stay put." She used a pillow to elevate his leg. "I'll get some aspirin."

"I took some before we went to the hospital. They didn't help."

"I'll fix you something," she said, leaving the room.

"Nothing ever works," he moaned.

Cassie grabbed three clean bath towels and headed to the kitchen. Heating a large stockpot of water until it boiled, she added a healthy dose of dried rosemary, then turned off the burner. Next she swirled a towel in the hot water, placed a lid on the pot and left it to steep.

Brice opened one eye when she lifted his leg to place one of the two remaining clean towels over the pillow. She poured a little olive oil into her hands and drizzled some over his leg.

"Closet cannibal or kinky fetishist?" The lackluster gleam in his eyes muted his cocky grin.

"This might hurt at first, but you'll feel better when I'm done." At least, she hoped he would. She could almost feel his agony throbbing in her own body as she kneaded the muscles above his knee.

"Ooh, S and M." Brice's fingers touched his lips. "Miss Albright, I'm shocked."

Cassie was, too, as heat flooded her body. Ignoring his

tease would've been easier if Brice wasn't flat on his back with a thin sheet accentuating every angle and line of his naked body. Her attention gravitated to the tent over his groin, and just that quickly, her common sense evaporated, leaving her defenseless and vulnerable.

She need to proceed carefully. Brice Walker had the power to turn her stupid. To make her want things she couldn't have. Things that would wreck her life if she stopped to pursue them.

His keen, smoldering gaze caressed her face and feathered down her chest to cup her breasts. If she hadn't seen his hands—one stashed behind his head, the other draped across his stomach—she would've sworn on her mother's urn that his fingers pinched her nipples. Exquisitely sensitive, the tight buds stung from straining against her shirt.

His charged gaze continued its downward journey and settled at the juncture between her legs. Cassie wore a T-shirt and jersey shorts, so he couldn't see anything. Still, a wicked smile shaped his mouth, and she knew he was picturing her naked.

He'd be disappointed. She wasn't generously endowed or overly curvy. Her breasts were small and slightly flared hips gave her a feminine silhouette, but she'd never be the willowy ingenue men seemed to crave. She was simply too short, too pale, and her tangled mop of red hair had earned her the nickname Raggedy Cassie in kindergarten. She doubted grown men thought any differently. After all, didn't they all prefer blondes?

Brice's eyes lifted to the spiral curls that had fallen over her shoulder. His gaze slid leisurely along the strands and landed back on her crotch. His brow lowered a little in a contemplative stare.

If she were a betting woman, she'd wager that Brice wondered if the carpet matched the curtains.

It did, to the exact shade, and Cassie pondered if he also speculated if the *carpet* was silky or coarse. Not that it mattered. Just because she saw his didn't mean she'd show him hers.

Because if she did, she'd want him to do more than look. For starters, if he stroked her nub with the thumb he'd brushed across her cheek...well, she wasn't quite sure what it might do to her, but thinking about it caused heat to flash in her core and dangerous thoughts to cross her mind.

A naked man lay in her bed. A man she was inexplicably attracted to, against all reason. She would be a fool to fling herself at her employers' son and her landlady's grandson. She would be out of her mind to have sex with a man who wasn't human.

Somehow, that last part wasn't the deterrent it should've been.

She didn't know much about wolves, but if they were anything like dogs, the males would jump any female in heat in order to impregnate her.

Cassie wanted to avoid that scenario at all costs. She wasn't on birth control because, frankly, she had no intention of having sexual relations with a man for a long time. She had goals to meet and dreams to achieve before she could give herself to a man.

Celibacy had been a no-brainer choice until he showed up, naked!

And touched her, and held her, and inspired all sorts of wicked ideas about things she shouldn't think about but her body now insisted on investigating.

"Damn. That feels good." Brice's voice yanked Cassie out of her reverie. His eyes closed in near-sleep, his body relaxed. Hers, however, had become a frazzle of nerves and need. Evidenced by damp panties and the urge to crawl up Brice's body and hump him to oblivion.

She scowled at him. After all, her predicament was all his fault.

She waited until her irritation and horniness mellowed before working her fingers over his knee and down his swollen calf.

Brice yanked his leg from her hands. "Goddamn, that hurts!"

"The massage will increase circulation and reduce the swelling," Cassie said. "Trust me. You will feel much better when I'm done."

"How do you know?" Brice propped on his elbow, his mouth scrunched in a suspicious grimace.

"It always helped my mom." Cassie coaxed his leg back onto the towel-covered pillow. Starting again, she rubbed slow, methodical circles over his rock-solid muscles. Of their own accord, her eyes followed the line of his thighs beneath the sheets, the swirls of dark hair and scars across his rippled abs and taut chest, the square cut of his chin, the fullness of his masculine lips, the perfectly proportioned nose, and once again locked onto the heart-stopping intensity of his breathtaking eyes.

A rebellious thrill zipped through her body. She saw his mouth move. Unfortunately, the "weeeeeee" ringing in her head drowned out his words. "I'm sorry. What did you say?"

An understated smile wavered on his lips. "What happened to your mother?"

"Oh." Just what Cassie needed—a reality check to keep her curly red head squarely on her sensible shoulders. "She died four years ago from end-stage liver disease."

"It must have been difficult," Brice said softly.

"I managed." Caring for an alcoholic parent for most of her young life had been the difficult part. Imogene's death had broken Cassie's heart. It also came as a relief, because it gave Cassie a chance at a new life.

"If I had known you then, I would've helped. If you need anything now, let me know."

Cassie found his sincerity disturbing. "Thanks, but I can take care of myself. I always have."

Soon Brice's calf muscles relaxed beneath her practiced

fingers, and she worked her way down to the sole of his foot, which garnered a contented sigh from him. "Don't move," she told him. "I'm not finished."

In the kitchen, Cassie soaped her hands, wishing the hot water could wash away the ridiculous tingle that coursed through her whenever she met Brice's gaze. She wanted to put duct tape over his stellar smile.

She fanned herself to ward off the shameless desire to learn what being a woman meant. After all, there was a naked man in her bed.

*Oh, no. Not going there.*

She could barely handle a fantasy. The real thing just might end her.

"Cas? Is everything okay in there?"

Only if spontaneous combustion was a normal reaction to his presence.

"Uh, yeah! I'll be there in a minute." She splashed cold water on her face. *I am not my hormones!*

She toted the rosemary-infused towel into the bedroom. Every move Cassie made wrapping his leg, Brice's sizzling gaze followed. Climbing into the freezer suddenly seemed a logical thing to do.

"Thanks, Cas." The huskiness in his voice electrified nerves in parts of her body that only he had managed to activate. "For everything."

"You're welcome." She didn't dare look at him. His smile might be devastating, but his eyes could outright slay her.

A wet heat worked its way through Brice's leg muscles and seeped into the bones. With Cassie's scent to soothe him and the pain in his leg melting away, maybe he'd finally succumb to a decent night's rest.

She tucked a dry towel over the hot, damp one around his calf. Her hands stilled, except for her thumbs worrying the edge of the pillow propped beneath his leg. Her eyes lifted to his face. "I should take the couch. I don't want to bump you during the night."

"Fine," he answered, challenging her with his gaze.

She rolled her bottom lip between two front teeth spaced a tiny bit farther apart than the others. He counted on that little bit of uncertainty to accomplish what he wanted. Her in bed, next to him.

"Oh, all right." The lights went out, and Cassie eased beneath the covers.

God, he could hardly resist touching her. Stripping her bare. Inhaling every inch of her skin. Burying his face between her thighs to imprint not only her scent in his nose but also her taste on his tongue.

He'd noticed how hot and bothered she became while massaging his leg. He'd almost yanked the sheet off himself so she could stalk up the mattress to ride him hard, fast and into tomorrow.

He didn't because of the conflicting emotions that marred her pretty little face. She probably thought boinking her employers' son would get her in trouble.

Likely it would, but not for the reason she suspected.

Her scent captivated him, and her spunk titillated him on a different level than any other female ever had. Every wolfan instinct buzzed with inherently misguided expectation. Until Brice gained better control, he couldn't risk coupling with Cassie, or he might make the mistake of claiming her and ruin the rest of their lives.

The dire consequence wasn't enough to curb his desire, but he respectfully appreciated the challenge.

"Remember. Stay on your side of the bed, and no hogging the covers." Cassie tucked her shabby comforter beneath his chin.

"Yes, ma'am." He saluted.

"Smart-ass."

Brice smothered a laugh. He enjoyed teasing Cassie as

much as he enjoyed her company. And it had been a long time since he'd enjoyed anything.

Within minutes, Cassie's soft, rhythmic breathing signaled a peaceful sleep. Brice touched a ringlet of her hair, winding the silky strands around his finger.

*Mine.*

The word droned with each beat of his heart. To which Brice's mind replied with an emphatic "No."

He dropped the curl and tucked his hands beneath his head. Each breath he took reeled her scent deeper into his lungs. His body hardened with desire and the effort to resist it.

As a distraction, Brice focused on counting. Somewhere around eight hundred, sleep dulled his lust. Until Cassie scooted next to him. He'd never fall back to sleep with the curve of her ass burrowed into him.

Ignoring the prudence of sleeping on the couch, Brice turned on his side. He spooned against her, his arm draped naturally across her hip. When her small hand cradled his, Brice slipped into blissful oblivion.

Pain exploded across Brice's face. He sat up, howling obscenities.

Cassie jumped out of bed and turned on the light.

Brice cupped his nose. "Why the hell did you hit me?"

"My head bopped your face when I jerked awake because you were squeezing my, my—never mind." The flush in Cassie's skin deepened. "It was an accident. I'm really sorry."

"You broke my nose." The throb was almost as bad as the pain in his leg last night.

"You should've stayed on your side of the bed." The worry etched on her face diffused his temper. Her brave but timid steps toward him ignited something more dangerous.

"It's my bed. Both sides *are mine.*"

Slowly her hands cradled his face, and she tilted back his head. Her lips parted slightly, and Brice no longer registered pain, because every cell in his body primed him for a kiss.

His muscles coiled like tightly wound springs. He dug his fingers into the mattress, fighting what he'd never wanted so badly in all his life.

"No blood, no swelling. Nothing crooked. I don't think it's broken." The strain eased from her face.

"Are you sure? A wolfan's nose is very sensitive. What if I can't smell you anymore?" The waver in his voice was instinctual, intending to draw her closer when he should have pushed her away.

"I'm sure it's fine." But she wasn't sure at all, because she bit her lip and skimmed her thumbs down the sides of his nose, sending shock waves throughout his body.

"You should kiss it to make me feel better." What the hell was wrong with him? He should have put distance between them instead of enticing her to continue.

Cassie's contemplative gaze searched his face. Brice's heart beat an erratic rhythm, and his lungs grabbed short, quick breaths.

God, if she actually kissed him, he'd lose all control.

"You big faker." Cassie shoved him.

Relieved, Brice caught her around the waist and buried his face in the curve of her neck. He needed her scent as consolation to temper his arousal.

"I have to get dressed," she finally said.

"Call in." He tried to tug her back into bed with a promise to himself to behave if she'd stay.

"I'm not sick." Bracing her knees against the mattress for leverage, she pulled free.

"I will be if you leave." The thought of hours bereft of her scent and her company churned his stomach.

"Maybe you should call a doctor." Cassie hesitated. "Or do you have vets?"

"The pack physician," he ground out, "is Doc Habersham, my dad's best friend. I can't call him or anyone else. I won't risk getting thrown out of the territory before Granny comes home."

"Figure something out. I'm not missing work." Cassie pulled one of her uniforms from the closet. As far as Brice could tell, those were the only clothes she had unpacked.

He flopped onto the mattress. "Come see me on your break."

"I won't have time. I have to reschedule my car service because you ate my pie."

Brice's tongue swept his lips. "What does one have to do with the other?"

"It's a barter with Rafe. He changes the oil in the clunker in exchange for a fresh-baked pie."

"I can't blame him. Granny's pies are delicious."

"Your grandmother doesn't bake." Cassie bent over to pick up her shoes, and the bottom of her shorts rode up her legs to give him a glimpse of her panties.

He swallowed a groan. "Granny made pies for me every time I came home from college."

Shaking her head, Cassie turned toward him, a corner of her bottom lip caught between her teeth.

"You made them?" Brice rose on his elbows. "For me?"

"Like I said—" Cassie avoided his gaze "—your grandmother doesn't bake."

"Damn, Sunshine. Your pies are the best." One more reason he should have detached himself from Cassie. Sex and food were a wolfan male's catnip.

"Thanks. I use my mother's recipes." Cassie's eyes misted. She flinched and hurried toward the bedroom door.

"I'm not sorry I ate the pie, but I'll pay for the oil change and anything else you need." It would be easy enough to transfer money from one of his accounts to hers.

She stopped, a disquiet fierceness in her eyes. "I don't want your money. I may not have much, but what I do have, I've earned."

She walked out, her spine and shoulders stiff.

Well, he'd unintentionally struck a nerve.

Brice sank into the mattress. He hadn't meant to upset her,

but if he followed her down the hallway to apologize, he'd only complicate his situation. No matter what his errant instinct demanded, he couldn't involve himself in Cassie's life.

No matter how damn good she smelled.

# Chapter 9

The old clunker needed five cranks before it started. Cassie backed the car out of the driveway and eased down the dirt road, headlights slicing through the darkness. The silent woods had never seemed more eerie or sinister. Of course, she blamed her knowledge that werewolves *did* exist on the change in her perception.

She glanced at the passenger seat Brice had reclined so far that it almost touched the backseat. If only last night had been a dream, or if he hadn't explained that the members of the Walker's Run Cooperative were really his entire pack, she wouldn't have been so nervous.

Brice insisted the wolf people were just as they appeared— honest, hardworking folks. The co-op provided housing and medical care for its members, paid for their college educations and helped them establish businesses. In turn, its members tithed 30 percent of their salaries or gross profits back to the co-op.

If members became unemployed or if their businesses failed, the co-op helped them get back on their feet. They had no need for unemployment checks or welfare. This pack took care of its own.

In contrast, Cassie's life lacked supportive connections. Imogene was gone, and Cassie could count on one finger the number of friends she'd had in her twenty-four years. A little girl named Grace had been her constant companion in the second grade, and Cassie had loved her like a sister.

One summer night, Imogene had packed Cassie and their few belongings in the car and left town. Once they settled in a new place, Imogene refused to let Cassie contact Grace. Imogene's philosophy had been never to look back. Only forward. That way, regret wouldn't drag her down.

Devastated by the constant upheaval, Cassie stopped making friends because no matter how many times her mother announced that was their last move, it never was. Until Imogene got sick and died, and left Cassie all alone.

She rubbed her neck to dispel the sorrow that fastened around her throat. Brice had an entire pack who cared for him. The idea they'd banished him couldn't be more absurd. As far as Cassie could tell, his parents loved him, and so did everyone else. Didn't he realize how precious it was to have the support of so many people?

She backed the car into the far corner of the resort parking lot. In case the clunker needed a jump start, it helped not to have her car blocked in on all sides.

Walking up to the giant lodge doors, Cassie gobbled a granola bar. More to settle her nerves than her hunger. After all, she lived and worked among wolves clothed in human skins. Her heart gave a little flutter, and she suffered a brief moment of hilarity. Her hysterical laugh echoed through the empty lobby.

From his post behind the registration counter, Shane McQuarrie looked up from his textbook. "Something funny?"

"No." The existence of werewolves wasn't a laughing matter.

*Wahya*, she corrected herself. Maybe if she stopped thinking of them as werewolves and saw them as people, she'd feel less nervous.

He closed his book and slid off his stool. He stretched, the same way he did every morning when she arrived to relieve him. He bent over to stuff the book into his backpack. His khaki pants molded around his thighs.

He wasn't quite as tall or as broad as Brice, but they shared a certain similarity in their movements. Quiet. Self-assured. Quick. One second she was assessing Shane from the back. The next he loomed in front of her, tall and pumped.

He stepped close. Too close. "Were you staring at my ass?"

"No." She snatched open the cabinet beneath the counter and stashed her purse. "Why?"

Passing behind her, Shane gave Cassie a sociable bump. "Just hoping. Maybe then I could convince you to go out with me."

"You're too young." Cassie logged into her computer time card.

"I'm nineteen." He circled around the registration desk and leaned on the counter.

"I repeat, too young."

A flirtatious gleam lit his smoky-gray eyes. "Come on. Give me a chance. We'll have fun. I promise."

"I don't want fun. I want stability." Cassie pulled up a list of the morning's expected checkouts.

"The two don't have to be mutually exclusive." Shane's grin betrayed far too much interest in her.

Cassie didn't feel any attraction toward Shane. Oh, she enjoyed his company whenever they worked together, and he was a sweet guy. A different time, a different place and maybe he could've been the little brother she never had.

Curious, she asked, "Are you a member of the Walker's Run Co-op?"

"Naw." His amicable expression didn't change. Still, something in the way his pupils flickered seemed off. "Maybe someday."

Abigail Walker emerged from the corridor leading to the Walkers' private residence. Her dark green Chanel suit complemented her golden complexion and deepened the mossy color of her eyes. She smoothed her tight chignon of coal-black hair, looking every bit the regal lady of the manor.

Until the image of a wolf poised on its hindquarters, wearing the same dress, pearl earrings and ruby-red lipstick, jarred Cassie's mind.

The insane calm of last night's shock broke. Her palms started to sweat. Acid bubbled in her stomach and threatened to expel her paltry breakfast.

No matter the proper term, the people she worked for were freaking *werewolves*. What was she thinking, coming to work as if nothing in the universe had changed?

"Shane, Cassie," the wolf queen greeted them.

"Good morning, Mrs. Walker," Cassie said without meeting her boss's gaze.

"Mornin', Abby." A subtle tension crept over Shane's body. His fingers squeezed the backpack straps slung across his shoulder, and the friendly curve of his smile tightened.

Strange. Shane adored Abby and often went above and beyond his job duties to please her. Not a brownnoser, he simply seemed to crave her approval.

"Any word from Brice?" Despite the softness of Shane's voice, his words sounded clipped.

"We haven't been able to reach him." Abigail's professional demeanor faltered as sadness leached color from her eyes and face. "He'll come home, though. I know he will."

The genuine emotion in her voice convinced Cassie that Brice's mother loved her son, banishment or not.

Shane relaxed. "If you need anything, call me."

"Thank you, Shane."

He nodded his goodbye to Abby and winked at Cassie as he left.

"Cassie." Abby's dark brows pinched her forehead. "If Brice calls or comes in, let me know immediately."

Guilt squeezed Cassie's throat. Brice hadn't mentioned if Wahyas were mind readers, but she begged her thoughts to focus on anything except him. Less than two miles up the road, inside the cabin, lying in bed, naked. Absolutely, deliciously naked.

Cassie nodded, not trusting her voice. She hated lies, but technically, agreeing to Abby's request wasn't a lie. Brice hadn't called or come inside the resort.

Unless he did, Cassie would keep his secret. He'd asked for her silence and trusted she'd be true to her word.

Still, the deception pricked her conscience. Ideally, Brice would come forward before the splinter of half-truth festered into a poison that would taint the rest of her life.

# *Chapter 10*

Brice sauntered out of the bathroom, towel-drying his hair. All day he'd missed Cassie's warmth. Her company. And he was jonesing for the smell of her skin.

Several hours ago, he awoke to crippling nausea. Cassie's scent had faded from the sheets. Out of desperation, he'd riffled through her laundry until he'd found something to settle his queasy stomach. Nothing, however, smelled as good as the real woman.

He moved quietly through the living room to the kitchen. His heart kicked up a notch at the sight of Cassie at the pantry. The slow, steady rise and fall of her chest drew his attention to the shapeless taupe blazer that practically flattened the gentle swell of her breasts. Breasts he knew were soft and pert, and just full enough to fill the cup of his hand.

His palm warmed. Damn if his hand didn't remember copping a feel in his sleep, and itched not only to do it again but also to strip away the drab, boxy skirt grievously camouflaging the slender curves that had tormented him all night. Twice he'd been forced out of bed to release his desire.

Still, he preferred those less-than-fulfilling interruptions to the cold sweats and panic that usually disturbed his sleep.

"How was work, Sunshine?"

Cassie jumped back from the pantry, wide-eyed, clutching a package of ramen noodles. Her startled look heated, charging the air. The current electrified his skin as her gaze devoured every inch of him.

"Do you ever keep that thing covered?" The huskiness in Cassie's voice caused his *thing* to twitch.

"You like seeing me naked. I can see it in your eyes." Securing the towel around his hips, Brice padded barefoot across the cold tile.

"What you see is my brain being fried from too much exposure to all your glory."

"You think I'm glorious?" Brice unfastened her silver hair clip. Red ringlets splashed over his hands and slid through his fingers. He held fast to one curl and stroked the luxurious strands across his cheek. A thrill zipped straight down to his groin.

"That's not what I meant." A slight tremble parted her lips.

Brice ached for a kiss and so much more. Her taste on his tongue, her scent on his skin, her luscious legs wrapped around his hips. A deluge of erotic dreams had eroded his resolution to keep things platonic.

Cassie's scent wove a spell of need and want that smothered reason. Helpless to resist, he slipped his arm around her waist and lowered his face to hers. She squinted and puckered her mouth, but not to receive his lips.

The unexpected rejection jolted Brice. "What's wrong?"

"I don't want this." She gestured a between-you-and-me hand signal. "I have plans for the future and you're not in them."

*Damn.* That stung.

Even though he agreed they had no future together, he disliked hearing her say it.

"You need ground rules." Cassie wormed out of his hold and faced him with a straight back, squared shoulders and both hands on her hips.

Her eyes slanted with censure. She pointed her jaw and scrunched her mouth like his fourth-grade teacher when he'd neglected to do his homework three days in a row. When he'd been a wolfling, the no-nonsense, better-get-your-shit-together look had mortified him into compliance. Now that he was an adult male in his prime, that look on a feisty, petite human female did something entirely different.

"I don't like rules." He smiled.

"Too bad." Cassie's frown deepened. "Rule number one, no more prancing around naked."

"Why?" Brice leaned back against the counter, stretched

his legs in front of him and crossed his ankles. "Are you afraid you'll jump me? Fuck me until I'm senseless? Go ahead." He held up his arms in surrender. "I won't resist."

Cassie's mouth opened in a silent gasp. The pinkness of her skin surpassed the shades he'd seen last night, and he wondered how far he could push before her choke hold on her passion broke.

"Where would you like to start? The bedroom? The living room?" Brice moved in front of her, hooked his finger beneath her jaw and tipped her face up. "Right here in the kitchen?"

Soft, rapid puffs flared Cassie's nostrils. The delicate vein beneath the porcelain skin of her neck pulsed with an escalating canter. Her pupils grew large and dark. "Um." She moistened her lips.

The scent of her budding desire reached his nose, but the disconcerted hesitancy in her eyes cooled his urgency. He wouldn't press her to do something she'd regret.

"When you're ready, tell me where you want me. I'll be there." *Primed and panting.* He walked to the sink and filled a glass to the rim with cool water. Pacing himself with small sips, he took his time draining the contents, giving Cassie opportunity to collect herself and him a chance to dam up the flood of testosterone gushing through his body.

Cassie audibly huffed. "Behavior like that is why you *will* adhere to rule number one."

Brice set the glass in the sink and turned around.

"And I'm not doing your laundry as a concession for you wearing clothes," she snapped.

God, he really liked her fiery spirit. If only they'd met a lifetime ago.

"Do I get bargaining privileges?" he teased.

"No. Since neither of us wants to sleep in your grandmother's room, pick either the couch or the bed. And stay there."

"Not a debatable issue," he said sternly. "Where I sleep, you sleep." Her scent kept the nausea at bay, and he'd do everything in his power to circumvent the crippling sickness, including tying her to the bed. Though he really hoped it wouldn't come to that. She'd demonstrated her trustworthiness by not reporting his trespass to his father. He'd hate to repay her loyalty by turning her into a prisoner.

A ferocious frown sharpened her jaw.

"It's only for a few days, Cas. Something about your scent keeps me from becoming violently sick. I barely made it through the day without you beside me." A slight stretch of the truth, but he wasn't about to explain how he had improvised.

Her expression softened. Mostly her eyes, which warmed the icy stare sharpened on him.

"Fine." She anchored her hands to her hips. "But stay on your side of the bed and stop looking at me like I'm a ham at Easter."

"Great." Brice loosely clasped his hands the same way he did when he'd successfully mediated an important issue during a negotiation. "What are the other rules?"

"Hmm?" Cassie's attention returned to the pantry.

"We agreed on the first rule. Are there more?"

"Yes, but I'll have to let you know when I think of them." Cassie's posture stooped a little. She grabbed a bowl for her ramen noodles, and he wondered how long it had been since she'd eaten a substantial meal.

"I'll make dinner tonight," he said. The chicken he'd found in the fridge during his lunch raid needed to be cooked before it went bad.

"You can cook?"

"Of course. Do you think I have a personal chef?"

From her sheepish expression, it appeared she did.

"Mamie taught me." The best cook the resort ever had. *God rest her soul.* "I'm not as good as she was, but I'm in no danger of starving. You, on the other hand, could use a few good meals."

The playful tease Brice intended flopped. Cassie stared at him as if he'd popped her with the back of his hand.

"I do the best I can with what I have. Not all people have

a co-op to take care of them." She smacked the ramen noo-dles package against his chest and stormed out of the kitchen.

"Whoa." Brice netted her in his arms.

"Let me go." Cassie's struggle lacked the hellcat fierceness of last night's battle.

Brice held her tight and stroked her hair. "Bad day?"

"I've been a freaking mess."

"Why? What happened?"

"You happened." Her long, heavy sigh scraped his bare chest. "I kept imagining everyone with fangs and fur and eye-balling me because I know their wolfy secret."

He rolled a silky curl around his finger. "No one wants to hurt you, Sunshine. Wahyas are ordinary people who live ordinary lives."

"Ordinary people don't maul each other." Her finger trailed down a scar on his arm.

"Have you seen the news? Violent crimes occur in every society. Ours included. There are good Wahyas and bad, same as humans. We aren't that different."

"Except for the teeth, the tails, the paws and all that hair." The electric charge in her tentative smile pulsed along every single nerve in Brice's body.

His heart thundered. His skin itched for her touch, and his insides jittered. "Anytime you're feeling a little wolf envy," he murmured, "you can pet mine. He'll even do tricks if you whisper in his ear and stroke his belly." Or something a lit-tle bit lower.

"No way, *Benji*." Cassie's tinkling laugh encouraged him.

"Too bad." Brice buried his face in her hair. Inhaling slowly and deeply, he allowed her scent to swirl along his senses.

Suddenly he clasped her cheeks between his hands. "I can smell the resort."

"From here?" Her cute button nose wrinkled.

"On you." He picked her up and swung her in a circle. "Your hair smells like cinnamon and cloves."

"That's great." Cassie's face radiated. She looked as happy

for him as he felt, which was pretty damn happy. A mischievous glint appeared in her eyes. "Didn't I tell you that your nose would be fine?"

"Yes, you did. Those bops you gave me jump-started my scent receptors." Actually, he suspected his mysterious recovery had more to do with Cassie's scent than anything else, but he had no idea why. "Maybe it'll be good as new by the time I return to Atlanta."

Cassie's smile drifted with her gaze. "When will that be?"

"Depends on Granny." Brice couldn't give a more definitive answer. She had refused to discuss her condition, and since he detected only Cassie's scent at the hospital, he couldn't determine if the stench of imminent death had tainted his grandmother's skin.

"You should call your mother." Cassie's words came out in a rush. "I saw her crying today."

Brice tensed as his good mood deflated. "When the time's right, I'll speak to her."

Cassie's anxious eyes didn't look satisfied.

"Is that what has you stressed out? Furry coworkers and my mother?" He lightly tapped Cassie's nose.

"Isn't that enough?" She backed out of the kitchen. "I have to study for a test tomorrow. You're making supper, right?"

"Sure." He placed her ramen noodle package with the others and stared at a sleeve of crackers and a small jar of peanut butter neatly arranged in a plastic bin labeled Cassie.

God, she had so little. He had so much.

And she wouldn't take a damn thing from him. Not his money to pay for an oil change. And not his help to ease her trouble.

The buzz in the back of his mind became a howling chant.

*Mine! Mine! Mine!*

Hell no, she wasn't.

What Brice was experiencing was nothing more than a mating urge gone wrong. No way would he allow his nose to fuck up his life, again.

# *Chapter 11*

"Still sneaking around to avoid your father?" Granny's raspy words carried a strong reprimand.

Hating the disappointment in her voice, Brice shut the window and sat in the chair next to her bed. The grayish color in Granny's skin twisted his stomach into tiny knots. "How are you feeling?"

"Tonight isn't about me, my boy."

"Of course it is. You're the reason I came."

"And when I'm gone?" Her soft words lashed his heart. Emotion swelled his throat. Granny had helped him so much through his teenage years, especially when it became evident that the animosity between him and his father would escalate to violence.

"Don't say that." The gnawing in his gut chewed into his chest and chomped at his heart. When he was growing up, Brice had gravitated to Granny for comfort. He should have turned to her after the attack, not Adam.

"You must let go of those no longer destined for this world." Her hoarse voice faded.

"I can't." Brice curled his large hand over her cold, bony one.

"You can." The squeeze of her fingers held no strength. "And you will. Everything will be as it should be. You'll see."

Brice wanted to be the little wolf who believed that when Granny said things would turn out all right, they did. The problem was that life had a way of black-and-bluing the innocence of childhood. Reality really did bite, and it hurt a hell of a lot more than a wolfan's teeth.

He'd spent the past five years angry and confused. When he'd leaped onto her porch last night, he'd craved her counsel, and her blessing. He wanted Granny to understand the rare opportunity offered to him by the Woelfesenat, and he wanted her to support his decision.

Now that he had the chance to tell her, Brice's courage failed.

"Don't look so sad, my boy." The love in Granny's eyes wrapped around Brice's heart and squeezed the breath from his chest. He didn't deserve her love, but he sure was grateful for it.

"Your mate will help you when I am gone." Granny stroked his cheek the way she used to dry his tears. "She will calm the storm that's raged in you for far too long."

"I don't have a mate," Brice said gently.

"You have Cassie."

Not really. Although meeting her had sparked something inside him, she couldn't alter his fate. The howl in his head, the attraction he felt, his reaction to her scent—all that meant nothing.

"She's been good to me. She'll be good to you, too." Granny's mouth twitched.

"I don't need someone to take care of me."

"Of course you do." Her shallow breathing remained slow, steady. "Except for your coloring, you remind me of your grandfather."

"I don't remember him," Brice confessed.

"You were only two when he died. I told him to see the doctor about that croup. Damn old wolf." Granny's finger covered her dry lips. "Don't tell anyone I cussed."

"I won't." Brice matched her conspiratorial grin, even though his heart was splintering into sharp little pieces.

"Gavin is like him, too. Stubborn as a plow mule, tender-hearted as a lamb." Granny's eyelids fluttered.

"My father doesn't have a soft spot in his body. If he did, he'd claw it out and eat it raw." The angry words slipped out before Brice had a chance to filter them.

Granny flattened the palm of her IV-tethered hand against

the bed. She waggled her one-fingered chastisement. "Gavin had to be stronger than most new Alphas because I'm human."

"Why? Wahyas have mated with humans since the beginning."

"Some prejudices run deep and dark. And deadly. Gavin made many sacrifices to protect us. To protect you." Her cough turned into a gasping wheeze.

Not knowing what else to do, Brice poured her a cup of water. She drank a few sips and waved him off. "I'm all right."

"You need to rest." Brice held her hand against his chest, trying to share his strength and knowing it would do no good.

He wasn't ready. He wanted more time.

"Do something for me." Granny's words were nearly lost in the drone of the machines.

"Anything." Brice leaned closer.

"Make peace with your father." Her chest began to heave as she struggled to take the next breath. "And look after Cassie."

A snow cone had a better chance at surviving hellfire than Brice and his father had at reconciling. As for Cassie, she was too damn independent to appreciate him sticking his nose into her well-planned life.

He said as much.

Granny pinned him with one uncompromising eye, waiting. Pleading.

The finality of her wish struck a bull's-eye in Brice's heart. Sorrow bubbled in his stomach. The caustic fumes rose in his throat, infiltrated his nose and stung his eyes. When he took a breath to clear the burning sensation, his lungs seemed to clog with ash.

It wasn't fair for her to ask him to do something that required someone else's cooperation. He couldn't control his father's attitude or Cassie's willingness to accept help. He'd be a fool to commit to Granny's outrageous request.

All the pieces of his heart throbbed in perfect time. The dirge scored his chest. How could he not give her the last thing she'd asked of him?

"I promise," he said with the conviction his grandmother expected, because a Walker never reneged on a promise.

Cassie awoke in Brice's bed, confused. The last thing she remembered was studying on the couch while Brice got ready to go to the hospital.

She sensed rather than saw him perched on the edge of the mattress. "Brice?"

"I didn't mean to wake you. I just needed—" His jagged breath drowned out the rest.

The heavy shroud of his grief blanketed her. *Oh, no!* Unexpected pain imploded in her chest, and the crushing weight squeezed the air from her lungs.

Cassie shook her head and forced a breath through her constricted airways. She needed to hold it together for Brice. He was the rightful one to grieve. Margaret was his grandmother, not hers.

"I'm so sorry." The need to offer Brice physical comfort warred with her need for self-preservation. Without permission, Margaret Walker had wheedled a place into Cassie's heart. She couldn't afford another breach. Still, she knew what it felt like to suffer alone and didn't want to abandon him in his time of need.

She touched his shoulder.

He flinched.

Thinking it might be prudent to leave him alone to deal with his loss, Cassie started to draw back. Brice's fingers grazed the back of her hand, stilling her retreat. He lightly squeezed her fingers, then curved her palm against his cheek.

In the woods, and every time he became nauseated, he'd done the same. Her scent calmed and soothed him, so he said. Since she had nothing else to offer for comfort, Cassie scooted closer and wrapped herself around him.

Brice's shoulders rose along with an audible, exaggerated breath. He exhaled just as slowly and slumped into Cassie's embrace. She refrained from filling the silence with the words of comfort others had given her. Hearing her mother had moved on to a better place without her hadn't given Cassie solace, and she doubted the empty words would dull Brice's pain, either.

She gently rocked him in her arms for untold minutes before the antiseptic hospital smell lacing the fabric of his shirt became too much for her to stomach. She helped him take off the shirt and tossed it in the laundry basket near the closet.

"I should've come home sooner. Spent more time with her." With sluggish movements, Brice finished undressing, then lay next to Cassie on the bed.

"Your grandmother loved you very much, and you loved her. That's all that matters."

"Granny loved you, too, Cas." Brice's whisper cut through Cassie. "She really did."

After the stun from the revelation passed, a silent wail broke loose from a place deep inside Cassie's being. Ever since Imogene's death, Cassie had assumed she was alone in the world. It never occurred to her that someone else could truly care for her. Now that someone was gone. The sudden knowledge made the loss sharper, the loneliness starker.

Praying for strength because of her weakness, Cassie inched close enough to Brice to feel his heat. He gathered her in his arms and kissed the crown of her head. She buried her face in the broad expanse of his chest. The strong, steady beat of his heart, a lighthouse to her weary soul, beckoned her to a safe harbor.

Until Brice came along, Cassie had weathered many storms quite well on her own. She couldn't allow this tempest to change her.

Tomorrow she'd repair the cracks in her resolve. For tonight—and tonight only—she needed the anchor Brice's presence provided.

# Chapter 12

Behind his desk, Gavin Walker sat Lincoln-style, his shoulders straight, hands slightly curled on the thick leather arms of the executive chair. The chiseled planes of his weathered face were a masterpiece of stoicism. The only indication that he was indeed alive rather than a marble statue was the watchfulness of his calculating blue eyes.

"Nice of you to finally show up." His father's sarcastic tone rubbed Brice like a briar between his paw pads.

Nothing courteous he'd rehearsed in his mind stuck. Angry declarations, ugly accusations bounced in his head until he pressed his lips together to keep from firing the words lined up on his tongue like poisonous darts.

Communication between them had never been easy. In the aftermath of Mason's death, it became impossible. Evidently time hadn't worked any miracles.

Palms up, Brice spread his arms wide. "Granny asked me to come." He sat in one of the two captain's chairs in front of the desk, rested his booted foot on the opposite knee and threaded his fingers together over his stomach.

Seconds ticked an eternity. Brice refused to be the first to give in. He rubbed his hand over his morning whiskers and down his throat to scratch the sensitive scars itchy from the stress.

As his father's gaze took in each vicious mark, a sickening grimace contorted his mouth.

"Still can't stand the sight of me." Brice thought he'd grown immune to his father's disdain. Somehow it needled into a tiny, foolish, unguarded piece of his heart and stuck.

More silence volleyed between them. The longer the quietness stretched, the more the anger, the hurt, the frustration simmering inside Brice bubbled. Everything he wanted to say, needed to say, tangled on his tongue.

As a lawyer in his uncle's firm, Brice routinely mediated hostile business negotiations. The Woelfesenat had even recruited him to arbitrate aggressions between warring packs. His success depended upon finding common ground.

Considering Brice and his father never saw eye to eye on anything, it might prove impossible to find a neutral starting point. Nevertheless, he had to try.

"I'm sorry for your loss." Nothing in his father's demeanor had expressed remorse over Granny's death. Still, Brice needed to acknowledge it. "I was with her at the end. She went peacefully."

A tiny fracture appeared in Gavin's stony manner. His shoulders rounded. His wrinkled brow slanted over troubled eyes. "She wanted you with her, though I imagine it must have been hard on you."

A sudden swell of grief brought Brice the acute awareness that his grandmother would never rock his children to sleep, soothe their tears or give them ice cream on a hot summer day. How strange that he would mourn something missed by children he never expected to father.

He brushed the tickle at the tip of his ear in an attempt to flick away the nearly imperceptible howl pestering his conscience.

Gavin straightened in his chair. "When I spoke to Adam this morning, he reluctantly admitted that you've been missing since Thursday. Needless to say, he was quite relieved when I explained that you had arrived safely Saturday night."

The blood in Brice's veins chilled. "How do you know when I returned?"

"Cooter spotted you at Gilmer's Bend." Gavin paused. "That's a dangerous waterway. Don't swim it again. I don't want the wolflings to emulate that stunt. It's bad enough they continue to tease Cybil because of that stupid prank you and Rafe played."

Brice didn't argue. He didn't want any of the young-sters getting hurt, either. If he'd known their teenaged pig-wrangling adventure would turn into a rite of passage for the wolflings, well, he probably would've done it anyway. He and Rafe had the best time of their lives freeing Cybil from the pen in their human forms, then corralling her as wolves. Cybil had been neither afraid of them nor willing to return to her sty. By the time they wrangled her back inside the pen, he and Rafe had more than their fair share of cuts and bruises and a few broken ribs.

"Anyway, Cooter called after your mother and I left the hospital. I brought Abby home and told her I needed to run. I was too late to catch you before you reached the cabin." The corners of his father's eyes stretched into a smile more than his lips. "You and Miss Albright gave me quite a show. I trust she didn't cause permanent damage to your balls."

If Brice didn't know better, he'd swear that his father was teasing him. However, he did know better. Gavin Walker never teased.

Brice placed both feet flat on the floor. "Why didn't you come for me afterward?"

"I didn't want you taking off again. Your grandmother needed you, and you needed to be with her. Now that she's gone, I want—"

"Allow me the decency to see her laid to rest before you kick me out again."

A dark, unsettling look crossed his father's face. "As you wish." He tossed Brice a set of keys and a cell phone. "Your mother prepared your old room in the hope you would return."

Brice wanted to project his negotiator's face. The blank one that gave no hint to his thoughts or emotions.

He failed.

First his eyes bugged. He felt the tightness behind the orbs as they bulged forward. An immediate dryness followed, since his eyelids were stuck wide-open.

Next his jaw went slack. Thank God his mouth didn't drop

open, spilling nonsensical prattle. For chrissakes, did his father think he would ever sleep under the same roof with him again?

Hell, no. Sixteen years were more than plenty.

"I'll remain at the cabin," Brice said, glad that his voice sounded normal.

"Ah, that brings me to the matter of Miss Albright." Gavin folded his hands over his waist and swiveled his chair side to side in a slow sweep.

"Granny's will deeds the cabin to me unless you force me to forfeit." Brice paused, bracing for an epic battle. A banished pack member couldn't own property inside the territory.

When his father shook his head to indicate he wouldn't interfere, Brice's insides jarred as if he'd stopped suddenly on a roller-coaster ride.

"Good." He cleared the rattle from his voice. "Granny asked that I take care of Cassie. I plan to give her full use of the cabin when I return to Atlanta. Until then, we'll share the space." And a bed, though his father didn't need to know that tidbit.

"Perhaps you should rent her an apartment in Maico, or give her money to find other accommodations."

"She refused to let me pay for an oil change. I doubt she'll take rent money."

"Son, people might misconstrue the circumstances."

"I don't care what people think."

"Do you know who her mother was?" Gavin's disapproval swamped the room.

"What the hell does that matter?" Brice didn't judge people based on their parentage or anything else except their own merit.

"Imogene Struthers."

The name detonated the room.

The deafening percussion banged in Brice's ears. Oh, yeah, he knew of Imogene Struthers. A pretty little drunk who'd slept with men for money when she ran out of her own. Brice's father had ordered the pack's unmated males to stay away from her. He didn't want the taint infecting the pack.

Brice hadn't known Imogene had a daughter. "Cassie isn't like her mother."

"You just met her. How can you be sure?"

Because yesterday morning, with steel in her eyes and grit in her voice, Cassie declared she didn't want or need Brice's money, and he believed her. The apple might not fall far from the tree, but it sure as hell could roll from beneath its shadow.

"I'll take my chances."

"Very well." Gavin's thumb tapped against the silver wedding band on his finger. "Go see Doc. Get a good physical and whatever else he feels you need."

Since his father dropped the issue of questioning Cassie's character, Brice's mood mellowed. "I had a checkup three months ago. Shots updated and everything."

Gavin's commanding look rubbed Brice raw; however, since he was no longer in hiding, Brice had planned to visit the pack physician for his bouts of nausea anyway.

"While you're in town, take time to visit the pack," Gavin ordered.

"I'm not here to socialize."

"They've missed you. And you missed a lot of important events in their lives."

Just when Brice thought they'd manage to remain civil for an entire conversation, his father had to bring up a matter that needed no spark before the explosion. Raging frustration unhinged Brice's control. He jumped to his feet and stalked to his father's desk.

"I've missed important events?" His fists slammed the mahogany desk, knocking over a crystal picture frame. He snatched up the photo of a tawny adolescent wolf and a black wolfling pup and shoved it toward his father's displeased face. "What important events have you missed?"

Brice didn't give him a chance to reply as he began to pace. "Where were you when I lost my first tooth or the first time I shifted? Oh, who took me on my first hunt? Sure as hell wasn't you.

"What about explaining puberty? Or teaching me how to drive? Didn't see you at either of my college commencements, and I bet you don't give a damn that I received a perfect score on my bar exam. On my first attempt."

Brice gripped the back of his empty chair. "You had time for Mason's important events. Never mine."

"Is jealousy what's been eating you all this time?"

"God, no." Exasperated, Brice wanted to wrap his fingers around his father's neck—not tightly enough to cause physical harm. He'd simply throttle him until he understood. Instead, he threw his hands in the air. "Mason *was* there for me, every single time, when it should've been you. Now he's gone and you still don't get it."

"Son, calm down." Gavin stood, his fingers spread wide as the motion of his hands echoed his words.

"Fuck you." Brice slammed the door on his way out.

# *Chapter 13*

Engaging the four-wheel drive, Brice turned off Shelley Highway onto a washed-out road that corkscrewed up Bluebird Mountain. Glimpses of the MacGregor antebellum flickered through a grove of large oaks dripping with Spanish moss.

From a distance, the homestead bespoke an old Southern charm. Up close, twining vines strangled the Roman columns anchoring the portico. Woody runners choked the wrought iron railings, and mutant veins streaked across the entire antiquated structure.

Two jostling miles farther, the dirt road dead-ended. Brice stopped and climbed out of the truck. The warm breeze caressing his face carried no distinguishable scent, yet his stomach, already churning, somersaulted.

Out of his hip pocket, he pulled a plastic zip bag containing a pair of Cassie's unmentionables. Ordinarily he didn't snoop through a woman's lingerie or steal it. Desperation over the debilitating nausea had forced him to become a petty panty thief.

He opened the bag and breathed in her scent. The unconventional remedy quieted his stomach. He hoped the effect would last until he saw Cassie later. Her scent was damn near irresistible. He planned to inhale her sweetness in giant lungfuls all night long.

She could fuss all she wanted about sharing his bed because regardless of her propriety, Little Miss Albright was a world-class snuggler. She enjoyed sleeping next to him, whether or not she admitted it.

Brice placed his folded clothes on the seat. The panty bag, keys and cell phone he tossed into the glove compartment.

Dropping to all fours, he craned his neck, then stretched his back. The mild shock from the shift energy rushed down his spine, stinging his nerves. Black fur sprouted from his skin as the morph of muscle, bone and tendons reshaped man into wolf. He lifted his muzzle and threw back a low, mournful howl.

Head and eyes lowered, he trotted to a small cove. Time had erased all traces of violence. Thin, towering trees shielded the lush foliage, although a few diligent sunbeams managed to trickle through the dense canopy in an attempt to warm the damp, musky thicket. He pawed the greedy ground that had lapped his brother's blood. The thick mud stuck to Brice's pads like a decrepit paste.

Five years ago, he and Mason weren't hunting to kill. They were simply exercising and enjoying one another's company. Absorbed in tracking an unfamiliar scent, Brice didn't notice the trap until the clamp of sharp metal teeth ripped through his flesh and snapped his bones. His first reaction had been a howl of pain.

Mason shifted into his human form to free Brice's leg. The old, rusty snare refused to budge. Neither of them knew rogues stalked the area until they appeared on the ridge.

Brice begged Mason to run. Instead, Mason went wolf, howling an alarm for any sentinels within range. Then he engaged the rogue pack alone.

Brice shifted into his human form to free himself, knowing the morph would cause more damage to his leg, but the rogues outnumbered Mason. Four to one, five to one. Brice couldn't remember.

So much blood poured from the wounds, his fingers kept slipping over the spring, wasting too many precious seconds. When the latch finally released, Brice shifted back into his wolf. Blocking the excruciating pain of his dangling leg, he charged three-footed toward the fight.

He bouldered two wolves off Mason. The first rolled to his paws, rounded on Brice and sank his teeth into Brice's side, slamming him to the ground. The other wolf launched for the kill.

Twisting his hips, Brice dislodged the first in time to catch the second by the throat. Dirt and fur coated his tongue, and the metallic taste of blood made him gag. Still, he clamped his jaw and yanked.

The sickening sound of ripping flesh and the gurgle of blood followed. The rogue wolf thudded to the ground, a lifeless man.

Snarling, his partner slashed Brice's shoulder to the bone. Brice's retaliatory bite laid open the wolf's hindquarter. Yelping, the wounded wolf scampered away. Two others charged.

Mason intercepted one, evening the odds.

Brice's head swarmed from the blood pouring from his wounds. The enemy wolf stayed just out of reach, wearing Brice down until he had little strength.

Brice glanced at his brother. One wolf had engaged Mason, distracting him from the mangy gray moving in.

*"Mason! Left!"* Brice's warning came too late. His brother collapsed, blood spurting from his throat.

The horror lasted less than a second before Brice became engulfed in a black rage. He sensed rather than saw the remaining wolves turn on him. Everything blurred in a fury of fur and fangs.

When his vision cleared, four rogues lay dead, their human bodies nothing more than bloody heaps. Barely able to walk, Brice struggled to reach his brother's side.

Brice shifted and hauled Mason's human form against his chest. He pressed his hand over Mason's gushing neck wound.

The thick, coppery scent of blood and the putrid stench of death cloyed Brice's nose. He gagged, yet the sound that escaped the tear in his throat sounded like gurgling wheeze.

Willing his life into his brother, he clung to Mason until, weak from his own blood loss, Brice slipped into darkness without ever saying goodbye.

Saying it now seemed too little, too late.

He circled the spot where he'd lost his brother, his mentor, his hero. Grief turned to anger. Brice's throat ached from the strain of unshed tears.

*You should've left me, Mace. I should've died. Not you. Now Granny's gone, too.*

Brice plopped on the ground, his head resting between his paws. His heavy sigh lifted a leaf from its spot in front of his nose.

A light breeze ruffled Brice's fur, though the woods were eerily still.

*Kill them. Kill them all.* Mason's last words resounded in Brice's mind as clear as the day his brother had imparted them to him employing the telepathic ability Wahyas manifested in their wolfan forms.

And Brice had done exactly what Mason had asked of him. He'd killed every last one of those damn fucking rogues. Hadn't he?

Waiting for her tea to heat in the microwave, Cassie scarfed down a container of yogurt. Loss and loneliness muted the elation of breezing through her exam. She missed sharing good news with Margaret.

Now that she was gone, the Walkers had no reason to continue Cassie's housing arrangement.

A quick rundown of her finances amounted to zilch. It had been only a few months ago that she'd paid off the credit card debt her mother had racked up under Cassie's Social Security number. And Cassie didn't want to spend her tiny savings to cover deposits on an apartment that she needed for only a few months.

The microwave dinged. Cassie collected her mug with all her dignity and a whopping load of anxiety, and left to clock in.

Dirty apartments, cheap motel rooms, a run-down RV, a tent, a dilapidated trailer—those were the homes Cassie and Imogene had shared. All were better than living on the streets, which is where Cassie would end up if she couldn't figure out an alternative. No matter how hard she worked, Cassie had no better luck than her mother.

"Cassie, come to my office." Abigail Walker continued past the registration counter.

Cassie's clenched stomach twisted into a pretzel knot. She sat in one of the mahogany chairs with button-tufted black leather. "I'm very sorry for your loss, Mrs. Walker."

"Thank you, Cassie. If you hadn't been there to help Margaret on Friday night, she might have slipped away before Brice had a chance to see her again." Abigail stroked the flat desk calendar, meticulously smoothing the curled edges into the blotter. "Gavin told me that Brice spent the last two nights at the cabin." Her gaze locked on Cassie. "With you."

Cassie kept her chin up, her shoulders straight, although her toes gripped the inside of her shoes. The words "Your services are no longer required" dangled over her head, a guillotine blade ready to finish the hack job delivered by bad karma.

"You should've had the decency to tell me." Abigail's censure slapped Cassie's heart.

"I didn't want to betray his trust." Knowing she'd done the right thing didn't ease Cassie's guilt.

"I am his mother. I had a right to know."

"Brice asked for my silence and I gave it. He's an adult. I am not his keeper."

"I see." The faint folds around Abigail's mouth elongated her frown. She gathered the papers on her desk.

Cassie inched down in her chair, envisioning her future capsizing in slow motion. If she lost her job, she would have to quit college. And Cassie couldn't let that happen. She'd worked long and hard and sacrificed everything to get this far. If she fell flat now, she might not gain the momentum to get up again.

Although her nerves jumped, Cassie's grip remained steady, accepting the printout Abigail handed to her.

Cassie skimmed the upcoming bookings. "Is something wrong with the reservations?"

"We're closing the resort for Margaret's memorial service. We expect a large number of friends and associates to come. I want you to call everyone on that list to reschedule their reservations. All the current guests need to vacate the premises no later than Wednesday afternoon. Express our regrets and make alternative arrangements as necessary."

Cassie thumbed through the pages. More names than not were guests she had assisted. Her rapport might make them more amenable to the disruption in their plans. In light of her own upheavals, she could fully empathize.

"One more thing," Abigail said crisply, and Cassie snapped her attention back to her employer. "Margaret's property now belongs to Brice. You will need to speak to him about your housing situation. Whatever he decides, Gavin and I won't interfere."

"I understand." Cassie kept her poise professional despite the sinking feeling rising in the pit of her stomach. She'd been homeless before, and Cassie had hoped and prayed that the latest time really had been the last time. But she knew all too well that her prayers were seldom answered.

# *Chapter 14*

The cell phone cradled to the dashboard rang. One of the resort's outgoing numbers flashed across the screen. Brice pressed the Bluetooth button on the steering wheel.

"Where are you?" his father demanded over the speakers.

Disappointment preceded Brice's annoyance. He'd expected Cassie. "Driving into Maico to see Doc as commanded. Why?"

The ensuing silence made Brice think the call had dropped. "Dad?"

"I hadn't expected your compliance so quickly." There was a pause. "Thank you."

His father's appreciation caught Brice off guard and made him incredibly suspicious. The man was up to something and Brice was sure he wouldn't like it one bit.

"We have an appointment at the funeral home at seven. Your mother and I expect you to join us. Don't be late." Whenever his father issued a command, his tone always implied an "or else."

"As you wish," Brice said, wanting to keep the promise to his grandmother at least in spirit. He doubted father and son could ever truly reconcile. There were too many disappointments and angry words to overcome. "Thanks for not turning me out, again. It means a lot to me to be here for Granny's memorial."

"I'm glad you're home, son." Was there a note of sincerity in his father's voice? "If you need anything, let me know."

Brice couldn't believe his ears. Maybe grief had softened his father's heart.

But, he wouldn't hold his breath.

His father cleared his throat. "We'll see you tonight."

"Wait." He might regret involving his father, but Brice's

second promise to his grandmother concerned Cassie and right now his worry over her outweighed his hesitation. "Has Cassie clocked in?" By now, she should've returned from the state college over in Brasstown Valley. If not, Brice wanted to know sooner rather than later. "She hasn't returned my calls."

"Hold on," his father said. Muzak filtered through the speakers.

Brice turned off Shelley Highway onto Chaney Boulevard, heading toward the small town of Maico.

"Thank you for calling Walker's Run Resort. This is Cassie. How may I help you?" Although her tone was all business, Brice found her voice as relaxing as the soft, bubbling warmth of a Jacuzzi.

"Hey, Sunshine."

"Who's calling, please?"

A stab of jealousy scattered the unusual, fuzzy sensation spreading through his body. "Who else calls you Sunshine?"

"Brice? Oh, I, um, didn't know you were on the line. Mr. Walker only said someone needed my assistance." She lowered her voice. "Are you coming to smell me?"

Brice's cheeks hurt from the grin splitting his face. "No, I found a way to manage for now."

"Oh, that's good."

If she knew what it was, she might not think so.

"How did you do on your test?" Brice expected that she did well. He'd found her to be quick-minded and doggedly determined.

"Passed, I think."

"You think?" Raising his voice in a tease, he wondered if a blush reddened her skin.

"Okay, I aced it."

Her bashful boast beckoned back the warm fuzzies. Their rushing invasion caused his hands, his skin, his groin to twitch. He couldn't wait to see her tonight.

"That's great, Cas," he said. "Hey, what time do you get off?"

"Nine thirty."

Brice whistled. "That's a long day." Although his wouldn't be much shorter. "I'm meeting my parents at the funeral home tonight. Want me to pick up supper on the way home?"

"No, I've got food…" Cassie's voice trailed.

Brice hit the volume button. "Are you sure? It's no trouble for me to grab some burgers or pick up a pizza. Whatever you want, name it."

"Some other time."

"All right, then." Brice kept his tone light, flipping the air vent away from him to dispel the sudden chill in his bones.

"Uh, Brice?"

"Yeah, Sunshine?" He brightened, thinking she'd changed her mind.

"About the housing arrangement I had."

"That's not going to work for me." He didn't need Cassie to be his live-in maid. He wanted something more personal.

Friends? Absolutely.

Between-the-sheets friends? Hell, yeah.

More than friends? He couldn't risk that one, but whatever happened, he expected them to be on equal ground.

"Oh, okay. Bye." Her voice sounded tight, choked.

"Cas?"

The line went dead.

A pinball pinged around in his gut. He activated the voice redial and asked for Cassie.

"Hey, stranger," Hannah Barkley, an old friend, said when she recognized his voice. "I'm glad you're finally home. Sucks about the circumstances, though. I'm sorry about Granny."

"Thanks," Brice mumbled.

"Things must've gone a little better with your dad this morning." Hannah's tone sounded light and teasing, just like always. "At least the lobby chandelier didn't crash to the floor like it did the last time you slammed the door to your dad's office."

Brice cringed. His father always pulled the worst out of

him, and Brice hated that he couldn't control his emotions around the man.

"Whatever Gavin said to piss you off, your mom sure took him to task," Hannah continued. "I thought your temper came from your dad. After today, I think your mom might've played a role, too."

"I'm not particularly fond of the trait, no matter who passed it on to me." Brice paused. "Maybe we can catch up later. I need time to get my bearings, and I have a lot weighing on my mind."

"Is Victoria Phalen one of those weights?"

Brice's gut clenched, and an unpleasant taste sprouted on his tongue. "Why?"

"She called asking for a key to your suite. I told her you didn't have a reservation, so she booked the honeymoon suite in your name."

"I'm staying at Granny's cabin." After the stunt Victoria pulled in Atlanta, Brice wanted to stay the hell away from her.

"Um…" Hannah hedged. "Your grandmother had a boarder, Cassie Albright. We work together, Brice. And she's a friend. Don't kick her out. She has nowhere else to go."

"I'm aware of Cassie's situation, and we have a mutually beneficial arrangement." Or they would as soon as he spoke to her about it. "Can you put her on the line?"

"Sure!" Relief lightened Hannah's tone. "Hold on a sec."

Approaching Maico's city limits, Brice remembered Mason's stories of a small group of Wahyas who integrated into this dying human settlement more than three hundred years ago. Farmers by day, wolves by night. Growing crops, hunting game. Hiding their dual identities while cohabiting with their human neighbors to build a better life for all.

Tired of the turmoil caused by constant challengers to Alphaships seized in trials of combat, the Maico Wahyas elected Abram Walker as Alpha and established a familial line of succession the pack continued to follow. Abram laid claim to Maico and the surrounding area, and acceptance by the

Woelfesenat legitimized the fledgling pack. Each subsequent generation saw the pack and their human neighbors prosper.

Passing Maico's welcome sign, Brice noticed the paint peeling from the board. The farther into town he drove, the antsier he became at the number of abandoned buildings and broken sidewalks and the amount of roadside litter.

Maico had been a pristine community that could've popped off the pages of a fairy-tale book. For some reason, the quaint village had deteriorated into a shabby soon-to-be ghost town. His disappointment grew when a glance down Sorghum Avenue revealed the R&L—Rafe's automotive repair service— looking as bad as the other places Brice had passed.

Hannah came back on the line. "Sorry, Brice. Cassie is on another call. Your mom assigned her to rebook all the reservations scheduled through Sunday."

"Have Cassie call me when she gets a break." Brice rattled off the cell number and disconnected the Bluetooth call.

Turning left at the fourth red light, he drove to the Maico Medical Plaza across the street from the hospital and parked in front of the second brick-and-mortar building. He held open the office door for two of his grandmother's elderly human friends. They offered profuse, sincere condolences, which he graciously accepted.

Popping her gum, the young human receptionist at the check-in window buzzed him in. He limped to Doc's office, less able to ignore the pain flaring since his jaunt through the woods.

Following the obligatory hug and bantered greetings, Doc hitched up his pant leg and perched on the edge of his desk. More silver streaked his godfather's hair than Brice remembered.

"When Gavin said you'd drop by, I didn't expect you to be so prompt."

Brice rubbed his chin. "When did he call?"

"About fifteen minutes ago."

"That's around the time I told him I was on my way."

"When did he ask you to come?" Doc cleaned his glasses using the corner of his lab coat.

"This morning." Brice scratched an itch behind his ear.

Doc laughed. "At least the delay got shorter. I remember when you'd wait at least a week before doing anything he asked."

"He doesn't ask. He demands."

"That is a matter of perspective, son." Doc clapped his hands. "Let's get started, shall we?"

Brice provided the date of his last physical and rabies immunization, listed pain medications prescribed but not taken, described the same trouble sleeping, mentioned a few other things and then got to the real issue.

"The nausea began when you scented this mystery woman?" Otoscope in hand, Doc tipped Brice's head up.

"After her scent faded." Brice gurgled a sneeze. Having something shoved up his nose was as uncomfortable as gagging on a tongue depressor.

"How long has this been going on?"

"I'd rather not say." Brice hadn't mentioned Cassie by name. Providing a time frame would pretty much shine a spotlight on her. Something, he thought, she wouldn't appreciate.

"It's important to give me all the details."

"You know that after the attack I smelled blood and guts 24/7."

"A posttraumatic olfactory hallucination. I told you it would fade in time."

"When it did, I lost my sense of smell completely." Brice paused.

Doc's clinical expression didn't change, so the information wasn't new to him. Adam must've updated the Walker's Run pack physician when it happened, although Brice wondered why. Generally, a pack didn't concern themselves in the affairs of shunned wolfans.

"After I met this woman, I started scenting again, but the smells make me sick unless she's with me."

"How do you feel now?" Doc clicked off the lighted scope and tossed the plastic speculum into the trash. "Any nausea?"

"Not at the moment." Brice pulled the baggie from his hip pocket.

"That's creative. Carried it all the way from Atlanta, did you?" The crinkles around Doc's light brown eyes deepened.

Brice remained silent.

"Well, your nose looks fine." Doc scribbled in Brice's medical chart. "My guess is that you're simply regaining your sense of smell."

"Why would that make me sick?" Brice stuffed the plastic bag into his pocket.

"You've been scentless for five years. Now that you can smell, your stomach is reacting to the sensory overload. The nausea should stop once you adjust. In the meantime, you might experience a confusion of scents until your brain relearns how to decipher the smells."

"Great," Brice said not feeling the sentiment. "Any ideas as to why this woman's scent triggered all this?"

"A Wahya's nose is quite remarkable, imprinting every scent it detects even if the wolfan doesn't register it in his or her human form." Doc tugged on the stethoscope looped around his neck. "Your mystery woman probably isn't a mystery to your wolf. She may have stood behind you at the grocery store or sat near you in a restaurant at any point in your life."

"Then when I run into her again—" Brice snapped his fingers "—my nose starts working? Sorry, Doc. Not buying it. Trust me, I'd remember her if we'd met before."

"Your wolf remembers even when your human self can't. The wolf always remembers." Doc sat behind his desk. "Have you considered the possibility that you've found your true mate?"

"Considered and dismissed."

"Keep an open mind. You might be surprised by what you discover." Doc reached for the phone.

The howl in Brice's mind that he had twice banked reared triumphant. For a third time, he silenced the whine.

He liked Cassie. Hell, he couldn't deny his attraction to her, but that was lust, plain and simple. Besides, Cassie didn't show signs of a deeper, inexplicable connection between them or any sense of knowing that they belonged together. Instead, she had made it clear he wasn't a part of her destiny.

True mates began bonding from their first meeting, the ethereal tendrils entwining and strengthening with each subsequent encounter. If he'd met Cassie in the past and if they were indeed true mates, Brice's mating urge would've sparked in those first moments.

It happened that way for Rafe and Lexi, and they were only eight. Of course, they didn't pursue an intimate relationship until they were the proper age. They didn't have children when Brice left. Rafe always said they were working on it.

Brice hoped they had a houseful of wolflings now. And he planned to spoil each of them, if Rafe allowed him. Not once in five years had Rafe contacted him, and Brice had been too emotionally raw to reach out to his best friend.

Doc placed his hand over the phone's mouthpiece. "I want you to get a CT scan so I can compare it to your previous one. The imaging center has an opening now. Will you go?"

Brice answered that he would. Doc finished the call and Brice asked, "Do you think Rafe and Lexi would mind if I stopped by their place?"

Doc stooped forward as if he'd taken a punch in the stomach. He braced his hands against his desk and took a deep breath. "Brice, Lexi's dead."

A breath-stealing pain crashed through the center of Brice's being. The shock wave stemmed not only from the news of the death of a lifelong friend but also the sorrow and sympathy he felt for Rafe's utter devastation.

Brice never wanted to experience the depths of pain, despair and often guilt the loss of a mate-bonded partner would wreak on male wolfan. Thankfully, an apprenticeship with the Woelfesenat would assure he never would.

# *Chapter 15*

Brice came home to an empty driveway and a deserted cabin. On the answering machine playback, his tired voice cracked the silence, urging Cassie to pick up the phone. After a pause, concern rang through his message for her to call him when she got home.

For the umpteenth time, he fished the cell phone from his pocket. No missed calls.

He dialed the resort. The night auditor, Shane McQuarrie, as he identified himself, swore Cassie clocked out on time and left.

Maybe she had car trouble and called Rafe, though Brice wondered why she hadn't called him, too. He'd left several messages for her at work, asking her to do just that.

After three unsuccessful telephone attempts to reach Rafe, Brice drove to R&L Automotive. The tow truck, Rafe's old Jeep and a few other cars were parked inside the locked fence. Doc said Rafe often ran the woods at night. Brice's heart hurt for Rafe's loss, and he intended to do whatever he could for his friend. Right now, though, Brice needed to find Cassie.

He circled through town in case she'd opted for takeout over another ramen noodle supper. Not seeing her car, he drove to Taylor's Roadhouse on the outskirts of town. Mondays used to be singles night. Maybe she went for drinks after work.

Kicking back with Cassie and dancing to a song or two would be a nice way to wind down the evening, unless she wasn't alone. He hadn't considered that she might be dating someone.

Sight unseen, he immediately detested the guy. Anyone who showed the slightest interest in Cassie would have to go through him. After all, Brice had a promise to keep.

The parking lot had no open spaces, and not one of the vehicles belonged to Cassie. He drove through the residential sections of Maico, conflicted. What if he found her car parked at some yahoo's house?

His ambivalence blossomed into anxiety when he didn't. He sped over to Northeast Georgia College in Brasstown Valley, cruised the campus parking lots. He no longer cared if he found Cassie with someone. He just wanted to find her.

On the return trip to Maico, Brice searched the condemned trailer park where Cassie had lived. Each call for her that went unanswered fed his imagination of finding her broken and bleeding.

Panic frayed his self-control. His fingers gripped the steering wheel so hard that the rod inside the ring began to bend. At the red light, he pried loose his hands and shook them out.

*Cas, where the hell are you?*

*Are you okay?*

The uncertainty ate at him like a cancer, devouring him cell by cell. He turned toward the last place he knew to look. The hospital. His already fast-beating heart launched into ludicrous speed at the sight of Cassie's car parked close to the ER entrance.

He wheeled into the parking lot, jammed the gear into Park, ran inside the building, checked every bay, questioned every person. No one had seen Cassie.

The tightness in his chest threatened to put him in a hospital bed if he didn't find her soon. All the things people swore when begging God for a favor, he offered and more.

He'd promised Granny he would take care of Cassie. *Promised!* After only one day, it seemed he'd already failed them both.

Walking toward Cassie's car, Brice dug the cell phone from his pocket.

"Yeah?" Pack sentinel and sworn sheriff deputy Tristan Durrance's sleepy voice answered.

In bed asleep was not where Brice expected Mason's former best friend to be on singles' night. Tristan and Mason were notorious ladies' men. Brice had assumed Tristan, a resolute bachelor, would be at Taylor's, carrying on the tradition.

"Who's calling?" Tristan sounded more alert, suspicious.

Brice's tongue stuck to the roof of his mouth. In the past, he wouldn't have thought twice about asking Tristan for help. Now Brice didn't know how well Tristan would receive him.

Reaching Cassie's car, Brice's fingers swept the cool hood. Tristan's threats about what he would do to his prank caller if he caught him assaulted Brice's ear. He peered into the driver's window. Empty, the front seat held no clues to Cassie's whereabouts.

Peeking in the rear door window, he noticed a swaddled lump in the backseat. Then he saw the ringlets of red hair fanned over the pillow. Tucked beneath a delicate chin, small hands clasped the frayed edges of the comforter. Coppery lashes fringed her porcelain skin.

*Cas!* Brice snapped the phone shut. The invisible bands around his torso popped, releasing a tide of relief. Cresting on the waves came the urge to seize, to dominate, to claim.

"No." Brice stepped away to avoid ripping the car door off its hinges.

Animal instinct would not rule him as a man. Massaging the bridge of his nose, he counted. He would count to the world's population if that's what it took to regain control.

Careful not to break the window, Brice knocked his knuckles against the glass. Cassie snuggled deeper beneath her comforter.

"Cas, wake up!"

Her eyelids eased open. Slowly she sat up. Sleepy. Sexy. Safe.

"Brice?" She yawned.

"Unlock the door, Sunshine." He waited for the click, yanked open the door. In one swift move, he hauled her from the backseat and pinned her against the car.

"Stop that!" Fully awake, she shoved him.

"I thought something happened to you." Brice nosed her

hair, her neck, gulping her scent to calm his frantic heart. "What the hell are you doing here?"

"Sleeping." She squirmed out of his clutches.

"For God's sake, why?"

"You were going to evict me anyway." She tucked her fists beneath her arms. "The hospital parking lot is safe. It's easy to sneak through the ER to the employee showers. The cafeteria has decent food. There's also a nice nook in the waiting area where I can study."

"Dammit, Cas." The blush staining her cheeks reminded him of her fragility regardless of her grit. He softened his tone. "When I said the arrangement doesn't work for me, I meant that I'm not an old woman who needs a caretaker."

"Yeah, I got that."

"Just because I don't need a caretaker doesn't mean I don't want your company."

"What are you saying?" Hope flashed in her sharp, not-quite-trusting eyes.

"I don't want you to leave." No way in hell was he going through this upheaval again.

"You aren't evicting me?" Cassie nibbled her bottom lip. Something he had a sudden hankering to do, too.

"Hell, no." He wanted to know where she'd be at all times.

Instead of jumping for joy or hugging and kissing him in gratitude, as Brice expected, Cassie walked a few steps away. Nervous that she didn't immediately agree to share the cabin with him, he shuffled the weight on his feet.

"How much is rent and what are the rules?" she asked, her back to him.

"No rent. No rules." He shoved his hands into his pockets so he wouldn't sling her over his shoulder caveman-style.

"I don't take freebies." Cassie spun around, hands on her hips, shaking her head.

The sight of those wild curls bouncing against her shoulders triggered another gush of testosterone. He hardened instantly. Primal instinct strained against his restraint to comply with the wolf's demand to seize and claim. The animal was gaining strength, the mating urge growing stronger. If his wolfan nature took control, Brice wouldn't be able to stop himself from taking a mate, whether or not Cassie wanted to be claimed.

*Unless you want to frighten her, hurt her, turn her against us and make her hate us...settle the fuck down!*

The restless snarling quieted to a few disgruntled growls. The overwhelming urge throbbing in the forefront of his mind to take everything he could, right here, right now, retreated into the dark recesses of his wolfan consciousness, tempered. But for how long?

"Can we discuss this later?" Brice plowed his fingers through a tumble of hair falling across his forehead. "It's late and I want to get you home, safe."

Cassie more than appreciated Brice's concern for her welfare. He awed her, actually. Kind, protective, not to mention devilishly handsome—oh, it wouldn't take much to fall hard for him, and if she didn't stay on her guard, she'd tumble all the way down Heartbreak Boulevard and land in the trash compactor of the junkyard of shattered dreams.

"What are your terms? I can cook and clean in lieu of rent. No sex, though. That's a deal breaker."

"God, Cassie." The planes of Brice's appalled face sharpened in the glow of the parking lot lights. "How could you think I would expect that from you?"

"Sometimes my mom slept with men so we'd have a place to live and food." Cassie didn't actually believe Brice the type to barter for sex, but better to know now than when he tried to collect payment. "I won't do it, though. I'd rather sleep in my car."

"I'd rather you didn't." The deep creases between Brice's eyebrows softened. "The cabin is your home. For as long as you want it to be."

"So, cooking and cleaning it is." She extended her hand.

"I don't need a housekeeper." Brice lifted her fingers to his cheek. "I don't need rent. I need to know you're safe."

"I can take care of myself." Cassie's typical adamancy waned under the influence of Brice's wispy breaths against her inner wrist. Her entire body stilled, though not from tension. Her muscles remained loose and pliable as he gently angled her arm slightly upward to rest her hand on his shoulder. He edged slowly into her personal space, testing her temperament toward the invasion.

"I'm not getting frisky," he said cautiously. "I need to smell you."

Words any woman would want to hear standing next to a wolfman in a deserted parking lot in the middle of the night.

Cassie nodded. He slowly placed his hands on her hips, lowering his face and skimming her cheek along her jaw. She concentrated on pacing her breaths to avoid sucking up the miniscule amount of air between them in one giant expectant gulp.

He nosed her earlobe, inching up to the shell. She bit her lip to stifle a gasp at the raspy pants in her ear as he nuzzled her hair.

His hands remained anchored on her hips. Despite her clothing, she felt every one of his long, tapered fingers burning into her skin. A cozy warmth spread through her body, softening her defenses like heated candle wax. She allowed Brice liberties she'd not given to any other man and wasn't quite sure why her acquiescence seemed so natural and comfortable in his presence.

A false sense of security...that's what he gave her. She shouldn't linger too long in the mirage. Better she should create her own stability by standing on her own two feet. Preferably when she wasn't swaying with Brice's every move.

"Um, while you sniff, think of something I can barter for rent. I won't accept something for nothing." Cassie refused to fall into the trap of relying on other people. In the end, they always disappointed.

Brice's heavy sigh gusted her hair. He pulled back slightly to study her. His mouth taut, an infinitesimal twitch on his lips made her think he'd started counting again.

He seemed to do that a lot.

She watched the slow slide of his Adam's apple. Standing on her toes, she might be tall enough to chase the lump with her tongue down to the jagged scars lining the base of his throat. Not that she would risk such a behavior. It was simply something to think while Brice decided on her rent.

"Pies." He flashed a sinful smile.

"Huh?" Cassie sank back on her heels after realizing she had rocked forward on her toes.

"Pies for rent. Sound reasonable?"

"Seriously?"

"I never joke about food," he deadpanned.

"I suppose you wouldn't, considering you're part wolf." Cassie slumped against the car. On her budget, she would be stupid not to take Brice's lopsided offer. Coming from anyone else, she would be suspicious. But everyone in town knew Brice's family had money, so he really didn't need hers, and she'd heard he was always a man of his word. "Deal. And you already ate my first payment."

Brice's high-wattage smile made his previous one look like a night-light in comparison. "I would ask for a kiss to seal the bargain, but I don't want to give you the wrong impression."

"A hug?" For crying out loud, what the heck was wrong with her? She needed to keep things strictly business with him. Wherever that irrational suggestion had come from, it was too late to retract.

Brice banded her in his warm, steely arms. Cassie intended to return the hug with a perfunctory pat on his back. Her body had other ideas, finagling as close as possible, welcoming his heat despite the moderate temperature cloying the late-night breeze.

"Let's go home, Sunshine." He stroked her hair and kissed the top of her head.

An unexpected vibration rippled down her spine, spread into nerves and dropped an electrified jumble at the apex between her thighs, a spot all too eager for the sudden stimulation.

*Yes, yes. Let's go home. A nice, comfortable bed awaits. And Brice will be in it.*

If Cassie kept thinking those errant thoughts, she'd be better off sleeping in her car.

So close to outrunning her mother's bad luck, come hell or high water, or the devil himself, Cassie wouldn't trip up now.

Slightly weak-kneed, Cassie keyed the old clunker's ignition and pulled out of the parking lot. Brice's truck lights reflected in her rearview mirror.

*Yeah. Come hell or high water or the devil himself.*

Cassie cranked up the radio to drown out the huge raspberry the evil one blew in her ear.

# Chapter 16

Pillow and comforter packed in her arms, Cassie hesitated at the threshold of Margaret Walker's bedroom. "Maybe I should stay in the other room. You take this one."

Brice's large frame filled the doorway. "I can't. It's wolfan taboo."

"I don't mind taking the couch." It didn't feel right to move into Margaret's room right after her passing.

"This is your home now. I won't have you sleeping on the couch. If you don't want to sleep in this bed, come back to mine."

Cassie wouldn't tempt fate. She inched to the king-size platform bed, studying the intricate forest scenes of wolves carved into the head and footboards. Elaborate designs of ferns and leaves decorated the sides, and the legs anchoring the frame boasted snarling wolf heads, reminiscent of ancient grotesques.

Such a shame Brice had an aversion toward the exquisite family heirloom. The only legacy Cassie had was bad luck. She prayed not to pass that on to her children.

"Do you like it?" The rawness in Brice's voice resonated in her body.

"It's—" she searched for the right term "—breathtaking." Now Cassie understood what art lovers meant when they talked of paintings moving them beyond words. She sensed the echoes of love from those who had rested here.

"Don't sell it." She spun around to find Brice a hairbreadth away.

His gaze touched her hair long before his fingers did. "I won't."

"What will you do with it?" Cassie asked, though it wasn't any of her business.

"The taboo applies to the bedding, not the frame. If I take a mate, I'll order a new mattress set before I claim her in this bed."

From the molten look in Brice's eyes, Cassie didn't need to ask what *claiming* meant.

"Oh!" Heat swept up her neck into her face and fanned out to the tips of her ears. "Maybe I should make a pallet at the foot of the bed."

His deep chuckle made her feel fuzzy and warm.

"Granny wouldn't want you to sleep on the floor. Neither do I." He yanked the bedding off the mattress.

Cassie's sheets didn't fit the oversized mattress, so they used clean linens from the closet to remake the bed. She flapped her worn comforter over the crisp sheet. Brice's face scrunched in disapproval.

"What?" She smoothed out the wrinkles, not caring the old comforter didn't quite stretch to the corners of the bed.

"Why haven't you scrapped that raggedy thing?"

An acidic prickle scalded Cassie's throat. The faded bedspread had once been an obnoxious patchwork of purple flowers, lime-green swirls, cotton-candy-pink stars, yellow hearts and orange diamonds. While she couldn't say that she loved the pattern, she adored the comforter. "It's the only Christmas present my mother ever gave me."

She shuffled past Brice. He wouldn't understand. No one did. People might say she was better off now that Imogene was gone. But the woman was her mother, and Cassie missed her very much.

"Get some rest, Sunshine." Brice wanted to kiss away the pain distorting Cassie's pretty face. His inner wolf howled in protest as he backed out of the room. "I'll see you in the morning."

Every instinct demanded that he hold her, touch her. Soothe her troubles.

None of which he could do right now and keep a reasonable thought in his head. His cock hurt so badly, any minute the damn thing would explode.

In the bathroom, he stripped and stood in the shower's icy water spray. Teeth chattering, he lathered a body wash that hinted of cherry blossoms on his skin. Thanks to Cassie, he was more cognizant of a variety of smells, and the bouts of nausea were lessening.

She affected him in ways he couldn't understand. The more he tried to deny the howl of his wolf declaring his mate, the more he became hopelessly entangled.

Passingly pretty, Cassie's understated beauty would never drop a man's jaw like a gussied up she-wolf on the prowl. Her sexiness sprang from steeled inner strength and infuriating stubbornness. And of course her wild splay of red curls that made him instantly hard.

He shouldn't imagine those silky ribbons tickling the places he washed, or dwell on how right her softness felt pressed against his body, but the erotic torments wouldn't cease. Massaging his sack with one hand, he glided his other hand up and down his shaft.

God, he couldn't remember a time when he'd desired a woman as fiercely as he craved Cassie. Generally, he was a man of reasonable mind and fortitude, but something about her sucker punched his ability to think clearly. Whenever they were together more than five minutes—no, make that two seconds—he had a hard time focusing on anything other than bedding her.

It wasn't a matter of being sex-starved in Atlanta. He'd had his pick of partners, though over the past year, he frequented them less and less until dwindling to one. Victoria.

He didn't harbor any special feelings toward her. They were coworkers, putting in long hours at the firm. Sometimes they both needed to blow off steam. And then there were the moon-fucks, driven by the instinct to couple during the full moon, primal and self-preserving.

Sex. They'd shared nothing more than sex.

Actually, there wasn't any sharing involved. He took, she took. They both came away unscathed. Until the last full moon.

He slammed the door on the abhorrent memory, tuning his mind to how good it felt pumping his cock through his fisted hand and how incredible it would feel sliding into a woman's tight, slick softness. Knowing the woman he wanted was only a dozen steps down the hallway supersensitized him to every thrust.

He bet she looked tiny and lost tucked in the vastness of such a big, comfortable bed.

A bed he'd claim his mate in—if he claimed one. An impossible *if* once he accepted the apprenticeship to the Woelfesenat, since council members were forbidden to claim mates.

Unbearable need tightened his muscles. Harder and faster, his smooth, steady rhythm spiraled into jerky pumps. Sharp points of electricity pricked every nerve. The vibration awoke and charged every cell. Head to toe, his entire body teetered on the edge of ecstasy and oblivion. The balance tipped. A longing for the woman he couldn't have threaded through his being, drowning him in hollow release. A milky stream spewed from his tip in short bursts.

Spent, Brice leaned against the cool tile, trying to block out the urgency in his wolf's pitiful whine.

For his and Cassie's sake, he had to resist the mating urge. Unfortunately, his wolf wouldn't let him keep his eyes, his hands or his nose away from the trigger.

He was so screwed.

# *Chapter 17*

Brice snagged enough food for two from the resort kitchen. He would have lunch with Cassie whether or not she protested.

They had a few things to settle.

Mainly, the sleeping arrangements. Despite what they'd agreed to last night, Cassie had crashed on the couch.

Well, if she didn't want to sleep in Granny's bed, he'd make damn sure Cassie returned to his. He'd endured a fitful night without her, anyway. After only two days of waking next to her, he hated not smelling her first thing in the morning.

He'd had only one sniff session with her today, after she'd burnt her toast and smoked up the cabin. The acrid odor triggered merciless vomiting. Guilelessly, she'd offered her scent as a remedy, and an unexpected rush of tenderness had driven him to slip behind her and brush aside her curls. Starting at the dimple behind her ear, he nudged along her neck to her shoulder. The perfect place for a mate claim bite.

Only he couldn't make that mistake. She had plans for her life. He had plans for his. Neither included the other.

If he hadn't left Walker's Run five years ago, maybe something would've evolved. Since their paths lay in different directions, the most he could dare with her was friends.

He navigated the dining room dotted with the few remaining guests. The rest Cassie and Hannah had checked out before noon.

Their easy camaraderie had roused a pang of unexpected jealousy Brice hadn't had time yet to contemplate. He'd spent the first part of the morning arguing with his mother over her plan to set him up on mini-dates to introduce him to the single daughters of the Alphas arriving for his grandmother's memorial. Afterward, he met with his father and Henry "Cooter" Coots, the pack's chief sentinel, to discuss how to handle the influx of Wahyas soon to arrive. Although the Walkers had treaties with the Alphas expected to attend, not all were allies of one another. Extra security measures were required to minimize frictions.

Brice's uncle, Adam, would bring reinforcements from Atlanta. Family alliances guaranteed ready assistance at any time. Booker Reynolds also offered to provide sentinels, though Gavin had respectfully declined.

On that matter, Brice and his father had agreed. It would be foolish to entrust the safety of the pack to an outsider. Even if the outsider was Adam's best friend.

Reynolds had grown up with Brice's mother and uncle in the Peachtree pack and had moved away after he'd claimed a mate from Asheville. Not long after, his mate and her father, the Alpha of Black Mountain, died in a single-car accident. Reynolds inherited the Alphaship by rite of marriage since he had no challengers.

He never claimed another mate, insisting he couldn't bear to replace Priscilla. The assertion didn't quite ring true to Brice. As a young wolfling, he'd noticed how Reynolds's smiles were a little too wide, his looks lingered a little too long and his voice softened a note too much whenever Abigail Walker appeared.

Brice knew Reynolds would never be a real threat to his parents' mateship. They were true mates, fused heart and soul through a mate-bond.

Not all Wahyas were fortunate enough to forge those precious emotional ties. Those who did couldn't be divided, except by death.

While Reynolds might harbor an infatuation with Brice's mother, he wouldn't challenge Gavin. At least Brice hoped Reynolds wasn't that stupid. Abigail Walker would strike down any fool who threatened her family. Brice's father would do the same.

Brice entered the lobby and irritably sized up the tall, broad male slouched against the guest services counter. *Wol-*

*fan*, Brice's instincts told him. An intrinsic awareness alerted Wahyas to their own kind like a keen recognition of sameness but not necessarily kindred.

Drawing closer, Brice detected a curdled odor. He swallowed the bile gurgling in his throat. Cassie wasn't so far away that he'd succumb to another bout of vomiting. He hoped.

Cassie didn't seem to notice his approach, her eyes trained on the wolfan guest. As she slid a key card toward the male, his massive hand flattened her palm to the counter. He dragged beefy fingers along the back of her hand, then curled them around her wrist. A flush brightened Cassie's skin. Alarm flashed in her eyes.

Brice's slow canter revved into a fast trot. The soured smell smothering his senses grew more pungent. His stomach remained steady as the muscles in his back tightened to steel his spine.

"Get your fucking paw off her," he said with deadly calm.

"Mind your own business, *boy*." A growl in his throat, the man turned around slowly, confidently.

"Miss Albright is my business." Sliding the lunch tray onto the guest services counter, Brice restrained the urge to pound the man into the ground and keep on going until he came out on the other side of the world.

The man's gaze landed on the scars at Brice's neck, jumped to Brice's right eye and then moved to the left. Surprised recognition flickered across the man's blocky features.

"I take it you know who I am." Unease slithered through Brice. Something about the man seemed familiar, but Brice couldn't quite place him. "Who the hell are you?"

Instead of answering, the wolfan took his time sizing up Brice.

"Vincent Hadler," Cassie said, slathering liquid sanitizer on her hands. "He arrived with Mr. Reynolds a few minutes ago."

"Vincent Hadler," Brice spat the name. No wonder his hackles had risen. The man was known for being a cruel, sadistic bastard. "Your reputation precedes you."

Hadler tipped his head in a smug nod, and a sardonic smile twisted his mouth.

"That wasn't a compliment." Brice dropped his voice to a threatening whisper. "As a visitor to Walker's Run, you are required to abide by our rules. The first of which is not to harass our females. Failure to comply will result in immediate expulsion from the territory."

Hadler's smile stretched into a sleazy grin. "The redhead might be worth it."

Brice's tightened gut pounded against his rib cage. The wolf inside him snarled, slashing at the tethers of civility in a desperate power play for the freedom to shred the wolfan into a bloody pulp.

"Miss Albright is invariably off-limits." He forced his hands to relax at his sides. "If you violate that directive, the consequences will be quite severe. I doubt your Alpha will appreciate the fallout."

Despite his fondness for Brice's mother and his alliance with Walker's Run, Booker Reynolds was an elitist. He believed humans were, by nature, inferior to Wahyas. Having his security officer pick an intentional fight over a human female would likely have additional repercussions for Hadler, provided he survived the ass-whipping Brice would serve him.

From Hadler's smirk, Brice knew the man considered the warning a challenge. So be it. If he inched one fingernail out of line, the arrogant male would get his ass handed to him on a pure silver platter, not a knockoff sterling one.

A swoosh echoed through the lobby as a brass luggage cart pushed open the heavy wooden doors.

"Shane?" Cassie scrunched her brow. "What are you doing here? You're not on the schedule."

All the color had drained from his face and skin, turning him ashy gray. The young man averted his eyes and lowered his head when he stopped next to Hadler.

"He's my gofer for the afternoon," Hadler said, following with a cold, hard laugh.

An almost imperceptible cringe blinked over Shane's body. Icy contempt flashed in his eyes. The seething tension surrounding him was palpable.

"Let's go, *boy*." Hadler's boots clomped against the wood plank floor to the elevator.

Dutifully following, Shane appeared to hold his breath as his knuckles whitened in a death grip around the bars of the luggage cart.

Those two definitely had a lot of unpleasantness between them. Of course, considering Hadler's reputation, there would be a lot of unpleasantness between him and most people.

Brice knew what battles to pick and choose. His primary concern was Cassie, but he'd ask the sentinels to keep an eye on Shane. Quietly.

"I didn't need your help." Cassie arrowed her gaze at Brice. His butting in would only make Vincent Hadler more difficult to deal with. "This wasn't the first time he played handsies with me."

"What?" Brice's boom rattled the lobby chandeliers.

"Keep your voice down and relax. Your face is turning purple." Thank goodness the lobby was empty. She hated being a spectacle.

Brice sucked in a deep breath through his nose. When he exhaled, an inaudible count parted his silent lips.

All night Cassie dreamed those full, strong lips were kissing every inch of her body, making her beg for things she'd asked of no man, until she finally awoke on the couch, her face pressed against her pillow, wet from her slobber. As she watched the slight movement of his mouth, her lips tingled with the phantom pressure of their fantasy kiss. Her insides turned warm and gooey.

"I know how to handle jerks," Cassie announced a little too sharply.

Brice was the one she had no experience managing. Devastatingly beautiful men didn't take notice of her. Brice did only because of circumstance. He wasn't really seeing her. She blamed the Florence Nightingale effect. His misguided notion that her scent was healing his nose and his grief over Margaret's death colored his perception.

She had no such excuse for her doe-eyed behavior, and if she didn't want a bout of puppy love scrapping her plans for the future, she needed to get a firm grip on her Brice-inspired, way-out-of-control hormones.

"He's looking for a reaction," Cassie continued. "I refuse to give him one."

"I saw your blush from across the lobby, Cas." Brice reached leisurely across the guest services counter, the movement fluid, self-assured and direct. He lifted her hand. "Hadler is playing a game you can't win. Don't try."

Good advice, although she didn't need it where Hadler was concerned. She had no desire to ride happily ever after into the sunset with him. Brice was the one she needed to guard against. "I don't play games." Especially ones that could break her heart.

"I grabbed us lunch." He touched his nose to the inside of her wrist. Soft puffs tickled her arm as he breathed. Funny how the wicked heat flashing through her body caused chills to sprout on her skin.

"I'm busy," she said, too breathy for the slam-the-door impact she intended. "Eat by yourself."

"I did, after you skipped out on the pancake breakfast you promised to make up for burning the toast." Brice's loose hold on her arm held firm despite Cassie's tug.

"What was I supposed to do? Your mother called me in to cover for Natalie. She has morning sickness again." Cassie ceased her useless, halfhearted struggle. Her reward? Brice pressed his lips to the back of her hand in a slightly wet kiss, as if he were tasting her skin. She swallowed the giddiness before it manifested into a giggle. "For the record, I never promised pancakes. I merely suggested."

"Never tease a hungry wolf." Brice's soft growl rolled

through her body like a sensual wave. The floor seemed to disappear in the tide. Only Brice's steady presence kept her buoyed amid the dangerous surf.

"Now, have lunch with me." An irresistible smile fanned his face. "Or I'll starve due to lack of food and your company." Something darker than a light tease shimmered in Brice's eyes. Something primal and powerful. Something that beckoned her closer and closer. Like the promise of exotic cheese to a mouse about to be caught in a trap.

"I, uh, can't leave the front desk unattended." Cassie's stomach protested, even though skipping a meal was child's play. After Imogene became ill, Cassie ensured her mother had enough food to eat and the medicines were paid for, but Cassie existed on instant soup and peanut butter. Sometimes the cheap meals ran out before her next check, and she'd simply chomped ice until she had money. Then the cycle would start again.

She reached for the Styrofoam cup of ice stowed beneath the counter, skimming her eyes over all the food on the tray. A little thrill fluttered in her chest at Brice's kindness, and she refused to wonder if he'd gone to the kitchen with the intention of asking her to lunch, or if the invitation was merely an afterthought following the unpleasant incident with Hadler.

"Start without me. I'll join you when Hannah gets back at two. One of her sons had an event at school today."

Brice's gaze flickered to the huge harvest moon clock on the wall behind the guest services counter. He picked up the lunch tray. "Fifteen minutes. Not a second more or I'll swing you over my shoulder and carry you into the break room."

"You wouldn't dare!" Although every cell in her body knew he would. He absolutely would. Anticipation, rather than dread, caused her nerves to tingle.

"Fourteen minutes, fifty-nine seconds." Brice's singsong tone harmonized with his arrogant swagger as he walked away.

Oh, she hoped he choked on all that smugness. Then she'd have to give him mouth-to-mouth. Her body cheered.

*Stop!*

Mouth-to-mouth would be futile without attempting the Heimlich maneuver, which meant she'd have to stand behind him, press intimately against him, wrap her arms around his torso, feel the curve of his sculpted muscles beneath her palms as her fingers crawled to the spot below his breastbone and squeezed.

Electricity swept through her, shorting out the strength in her legs. Before Brice she'd never had trouble standing on her own two feet.

Grateful for the empty lobby, Cassie slumped in her stool and chomped the ice in her cup. She'd scrimped to pay for her college education, and with graduation on the near horizon, she couldn't afford Brice's distraction.

*Focus, focus, focus!*

She couldn't wait to get off tonight. Her biweekly run at the high school track would give her plenty of uninterrupted alone time to come up with critical additions to the roommate rules before crawling into bed and snuggling against Brice. Warm and cozy tucked beneath his arm, she slept better than she ever had. Her body sighed.

*No, no, no!*

She needed to think about the future. Brice's presence in her life was an aberration. Soon he'd return to his life in Atlanta. When he did, Cassie wanted no fallout from his departure. She simply wanted to continue her steady plod toward stability and financial freedom, because in the end, the only person she could depend on was herself.

# Chapter 18

With three seconds to spare, Cassie entered the break room. Brice sat at a round table for two, his right leg propped on the second chair. The tray of food in front of him remained untouched.

She expected that he would have finished his portion and most of hers by now. He was making a habit of doing the opposite of what she expected.

He squinted in concentration as his fingers skimmed the touch screen on his cell phone. Although he didn't immediately look up as she approached, a killer smiled curved his mouth, and the air crackled with electricity.

"Angry Birds." Standing, he shoved the phone into his pocket. "I'm addicted."

"I pegged you for a sudoku man."

"Why is that?" Brice pulled out her chair.

Cassie froze. No one had ever done that for her.

His hand nudged the small of her back, and a cuddly warmth spread through her body. She sat down to keep from snuggling against him.

"I've been your grandmother's housekeeper since I was fourteen. After your weekend visits from college, I'd find your crossword puzzles stuffed in the strangest places."

"Really? Where?" Brice settled in his chair. Curiosity brightened the vivid hues of his beautiful eyes. His lips parted with an expectant breath as he waited.

Cassie's heart raced with a panicked beat. Brice was nothing like Vincent Hadler. Putting them in the same category sickened her stomach, but if she was going to survive being Brice's roommate, she needed to handle him with the same indifference she'd shown Hadler.

Avoiding the hand Brice stretched toward her, Cassie

placed her napkin on her lap. "The most bizarre place I found your puzzle book was inside the egg carton in the refrigerator."

The sound of Brice's deep, rich, sexy laugh looped through her belly. Hadler's cold, harsh laughter, the few times she'd heard it, slithered over her skin, leaving behind a grimy film she couldn't wait to wash off.

"I must've been in the middle of a puzzle when I got hungry." Brice grinned. For the first time since they'd met, Brice resembled the buoyant little boy and mischievous young man captured in the photos decorating the walls in Margaret's home.

"It seems odd that we never met before Saturday night." His wistful sigh seeped into his eyes, and Cassie had a compulsion to confess the secret she'd kept from all but her mother.

"Or have we?" Brice scooted closer to the table. His knees brushed against hers and ignited a sinful tingle in her core. "Tell me, Cas. Have we met before?"

"Sort of." Cassie crossed her legs. A lot of good that did to stop the irresistible sensation of Brice seeping into the deepest places of her being. She wanted to get mad, bolster her defenses to keep him at arm's length as she did everyone else. Brice had ignored the tactic before, he probably would again and the effort to erect the walls he so effortlessly skirted required more energy than she had at the moment. "You were unconscious at the time."

A soft breath parted his lips. "You came to see me in the hospital?"

"I was visiting my mom." Cassie shrugged. "When I went down to the cafeteria for tea, I overheard some nurses talking about your parents' decision to take Mason off life support. They were speculating about you, too." She paused, remembering the irrational panic that drove her to find Brice's room. A frenzied fantasy, really, that if she could make it to him before they turned off the machines, if she saw him, touched him, he would be all right.

Of course, it had been a ludicrous delusion. At the time,

Cassie hadn't known Brice, although she fancied a strange connection to him. After all, every week she cleaned his room, washed the clothes he dropped on the floor, picked up the books he scattered through Margaret's house and discovered the puzzles he abandoned when something else had snagged his attention.

Cassie's heart pounded as hard as it did on the day she stepped into the hospital room and saw Brice wrapped neck to foot in blood-streaked bandages. Tubes protruded from his arms and covered most of his face. The erratic beep of the monitors and the mechanical hum of the machines that kept him alive chased away her sleep for months.

"I thought you were going to die." A sudden spasm seized her lungs. She coughed uncontrollably.

"It's okay, Cas." Brice knelt next to her, opened his arms and gathered her close. "I'm alive and well."

Close to hyperventilation, Cassie clung to his calm, steady strength. She'd faced far too many storms in her life alone. Though this one had long passed, the turbulent memory threatened to unleash a maelstrom of restrained emotion. She wouldn't cry, though. There was no need. Brice was indeed alive and well, gently rocking her in his safe, strong arms.

She pressed her cheek deeper into his chest. He rested his chin on the crown of her head and cupped her neck to knead the tight muscles while his other hand caressed her back in long, luxurious strokes that became more sensual as her anxiety faded.

Why couldn't the timing be better? She had so much to accomplish before she could risk falling in love, and Brice Walker would be at the top of her list—if she had one.

With him, she felt safe, protected. He pushed her boundaries but knew when to back off. He challenged her, and offered his support even when she didn't need it.

And she fit so snugly in his arms.

So much for indifference. Oh, that was a fine strategy if

they weren't within touching distance. Up close and personal always usurped the tactic.

Not wanting her future to end with a bad roll of the dice, Cassie straightened her shoulders and leaned back. Brice's hands glided down her arms, leaving a trail of chill bumps puckered beneath her uniform blazer. The gleam of primal sentience was back in his eyes. Staring into the deep pools, she could almost hear his thoughts. Not actual words, but impressions. Tender concern, fierce protectiveness. Blatant desire.

*Mine!*

The declaration reverberating in her mind held Brice's distinctive baritone yet clearly sounded like an animalistic roar. She smiled even though she shouldn't have. Encouraging delusional fantasies would put her on the fast track to devastation.

She forced her attention to the bulletin board on the far wall, breaking whatever spell there might have been between them. Brice reluctantly returned to his seat.

"Why didn't you come back to see me? After the first time?" The sad longing in his voice needled into her heart. He believed so resolutely that his parents didn't care about him that a stranger's visit mattered, and he was disappointed she hadn't returned.

"Actually, I couldn't stay away. Whenever I visited my mom, I'd sneak into your room, too. Even after her discharge, I came by every night to read you joke books."

"Dirty jokes?" Brice winked, and the mischievous sparkle enticed all sorts of delirious madness.

"No, of course not." Cassie shoved her straw into her drink and forced herself not to slurp down the iced tea in order to cool the heat flushing her skin.

"Why didn't I see you after I came out of the coma?" He unwrapped a sandwich and handed it to her before opening his own.

"Too many people." She dribbled mustard inside the ham and cheese sandwich. "I couldn't risk getting caught. If anyone found out how I'd been sneaking in, I wouldn't have been able to see my mom whenever she was hospitalized again."

An amicable silence filled the room. Cassie didn't expect it to last long. Brice liked to talk. Or rather, he had a way of getting her to say, and feel, more than she intended.

She chewed her sandwich, watching Brice toy with his food. For someone who'd professed starvation earlier, he didn't seem in any hurry to eat. Head lowered, his brows painfully scrunched, he seemed to be working a mental puzzle.

Cassie ate half her lunch before Brice spoke again.

"What do you do for fun? Belong to a sorority? Have a boyfriend?"

"I work and go to school. That's all I have time for until I finish my business degree in December." On the track that combined bachelor's and master's programs, Cassie's college course work sucked up most of her energy.

"And after that?"

"Find a job that gives me practical experience in the business aspect of managing a resort. I plan to own one someday."

"Fantastic!" Brice's unexpected enthusiasm didn't inspire Cassie. "Have you talked to my parents about your career goals?"

"No. They weren't interested in my suggestions to boost business, and there's little opportunity for advancement. Don't get me wrong. Your parents have been good to me. But I want to be more than a guest services clerk."

"I could talk to them, see if they're willing to make some changes." He finally took a large bite of his sandwich.

"Thanks, but no thanks. I'd rather not have my roommate involving himself in my personal matters."

"We're more than roommates, Cas." Brice swiped a brown napkin across his mouth, balled it and pitched it into the trash can. "At the very least, we're friends."

"I don't want to be your friend, Brice. Roommate is all I can handle." Although Cassie wasn't sure she managed that very well, either.

Brice stirred feelings in her that could lead to stupid mistakes. And stupid mistakes would ruin her future.

Thin lines formed around the unhappy curl of Brice's mouth. The expression reminded her so much of his mother that it was uncanny.

A pang of remorse tightened Cassie's chest. Although she had Imogene's red hair and small stature, Cassie didn't know if they had shared expressions or mannerisms. The musing Cassie most often heard was whether or not she'd turn out like her mother.

"I believe in you," Brice said quietly. "Have a little faith in me, too."

"Oh, I have faith." Faith that anything more than a roommate agreement with Brice would end in catastrophe. Cassie swallowed the last bite of her sandwich.

Brice dabbed the corner of her mouth. Instead of using the napkin Cassie offered, he indulgently sucked the mustard from his thumb. His radiant smile might have dazzled her if the brilliance of his eyes hadn't blinded her like a train she didn't have enough sense to jump out of the way of. Screeching brakes clamored in her mind, setting off a ripple effect that undoubtedly signaled the beginning of her future's derailment. Only a massive amount of damage control would minimize the impact. Unfortunately, the finesse it required was beyond Cassie's experience. All she could do was wing it and hope her efforts succeeded, because failure would leave her in ruin.

# Chapter 19

Brice crossed his ankles on his father's presidential desk. He picked at the yellow fleck beneath his thumbnail. Kissing the mustard from Cassie's lips would've been so much more fun than sucking it from his thumb. She would've turned all shades of pink and refused to speak to him until he found a way to sweet-talk her into forgiveness.

He craved her nearness. The turmoil inside him subsided in Cassie's presence. At lunch, when he learned of her secret hospital visits, he couldn't help wondering if she had triggered his mating urge all those years ago. Was she the reason he'd fought to live? Was their separation the reason he'd been so restless in Atlanta? Why he hesitated to accept the Woelfesenat's offer and became so desperate to return to Walker's Run?

He leaned back to stare at the ceiling. A few forgotten remnants of resin clung to the exposed wood beams.

"Admiring your handiwork?" His father entered the office.

"Someone's." As teenagers, Brice and Rafe had endured a brutal inquisition on who had painted the room with silly string. Neither admitted culpability. Not then or since.

Thankfully, the adolescent males coming of age after them had chosen pig wrangling as their rite of passage. Had they reenacted the silly string prank, their Alpha might've suffered a stroke from the repeated assault against his imperial throne room.

Relinquishing said throne to his father, Brice genuflected flippantly, which garnered a warning growl. He expected no less.

Abigail Walker swept into the room on the arm of her twin brother, her head bent close enough to Adam that her kohl strands were lost in his. The profile of her regal nose and the strong, angular cut of her chin mirrored Adam's profile. However, the contours of her face were soft, feminine.

There was nothing soft or feminine about Adam. A stonecutter could've carved his sharp features.

Brice more than favored his maternal side, and many had mistaken him for Adam's son. Brice bore no Walker coloring except for one blue eye and a one-inch tuft of blond hair at the base of his neck, obscured by thick, black waves.

His mother left Adam's side to haul Brice into an unrestrained embrace. "Oh, my baby. My baby."

"Mom!" Brice tugged her elbows. "For chrissakes. You don't have to do this every time we're in the same room."

"Get used to it. I have five years of hugs to make up for." She grabbed his cheeks. "I missed you so very much."

*Oh, no. Not again.*

Having his mother smother him, a grown man, with kisses was—well, embarrassing. He'd suffered through the humiliation in front of the funeral home director last night. In her office this morning, she put him through the ordeal again. Thankfully the blinds were drawn.

However, repeating the demonstration in front of Adam more than humbled Brice. At least his father and uncle had the decency to avert their eyes during his mortification.

Abby finally released him. "You have no idea what it does to a mother's heart when separated from her child."

Three grown Wahya males pretended not to notice the tension that eked into the room with the subtlety of a three-hundred-pound purple panda.

After stroking Brice's cheek, kissing her mate and squeezing her brother's arm, Abigail Walker waltzed unfazed through the invisible quagmire of male contention. She turned at the threshold, surrounded by a beautiful aura of happiness. "I love you all so very much. Now, don't kill each other."

The office door swooped closed.

Gavin took his seat behind the desk.

"Thank God you're all right." Adam pulled Brice into a

bear hug. "Why did you disappear without a word to me?" Adam stepped back; sadness shadowed the relief on his face.

"I had my reasons." Brice eyed his father. If Gavin hadn't consented to his presence in the territory, Brice didn't want his uncle to be culpable in the trespass.

Adam's eyebrows drew together, deepening the vertical lines between them. "Don't pull that stunt again or I swear I'll put a leash on you."

"I'm not a wolfling," Brice answered, unoffended. "I can protect myself."

"Yes, yes, but I was worried sick. You should've at least called to let me know you were all right."

The twinge of guilt Brice felt in his gut wasn't enough to make him regret his actions.

"Perhaps now you can understand what we've gone through." Gavin's deliberate enunciation carried an unmistakable reprimand. Elbow resting on the desktop, he aimed his index finger at Adam. "You worried for three days. We worried for five years."

"I kept you apprised of Brice's progress." Stiff-backed, Adam sat in one of captain's chairs in front of Gavin's desk. "Kept him safe."

"Stop the pretenses, Dad. No one in Walker's Run cared enough to call or come see me, least of all you." Brice dragged the other chair toward the corner of the desk, putting equal distance between his father and uncle.

"I did," Gavin snapped. "Several times."

The assertion didn't ring true, though Brice had never known his father to lie. "Did what, exactly?"

"Gavin, this isn't the time to hash this out. The boy has been through enough."

"I'm not a boy." Brice leveled his gaze at Adam. "What the hell is going on?"

Adam's tightened jaw pressed his lips into a grim line.

"Mason wasn't the only one with life-threatening injuries, son." Gavin rubbed his scrunched brow. "We lost him, but a miracle brought you back to us, though you weren't the same. Flashbacks tormented your sleep, and you became increasingly violent toward yourself.

"Adam suggested a change of scenery might help distance you from what happened, and since the city offered more rehabilitative services than we had here, I entrusted you to his care. You were only supposed to be in Atlanta until you got better." Gavin's piercing gaze didn't seem to ruffle Adam's placidity. "Instead, Adam stole you from us."

"Nice try, Dad." Brice tapped his fingers against the chair's armrest. "I know you banished me because I'm responsible for Mason's death."

"Is that what you told him, Adam?" Gavin's face darkened, and his hands curled into hammering fists.

Adam didn't balk. "I swear, I never said anything of that nature."

"You didn't have to." Uprooted, uncertain and an absolute emotional mess, Brice had been too embarrassed to ask for confirmation of what he knew in his heart to be true. "No one returned my calls or answered my letters. No one came to see me. Not even my grandmother." The hurt sliced through his voice, mocking his effort to sound unaffected.

"We didn't receive any of your calls or letters. And our cards and letters came back unopened. When we called, your secretary always said you were unavailable. Every time Adam invited us to visit, you were inconveniently out of town."

"You could've called my cell, taped a note to my office or apartment door."

"I called every goddamn day, Brice. Left hundreds of messages with your assistant. Your mother and grandmother sent cards and letters without fail. Even when Adam said you didn't want us to hound you, we never stopped trying to reach you."

"Adam?" Brice expected his uncle to provide a reasonable explanation. When none came, a sickening sensation churned the food settled in Brice's stomach. "You had my personal calls, my mail screened? You lied about me being out of town?"

"I never lied." Adam met Brice's gaze, then addressed Gavin. "He was out of town whenever you and Abby visited."

"Because you arranged it that way." Gavin jabbed his finger toward Adam.

Adam tipped his head.

An avalanche of questions slammed into Brice's brain. The only intelligible word he managed to utter was "Why?"

"Your guilt ran so deep, the pack doctors believed a clean break from Walker's Run was your only chance at recovery."

"*Your* doctors—" Gavin slammed his palm flat on the desk "—didn't have a fucking clue about how to help *my* son."

"Brice is alive and successful thanks to *my* doctors." Adam slapped the armrest and stood. "I did what I thought best for him. He needed the distance from you and your pack, so I cut him off from Walker's Run to save his sanity. He has a new life now. Let him go, Gavin, before you destroy everything I've built for him."

Brice should've jumped to his feet, shouted his anger. Instead, he sat there, barely able to manage a whisper as the enormity of Adam's actions pulverized everything Brice had believed.

"Do you realize what you've done?" Brice asked his uncle.

"Of course he does." Gavin's mouth twisted. "Adam took advantage of your vulnerability and isolated you from us to further his agenda."

Brice didn't think his stomach could drop any further than his feet, but it seemed the floor opened up beneath him and his stomach decided to keep right on going. He glanced around for the trash can in case he needed to hurl. "What agenda?"

"When you were born, Adam demanded to adopt you. Since you have the Foster coloring, he believes you belong to him."

"Brice is mine." Adam's fierce eyes and defiant jaw emphasized how much the man believed his preposterous claim.

"He bears my blood through my sister, and since the day he was born, I have loved him as my son."

"For the last time, Adam. Brice. Is. Not. Your. Son. He's mine!" Gavin sprang to his feet.

"He's always been more mine in spirit than yours," Adam snarled.

The air between the two Alphas felt thick enough to choke a Wahyarian—the foul, primitive beast civilized Wahyas regressed into only on rare and extreme occasions. Brice sat immobilized as the Novocain of his uncle's deception numbed him mind, body and soul.

"You know nothing about my son. Nothing about what makes him happy." Gavin shoved his chair. "Nothing about what he needs."

A flicker of hysterical amusement threaded through Brice's thoughts. His father had no right to accuse someone of something he was guilty of.

"I understand him better than you ever could." Adam's rising volume matched his rival's.

"Ha!" Gavin threw his palms in the air.

Their escalated voices waned in the veritable howl inside Brice's head. Neither man knew squat about him.

Since the age of four, Brice had looked to Adam as a father figure. Now Brice realized his devotion had been a mistake. If his uncle had cared more about Brice and less about gaining an heir, he would've understood that sequestering him from his birth pack would do more harm than good. Walker's Run was in Brice's blood.

How could Adam betray him? Separate Brice from all he'd known and loved, and lost in absentia? Brice's world tilted, sinking slowly into chaos. Even as he scrambled to hold on to the pieces, he drowned in the truth.

"Why, Adam? Why did you do this to me?" Brice's soft-spoken question silenced the room.

"To protect you. Your health and sanity were at risk." Conviction laced Adam's words, though the treacherous sentiment was a spinning arrow mutilating Brice's heart.

"My health, my sanity, my risk. Not yours. I spent the last five years believing that my pack had shunned me because of what happened to Mason." Brice rubbed the knot bunched between his brows. "I loved you, Adam, just as much as I would have if you had been my father. What more could you possibly gain from playing me like a fool?"

"He wants you to lead his pack." Gavin exhaled a long-winded breath, righted his chair and retook his seat.

"That's ridiculous. The Peachtree pack doesn't have a line of succession. The males fight for the Alpha position." Brice cut his eyes at his uncle. The man's face reflected the perfect confidence of someone who'd done nothing wrong. "Adam, if you knew me at all, you would've understood that I won't fight. I can't. Not ever again."

"My pack adores you, Brice. We agreed to forgo a trial by combat if you accept the Alphaship when I'm ready to step down. You proved your worthiness when you killed the rogues who invaded Walker's Run."

"Worthy? Goddammit, I got Mason killed. Your pack is delusional if they believe a fuck-up is qualified to lead. For chrissakes. Allowing me to believe my own pack didn't want me because yours did is ludicrous. What were you thinking?"

"I wanted you to be happy." Adam's shoulders began to stoop.

"Do I fucking look happy?" Brice crammed his fingers into his hair and pressed his skull between his hands. Bitter, angry, hurtful emotions whirled inside him, a tornadic force wrenching out the trust he had in his uncle, leaving behind jagged, pulsating wounds in his heart.

"I didn't do this to hurt you." The sincerity in Adam's voice did little to dissuade Brice's growing outrage.

Five years of longing, of wanting to come home. Five years of time lost among friends, family and his *mate*?

If Cassie was his true mate, then Adam's deception had cheated him out of five years of knowing her, loving her.

A ferocious growl reverberated through the room. Brice seized Adam by the throat and plowed him into the floor-to-ceiling bookcases. Rare first editions splattered on the floor.

"You have no idea how deep your betrayal runs." Brice growled through clenched teeth.

Adam's hand covered the one Brice held clutched around his throat. "Sometimes our best intentions are our worst mistakes. Forgive me for mine."

Nose to nose, Brice glowered into his uncle's eyes. In them, he saw a deep, abiding sorrow and an unwavering love. The curses burning Brice's tongue disintegrated.

Adam had opened his home to Brice, mentored him through law school, appointed him a junior partner in his firm and wanted to entrust him with the livelihood of his entire pack. On some level, Brice understood that Adam's actions carried no malice.

He pulled back his hand. A nauseating sweat disrupted his balance. He stumbled away and slumped against the window, the glass a cool welcome against the heat of his anger.

"Would you have let me kill him?" he asked his father.

Relaxed, even amused, Gavin sat with his feet propped on the corner of his desk. "Had you been set on killing Adam, you would've done so before I could stop you. Your anger is justified, Brice. You needed to act on your frustration, and I trusted you not to do irreparable harm to your uncle."

"It wasn't your throat in jeopardy." Returning to his seat, Adam rubbed the red imprint on his neck.

"I told you, Adam." Gavin's flat lips gave no hint of the smile crinkling his eyes. "I know my son."

Brice's heart pinched. Was his father actually proud of something Brice had done? The ill-conceived notion disturbed him as much as the confrontation with his uncle.

Adam's betrayal would not be forgotten, though in time,

Brice would forgive him. Maybe one day he could also forgive his father.

"Now, to the matter of Brice's future." Gavin swung his feet to the floor.

"I don't see how either of you has any business dictating my future." Brice returned to his seat.

"Walker's Run is your birthright. You are the Alpha-in-Waiting. One day you will lead this pack." Gavin didn't have the courtesy to look at Brice during the metronomic rote. His father didn't mean the words any more than Brice believed them.

"Here we go." Brice squeezed his head between his hands again. "The Alphaship belonged to Mason. Before he died, you didn't care two hoots about me."

"I understand that you believe that, Brice. However, it isn't true." Gavin laid his arms on his desk blotter and steepled his fingers.

"Actions don't lie." Brice's declaration garnered him a full-face grimace from his father.

"No, but they can be misinterpreted." Gavin sighed.

Brice counted to thirty and swallowed the same old defensive argument. He'd been wrong about Adam. What would it hurt to give his father the benefit of the doubt?

Granny asked Brice to reconcile with his father. Maybe the time had truly come to do just that.

"I'm not ready to commit to the responsibilities of the Alpha-in-Waiting." Brice's upheld hand stalled his father's interjection. "I have commitments, Dad. Important ones that I can't walk out on. I need time."

"Take all the time you need. I'm in no rush to retire." Gavin leaned back, stroking his short-cropped snow-white beard. "Now, to the next matter. You have until Christmas to claim an acceptable mate."

"What?" Brice and Adam responded in unison, though Brice's shout drowned out his uncle's exclamation.

"You can't force him into a mateship," Adam argued.

That's not what concerned Brice. His father's emphasis on the word *acceptable* was what troubled him. Especially since Gavin had pointed out Cassie's less than stellar pedigree yesterday. If she turned out to be Brice's true mate, he'd have no other but her, his father be damned.

Standing, Gavin flattened his palms against his desk. "Brice, this pack needs to see your commitment to them. What better demonstration of your loyalty than settling down and producing the next generation of Walkers?"

In that moment, an oil wick in a furnace had a better chance of surviving an inferno unscathed than peace settling between father and son. Brice jumped to his feet.

"Always the Alpha. Never my father," he seethed as years of resentment erupted from the darkest place in his heart to gush poison through his veins. "You don't want me as your heir. You want my firstborn."

He towered over his father's desk. "Is this why Mom came up with the crazy speed dating marathon for tomorrow? I'll tell you the same thing I told her. Hell, no! I won't do it."

Gavin's eyes darkened like an angry storm. "If you want to remain in Walker's Run, you will follow my orders. If you don't make a concerted effort to find a mate, come the New Year I will put you out of the territory and strike at any Alpha who offers you sanctuary. Including your uncle."

"Gavin, you've gone too far." Adam approached, open-handed. "Think about what you're doing."

"Fuck off, Adam." Gavin shoved him aside. "This is for your own good, Brice."

"Nothing you've ever done has been for my benefit. Consider carefully the trap you've set for me. You know what happened the last time I stepped in one."

"Settle down before this spirals into a full-blown war." Adam barreled between Brice and his father.

Good timing, because if things had continued, patricide would have become a real and present threat, despite Brice's vow to never to kill again. The anger he harbored against

Adam paled in comparison to the pure, unadulterated, primal rage concentrated on his father.

"I've set no trap. Once your temper cools, you'll recognize this as the opportunity it is." Gavin returned to his desk and sat down, confidence stretching the limits of his lips.

Brice stormed out of the room before he knocked that smug smile right off his father's triumphant face.

# Chapter 20

Brice's fingers slipped through Cassie's hair as she slept. Curls slid over his knuckles and spilled down his forearm, a cascade of red silk ribbons. The next time they watched TV at night, he needed to be shirtless. He wanted those ringlets splayed across his bare chest, among other places, if he could endure the tantalization. Already every strand that brushed his skin sparked an electric charge that shot up his arm, pinged across his torso and zipped straight down to his groin.

He closed his eyes, inhaling her sweetness. Such a perfect moment. Peacefully asleep, Cassie curled against him, her small hands resting on his arm secured around her midriff.

She reminded him of a china doll, tiny and fragile. A rarity to be guarded and treasured. He recognized her worth, even if no one else understood her value.

*Mine*, his wolf insisted. Tonight, Brice wasn't so quick to dismiss the instinct.

His father's ridiculous edict made Brice realize two things. One—Gavin Walker was an idiot. At least when it came to handling his son. If he'd simply commanded Brice to find a mate, he would've complied. Maybe even within the time frame specified. Because in the aftermath of an afternoon gone wrong, the second thing Brice had realized was that Cassie was indeed his true mate.

Gavin's disapproval of Cassie and Brice's fear that his father would keep them apart had triggered Brice's primal rage. Only when he calmed did Brice understand the truth, and the consequences of breaking his father's edict.

He kissed Cassie's temple. The delicateness of her skin quickened his pulse. She turned her face into the curve of his neck, and inexplicable hope wormed through his soul. Warm, rich, redeeming.

He didn't have the willpower to force Cassie to sleep in his grandmother's room or the tolerance to leave her on the couch, so he carried her to his bed.

She looked so enticing that he ached down to his toes. He backed out of the room, listening to her soft, even breaths.

Cleaning the kitchen became his first task of distraction. When that didn't temper his thoughts, his nerves or his raging hard-on, he decided to get some fresh air. After shedding his clothes and locking the kitchen door, he fastened the silver-corded house key around his arm.

Bounding off the porch as a wolf, Brice found the tease of the late summer evening's woodsy fragrances deliciously satisfying. The crispness of the night air ruffled his fur, and the instinct to run full-throttle burned in his legs.

Movement just beyond the gazebo where the backyard sloped snagged his attention. Using his ears rather than his nose to track his prey, he stalked the worn path that led down to the creek.

Beneath the whispers of the wind, the muffled snap of a twig might have gone unnoticed by another Wahya less dependent on his auditory senses. The hair along Brice's spine spiked. He issued a warning growl.

The rustling ceased. A few seconds later, Brice heard a low, familiar growl followed by the sounds of paw steps. Emerging from the darkness, the trespasser continued in a methodical, unhurried pace down the moonlit trail.

Brice trailed him down the mountain to the stream, where the moonlight glinted off the water in a shimmering splay that mirrored the sparkle of stars in the sky. Planting surefooted paws on the polished pebbles, the red wolf lapped at the river's edge. A fish jumped. The wolfan pounced. Moments later, he stretched on the riverbank to eat.

*"Rafe,"* Brice called telepathically.

The greeting went unanswered. Brice cautiously approached.

*"Rafe, we need to talk."*

A series of short, snarky barks said Rafe wasn't interested.

Undeterred, Brice dropped his rump on the ground. He and Rafe had gone through a similar ritual the first time they'd met.

When Doc adopted a seven-year-old wolfan pup from a pack decimated by a tuberculosis outbreak, Rafe had been sick, frightened and confused. He'd lashed out at everyone who'd tried to help. Nine at the time, Brice had decided that even near-feral wolflings needed a friend and vowed to become that friend.

Tonight, he didn't know who needed their friendship more.

Rafe took an inordinate amount of time consuming his meal.

Another fish jumped in the stream. Unable to resist, Brice splashed after it to play, not harm. When he grew tired, Brice swam to the edge of the stream. Jumped out. Shook.

Rafe snapped at the water spray.

*"What?"* Brice trotted closer. *"It isn't as if you aren't already wet."*

Rafe continued ignoring him.

*"This is ridiculous."* Brice shifted to his human form. "I'm not leaving until you talk to me."

Rafe licked the fish bones clean. Licked his paws. Licked his lips.

Yawned.

His vivid blue eyes settled on Brice's unprotected feet.

"I swear to God, Rafe," Brice snarled. "Do it and I'll kick those canines right out of your mouth."

Growling softly, Rafe bared his teeth. A second later, he stood before Brice as a man. A few inches shorter with a slimmer build, Rafe would still be a formidable foe if he chose to be.

"Next time you stick those stinky toes in my face, Walker, expect to lose them."

"Don't put me in a situation where I have to wiggle them under your nose to get your attention."

They glared into each other's eyes, unfazed by their nudity, which was as natural to them as their wolfan forms.

Brice broke the stance first. He tipped his head slightly and shifted his gaze. Rather than a sign of weakness, the action demonstrated respect and contrition.

Rafe touched Brice's shoulder in acceptance. Though Brice knew this was one of many steps toward rebuilding their friendship, Brice took his first easy breath.

"Lexi's dead." Rafe's bluntness reflected his manner, candid to a fault.

"I didn't know until yesterday." Brice placed his hand over the pain slicing through his heart for his friend's loss. "You weren't at the R&L when I came by, and I didn't bother going by the house. Doc said you've never gone back."

Rafe gave a curt nod. He tramped to the giant flat rock at the water's edge and gathered some pebbles. "Did he tell you that we'd just found out she was pregnant?" Grief rolled off him in waves. "Goddamn hunter."

Joining Rafe, Brice gathered his own stones. "I should've been here for you."

"Why? To pat my hand? To tell me it's gonna be all right? Well, it isn't." Rafe paused. "Chafes my ass the way people tell me to put it behind me. To move on. Dammit, I don't wanna *move on*, got it?" He turned cold, soulless eyes on Brice. "Don't make me your mission again. If you want things to be right between us, just let me be."

They took turns skipping rocks across the glassy river.

"Sorry about Granny." Waning moonbeams cast a silvery haze over Rafe's upturned face.

At the mention of his grandmother, the pain of her loss seared Brice's heart. Coming home, he'd been prepared to say goodbye. He just hadn't expected his farewell to be so permanent.

"I should've come home sooner." Brice cast his last stone. "Adam manipulated me into believing I was banished."

Rafe snorted as if to say Brice should've known something was off. And that he should've realized the Walker's Run pack wouldn't turn their backs on him.

Or maybe he did know and was just too ashamed to come home.

Brice wondered how Rafe managed to convey so much without uttering an actual word. Well, the chastisement stuck, so there wasn't any reason to whine about something he let happen. Besides, as much as Adam's betrayal hurt, his real worry lay elsewhere.

The constant, dull ache in his leg began to throb in earnest. To ease the pressure, Brice leaned against the boulder jutting into the river.

After a few minutes of silence, he spoke again. "Dad ordered me to claim a mate before Christmas."

Rafe snapped his head toward Brice. "He can't be serious."

"Said he'll banish me for good if I don't."

Rafe's eyes narrowed and his upper lip curled. "He's an idiot."

"I came to the same conclusion. But finding a mate isn't the problem. She's been right here all along."

Rafe cocked his head, then slowly turned in the direction of the cabin. "Red?"

"Dad doesn't think she's an acceptable choice."

"Since when have you cared what he thinks?"

Deep down, Brice always cared. So would Cassie.

Cassie's eyes stung from not blinking. Not that it improved her vision in total darkness, though the effort sharpened her hearing.

She wouldn't have been frightened if the front door hadn't rattled so hard before the distinct click of nails against the porch's wooden planks drew closer to the bedroom window. She sat crossed-legged in the center of Brice's bed, her fists balled in the threadbare folds of her comforter, telling herself that she was safe all the while her gut screamed that she wasn't.

Where was Brice? Why wasn't he here to protect her?

Before the thought had time to take root, Cassie threw back the covers and slipped from the bed. She would not fall into a helpless-woman trap.

Careful not to make any sound, Cassie reached into the far corner of the closet. The night Brice had ordered her to find his shoes, she'd discovered his old baseball bat and because of his bossiness had indulged in the brief fantasy of clunking it over his head.

Gripping the battered handle, she tiptoed from the room, only to hesitate in the hallway. Her panicked heartbeat muted all other sound.

Cassie lost count of the seconds that passed before she inched her way into the living room, only to pause next to the couch. Tomorrow would come before she reached the door at this pace. That didn't motivate her to move any faster.

Last week, a commotion outside wouldn't have terrified her. She would've been more certain in her ability to defend herself. Not even waking up to a scruffy, naked man in her room had caused her to freeze. Of course, she hadn't known of the reality of werewolves then.

*Wahyas!* she corrected herself.

Brice said they were civilized. She had no reason to be afraid.

Her stomach seesawed between stark fear and the indignant irritation that something had spooked her this much. Enough was enough, though. Whatever lurked outside, she planned to greet it with a Babe Ruth swing.

Turning on the porch light, she threw open the front door. "Get away from here!"

Nothing scrambled off the porch. Nothing darted into the woods. In fact, nothing seemed to be happening at all.

Satisfied that she'd made a complete idiot of herself, she retreated inside, shut off the light, relocked the door and turned.

A huge figure blocked her path. "What the hell are you doing?"

Cassie hollered something intelligible and wielded the bat. The shadow stopped it midswing.

"Easy, Sunshine." The smirk in Brice's tone grated on her nerves.

"Are you trying to give me a heart attack?" she snapped.

A heavy chill blanketed the subsequent silence, and Cassie recognized her poor word choice.

"I'm sorry. It slipped out."

Brice released a weighted breath. "Where did you get this?" He wrestled the bat from her death grip.

"From the closet. I heard something on the porch." She hoped the darkness masked her embarrassment.

"Next time, stay inside with the doors locked. I'll handle unwanted visitors."

"You weren't here!" Directing her anger at him instead of herself made Cassie more cross. She knew how to take care of herself; she didn't need him to do it.

"I was marking my territory."

"Please tell me you weren't peeing all over the porch."

"Of course not," Brice grumbled. "Just the perimeter of the cabin, the truck and—"

"The driveway?"

"Your car."

"What?" she shrieked.

"For chrissakes, it was just the tires."

"Great, now I have to find time to wash my car."

"Don't you dare rinse off my scent." His punctuated growl spiraled down her spine and threaded an inconvenient tingle in her core.

Thank goodness her mind, not her hormones, was in control or she might have forgotten the point she wanted to make.

"Listen, *Benji*." Most men took the hint when she rebuffed their advances. If they didn't, an introduction to her knee usually did the trick. Brice, however, was a different breed. His penis and her knee had met with considerable force the night of his arrival, but the unfortunate incident hadn't quelled his interest.

She shouldn't have been flattered, but a teeny, tiny, idiotic part of her rejoiced, because for heaven's sake, what woman wouldn't covet Brice Walker's attention?

"My car is *not* your territory. And neither am I, so keep that *thing*—" she pointed in the general direction of his groin "—away from me and my belongings."

Brice dropped the bat and hauled her against his rock-hard body. "You don't want me to stay away." His broad hand splayed the small of her back, holding her flush in all the right places. As her body softened against the rigid planes of his formidable strength, her thoughts splintered and scattered as far and wide as her resistance.

A small mewling rose from the back of her throat. It didn't sound like the protest a sensible woman should've made, and Brice didn't take it as discouragement.

He backed her against the wall and leaned down to sprinkle delicate kisses across her cheeks. The feathery sensation penetrated her senses, muting the wisdom to push away and run. What was the point? She'd already learned the futility of trying to outrun a wolf.

She tipped up her head, exposing her neck. He could rip out her throat if he wanted, but he seemed content to nip and lick and suck every inch. Trembling, she felt no less devoured as her strength failed from the hum of sheer pleasure.

Dangerous, oh-so-dangerous. Despite her best effort, she couldn't continue to pretend that he meant nothing to her. She'd crashed that hurdle the first time she foolishly slipped inside his hospital room. After hours of watching over him during his darkest time, offering her touch to ease his pain, lending her voice to vanquish his nightmares, her heart simply refused to turn him out cold.

Earlier Brice had asked her to have faith in him. Right now, that's all she had, because following suit behind her heart, her mutinous legs refused to usurp his support to carry her away from the danger. With her arms banded around his sleek, muscled torso, she sighed her surrender against his chest.

He cradled her for the longest time. Patient, warm, understanding.

When he finally moved, his mouth christened her lips with a kiss, soft and wispy, like the fluttering of butterfly wings. There was a promise in the whispered touch. A promise to be kind and gentle. Never to expect more than she offered. Never to demand more than she could give. She might've considered the notion a wishful fantasy except for the deep-seated knowing in her spirit.

Surrendering to the need to taste more of him than a breeze, she captured his face between her palms and pulled him to her lips. His breath hitched. Then he crushed open her mouth. Lightning sparked at the point of contact and zipped through her body, a white-hot bolt of electricity that left no nerves, no cells uncharged. Fingers twisted in her hair, he tilted her head for a better, tighter seal. Spearing into her mouth, his tongue gentled when it met hers probing in soft darts.

He tasted like a storybook Christmas, sparkly, exciting and overwhelmingly wonderful. Her body quivered from the starburst of pure joy.

Brice deepened the kiss, his heat blanketing her in a snug comfort that made her feel safe, secure and anchored. She'd craved those things as a child and as a woman, they were her defining brass rings. If only for a moment, to know in his arms she had all three made her heart swell to near bursting.

She pressed closer, basking in his intimate warmth. Awareness threaded through her, sexual, decadent. Tingles became throbs in the most inconvenient places. Instead of concentrating on the kiss, her focus centered on her wet, clenching sex.

Air! She needed air.

Cassie tore away, her mouth separating from his with a wet smack. Brice's hard, fast breaths swirled around her. She wished the house wasn't too dark to see his expression. To see his eyes. She loved his eyes, how they sparkled when he teased, burned in an argument, brightened with curiosity, softened as he coaxed, and gleamed with feverish intensity when aroused, like now.

She knew he was because the hard evidence pressed against her abdomen. An arid heat whooshed across her skin. She would've broken out in a sweat if the moisture in her body hadn't pooled somewhere else.

No matter how many billions of years of evolution had

passed, three things were certain. He was male, she was female and primal instinct was just that. Primal.

Cassie grabbed Brice's face and savaged his mouth, drawing a growl from the back of his throat and swallowing it. An animalistic fervor flooded her conscience. She rubbed against his body, clawed at his skin, wanting to get as close as she possibly could.

It wasn't enough. More, she needed more.

Fire erupted in her womb, its tendrils licking through her body, enflaming every cell. She couldn't imagine anything hotter than hellfire, but this was a close second.

*Easy, Cas.*

Brice's voice lilted through her thoughts, a gentle commanding beacon amidst the passionate maelstrom. She knew he hadn't spoken because their mouths were sealed around their dueling tongues.

He captured her wrists, pinning them behind her. Oh, she didn't like the absence of his muscles flexing beneath her strokes. Not. One. Bit.

Then he trailed his fingers leisurely up and down her spine. Her heated skin cooled upon the mighty invasion of delicious chills. She snuggled closer without trying to climb to his body.

The rhythm of his touch created a calming, centering wave that didn't douse her desire. It merely changed the tempo.

Their frenzied kiss became a series of softer, shorter ones until Brice drew back on a ragged breath.

"Good night, Sunshine," he whispered hoarsely. His knuckles grazed her curls. Then he turned and left her standing in the dark, alone.

Stunned, all Cassie could do was stare into the empty space.

When she'd said she wanted to see his ass walking out the front door on the night he arrived, this was so not what she had in mind.

She trudged to the bedroom, irritation slicing through the adrenaline high to expose a raw nerve. Brice had done exactly what she needed him to do. Shut down her hormones before things escalated to a point of regret.

*How noble.*

She climbed into bed. Tomorrow she would be thankful he'd kept his head clear while hers overdosed on him, but right now… She grabbed his pillow and punched it with all her might. Oh, he was so lucky to have walked out that door.

# Chapter 21

Brice disconnected the Bluetooth call to his father and parked in a reserved space in front of a large roadhouse. A blue neon sign on the roof flashed TAYLOR'S.

"I'll wait," Cassie mumbled. She'd been in an inhospitable mood all day, embarrassed by her behavior last night and stoked by a front-row view of the round-robin parade of women Mrs. Walker had arranged to meet Brice.

"You agreed to get a bite to eat with me."

Only because as she'd started to say no she looked into his eyes. Big blue-and-green pools of kryptonite, that's what they were. Sucking every bit of willpower right out of her body.

"I thought we were going to a drive-through. I can't afford steak-house prices. Besides, I'm not that hungry." Her stomach protested, obnoxiously loud and pitiful. She pressed her arm into her abdomen to quiet the traitor.

"Dinner is on me." He leaned over to snuffle her hair.

A capricious heat flooded her body and fueled her bad mood. After the fool she'd made of herself last night, Cassie didn't want his lips anywhere near her body. She brushed him away. "I don't want your charity."

"I'm not being charitable. I'm hungry and don't want to eat alone." Brice netted her hand and took the liberty of another sniff.

"The parking lot is full. I'm sure someone will join you." She reclaimed the appendage, which hummed from his touch.

Brice closed his eyes. His lips parted in a silent count. When he looked again at Cassie, his expression was perfectly clear of annoyance. She wished he'd teach her his Zen counting meditation. Being pissy was exhausting, and she didn't like it very much.

"What's wrong, Sunshine?"

"You." She woodpeckered her finger into his bicep.

This was the first opportunity she'd had today to clear the air about what happened last night and establish rules to avoid a repeat.

"What, specifically, about me bothers you?"

"Let's start with last night's kiss."

"It wasn't to your liking?" He ate his smile, but the flattened seam of his mouth continued to stretch and the corners hitched up, so obviously he wasn't trying very hard not to be amused.

"It was…okay." She held her breath and schooled her features, hoping her expression portrayed unaffected boredom.

"Okay?" Brice's eyes flashed and his spine stiffened. Puffing his chest, he said, "It was a hell of a lot more than *okay*!"

Not the point, so she moved on.

"You walked out on me." *Do you have any idea how that made me feel?*

Confused. Frustrated. Embarrassed. Worst of all, abandoned.

The whole mess was her fault, really. Inexperience caused her to become overly excited. She could admit her blunder. Would have, in fact, if he had come home.

She expected him to be more upfront about the uncomfortable situation she'd created. Instead, he dodged and ran, the same tactic her mother had employed.

"Last night, I faced two choices. The first, walk away. The second, stay and let nature take its course." He paused. "I didn't want to fail the first test of your trust."

She suspected as much. What really hurt was that he didn't say that to her last night.

"You were sleeping when I came home." Intense and purposeful, his gaze commanded her understanding. "You were exhausted, so I didn't wake you."

Cassie's heart kicked an extra beat. "You weren't home when I got up for class. I thought you had stayed out all night."

"With you snuggled in my bed? Never!" He winked.

A calm, cuddly, comfy feeling spread from the top of her curly head to the tips of her unpolished toes. She could get used to this toasty reaction.

Before the feel-good sensation soaked into her bones, a cold splash of reality passed in front of the truck. The trio of beautiful women had been among the throng of Brice's admirers today.

Dropping his shoulders, he leaned slightly forward on the steering wheel, eyes slitted. Despite the flare of his nostrils, his respiration slowed to an imperceptible breath as the lady wolves dressed in expensive-looking low-cut minidresses and spiky heels sashayed into the restaurant.

Cassie's gaze sank to her worn, baby-pink capris, plain white sandals and basic white three-quarter-sleeve cotton top with tiny golden studs framing the scoop neckline. Attire fit for a drive-through, not for clubbing. "If you'd rather eat with them…" She let her voice trail.

Brice's head swung toward her, his brows drawn together. "Then I wouldn't have asked you."

His reassurance wasn't reassuring. He climbed out of the truck. She waited.

At the cabin, she needed his help getting into the raised vehicle, and she wasn't too proud for him to help her down, especially since falling flat on the asphalt was a likely outcome if she refused his Southern chivalry.

The door jerked open, and Brice's hands fastened on her waist. Little bites of electricity nipped her skin despite her clothing. Her nerves crackled and snapped with awareness.

*Great, just great.*

At least a table would provide a decent barrier for the next hour or so.

Brice lifted her from the seat and slid her down the length of his exquisitely tortuous body. By the time her feet touched the ground, the prickle throughout her body had converted to an expectant throb. The sandpapery feel of his cheek against her jaw as he scented her delighted Cassie's all-too-eager senses. She lifted her chin, giving him greater access.

"God, you smell good," he breathed across her skin. The hot, wispy puffs evoked an involuntary shiver.

"Define *good*." She leaned into his nuzzle.

"Like sunshine after a terrible storm," he whispered.

Wow. The wildflower line at the hospital had been sweet, but this response caused her breath to catch in her throat. Brice hadn't simply given her a one-size-fits-all-women nickname. He gave her one with deep personal meaning.

He moved closer, eliminating the infinitesimal space between their bodies. Despite the August evening heat, her body curved into him out of pure conditioning. Sharing his bed and spooning every night wasn't much different from Pavlov's bell. Only Cassie didn't drool at the stimulus. She became wet in other places.

*Get a grip!*

Her arms slipped around his neck.

*No, no, no! That's not what I meant.*

The smile plumping her cheeks refused to give in to the frown her brain tried to force on her mouth. She needed to clear her head before she did something stupid.

At fourteen, Cassie briefly imagined what it would be like to step out of her hovel into Brice's world. Until her fairy godmother slapped her with a reality stick and screamed like a drill sergeant that Imogene Struthers's daughter was no freaking Cinderella. And if Cassie didn't have the good sense to keep her curly redhead out of the clouds, she'd end up just like her mother.

Sound advice Cassie intended to heed. She wouldn't allow her foolish heart to make decisions. It was too soft, too gullible. It would be too easily broken.

Brice's mouth hovered a hairbreadth from her lips. She dropped her hands to his chest and pushed him away.

"We're temporary roommates, nothing more." She turned her face, causing his kiss to graze her ear.

He released a soft, frustrated groan. "We're so much more. I know you sense the connection."

"It's called biology. A male and female in close proximity during a period of high emotions. You would have the same draw to any woman under the same circumstances."

"I can say with certainty I wouldn't." He pulled the loose band from her hair, tossed it on the seat, slipped his fingers through her hair.

"Maybe just curly redheads." She batted his hands.

"One curly redhead in particular."

Cassie slipped around him before he kissed her. "I've thought of more roommate rules. Touching, kissing or otherwise getting frisky is not permitted."

Without a second's worth of hesitation, Brice said, "Agreed."

"Really?" Her voice sounded more disappointed than relieved. Cassie clamped her arms across her chest.

"Absolutely." A mischievous air broadened his wide, bright smile. "I'll pound any man into the ground who does those things to you." Brice draped his arm over her shoulders and walked her up the steps of the restaurant. "You're mine, Cas. After dinner, I'll explain exactly what that means."

A profound sense of Brice flooded her being in a wave of intense emotions. She'd felt the same rush years ago in his hospital room and blamed her imagination.

A kernel of hope bloomed. If she didn't find a way to strangle the menace before it took hold, it would spread like ivy and choke out her good sense. Good sense she seemed to have less and less of whenever Brice was around.

"I need to use the ladies' room." The simmer in Cassie's eyes cooled.

"Just one more dance." Brice rehooked Cassie's arms around his neck.

During their first dance, she'd been overly self-conscious, so Brice took her face into his hands and ordered her to block out everyone around them. To focus on him, then the music.

Two songs later, she giggled when she misstepped, and her skin glowed. He wanted to believe the flush came from the excitement of being with him rather than the exertion.

That's how it was for him, at least. They could be doing yoga in an ice pond and his heart would pound, his skin would tingle and his cock would be just as hard.

In a matter of days, he'd grown to crave Cassie's company. Whenever he looked at her, a feeling of rightness settled in his bones. Her sharp wit and dry humor enchanted him, and that stubborn streak of hers fairly matched his own. Mostly he loved the warm, soft feel of her in his arms, especially when she wiggled against him in her sleep. Those unguarded moments were the highlights of his day.

Now that the music tempo slowed and he had the opportunity to hold her close, he wasn't about to let her run for cover. Savoring every second of the crazy, maddening feel of her in his arms, he sensed the tethers of the mate-bond stitching together their souls. He could have stayed entwined with her forever.

Except the song ended and Cassie pulled away. "Meet you at the table."

Then she was gone.

"Cheer up." Tristan Durrance slapped him on the back. "The lady only went to powder her nose. She hasn't left you at the pound."

Brice stared into the face of his brother's best friend and swallowed bitter regret. He didn't care about titles or position. Only whether or not Tristan could forgive him for Mason's death.

Tristan draped his arm over Brice's shoulders, steering him to the booth. "I heard about Granny. You have my sympathies."

Brice accepted the condolence with a quick nod.

"You know what happened to Rafe, right?" Tristan's happy-go-lucky expression faltered.

"I do now." Even though Rafe insisted Brice's presence

wouldn't have helped him get over the loss, Brice knew he'd failed his friend. "Adam didn't tell me when it happened. Among other things."

"I figured as much. Hell, we all knew something wasn't right." Tristan stretched his arm over the back of the booth. "You were in a bad state when Adam took you away."

Though Tristan's soulful eyes fixed on him, Brice knew the older wolfan's other senses were scoping the increased bustle of the restaurant. A pack sentinel was always on duty, even when he wasn't.

"Mason's dead because of me. Everyone should hate me." For chrissakes, Brice sure hated himself.

"Mason loved you more than anything. He would be proud of the way you fought and survived. We all are." The sincerity in Tristan's tone mocked Brice's shame.

"I howled in a moment of weakness, and the rogues found us."

"You almost lost your leg in a steel trap. I don't know any wolfan who wouldn't have howled. Your reaction was normal, Brice. Quit feeling sorry for yourself and give this pack what we want."

A golf-ball-sized knot of tension formed at the base of Brice's skull. He'd brought Cassie to Taylor's to relax and have fun. Tristan's dose of reality put a damper on the evening.

"What does the pack want, Tristan?"

"You, home and happy. You are the heart of Walker's Run, and Mason took great care to foster you. Don't waste his efforts."

"Foster me for what?"

"Gavin should've told you a long time ago." Tristan's expression hardened. "Mason abdicated the Alphaship when you were born. You are and have always been our Alpha-in-Waiting."

The words bounced in Brice's head like a box of Ping-Pong balls dumped on a game table. His head spun, and it wasn't from the two beers he'd drunk earlier. "Mason was eight when I was born. He wasn't old enough to abdicate."

"Not officially, but your parents knew." Tristan leaned his arms on the table, his hands relaxed and open. "Mason planned to tell you the day he took you hunting."

How ironic for his brother to die on the day he planned to abdicate the Alphaship.

The timing of the revelation seemed too convenient, too orchestrated.

"My dad put you up to this." Brice directed no anger toward Tristan. A sentinel had a duty to carry out the Alpha's wishes. Tristan had merely been ensnared in Brice's father's latest manipulation ploy. "What's he playing me for now?"

"This isn't an Alpha game." Tristan's features sharpened. Baring his clenched teeth, he took on the look of a really pissed wolf. "You are our Alpha-in-Waiting. The future of the pack rests with you."

"Maybe the pack should consider alternatives to the tradition of Alpha succession. Everyone says I'm more Foster than Walker."

"Only in coloring."

Brice's stomach, churning ever since Tristan had greeted him, precariously rolled and dipped. He laced his fingers behind his head to cradle his skull as he pointed his nose upward.

*Where the hell was Cassie?*

The myriad of smells was annoyingly bereft of Cassie's scent; however, the singular feminine fragrance that overwhelmed his senses raised his hackles a second too late.

"What the fuck?" Brice tangled with the octopus-like arms of the woman who fell into his lap. She peppered his face with ardent kisses, and her strong, heady scent scalded his nose with each breath.

"Enough, Victoria." Brice attempted to extricate himself politely. If not for the growing number of spectators, he would've dumped her on the floor.

Her underhanded attempt to trap him in a mateship had

stripped away any respect he once had for her. After their last encounter, he awoke in her bed disoriented and with a killer headache. Victoria sprawled beside him, buck naked. The air was heavy with the scent of sex and not one used condom in sight.

He had no memory of the entire evening and suspected that she'd dosed his drink with the hope of convincing him to claim her.

He'd checked her twice for bite marks. Finding none, he dressed and hightailed it to his apartment.

Afterward, Victoria made it clear that she expected a mateship. Brice, on the other hand, would chew off his cock before he climbed back into Victoria Phalen's bed.

# Chapter 22

In the few minutes Cassie had been in the restroom, Taylor's occupancy had swelled beyond capacity. She wedged between people gathered around the bar.

"Well, hello." Vincent Hadler's arm slithered around her waist to pull her from the crowd.

A sickening sensation crawled Cassie's skin. "I'm here with someone."

"He's busy. Why don't you keep me company instead?" Though she suspected Vince was wolfan, his smile reminded Cassie of a hyena. Comical and dangerous.

"I don't socialize with resort guests." More irritated than afraid, Cassie unhooked his arm from her hip.

"From what I've seen, you don't socialize at all." He laughed harshly against her ear. "But since you're out tonight, I insist on a drink and a dance."

"I don't drink." Her attempt to sidestep him failed.

"All right, let's skip straight to a dance. I've got better moves than that Walker *boy*." Hadler's lips puckered as if he'd swallowed something sour.

"Not interested. If you'll excuse me, Brice is waiting for me."

"Don't bet on it." Hadler jerked Cassie against his body.

Fear and disgust rippled through her. She couldn't see Brice through the crowd, so he probably couldn't see her. So much for him being there when she needed him.

She would handle Vincent Hadler, alone.

He wouldn't be the first man she'd dropped to the floor for his unwanted attention. Imogene's suitors weren't always interested only in Imogene.

"Let me go." Cassie had trained her voice to sound braver than she felt.

"Not until we've had that dance." From his suggestive tone, Cassie knew he wasn't talking about a twirl on the dance floor.

He drew her closer, rubbing his nose in her hair. "You smell delicious."

Cassie thanked him with a hard thrust of her knee to his groin. He doubled over.

"I'm not on the menu." Shaking, Cassie pushed her way through the throng to find Brice and a gorgeous blonde femme fatale locked at the lips.

Cassie's get-real talk in the bathroom had been a bunch of hooey. The sight of him kissing another woman cut her to the quick. A void opened in Cassie's chest and sucked out her heart.

"The ladies' room is empty. You can finish in there." She clamped her lips to keep her dinner from landing on the table.

The woman dragged her slutty mouth from Brice's lips. "Who the hell are you?"

"I'm wondering the same about you." Cassie resisted the urge to storm away. She had no right to be jealous.

Roommates, she reminded herself.

Yeah?

Well, hell. Being roommates sucked.

Brice pushed the woman to her feet and scrambled up beside her. "Victoria Phalen, this is Cassidy Albright." Using the back of his hand, he rubbed the wetness of Victoria's kisses from his guilty face. "We'd appreciate it if you wouldn't slobber all over me."

"I'd appreciate it, too." The tawny-haired man at their booth stood.

From the mischievous twinkle in his dark chocolate eyes and the infectious smile that was almost too much to take in, Cassie immediately recognized Maico's most talked-about bachelor. Although from Tristan Durrance's reputation, she would've expected him to be the one making out in public rather than Brice.

"I'm all for PDA, but damn, that was painful to watch. You

didn't enjoy that one bit, did you, kiddo?" Tristan gave Brice a sympathetic look that chilled when his gaze passed to Victoria.

"Not in the least." Brice nudged Cassie into the booth, although all she wanted to do was find a ride home.

Tristan retook his seat and turned his high-powered smile on Cassie.

"Victoria, I meant what I said in Atlanta." Brice rubbed his temple.

"You'll come around." Victoria's tapered brows lifted in perfect twin arcs. "You can't fight fate. Christmas isn't too far away, and we have a wedding to plan." She sauntered to the bar, stomping on Cassie's heart each step of the way.

Knowing Brice would eventually marry someone as sophisticated as Victoria was one thing. Having the reality of it shoved in Cassie's face stung to high heaven.

"I can explain." Brice slid beside Cassie, crowding her with his overwhelming presence.

"Your affairs are not my business." She reached across the table. "Hi, I'm Cassie Albright."

"Tristan Durrance, at your service." He gave her fingers a gentle shake. "I'm a great fan of your pies."

"Really?" She repaid his tact in changing the conversation with a grateful smile.

"Yep. The first one cost me a chomp in the ass when Rafe caught me polishing off one you gave him." Tristan draped his arms over the top of his seat. "The last one cost me sixty-five bucks at the Fourth of July charity auction. Both were worth the price."

"Thanks." Pride tempered the ache in Cassie's chest.

"Ever thought about going into the pie business?" The tip of Tristan's tongue peeked between his lips and slid across the seam of his mouth in a manner that said he'd be her first customer if she did.

She gave a throaty laugh. "I love baking because it reminds me of the good times with my mom. If I had to make pies for a living, it would ruin the memories."

"Well, if you ever need a taste tester, I'm available." Something beyond their table stole Tristan's attention. "I've got to run, love. I look forward to seeing you again." He tipped his head toward Brice, then slipped out of the booth to disappear into the crowd.

"There's nothing between me and Victoria," Brice blurted.

"Like I said, your affairs aren't my business." Cassie choked on the lump constricting her throat. "Take me home. I want to forget this night ever happened."

# *Chapter 23*

Home was the last place Brice wanted to take Cassie. He turned onto a worn trail that cut through the heart of the co-op's wolf sanctuary. A half mile in, a sentinel opened the gate for them to enter.

Brice engaged the four-wheel drive and followed the dirt path up the mountain. The truck bounced over the rough terrain, jostling them despite the seat belts. Cassie maintained a two-fisted death grip on the armrest, her mouth pulled tight.

Moonlight dappled the woods in a silvery mist, though Brice was too annoyed to enjoy its serenity. Judging from Cassie's glazed stare, she didn't appreciate the evening beauty, either.

At the pinnacle, Brice killed the engine and set the emergency brake.

"If you wanted to get rid of me to be with your fiancée, you could've asked me to move out. Throwing me off a mountain is a bit dramatic, don't you think?"

Cassie's sarcasm didn't rile Brice as much as her continued references to his *fiancée*. How many times did he have to explain that Victoria meant nothing to him?

"I want to show you something," he said softly.

"I'm not up for sightseeing." Cassie focused on the windshield rather than looking at him.

Too edgy to cajole her compliance, Brice clasped her arm and hauled Cassie out of the truck.

She dug the heels of her sandals into the ground. "I'm not going anywhere with you, except home to pack my suitcases."

Undeterred, Brice picked her up and swung her over his shoulder.

"I. Am. Not. A. Rag. Doll. Brice. Walker. Put. Me. Down." She punctuated each word with a punch to his backside.

The strikes weren't forceful enough to make him comply, though it did seem funny—such a slight woman railing against his hulk, her feet kicking in the air amid a swirl of curse words that he hadn't known she knew. The baritone of his laughter echoed through the woods, making it a symphony of hilarity.

Until she clamped her teeth on the back of his arm and he almost dropped her. His vision blurred, and the pain became lost in the surge of testosterone.

*Cassie claimed me!*

The wolf fought to make the claim official. The man struggled not to fuck things up.

"Settle down." He smacked her rump.

"I used to think you were a nice guy." She returned the smack. "The more I get to know you, the less I like you."

"So, you admit that you do like me?" He smiled at her disgusted groan.

"Is that what you learned in law school? How to twist someone's words into something she didn't mean?"

"Truth is truth, Sunshine. You'd see it for what it is if you stopped running." The words struck a chord. Hadn't he been running, too? From his family, his friends, his pack? His destiny?

"What I see is spots in front of my eyes from all the blood rushing to my head." Her voice waned.

"Relax." Brice set Cassie on her feet and held her steady until she stopped swaying.

"Why am I here?" Shoulders straight and spine rigid, she crossed her arms and arrowed her chin at him.

Brice turned her around. His heartbeat suspended for each second it took for the harsh suspicions weighting her brow to give way to round-eyed amazement.

Countless stars twinkled against the dark blue velvet of the night sky. A celestial glow cast by the waning moon colored the valley and shimmered over the winding river that had brought him home. To her.

"It's beautiful," she breathed. "Where are we?"

"Walker's Pointe." Brice urged Cassie to sit on the soft moss where he'd spent rapturous hours listening to his brother recite the chronicles of Walker's Run. "Legend has it that when my forefather, Abram Walker, came to this place, something settled in his blood and made it impossible for him to be happy anywhere else in the world. Every generation of Walkers has experienced the same calling." Including Brice.

Walker's Run was in his blood.

So was Cassie. Even now, a part of her circulated through him. Her bite had broken the skin, allowing her saliva to seep into the wound. Although her human bite wasn't binding under wolfan law, Brice believed the instinctive act would strengthen and solidify a mate-bond. Until Cassie believed, he needed to exercise care not to rush her or he'd lose her.

"It must be wonderful to have such a strong sense of belonging." Cassie pulled her knees to her chest.

Brice put his arm around her. "I came home to tell Granny that I planned to give it all up. I lost faith in my friends, in my family. In everything."

"They never lost faith in you."

"I'm learning that."

"It must have been hard when you moved away." Cassie relaxed against him.

"Even harder coming home." Brice's next breath sounded ragged.

Cassie's small hand cupped his larger one. A warm, dizzying wave surged through the mate-bond. She had opened herself to give him comfort, and he'd take whatever she offered.

He brushed his cheek against Cassie's hair. A soured milk smell clung to the strands. The hairs on the back of his neck stood up, and the muscles along his spine tightened. The scent reminded him of the one he picked up outside the cabin last night.

"Who were you with tonight, Sunshine?" He kept his tone light despite the tightness in his throat.

"You." The softness in her shoulders hardened. "Two beers.

You said you could handle two beers. Apparently you can't if you don't remember eating dinner and dancing with me."

"I can recall every minute we spent together. What I don't understand is why I smell another man's scent in your hair."

"What?" She looked at him, guileless and innocent. Then her mouth dropped in a disgusted grimace. "Oh, that's gross. I'm washing my hair as soon as we get home."

"Was it Shane?" Brice had seen the Black Mountain pack member near the bar when Cassie headed to the restroom.

"Shane? No. I ran into—" Cassie hesitated.

"Who?"

"Some jerk who wanted a dance."

A possessive growl vibrated in Brice's chest.

"Take it easy, *Benji*." Cassie laid her hand on his thigh. "I handled him."

"What?" Brice's snarl silenced the forest's nocturnal sounds.

"Jeez." Cassie jumped. "I don't know why you're all pissy about a guy wanting a dance. I caught you and your fiancée tongue-wrestling."

"Cassie." Brice's blood pressure skyrocketed along with his voice. "For the last fucking time, Victoria is not my fiancée, and she will never be my mate. Now tell me, who the hell did you dance with tonight?"

"You! You big dope. I only danced with you." Cassie scrubbed her fists down her arms. "That other guy was a creep."

Just as Brice's blood pressure leveled she added, "He got the message when I gave him the knee. I doubt he'll grope me again."

Black spots mottled Brice's vision. His head pounded until he felt the force might crack his skull. Primitive instinct demanded that he track down the man and render him a bloody pulp.

"Are you playing me against Victoria?" Cassie's expression held no anger, only a disappointed resignation.

"No," Brice said, reeling in his emotions. "I know how it feels to be manipulated. I won't do that to you."

Brice lifted her hand to his face and brushed his cheek along the delicate side of her wrist, allowing her scent to soothe him. "But there is something you should know. In Atlanta, Victoria and I were coworkers who had sex."

Cassie pulled away from his touch and hugged her knees beneath her chin.

"She and I were never a couple, Cas. Wahyas need sex, especially during full moons, to regulate the wolfan hormones. A lack of sex can cause us to regress into our primitive state, a bipedal wolf hybrid that has no human conscience."

Cassie scrunched her nose. "Are you saying that if you don't have sex, you could become a—" she lowered her voice—"a werewolf?"

Brice nodded. "Victoria and I had an understanding. Until she drugged me and I ended our affair."

"She's planning a wedding."

"Not mine," Brice said. "The truth is, my dad does want me to settle down before Christmas."

"Oh." Cassie's voice followed her gaze to some nebulous spot in the distance.

"Cas, I don't love Victoria. Never have, never will."

"She is quite attached to you."

"Only because of what she can gain. Victoria wants a mate who can elevate her status. If I become an Alpha, my mate will be an Alphena."

"I'm sure Miss Phalen will be a great help to you." Cassie traced her finger over a smooth stone near her foot.

"I don't want her help. I need yours."

Cassie cast him a sidelong glance. "We should go home so you can sleep off those beers."

"We share a bond, Cas. A mate-bond." Scooting behind Cassie, he cloaked her with his arms. God, he loved how her heat soaked through his muscles and down into his bones.

Cassie bristled. "The only thing between us is a series of unusual circumstances."

"That's not true. When I was in the hospital, the bond drew

you back to me. But once I woke up, you stopped coming, so I didn't consciously know a bond had formed. For the last five years, I've been nearly out of my mind, needing something that I couldn't quite define. Until I came home and found you."

"You're out of your mind, all right. Drunk out of your mind."

"The only thing I'm drunk on, Sunshine, is you." Brice nuzzled her hair to re-mark her with his scent. "The night we met, right before you kneed me, you triggered my mating urge."

"Well, *Benji*. Point that nose of yours at someone else." She edged away from him. "I can't be your mate. I'm not like you."

"So? Wahyas can take human mates. Our children won't be human, though. Wahyan genes are dominant."

"I wasn't talking about you being wolfy." Cassie's delicate brow dipped over worried eyes. "You have everything, Brice. I have nothing."

"I don't care." Social standing and financial status had never been important to him.

"I do." An unsettling fierceness resonated in Cassie's voice. "All my life, I've worked hard, sacrificed everything, and I still have a long way to go before I get what I want."

"Your own business?"

"Stability." She gave an aggravated sigh.

"Let me be your stability," Brice insisted.

"No." Cassie's curls bounced as she shook her head. "I need to make it on my own."

Brice let the matter drop. Cassie hadn't outright rejected him. Just sent a warning that now wasn't the right time for her. He could handle a delay. After all, in spite of his father's edict, Brice had obligations to attend to before he claimed a mate.

Besides, they needed time to learn each other. Time to fall in love.

"Victoria is a better match. She's beautiful, sophisticated. You run in the same social circles." Cassie hiccupped a humorless laugh. "In and out of the woods."

"She isn't the one who gave me this." Brice showed Cassie the bite mark.

"I got carried away." She tucked a loose curl behind her ear and shrugged. "Sorry."

"Don't be. I'm proud of your mark. Wahyas claim their mates with a bite." A primal need surged through his body, tempered only by his desire to live as a man, not an animal.

"That wasn't my intention." Cassie's flat voice wasn't encouraging.

"Doesn't matter. A bite is a bite, and Wahyas mate for life," he answered playfully to offset her seriousness.

"This isn't funny." Cassie gazed over the valley.

Brice stretched out beside her, cushioning his head in his hands.

"Just out of curiosity," Cassie said, "what is this mate stuff all about?"

Brice pressed his lips between his teeth to hide his smile. Curiosity was good. Very good. Except in cats.

"Human marriages are legal contracts that can be dissolved by annulment or divorce. A Wahyan mate-claim is an unbreakable union under wolfan law."

Cassie wrinkled her cute little nose. "What if someone's mate turns out to be a jackass?"

"We can't mate with equines." He tried to sound serious, but amusement cracked his voice.

"That's not what I meant and you know it." She tossed a blade of grass at him.

"Mate-claims are sacred, Cas. Wahyas aren't rash about commitment. If a couple makes a poor choice, the claim can't be reversed."

"Why?"

"It's an evolutionary instinct. A Wahya male can't father children until he's bitten a female during sex. Marking her with his scent hormone triggers a physiologic change that allows the male to secrete viable sperm as opposed to—"

"Duds," Cassie interrupted. "I don't need a biology lesson."

"I want you to understand how important a bite is to Wahyas. A male becomes intuitively possessive and protective of the female he bites."

"In case you didn't notice, I'm not a Wahyan male, and we weren't having sex when *I* bit *you*."

"A human bite can be just as binding if a mate-bond exists."

"Nothing is between us, okay?" Cassie's irritation flooded into Brice, as did a thread of hope. Proving to him how wrong she was.

He allowed what he knew to be true to flow back to her in a calm, steady stream. "There's another dynamic called a mate-bond. It sparks between true mates the moment they meet. Each subsequent encounter allows their life forces to weave together. It binds them heart and mind, body and soul. This allows the couple to feel what the other feels and hear one another's thoughts."

"They become telepathic?"

"With each other, yes." Brice lifted on his elbows and shook out the cramp in his calf. "Unfortunately, not all Wahyas develop this type of bond with their mates. Many think it's a myth."

"Do you believe it exists?" Cassie flicked her loose curls over her shoulder, then pulled his sore leg onto her lap. She pushed up his pant leg and began a slow, gentle massage.

"I've seen how the bond works between my parents. Rafe and Lexi were bonded, too."

"He's so lost without her." Cassie's voice squeaked. "I can't imagine someone loving me that much."

"I can, if you'll let me."

Cassie's back stiffened. "I'd prefer if you kept me out of your wolfy courtship rituals."

In the early stages, a mate-bond could be rejected by either party. If that happened, Cassie would never find another man who would love her as completely as Brice when fully bonded. And he would spend the rest of his life mourning her loss.

Fighting against utter desperation, Brice peered into the black expanse of the night sky and, with all his being, wished on the twinkling stars that he and Cassie wouldn't suffer that fate.

# Chapter 24

Surrounded by bloody feathers and mutilated chickens wasn't how Brice had planned to spend the morning after last night's confessions to Cassie.

At breakfast, he couldn't have been happier with the aroma of bacon and pancakes, butter and syrup. He even detected the fragrance of Cassie's hot tea and the milk he guided her to pour into his coffee.

As much as he loved those smells, he was most grateful for the scent of Cassie's desire when they'd kissed. Leaving her had been damn near painful.

This morning, she opened herself to him. Brice saw it in the way she looked at him, felt it in the way she touched him. He wouldn't have taken things as far as he did if he hadn't sensed her readiness.

Now, instead of making love to Cassie, Brice stood in the midst of a massacre inside Mary-Jane McAllister's farmyard, suffocated by the stench of death. Sickened by the brutal carnage, Brice's stomach churned mercilessly. Maybe wolfing down those pancakes before he'd left wasn't such a good idea.

"Why would someone do this?" He studied his father, who seemed to stomach the slaughter much better than Brice.

"Maybe some wolflings came for Cybil and decided to have a go with the chickens instead." Gavin swiped the back of his hand across his nose. "This is why I always told you and Rafe to be mindful of your pranks."

Brice refused to believe that any of the Walker's Run wolflings were responsible. "Where is Cybil?" he asked, alarmed by her empty pen.

"In the house," his father replied. "Mary-Jane spent last night with her cousin in Blairsville. She locked Cybil inside so she wouldn't get loose and roam the woods."

Mary-Jane loved that pig like a child. Brice couldn't imagine how heartbroken she would've been if something had happened to Cybil.

"When Mary-Jane came home to this mess, she called Cooter. He's with her now," Gavin said.

Noting the gouges in the dirt made during the frenzied attack, Brice limped to the coop that until last night had been a haven for Mary-Jane's chickens. Half of her stock never made it out of their pen.

Inside, the stink was twice as concentrated as the smell in the yard. Turning to leave, Brice caught wind of a faint, sour odor.

He stood in the middle of the coop, hoping to isolate the scent.

After a few seconds, beads of sweat broke out across his skin. The uncomfortable prickle in the pit of his stomach rushed into his throat. He made it outside and around the corner of the coop before his hands and knees hit the ground, followed by his partially digested breakfast. Even after his stomach emptied, he continued to heave.

"Easy, son." Adam gripped Brice's shoulder.

"Don't touch me," Brice snarled. "And I'm not your son."

Adam removed his hand.

"What are you doing here?" Brice spat out remnants of bile.

"Abby told me what happened. I knew Gavin would drag you here."

Brice rolled from his hands-and-knees posture to a seated position and leaned against the chicken coop.

"Go back to the resort, Adam." Gavin knelt beside Brice. "You aren't needed here."

"He isn't ready for this, Gavin. You push too hard, too fast. Let me take Brice with me."

"Never again, Adam." Gavin's tone held a definite finality that Brice appreciated.

Adam hesitated, his eyes fixed on Brice.

"I don't need you, Adam. Tell Mom I'm okay."

Adam nodded. His shoulders sagged, and for the first time, Brice thought his uncle looked old and haggard. He trudged toward his car, the driver's door wide open, the engine still running.

Irrational, bordering on idiocy, a little piece of Brice's heart hurt for Adam. His uncle loved him to a fault but his betrayal, no matter how well-intended, was too new to forgive.

Gavin clenched the scruff of Brice's neck and Brice tensed. A grown wolfan upchucking at the sight of a feeding frenzy signaled a weak stomach and a lack of self-control.

"Easy, son." Gavin's thumb slipped beneath Brice's hair to the secret patch of blond. He applied a gentle pressure, massaging slow circles into Brice's scalp.

The gentle gesture soothed and confused Brice. His father had never coddled or comforted him. He'd never had the time.

The contractions in Brice's stomach eased.

Gavin offered him a frazzled cotton handkerchief with threadbare embroidery that once declared Best Dad Ever.

A different kind nausea rocked Brice.

Mason had taught him how to draw those letters. Afterward, Granny helped Brice stitch the words so the sentiment wouldn't wash off in the laundry. He had been so excited to give the handmade present to his dad on Father's Day.

And utterly devastated when Gavin tossed the unopened box into a drawer and rushed off without so much as a thank-you.

"No, thanks." Brice used his shirtsleeve to swipe the sweat from his face.

"I've carried this in my pocket for almost twenty-five years." Gavin fingered the frayed letters. "It's the best gift I ever received."

Those words would've put a four-year-old on the moon. A lifetime of shuns and slights kept Brice grounded. Since he hadn't signed his name to the present, Brice assumed his father had forgotten which son had given him the gift.

A forest-green SUV flashing the emergency lights embedded in the grill pulled to stop behind his father's black truck. Tristan stepped out and walked the maze of dead fowl. "What a damn shame."

"Find who did this," Gavin said to Tristan, then offered Brice a hand up, which he grudgingly accepted.

"Dad believes our wolflings are involved." Brice dusted the dirt from his jeans.

Tristan scratched his head just above his ear. "We have a few pranksters in the pack. None with a vicious streak, though."

"What about Vincent Hadler?" A worry knot tightened in Brice's gut. "Considering his reputation, it isn't hard to imagine him doing this."

"Never had problems with him before." Tristan squatted next to a patch of mud in front of the chicken coop and inspected a small depression. "But, I broke up an argument between him and Shane last night at Taylor's."

*Hadler was at Taylor's last night?*

Brice's gut began gnawing at him. When Hadler had harassed Cassie at the resort, Brice had detected a sour odor. Later, he'd tracked a similar scent around the cabin. Last night, he smelled it again in Cassie's hair.

Doc had warned of the likelihood that Brice would experience a confusion of scents for a while. Each time he'd encountered the odor, his emotions were running high. He hope it was a coincidence because if he discovered Hadler was stalking Cassie, Brice wouldn't hesitate to put an end to it, permanently.

# Chapter 25

"It's a shame to call these Georgia peaches," Cassie muttered to no one in particular. Disgusted, she walked past the arrogantly labeled fruit. Bland in color and lacking the trademark fuzz, the state fruit looked no better than the last batch, which was why Cassie had baked Rafe a cherry pie rather than his favorite, peach cobbler.

This morning, she'd hoped he would change the clunker's oil while she picked up a few items from the market and helped Brice pick out his grandmother's memorial flowers at the florist across the street. However, Rafe had greeted her at the R&L with bloodshot eyes, a rough beard and uncombed hair. In no shape to work today, he said if she stopped by after class tomorrow he would complete the oil change before she had to be at work.

Cassie wouldn't have minded postponing the service another week, but Rafe insisted it had been too long since the last automotive checkup. Because of the car's age, he didn't want to delay service longer than necessary.

She strolled down the produce aisle. Blackberries occupied the space where the cherries had been last week. They didn't look any better than the peaches. On her small budget, she refused to pay the outrageous price for the blueberries.

Tapping her nail against the plastic handle of the shopping basket, Cassie dismissed the notion to purchase a can of pie filing. Imogene had thumbed her nose at that particular convenience and taught her daughter to do the same.

Cassie's heart smiled. The good recollections of her mother were rare and all involved the kitchen. Those memories were a radiant shield against the fallout from her mother's reputation.

Imogene had shacked up with any man who'd take them in. *Sugar daddies*, she called them, although Cassie saw nothing sweet or fatherly about them. All of them had used her mother. Then again, Imogene used them. For food. Shelter. And whatever else mother and daughter needed.

The irony of Cassie's current situation wasn't lost on her. Neither were the lessons she'd learned from her mother's mistakes. A man couldn't give her a better life, but he sure could wreck it.

Regardless of the undeniable attraction between them, Cassie would not sleep with Brice.

Okay—technically, they slept in the same bed. However, they wouldn't have sex. And she would not fall in love.

Their breakfast make-out session had nothing to do with magic bonds or soul mates or destiny, and everything to do with hormones. Hormones she could handle. She just needed to keep an iron grip on reality.

Cassie stopped at the apple bin. Margaret loved her apple strudel.

Remorse heated Cassie's throat. She should have called Margaret Granny, at least once. The opportunity had passed, and there would be no more.

Cassie adjusted the basket in her hands. Wallowing in regret made for a miserable life. Another lesson learned from Imogene.

Cassie picked through the apples for those bright green in color with a tart, mouth-watering smell and just beginning to soften. Careful not to bruise the fruit, she placed eight in her basket.

At the checkout, two women stepped in line behind her. Cassie guessed they were close to her age, but their vivacious energy made her feel dowdy and old.

Through the storefront window, Cassie watched a black truck park next to her beat-up clunker in front of The Flower Stop on the other side of the town square park. A few seconds later, Brice climbed out, then leaned back inside the cab.

"Mmm, mmm," one of the girls behind Cassie hummed. "He has a fine ass."

*I know how fine his ass looks without pants.*

Cassie squelched her grin before she got herself in trouble.

Brice closed the truck door and looked across the park, seemingly through the market's storefront window and straight into Cassie's eyes.

*"That better be my ass you're thinking about, Sunshine."*

Crisp and clear, Brice's voice tickled her ear. Confused, she nonchalantly scanned the store to see who'd actually said what she heard. There wasn't a man in sight, at least not inside the store.

Annoyed with her imagination, she flipped through the latest edition of *Monstahz* magazine to an article on the sightings of Big Foot in the Everglades. Yikes! Not that Cassie believed in Big Foot; however, a few days ago she hadn't believed in werewolves, either. She shoved the magazine into the rack and stepped forward as the customer ahead of her finished.

"Oh, here he comes," the girls behind her gushed.

Against her good sense, Cassie watched Mr. Tall, Dark and Handsome as Sin limp across the grassy square. Her heart fluttered the same funny little trill that first appeared when she hovered at the threshold of Brice's hospital room and recurred every time she saw him.

He waited at the curb for a car to pass on the one-way street. Cassie met his gaze through the window and offered a weak shrug. Something warm wrapped around her shoulders, and her neck tickled. She stopped herself from flicking away the fabricated sensation, afraid that the action would give credence to her ridiculous imagination.

*"You're beautiful, Sunshine."*

The tips of Cassie's ears heated as hot as her cheeks. Jeez, if she fantasized about Brice calling her beautiful after nearly a week, what would happen to her brain after a month or two?

Placing her items on the checkout conveyor, she wondered if the hallucination might be a manifestation of the bond Brice mentioned. Excitement rushed through her head to toe. For all of three seconds before common sense flushed it out.

Brice drank two beers last night. Nothing he said afterward was trustworthy. Imogene made many promises when she drank. None came to fruition. Ever.

Cassie paid the cashier. Meager basket in hand, she walked outside, head held high and heart mopping the floor.

Brice stepped onto the sidewalk. Cassie's stride faltered beneath the turmoil in his eyes. "What's wrong?"

He gathered her in his arms, pressing intimately into her. His warmth soaked into her essence, and she was too indulgent to push him away.

"Someone killed Mary-Jane McAllister's chickens last night. Her farmyard is a mess," he said in a soft heave.

"Is she okay?" Cassie bought eggs from Mary-Jane. Poor woman fussed over her chicks like a mother hen.

"Shocked, mostly." Brice stroked his thumbs across Cassie's cheeks. "We think Wahyas are responsible. I doubt it's anyone from our pack, but we have a lot of wolfan visitors here for Granny's memorial."

A tremor of unease ran through Cassie's body. Hadn't he told her wolf people were civilized?

He pulled a cell phone from his back pocket. "I got this for you."

"I don't have anyone to call."

"Me, Cas. Call me." Brice smacked the device into her palm.

"This isn't necessary," Cassie began. Brice's fingers fastened around her hand, his jaw frozen in a stubborn clench. "But if you insist." She dropped the phone into her purse.

"I do." Brice slung his arm over her shoulder. "And until we find the culprit who raided Mary-Jane's chickens, I don't want you out alone at night."

They strolled leisurely toward the florist. When Brice opened the door, Cassie expected the heady scents of fresh-cut flowers. Perhaps Brice didn't. He sneezed several times. His eyes glazed, and he looked a little peaked.

Cassie touched his face, allowing him to rub his nose against her wrist.

"Good afternoon," Alethea Duncan, the florist, greeted them. "I'm sorry for your loss, Brice."

"Thank you." His grip on Cassie's shoulder tightened, and she stroked his hand until he relaxed.

"Please make yourselves comfortable." Alethea walked them to a table. She opened one of four large three-ring binders. "I'll give you a few moments to look at the selections. Let me know if you have any questions."

Brice's cottony mouth made it hard to speak. His heart beat out of rhythm, and he had a feeling of no longer being in his body. Only the heat from Cassie's hand resting on his thigh kept him anchored.

"Take a deep breath." She brushed his hair from his damp brow.

Brice struggled to follow her instruction.

"Now let it out, slowly."

He tried, but his breath came out in a rush.

Wouldn't his father be proud? His heir to the Alphaship not only barfed at the sight of blood but also fainted, or soon would, inside a fucking flower shop.

Cassie tapped his face. "You can do this."

God, he was thankful she had come along. Her touch, her scent, her very presence soothed him.

"Breathe in." She demonstrated. "Breathe out."

Brice exhaled when she did.

"Good. Do it again."

Such a trooper. He loved that about her. After a few more attempts, the probability of him collapsing on the floor passed.

Leafing through the selections, Brice linked his fingers with Cassie's. What did he know about flowers or what would be appropriate for a grandson to order for his grandmother's memorial? He didn't want to pick out the wrong thing.

"What is this?" He pointed at colorless buds woven together in a floral carpet.

"A white rose funeral spray." Alethea appeared behind them. "It's placed on top of the casket during the service, then laid on the ground at the burial."

"No, no. That won't do." Brice wiped the perspiration from his forehead on his sleeve.

"Can I get either of you something to drink? Coffee? A soda?"

*A bottle of bourbon would be nice.*

Cassie frowned in the most disapproving way.

"No. Thanks." Brice slapped the last book closed. "May I look at these?" He grabbed two more binders from the shelves above the table.

"He needs more time," Cassie said to Alethea. "I'll let you know when he's ready."

Brice thumbed the pages. Why hadn't he thought to buy Granny flowers before she died? Why was he expected to give them to her now that she couldn't enjoy them?

"These won't do." He shoved the books away. Some tumbled to the floor. His elbows on the table, he pressed his forehead into his palms. "What kind of grandson am I? I can't even pick out the right flowers, for chrissakes."

"Margaret thought the world of you," Cassie whispered in his ear. "That's the kind of grandson you are. Forget those books. What kind of flowers would you give her right now if you could?"

Brice remembered the armful of bright-colored blossoms he'd picked from a meadow for her birthday when he was six. Granny said she loved the bouquet more than all of her other presents.

"Wildflowers." He lifted his head.

Cassie motioned for Alethea. "Do you have wildflowers?"

"Yes, I have plenty of those. It's the roses and lilies that are running low."

"I want your largest bouquet of wildflowers," Brice said, his heart lighter than when he walked into the florist shop.

"Are you sure you want those for the funeral service?" Alethea's concerned expression made Brice uncertain about his decision.

Cassie's smile chased away his doubts.

"Granny would've loved them," he told Alethea. "Can you deliver them to the church before the service on Saturday?"

"Of course." Alethea scribbled on her order pad.

As he paid for the arrangement, Alethea handed him a card to sign. He couldn't fathom why Granny needed a card when she wasn't alive to read it. But she couldn't smell the flowers, either. Grabbing a pen, Brice wrote:

Granny, you are in our hearts forever.
Love, Brice and Cassie

He escorted Cassie to her car, cursing each step that would separate them for the remainder of the afternoon. He brushed the loose strands of her hair behind her ear. The innocent touch caused his fingertips to tingle. "I'm glad you came."

"Happy to help. Have a nice lunch at Mabel's with Mr. Krussen and Mr. Bartolomew." Cassie turned her face from him. She was blocking the mate-bond, again.

He wasn't worried. He knew she heard his thoughts at the market. Although she didn't respond telepathically, she had looked around the store as soon as his thoughts transferred and hid behind a magazine after his compliment. For now, he needed to be patient. Allow her to accept what was happening at her own pace, and give himself time to adjust to it, as well. This was a new experience for them, and there was no need to rush.

# Chapter 26

"Brice Walker!" Mabel Whitcomb's loud Southern twang silenced the commotion inside her diner. Seventyish, robust, dolled up in an unnatural red-colored beehive hairdo and sky-blue eye shadow, Mabel took her time rounding the counter. Arms open, she flapped her fingers in a come-here-and-give-me-a-hug signal. So he did, squeezing her until she squealed like a schoolgirl.

"Lordy, it's been a dinosaur's age since I last saw you. So sorry about your granny. Sweet lady. God bless her soul."

"Thank you, Mabel." Brice marveled that she looked the same as when he and Rafe used to sit at the counter scarfing cheeseburgers and slurping strawberry milkshakes after school.

"Gracious." She fanned herself with a menu. "Why, if I was forty years younger."

Her gaze trolled past Brice's shoulder and snagged on the elderly gentlemen behind him.

"My, my." She pushed Brice aside. "Who are your handsome friends?"

"Seriously?" Brice lifted his hands, palms up. "I just got here and you're dumping me?"

Mabel pinched his cheek. "You're too young, sug. But your friends…aren't you gonna introduce us?"

"Mabel Whitcomb, this is Philip Bartolomew and Michael Krussen."

Both councilmen gushed extolments of her beauty and the praises they'd heard about her fine establishment.

Worn carpet, '80s-style decor and a menu fit for a greasy spoon, no one in their right mind would mistake Mabel's Diner for a five-star restaurant. Still, Mabel beamed, and Brice appreciated the older men's graciousness.

"What can I get you gents to eat?" she asked, seating them in a booth.

"The adorable young lady who checked us into the resort said you had the best open-faced roast beef sandwich platters in the area." Philip flashed a pearly smile at Mabel, but his gaze drifted to Brice.

"Well, she didn't lie, hon. Some say it's the best in the state." Mabel touched her hair, grinning broader than a debutante at her coming-out party. "But I'm not one to brag."

"Ah, my dear, it isn't bragging if it's true." Philip leaned back in his seat. "One platter for me and a glass of iced tea, please."

"I'll have the same." Michael winked.

"What about you, sug?" Mabel asked Brice.

"A glass of water," he answered, not trusting his stomach.

"Let the gals know if you change your mind." Mabel moseyed to the kitchen.

"We saw you across the street with Miss Albright when we arrived." The calculated interest in Philip's eyes undermined his conversational tone.

"How long have you known her?" Michael asked.

"We met Saturday night." No need to confess that an innocent encounter five years ago had sparked a mate-bond. "Is your interest idle curiosity or something else?"

"The question is, Brice, what is your interest?" Michael's expression gave no hint as to what he expected to hear.

A waitress dispensed their drinks and scurried to the next table.

"I promised my grandmother that I would take care of Cassie." Brice dropped his wadded straw paper next to the silverware wrapper Philip had placed at the edge of the table. "Not that it should concern the council."

"Your affinity for Miss Albright does concern us. A great deal." Philip folded his paper napkin over his lap. "The Woelfesenat appointed you to an apprenticeship."

"I haven't accepted yet." A week ago, the opportunity had

been a sweet song of redemption. Today it sounded more like a screeching bagpipe.

"The offer is unprecedented, Brice." Michael squeezed a lemon into his tea glass. "A unanimous vote. You've impressed everyone on the council."

"The assignments they asked me to handle were sticky, but not complicated. Any experienced negotiator would've had the same outcomes."

"It is your method that intrigues the council." Philip rested his arms comfortably on the table. "Particularly with the Maldean incident. In the past, we eliminated anyone unfortunate enough to discover what we are and threaten exposure. You resolved the situation without violence."

"How, exactly, did you convince that reporter not to release the footage of Congressman Maldean's nephew turning Wahyarian?" Michael asked.

"Negotiation with a side of intimidation." Working for a legal powerhouse provided immeasurable leverage. "He thought a *werewolf* tape would get him noticed by the networks, so I hit him hard with the unbelievable factor and convinced him that a public release of the questionable video would damage his credibility and ruin his chances of ever landing a job with any reputable news agency. Eventually he understood the ramifications and surrendered all the evidence. In turn, I arranged a job interview at WNN."

"Did he get the position?" Michael asked.

"When a partner in Adam Foster's law firm asks for a favor, not even a news conglomerate will say no." Although Brice never abused his uncle's influence, he was grateful for its far-reaching scope. Only time would tell if they would continue their work relationship.

The waitress plunked two lunch platters on the table. "If you need anything else, just holler," she said before rushing back to the kitchen.

Eyes closed, Michael inhaled the scent of his food and

sighed. "Our secret is safe and the human lives. You're very resourceful, Brice."

"Which is why the council wants you." Philip cut into his open-faced roast beef sandwich, lifted the bite to his nose for a sniff and popped it into his mouth. A satisfied smile curved his lips as he swallowed. "Times have changed. The council wants to change, too."

"Will those changes allow council members to claim mates and have families?" Brice downed his water in two gulps.

"Never." Michael put down his silverware and fisted his hands on the table. "The Rule of Unattachment ensures the Woelfesenat remains impartial and uncompromised."

"I know it seems harsh, but the council can't risk divided loyalties." Philip's white brows knitted together. "Have you changed your mind about bachelorhood?"

"I've always wanted a family. After I lost my scenting abilities, I didn't believe I would find a mate."

"And now you have?" Philip's black eyes softened.

Brice nodded.

"Don't be foolish," Michael snapped. "The Woelfesenat has gift-wrapped a council seat for you. Some wolfans would kill for this honor."

Brice leveled his gaze. "I'm not killing anyone."

"No one expects you to." Philip frowned at Michael. "There is, however, another matter that needs our attention."

"Our attention?" Brice stretched his right leg, careful not to extend it too far into the aisle.

"A pack of insurgents are terrorizing a remote area of Romania. The council wants them handled before the situation gains unwanted global attention." Michael wiped his chin and squinted at Brice. "You will assist Philip with the negotiations."

"My grandmother's memorial is Saturday. Find someone else." Brice tipped his glass to his lips and caught an ice cube between his teeth.

"There is no one else. Keep a bag packed. You may need

to leave at a moment's notice. And if you refuse—" Michael's gray eyes turned arctic "—know that although the council wants to change its ways, some things inevitably remain the same."

Brice's gut fisted. The force of the reaction ricocheted up his esophagus, and he choked on the tiny ice chips he had just swallowed.

"That wasn't necessary." Philip glared at Michael. "If the situation deteriorates, I'll travel ahead. Brice can join me later."

Brice stopped coughing, and a deathly chill invaded his blood. "I'll do whatever I can to help Philip after the memorial, but threaten me again, Michael, and Romania will be the least of your worries."

"Jeez!" Cassie slapped her chest. "How long have you been standing there?"

"A couple of minutes." Mouth stretched in a lopsided grin, Brice reminded her of a mischievous imp. A mischievous, six-foot-four imp whose stormy eyes and tousled hair would've made her heart race even if she wasn't tachycardic from dancing and the fright of getting caught.

Clutching the broom, her makeshift dance partner, Cassie hurried across the living room to turn off the small radio on the entertainment center.

"Practicing the moves I taught you last night?" The seductive amusement in Brice's voice caused her thready pulse to gallop.

"No." Cassie fanned her face. "Exercising."

In two strides, Brice stood beside her, reached around her shoulder and readjusted the radio dial. A soft ballad replaced the country rock tempo she'd turned off.

"You need to cool down your body or your muscles will cramp."

Before she could protest, Brice tossed aside the broom

and spun Cassie into his arms. She felt much too comfortable with the proximity, yet she had no willpower to break away.

The hypnotic melody charmed her body to follow his lead in a slow, erotic sway.

Wispy romantic thoughts cluttered her mind. Useless thoughts that had no place in her head. But there they were, drifting along, serene and nonimposing. Like the iceberg that sank the Titanic.

All afternoon, Cassie had lectured herself against the dangers of getting too cozy with Brice. He was the piper. She was the hypnotized mouse. Following him down this path would ruin everything she worked so hard to achieve.

If she had listened to her own good advice, they wouldn't be slow-dancing right now, and she wouldn't be thumbing her nose at the future. Nothing good would come from moving beyond the friendship stage. Despite Brice's ridiculous revelation that she was his mate, Cassie knew better than to believe in fairy tales.

He hooked his thumb beneath her chin. Hypnotically, Cassie rose on her toes as he leaned down. The instant their mouths touched, she forgot why kissing him was a bad idea. The possessive way he held her, wrapped in a protective bubble of suspended time and space, made her want to believe in the strange connection he claimed existed.

In a few short days, she'd not only grown accustomed to his company but also craved his nearness, and his touch. Her defenses refused even a pretense of raising a shield to protect her from the fallout.

Vaguely aware of Brice walking her backward as they kissed, Cassie offered no protest when he nudged down on the couch. His hands roamed her body, his mouth skimmed her throat and his teeth scraped against her tender earlobe.

A waterfall of sensations cascaded through her senses. Dizzying. Daring. Devastating.

She scrunched her fingers in his hair. Pulled him closer. Claimed his lips in an urgent, sweeping kiss.

Brice cupped her bottom, pressing her pelvis against his erection. She scraped her fingernails down the back of his shirt, scaling lower and lower until her fingers slipped beneath the waistband of his jeans.

The barest movement of their compressed bodies pulsed a sexual fever through her veins. On fire, she squirmed. His hand slid beneath her shirt, glided up her abdomen and cupped her small breasts. He flicked her nipples, and fiery ribbons of desire streaked her core causing her to wiggle her hips.

Brice groaned, deep, primal, possessive, making her sex wetter. He tugged and angled her beneath him. Although they were fully clothed, the exquisite friction of his palm grinding against her mound caused her sex to clench with need and expectation.

How in high heaven did she keep getting herself in this situation? The madness had to stop before she lost herself completely.

His fingers slipped inside her panties and his mouth swallowed her protest. She bucked at the sensation of his fingers sliding along her folds in a maddeningly steady rhythm until her entire body was primed.

Brice's lips brushed her ear. "Come for me, Cas."

She didn't need his permission, but the sexy desperation in his gravelly voice broke the last string in her restraint. She exploded as a deluge of mind-numbing sensations pounded her being. She tasted Brice's kisses on her tongue, smelled his scent in the air, heard the erratic race of his heart slow to a leisurely canter and sensed his presence all around her, buoying her through the rapids.

An eternity of bliss marked the minutes it took for her senses to return to reality.

Her brain was ready and waiting.

*What have I done?*

She shoved away from Brice. "No, no, no, no!" Panic shrilled her voice. "I shouldn't have let this happen. I don't know what came over me." Her statement wasn't entirely true.

What came over her was an incomprehensible lack of judgment induced by an undeniable and totally irresponsible affection for Brice.

"Easy, Cas." Brice caught her arm. "We did nothing wrong."

Wrong, no.

Catastrophic? Yes.

"We cannot do this again."

Brice was the type of man with whom she could fall helplessly in love. Any intimacy with him opened up vulnerabilities she was too weak to defend. She wasn't prepared to contend with his rejection, wasn't strong enough to survive when it inevitably occurred.

"Never. Ever. Understand?" She disentangled from his hold to the sounds of muttered curses. Running might trigger his animal instinct for chase, so she walked away. Each purposeful step anchored her to her course—the kitchen. A much better choice than the bedroom in case Brice attempted to seduce her again. The kitchen had a lot more artillery, including iron skillets.

Cassie peeked through the oven glass. The tarts were perfectly golden. She pulled them out and placed them on the cooling rack, then began wiping down the counters, pretending what happened between them was no big deal. Too bad it was truly momentous.

Brice was the first man she'd kissed, the first man to touch her intimately and the first man to bring her an orgasm not achieved by her own hand. *Damn him!*

A few years into the future, she would be willing and ready to venture down the path of mutual sexual gratification. Now was too soon. She still had too much to lose.

A few strands of hair fell around her face. She unfastened the silver barrette. The moment the clasp sprang open, Brice's fingers dived through the freed curls.

"Stop." Cassie stepped back and pointed at the counter. "Don't eat those strudels. If you'll excuse me, I have things to do." Gathering her dignity, she marched through the claus-trophobic kitchen.

"That's it?" Feet planted, arms barricaded across his chest, Brice blocked her exit.

"What else is there to say?" The flush creeping over her skin undermined her forced nonchalance.

"I have a hell of a lot to say." Brice's agitated voice bounced around the small kitchen. He rubbed the worry lines in his brow. "I'm trying to be patient, but this seesaw of you wanting me and then shutting me down is driving me bat shit crazy."

"I made a mistake." Cassie's own frustration sharpened her tone. "I'm not interested in becoming anything more than friends."

Brice shoveled his fists through his hair, knotting the strands in his fingers. "Goddammit! Weren't you listening to me last night? You're my mate. My *true mate*." The confu-sion and frustration in Brice's eyes drove guilt into Cassie's soul. "What are you afraid of?"

"You," Cassie answered forcefully, because it was true. En-tertaining Brice's affection would set up her heart for a long, hard fall. "You're going to wreck my life."

"I won't, I promise." Brice's reassurance flooded her heart and soul. All the while, her mind entertained images of him whistling a tune while she fell off the cliff at Walker's Pointe.

"I'm not your alcoholic mother. I'm not going to hustle you from place to place. I'm not going to promise you things I can't deliver. And, I'm never going to abandon you." He blocked her against the counter. "You can depend on me."

"I don't want to depend on you. I don't want to depend on anyone." Cassie ducked beneath his arm to escape before his male wolfiness overpowered her good sense. Again. "I think it's best that I sleep on the couch tonight."

"Hell no!" He towered over her, shoulders broadened, chest puffed, hands cinched at his waist, fingers thumping his hip pockets. "Even if I need to tie your hands to the headboard tonight and every night hereafter, you will sleep next to me where you belong."

"I don't belong. Not with you. Stop pretending that I do." Cassie bulldozed past him before he changed her mind.

"Fuck it!"

The slamming kitchen door tolled through her being like an ominous church bell.

Cassie collapsed onto the couch. Clutching the throw pillow to her chest didn't smother the ache in her heart. She'd made the right choice, for both of them. Despite his insistence to the contrary, Cassie didn't belong with him among the rich and wolfy. No matter how much she might wish that she did.

# Chapter 27

Brice lifted a tumbler to his lips and gulped plain, cold water instead of whiskey so the smell of liquor wouldn't stain his breath when he returned home to assure Cassie that his feelings weren't a fluke. No woman had gotten under his skin the way she did. No woman had plagued his thoughts or turned him inside out the way she could.

Walking out of the resort lounge, Brice watched his parents greeting the pockets of people gathered in the lobby. So far, everyone seemed genuine in their sympathies and alliances. Yet somewhere in the midst of smiles and social politeness lurked a menace. The sentinels, after relentless security drills, were on full alert.

Brice's instinct urged him to interrogate the entire room, though he conceded Tristan's effervescent charm would yield better results. Especially since Brice's mood wasn't conducive to niceties tonight.

He breathed in a lungful of cinnamon and remembered the first tease of the scent in Cassie's hair. The radiant happiness for him on her face.

*Mine!* his wolf insisted.

Brice only had to convince Cassie of the same. From the start, he knew she'd be a challenge. Her resistance stemmed from her inability to trust him. He needed to find a way to prove her heart, her life, her future were safe with him.

"Nice to see you socializing." Doc joined Brice.

"Did I have a choice?"

"You always have choices, even if you don't like them." Doc took a handkerchief from his pocket to clean his glasses.

"Where's Rafe?" Brice had hoped to commiserate with his friend.

"Running the woods." The sparkle Brice remembered in

Doc's eyes seemed diminished. "Ever since he lost Lexi, he refuses to participate in pack events. Don't take his absence personally. You know that if you ever need him, he'll be there for you."

"I wished I had been around for him," Brice answered quietly.

Doc gave Brice a quick pat on the back. "All that matters is that you're here now."

But for how long?

At any moment, the Woelfesenat could demand his presence in Romania. He needed to work fast to cement his relationship with Cassie and patch the one with his father. Granny would expect no less.

"Try to relax tonight. Doctor's orders." Doc waved at Philip and Michael headed toward the lounge, and he left to join them.

A possessive arm latched around his waist. "Hello again, lover."

Brice's stomach dropped in a dead armadillo roll.

Wearing a white silk gown slit up the sides to reveal mile-long legs in strappy heels, Victoria stood nearly nose to nose to him. Her flawless skin shimmered beneath the soft lighting.

Brice pried her fingers from his side. "A bit overdressed for a casual cocktail party."

"I wanted to look divine for my mate." Her cold lips chilled his mouth.

Brice turned his face. "Don't kiss me again or I will put you in your place."

"My place is in your bed." Unflappable assurance oozed from her practiced smile. An exquisite beauty most men, wolfan and human, would covet.

Before her betrayal, he'd considered her a friend. Now he found nothing remotely appealing about Victoria Phalen.

"I've said this twice before. This time, you need to listen." Brice lowered his voice to a threatening growl. "You will never be welcome in my bed."

"I know you're angry I tried to trick you into a mate-claim."

*Tricked?* She'd fucking drugged him, and if he had claimed her, he would've been miserably and irrevocably bound to Victoria.

He would've missed out on Cassie.

Primal wolfan hormones flooded Brice's body.

A mate-claim with Victoria would've shortened one of their lives. Only death severed a mate-claim and he'd allow nothing to keep him from Cassie for long.

"Your father commanded you to take a mate by Christmas and expects a wolfling on the way soon after, so let's forget the past and jump straight to the good stuff." Victoria's smile turned manically Cheshire.

Brice closed his hand over hers and squeezed until she grimaced. "I'll decide when it's time to claim my mate, and she isn't you. So sink your paws into some other wolf and leave me the hell alone."

Instead of heeding his words when he released her hand, Victoria hooked his arm. "Let's join your parents."

Brice's temper strained against his propriety. Victoria practically floated as they navigated the lobby. Her aristocratic nod to the guests they passed tested Brice's ability to refrain from rolling his eyes. By the time Brice and Victoria reached their destination, his mother had splintered off, encompassed by several visiting Alphenas and a rather annoyed Booker Reynolds. Brice's father, Adam, Dennis Stratton, Alpha of the Eau Gallie pack from Florida, and his son, Eason, were ensconced in the pros and cons of Alpha succession versus trial by combat.

Despite the nails clamped in his bicep, Brice lifted Victoria's hand and passed her to Adam. "Please keep your packmate on a shorter leash. I'm tired of her yapping at my heels."

Before Brice spun away, he caught the desperate look of a drowning man in the eyes of Stratton's son.

"Eason," Brice said. "Join me in the lounge? I've heard

you're researching the Bimini Road. Discovered any mermaids?"

Relief eased Eason's pinched features, and he laughed. "Not yet, but I keep hoping." He bowed his head, first to Gavin and then to his father, before accompanying Brice.

Even though Brice couldn't see Victoria's seething glare, the volcanic heat of it seared his back as he walked away. No doubt he would later find the truck's tires slashed and the sides of the cab keyed.

*Oh, well.* He grinned. It wasn't really his truck anyway.

Cassie opened the gate to the deserted high school track field. The tiny can of pepper spray tied to her wrist clanked against the ground as she grabbed her ankles to stretch her back and calves.

Her empty stomach gurgled. The fight with Brice had stolen her appetite. The harder he tried to smooth things over, the more adamant—and hysterical—she became.

She couldn't give in to the errant feelings he awakened. Doubting that she could handle heartbreak any better than her mother, Cassie refused to start down any romantic path until she was utterly and completely self-sufficient.

Cassie never knew her father, but Imogene had loved him 'til the day she died, even though he'd left her devastated. The Struthers curse, she called it when drunk. Apparently Cassie was descended from a long line of women who fell hopelessly in love with the wrong men and never recovered.

Well, she wouldn't fall victim to poor choices. Brice and his misguided notion about her being his mate was utter nonsense. She hadn't believed him for one second. The yearning in her heart meant nothing except that this had been an emotional few days. Next week, everything would get back to normal.

Returning to an upright position, Cassie pulled her foot behind her until it rested against her thigh. Counted to thirty. Switched legs.

A few more stretches, then Cassie started a light jog around the track. On the second lap, she found her groove. Tiny dots of sweat beaded on her skin and moisture seeped into her eyes. She dabbed at the sting.

By the time she finished her seventh lap, the sun had set and the field lights illuminated the track. The steady plod of her feet against the pavement hammered out all conscious thought; and Cassie was simply in her zone. The place where she had no constraints. The place where she could breathe without responsibility, without worry, without fear. The place where she was free.

Something blurred in her peripheral vision as she rounded the turn. Suddenly a large wolf with fur the color of freshly baled hay darted in front of her. Cassie skidded to a stop.

Her heart thudded from exertion, fear and more than a little irritation. Her palm tightened around the cold aluminum canister.

Cassie recognized the highfalutin disdain in the animal's glittery eyes as it jumped at her. Knowing better than to run, she stamped her foot. "Get out of here, you flea-bitten fur ball."

The wolf's face contorted. A second later, Victoria Phalen rose from where the wolf had squatted. Her angelic features twisted in a wicked sneer. "How dare you? I have impeccable breeding." Contempt weighted every word. "Unlike you."

Years of enduring whispers, snubs and downright rudeness had hardened Cassie against jabs from her so-called betters.

"You shouldn't parade around naked, Miss Phalen. In the civilized world, we have laws against public indecency, so why don't you scamper into the woods where you belong."

Elegant and proud, Victoria strode toward Cassie. "Where I belong, Little Miss Ragamuffin, is with Brice."

"Well, he isn't here." Cassie rocked on her toes to stretch her calves. "If you'll excuse me, I need to finish my run."

"Trampling an asphalt loop isn't running." Victoria snickered.

"At least I don't have to worry about ticks." Cassie got some satisfaction in Victoria's waning smugness when the lady-wolf saw the black dot stuck to her stomach.

Victoria plucked the nuisance from her skin and flicked it at Cassie. Instead of landing on the intended target, the tick fell harmlessly to the ground. Cassie squashed it beneath her sneaker.

"Have a nice evening," she said, not feeling the sentiment.

"Not so fast." Victoria blocked Cassie's path. "I'm only going to say this once. Brice is mine."

Hearing someone else claim him didn't bother Cassie.

She bit her lip. Okay, it did bother her, which prompted Cassie's mouth to disengage from her brain and operate independently of her common sense. "Brice said you meant nothing to him. And ever since I bit him, he has insisted that I'm his mate."

"You little *bitch*." Victoria's fingers clamped around Cassie's throat, lifting her so that she stood on her tiptoes.

Gasping, Cassie aimed the pepper spray can at Victoria's face. A faint, empty hiss escaped the nozzle.

Victoria laughed, then choked on a scream when the hiss became a potent spray. She dropped Cassie to claw her own face.

"I don't care who you are or what you are, Miss Phalen. Stay the hell away from me or you'll get more of the same." Cassie stomped to her car.

Plopped behind the steering wheel.

Slammed the door.

"Freaking werewolves!"

# Chapter 28

The cabin was dark, except for the light beneath the bathroom door. Brice knocked. "Cas, I'm home."

He heard her bumping around before she answered. "I'll be out in a minute."

The odd feeling that had preyed on him for the last hour intensified. "Everything okay?"

"Yeah." She opened the door. "I'm sleeping on the couch, and I swear if you don't leave me alone, I'll sleep in my car."

Brice's night vision sharpened. The way she clutched the collar of her worn terry cloth robe bothered him. He blocked her exit. "What's wrong? You okay?"

She stared straight through him. "Leave me alone."

"I'm not inclined to do that." Brice's tugged Cassie's housecoat.

"Stop!" An uncharacteristic tremble softened her demand.

The tug-of-war didn't last another second. He yanked opened the collar of her robe. "What the fuck?"

He slammed the bathroom door shut to prevent her from leaving.

"You can't do this. It's kidnapping," she hissed.

"Sue me." He pointed at the commode. "Sit down."

She flipped the lid down and shot him a look that said she'd like to flip him off. Her knuckles turned white from clenching the robe beneath her chin.

Worry twisted everything inside him. "I won't touch you if that's what you want, but I need to see your neck." Brice knelt in front of her. "Please, Sunshine."

Finally she dropped her hands.

Brice slowly parted Cassie's robe. The bruises around the slender column of her throat appalled him. Brice's hands shook as he inspected her for a bite mark. Finding none didn't temper his anger. "Who did this to you?"

"It doesn't matter. I took care of it." Cassie closed the robe.

"Why would you hide this from me?"

"I didn't want you to overreact."

Overreact? She had a goddamn handprint on her throat. If there was ever a time to overreact, it was now.

"I defended myself," Cassie continued, "and came out the better of the two of us. I don't think she'll bother me again."

"She?" Brice screeched. Immediately he thought of Victoria.

Cassie worked her mouth over her bottom lip, her eyes anxious and uncertain.

Brice reined in his temper so she wouldn't think he was angry with her. "Are you all right? Should I call Doc? No, I'm taking you to the ER."

"I'm fine," she insisted. "My throat isn't swollen. I can breathe and swallow without pain. I'd rather avoid a medical bill for a stupid, ugly bruise." She dropped her gaze, and a little color reddened her cheeks.

Cradling her against his chest, Brice pressed his lips to the crown of her head and stroked her hair.

"This isn't necessary," she muttered into his shirt.

"It is for me." He could've lost her so easily, and the last words they exchanged had been angry and terse.

Cassie thumped his back. "You can let go now."

Brice touched his nose gently to her neck to verify the lingering scent on her skin. Another burst of anger surged through him. He banked it for Cassie's sake.

"I know you don't want to talk about this." He pulled back to see her face. "But I can't ignore that someone assaulted you in our home."

A guilty look flashed across her porcelain features. "I was at the high school track."

"What?" Brice clamped his mouth closed. "I didn't mean to yell at you." He'd warned her that morning about going out alone, but this wasn't the time to tackle that subject. "What happened tonight isn't your fault."

"I know it isn't." She frowned. "You pointing it out makes me believe that you think it is."

God, she stretched his patience. He had to stay focused and not take the bait of her deflection. She put up a brave front, but he knew she was afraid. "Baby, trust me enough to tell me how this happened."

"I am not your baby." She fidgeted with her hands in her lap. "I run the track twice a week and never had a problem until tonight."

Brice's heart squeezed. Cassie had lost another important thing in her life. From now on, she would always associate the track with the attack. "Go on."

"A wolf cut me off." Cassie tucked her hands beneath her legs with her feet turned inward. "It was Victoria. She said that you were hers. I told you I don't want to be anyone's competition, Brice."

"You aren't, because I only have a nose for you," Brice sang the last few words.

"Don't patronize me," Cassie snapped.

"I'm not." Frustrated, Brice rubbed his jaw. "I choose you as my mate. Not Victoria." Brice tucked a curl behind her ear. "I'll make sure she doesn't bother you again."

"No need." Weariness shimmered in Cassie's eyes. "I handled the problem."

"It isn't that simple. Wahyas have laws to protect humans."

"This wasn't an interspecies incident, okay? She was just being bitchy, and I ended her tirade with pepper spray. Situation resolved."

"You pepper sprayed her?" Brice felt his smile to his ears. His delicate little human mate-to-be stood up to a jealous she-wolf twice her size and bulk and came out the winner. Damn, he was proud.

"In the face." A bashful glow brightened Cassie's skin.

"That's my girl." Brice pressed her knuckles to his lips,

then helped her stand. "Come on, let's go to bed." He snagged her comforter off the couch on the way to the bedroom.

"You know this isn't appropriate." She stalled at the foot of the bed. "I can understand why you wanted me to sleep next to you the first night. You were exhausted, in pain, and didn't want me to tell anyone you were home. And then Margaret died." She paused. "Last night you were drunk and I was tired. Well, that sounds bad. You know what I mean."

"I wasn't drunk." He unbuttoned his shirt. "I sleep better when you're beside me." He winked. "Admit it. You like sleeping next to me, too."

"I admit nothing." Cassie climbed into bed. "Except that I don't want to argue all night. Since you're too stubborn to give in, I have to. You might be able to sleep all day if you wanted, but I have places to go and things to do."

Brice kicked off his shoes and traded his pants for the cutoff sweats he donned for her modesty. He slid beneath the covers and curled against her.

She huffed. "You're supposed to stay on your side of the bed."

"Remember, Sunshine, both sides are mine."

Within minutes, Cassie fell fast asleep. Once he knew she wouldn't wake, he slipped out of bed, redressed and headed to the resort.

He'd expected Victoria to retaliate by attacking his personal possessions. Instead, she'd struck straight at his heart.

Renewed anger welled inside him. He stalked to the elevator. The mechanical drone of the hydraulics intensified the molasses crawl up the shaft. Jackhammering the button didn't prod the lift to ascend any faster.

Brice slumped against the brushed gold paneling. What the hell was wrong with him? Five years ago, his carelessness had killed Mason. Tonight, his carelessness in handling Victoria could've seriously injured Cassie.

A polite ding announced arrival at the fourth floor. Brice

peeled the doors apart the second the elevator stopped. Walking down the corridor, he counted silently to bank his temper.

Heads bent together in muffled conversation, his mother and Doc stood in the alcove outside Victoria's suite.

"Is Victoria all right?" he asked Doc through clenched teeth.

"No permanent damage. She'll be fine."

"Victoria said Cassie attacked her in the parking lot without provocation," Brice's mother said. "The accusation is ridiculous, but your father and I will need to speak to Cassie."

"No." Brice anchored his arms over his chest. "Victoria stalked Cassie at the high school track in her wolf form. When Cassie didn't cower, Victoria shifted and wrapped her fingers around Cassie's throat. Cassie used pepper spray in self-defense."

"Is Cassie all right?" His mother fingered her mouth.

"Yes, except for the handprint on her throat."

"Where is she?" Doc folded his coat over the arm carrying his medical bag. "I want to check on her."

"She's asleep in the cabin and I don't want her disturbed. She didn't have any swelling or problems swallowing or breathing. I'll get her to the ER if anything changes."

"Make sure you do," Doc said.

"Your father is coming back from a patrol with Cooter and Tristan. He'll want to talk to you when he arrives."

"He knows where to find me." Brice glanced at the electronic lock on the door. "Mind letting me in?"

His mother held his gaze, assessing his threat level. Despite his anger, Brice had no intention of harming Victoria. However, he would make sure she left the territory tonight, even if he had to hog-tie her and toss her in the back of the truck.

Apparently satisfied Brice wouldn't physically retaliate, his mother swiped her master card through the electronic lock. A warning flashed in her green eyes before she left with Doc.

Brice punched open the door, driving the handle through the drywall. "Victoria!"

Propped in the middle of a fluffy four-poster bed, the pitiful looking she-wolf appeared almost comical. Golden hair matted around her splotchy red face, Victoria aimed her swollen eyes and pointed her puffy nose in his direction.

"See what your tramp did to me," she howled. "I want her punished."

Brice's nails dug into his palms, and he locked his fists behind his back.

"Consider yourself lucky, Victoria." Brice hated that she reclined in a luxurious bed, surrounded by overstuffed pillows. Cassie deserved that kind of royal treatment, not Victoria.

"Lucky?" Hands balled in her fluffy bedding, Victoria glared. "That rabid redheaded tramp tried to kill me!"

"You should have come after me, Victoria," Brice said. "Not Cassie."

"I didn't lay one finger on the runt." Victoria's haughtiness matched the smugness on her face.

"How about five?" Brice countered.

Victoria threw him a halfhearted shrug.

"What the hell were you thinking?" Brice leaned against the bedpost. "You attacked a human. One under my direct protection."

"The gutter rat had no right to claim what is mine," Victoria hissed.

"Cassie told you that she bit me?" Through his anger, Brice's heart thumped a happy, ridiculous beat. Whether she realized it or not, Cassie believed in their bond. And defended it.

"Her bite gives me justifiable cause. It's my right to fight for what's mine."

"I'm not yours."

"You will be." Victoria's haughty eyes glittered. "Your father wants your mateship to be with someone acceptable. Something your human will never be."

"*My* mateship isn't about what my father wants. It's about what I want."

"What you want is irrelevant. Your father wants a suitable heir to continue the Walker lineage, and Adam wants someone by your side who won't embarrass the firm. Gutter rats need not apply, if you get my drift." Victoria's malicious laugh soured his stomach, and he wondered how the hell he'd become involved with her.

"Get out." Brice yanked Victoria from the bed. "Out of Walker's Run and out of my life."

"No." She twisted free. "If you would get your head out of that redheaded tramp's lap, you would realize we are a perfect match. We're both on the fast track at Adam's firm. We have the same tastes, the same friends, the same interests. And I have an excellent pedigree."

"All we have in common are the projects we've worked on together. Your tastes are not mine, your friends are pretentious, your interests are tedious and I don't give a fuck about your pedigree." Brice tossed a suitcase on the bed. "Start packing."

When she didn't budge, he gathered some of her belongings and threw them into her luggage.

"How dare you choose that scrawny bitch over me?" Victoria gnarled her fingers in Brice's shirtsleeve. "Come the next full moon, you'll regret this, Brice Walker."

Brice seriously doubted he would.

# Chapter 29

"Come back to bed."

Contemplating Brice's sleepy grumble, Cassie grinned.

Barefoot and wearing the cutoff sweats he slept in, he rubbed his fingers through his bed-head hair. His eyes drooped in a grumpy, it's-too-early-to-be-awake scowl. Elbows pointed outward, fingers laced over his mouth, he stretched his back in a full-body yawn.

Tall. Sleek. Magnificent.

The scars slashing his golden skin only added to his powerful beauty and larger-than-life presence. Cassie would have been a liar if she claimed that she didn't like cozying into the heat of his body. Truth be told, she enjoyed the comfort of his warmth far too much. Especially early in the mornings when his temptations were strongest and her resistance at its weakest.

It would be so easy to succumb to his assertions to provide, protect and pleasure. If she were in a more secure position, financially and emotionally, she might give in.

*Might?* Who was she kidding? She'd be the one dragging him back to bed.

Forcing her gaze off his sexy reflection in the bathroom mirror, she finished pinning her hair. "I won't skip class. After the first absence, it's too easy to miss the second, then third."

Dressed in her drab resort uniform and an old, faded scarf around her neck to hide the ugly bruises, Cassie could've been a billboard ad for hideous fashion don'ts.

Being poor sucked. Someday she'd be able to afford the stylish accessories she saw in the magazines at the campus library. She'd even splurge for a decent haircut instead of trimming the ends herself. Until then, spending one unnecessary penny was as much a fatal distraction to her future as entertaining romantic notions about Brice.

His hands cupped her waist and her pragmatic resolve wimped out. She loved how he never let an opportunity to touch her pass. Maybe it was rapid conditioning. In the beginning, he'd pulled her close for her scent and she had offered no resistance. Lately he didn't stop at smelling her skin. He boldly proceeded to lick and kiss the trail he nuzzled. Since she failed to protest the progression, her body whirred with expectancy.

The sandpapery rub of his morning stubble against her ear caused her nipples to pucker against the satiny bra cups covering her small breasts. They ached to be fondled and teased by his long, magically talented fingers. Other places ached, too.

Close proximity to him was not in her best interest. Every reasonable thought in her head dissipated whenever Brice stood too close. Or touched her. Or looked at her with the molten gaze that melted her in place, making it impossible to escape.

"Have I told you how much I appreciate everything you did for Granny?" Hot puffs of air wisped against her neck. "And for me now that she's gone?"

Just what she needed. A good dose of reality to remind her the bubble she lived in this week would pop within a few days of Margaret's memorial.

Grief swelled in Cassie's chest over the loss of a woman as dear as a grandmother, and the stark loneliness that would return upon Brice's departure. Like Margaret, Brice had bore a tiny chink in the armor guarding her heart. If he broke completely through the barrier, he'd break her, too.

Cassie peeled away from him. "Margaret was a special woman. I'm privileged to have known her."

"There's nothing wrong with admitting that you loved her, Cas."

A burning lump rose high in Cassie's throat. Love was an extravagance she couldn't afford. "I have to go. I'm dropping off a strudel at the lodge for your mother's brunch with Margaret's bunco group, and I don't want to be late for class."

Brice followed her into the kitchen. "I'll take it. I'm expected to make an appearance there, anyway."

"Thanks, but I'll do it so you won't be tempted to eat it before the brunch starts." Cassie slung the oversized purse she used as a book bag over her shoulder and tucked two pastry carriers beneath her arm. "Oh, I'm stopping by the R&L after class and then going to work."

"What time do you get off?"

"Eight thirty."

Brice frowned. "Can someone cover for you? I want you to join me at the dinner tonight."

"No way." She'd feel awkward eating with wolfdom's elite, especially since she had either checked in or handled room issues for most of them. Besides, she didn't know which fork or spoon to use. Nor did she have an elegant dress to wear.

"Maybe you'll change your mind." Brice flashed a fiendish grin. "I have all afternoon to convince you."

"I'll be busy with work."

"Not if I chase everyone away." Brice's sleepy eyes simmered with mischief. He cradled Cassie's face and gave her the softest, most alluring kiss.

Temptation incarnate, that's what he was. Good thing he ushered her out the door before she yielded.

"Drive safe." He waited on the porch while she backed out of the driveway.

Her dreamy sigh became lost in the screechy voice in her head, reminding her again that she was no Cinderella, and Brice was not her Prince no matter how much he tried to charm her.

In a little over three months, she would graduate from college. Then phase two of her plan would begin. Finding a new job where she would gain the professional experience and clout needed for phase three—operating her own business. Her investment would be small-scale, but she had plans to grow and expand.

Sadness tainted her usual excitement. Somehow the future seemed less golden than she'd once imagined, and it was all Brice's fault. He'd mucked up her realistic expectations with his fantasy wolf tales. She needed to get a handle on her hormones and shore up her common sense before she stumbled down a path she couldn't turn back from.

"What the fuck is going on?"

Too late to prevent Vincent Hadler's knuckles from slamming Shane's jaw, Brice barreled between them. Ever since the despicable wolf had pawed Cassie, Brice's inner wolf would snarl at the sight of him.

"Best to keep your nose out of my business." Cracking his neck, Hadler straightened his shirt and sleeves.

"What happens in Walker's Run is *my* business, particularly when it plays out in the parking lot of my family's resort."

"This is between me and the *boy*." Hadler made a sucking noise through his teeth. "Why don't you scamper inside to hold your daddy's hand while he cries over his dead mama and let me finish teaching this little shit some manners?"

The muscles along Brice's spine tightened all the way to his neck. Without taking his eyes off Hadler, he cocked his face toward Shane. "Is he blood kin?"

"Hell, no." Shane spit on the asphalt. "And no longer pack. I've declared disassociation from the Black Mountain pack to join Walker's Run."

"Doesn't mean you've been released." Hadler's sharp laugh held no humor and a lot of malice.

"Semantics best left to Alphas, not their henchmen." Brice fully faced Hadler. "I doubt Reynolds cares to make this matter a bone of contention. However, I will."

"I don't need your help," Shane snapped. "I can handle him."

Brice didn't take offense. The young wolf wanted to prove

himself against an obvious longtime bully. Unfortunately, he didn't have the experience to win a dogfight with Hadler.

"As an initiate, you're entitled to the same protection any Walker's Run pack member would receive. Your fight is our fight, should it come to that. No wolf stands alone."

Holding back his words, Shane's teeth clicked in restrained frustration. Finally, he nodded on a heavy breath and lowered his eyes.

"Share and share alike, is it?" Hadler's upper lip lifted over his sneering smile. "If that applies to your women— particularly the redheaded one—I might be persuaded to join."

Brice's vision darkened. The rush of adrenaline and testosterone rang in his ears, begging him to pound Hadler into the ground along with his persistent sour scent. "This is your only warning—Stay. The. Fuck. Away. From. Her."

"It's my right to scent and scope possible mates. Little Red smells as sweet as always, which means you haven't claimed her." Hadler's smugness dirtied the air. "She's open season."

"With or without my bite, she's *mine*!"

A dangerous gleam lit Hadler's eyes as he mouthed the words, *Not if I claim her first.*

Brice's fist flew true, connecting with the intended target in a smashing crunch he repeated over and over again.

Shouts rose over the howls in his mind. He tasted blood before he registered the smell. Still, he hammered ruthlessly until half a dozen hands pulled him from the frenzy. Sentinels surrounded Brice as Cooter escorted Hadler from the parking lot.

"Stand aside," Gavin Walker snarled. The sentinels parted for him to approach Brice. "What the fuck is going on?"

"If Hadler lays one finger on Cassie, I'll rip off his goddamn balls and stuff them down his throat."

"Everyone, return to your posts." A ferocious frown weighted Gavin's mouth. From his back pocket, he pulled the worn handkerchief he'd offered yesterday and handed it to Brice. "Are you all right?"

Brice nodded, wiping a trickle of blood from his lip.

"You're the Alpha-in-Waiting of Walker's Run, not some brawler in a biker bar. What the hell were you thinking?"

"I wasn't." Brice tossed the handkerchief back to his father. "He threated Cassie and I responded."

"Considering the circumstances, I understand how you might feel protective of Cassie."

Brice doubted his father understood anything about the depth of what he felt or the lengths he would go to keep her safe.

"So much has happened since you've returned," Gavin continued. "Your emotions are raw. Don't confuse duty with affection."

"I'm not confused." A mate-bond had formed between him and Cassie, and he wouldn't allow anyone to threaten their budding relationship.

"When I set a time frame for you to claim a mate, I simply wanted to see you settled, here, where you belong." Gavin scratched his short white beard. "I don't want to lose you a second time because you unwisely chose an ill-suited mate to spite me."

"Did you consider I may have found my one true mate?"

Gavin's eyes drifted from Brice's face. A slight twitch rippled along his jaw.

Brice humphed. His father's silence told him all he needed to know.

The thick gray haze that overshadowed Cassie's morning drive to the campus lightened beneath the midday sun. Glimpses of the majestic mountain scape flickered in her peripheral vision.

She pressed the accelerator to give the old clunker more gas before the engine stalled. The incline in the two-lane road wasn't steep, but the car always needed a little oomph to coax it over the top.

A vehicle pulled next to her, blasting an impatient horn.

The driver appeared unconcerned about cresting the hill in the wrong lane with no visibility of oncoming traffic.

Cassie tapped her brakes. They felt a little sluggish, but her speed dropped and the silver convertible zipped past.

At the top of the hill, Cassie eased off the gas. The weight of the car and forward momentum carried her down the other side. Mindful of the road signs warning of dangerous curves and falling rocks, Cassie took her time rounding the bends. Each time she pushed the pedal, the brakes felt squishy. She glanced at the strudel secured in its carrier and made a mental note to ask Rafe to check her brakes when he changed the oil.

Ahead, the little sports car hugged the curves without slowing. Cassie imagined that the driver lived life the same carefree way.

It would be nice—no, not nice. Liberating, she decided. It would be liberating to be unconcerned about responsibilities and consequences. Imogene never worried about anything. She flitted from one place to another, barely scraping together enough money to buy MoonPies and sodas from the gas stations along the interstates and highways and back roads that carried them to more than two dozen this-is-our-new-hometowns in half as many years.

Imogene could be footloose because she had Cassie to worry about their circumstances. Cassie, the practical penny-pincher. Afraid to step outside the plan because she didn't want to end up broken and destitute like her mother.

Greeted by another curve, Cassie touched her foot to the brakes. The car didn't respond. She pressed the brakes again and again. Her heart pumped forcefully with each frantic stomp on the pedal. The car wasn't traveling very fast, but the next three miles were all downhill.

She carefully downshifted one gear at a time until she reached first. The needle on the speedometer dropped, jiggled and resumed its climb. The corkscrew curve ahead was too sharp to navigate at increasing speed.

Beneath her breastbone, Cassie's heart hammered a white-hot searing pain through her chest. Every breath seemed to singe her throat and lungs.

Resisting the urge to yank with all her might, she engaged the emergency brake, slow and steady to avoid throwing the vehicle into a spin. She tried to create friction, weaving the car from side to side. Nothing worked.

She edged onto the shoulder of the road. Beneath the tires, gravel flew in all directions. Since there wasn't a guardrail, she dragged the passenger side of the car along the clay embankment. The screech of metal scraping the barrier vibrated through her clenched jaw like the raw, pulsing pain of a tooth in need of a root canal.

The car finally jerked to a stop. Cassie's entire body shimmied except her hands. Her hands were rock-steady, cemented to the steering wheel.

Cassie had no idea how long she sat locked in that position before she had the strength to lumber out of the car, clutching her shoulder bag. Her wobbly legs forced her to lean against the open car door for support.

The clunker's hood had crumpled. Only a twisted, empty socket remained of the right headlight, and the bumper dangled at a vicious angle. Because the passenger side had wedged against the embankment, Cassie couldn't see the rest of the damage.

She didn't need to.

Her stomach, which had climbed high in her chest, dropped suddenly to her feet. The pastry on the front seat wouldn't come close to covering the costs of repairs.

She slammed the car door. A dozen pebbles tumbled down the cracked front windshield, followed by a handful of small rocks that bounced off the damaged hood. A loud pop echoed down the jutted face of the looming mountain. A deafening rumble shuddered the ground.

*Of all the freaking luck!*

Cassie ran to avoid falling debris. She had seen the roadblocks when highway maintenance crews worked to clear the occasional rockslides. Most of the time, the damage reported was minimal.

This was not one of those times. From the crunch of metal and the shatter of glass, she judged the odds of winning the Powerball without a ticket were higher than the clunker's chances for salvage.

Cassie began to shake even as the ground fell silent. As long as she had a vehicle, Cassie had the means to work and go to school. And, when necessary, a place to sleep. Now all her hopes and dreams lay crushed beneath a pile of rubble.

She seemed destined for failure, no matter what. She worked hard, made the right choices, tried to do her very best with what she had.

What had that gotten her?

*Nothing. Absolutely nothing.*

# Chapter 30

Brice sensed Cassie coming. He turned from his father, watching for her. An unsettling feeling streaked his gut as Rafe's tow truck came into view. Her car wasn't on it.

Something wasn't right.

Forgetting his father, Brice jogged to where Rafe pulled to a stop. Brice opened the passenger door. "Hey, Sunshine."

Eyes wide and vacant, she stared straight through him. He pulled her from the cab and set her gently on her feet. "What's wrong?"

"Car accident," Rafe answered when Cassie didn't.

Brice's chest tightened as the blood in his veins stilled.

"Gotta go," Rafe said, tight-lipped. "Told the road crew I'd help dig the car out from under the rocks."

*Car accident? Rocks? What the hell?*

"I'll call later." Rafe reached across the seat, yanked the passenger door closed and drove off before Brice found his voice.

"God, Cas. Are you hurt?" Brice gently rubbed a streak of dirt from her face and ran his hands across her shoulders and down her arms. No blood seeped from any obvious cuts or scrapes, and he saw no signs of broken bones. Relief poured over him in a thick, cold sweat.

"I'm fine," she said with a tight smile. Then her eyes rolled back and her body went limp.

Brice swept her up into his arms. Cradling her to his chest, he did the only thing he knew to do. *"Dad!"*

Within seconds, his father appeared at his side. Followed by a flurry of people, including Doc. Sentinels held open the door and cleared a path through the lobby. Gavin led them down the corridor to the family quarters and directed them into the family room.

Cassie shook so badly that Brice didn't want to put her down, so he sat on the couch with her on his lap. "Shh," he whispered against her head as he rocked. "I've got you."

He tried to feed calm assurance to her through the mate-bond, but his own panic kept getting in the way.

Doc sat on the edge of the coffee table. "I need to examine her."

Brice agreed, despite the threatening growl that rose in his throat. Doc slowly drew back his hand.

Gavin gripped Brice's shoulder. "Easy, son. Doc is here to help."

"Brice?" Cassie's voice sounded so soft and small.

"What, Sunshine?"

"I can't breathe."

"She needs oxygen," he yelled. "Her lungs are collapsing!"

"Loosen your grip." Doc tugged Brice's arm.

"Yes, please." Cassie nodded against his chest.

Brice unbanded his arms from around Cassie's torso, though he kept a light hold on her waist.

"Better?" Doc asked.

"Yes." Cassie sat up. "I'm fine."

"You passed out in the parking lot. That's not *fine*," Brice said, taking his first easy breath at hearing the stubborn sass return to her voice.

"Since I'm here, how about allowing me to authenticate the 'fine' diagnosis?" Humor crinkled Doc's eyes behind his thick glasses. He put the stethoscope tips into his ears and tucked the chest piece against her blouse. Next he poked a thermometer into her mouth, checked her blood pressure and inspected the bruises on her neck.

"You're a little dehydrated, and your blood pressure is slightly elevated, probably from all the excitement." He patted her leg. "Drink a lot of fluids and get plenty of rest."

Doc packed his medical bag. "I'm headed to the clinic." He looked at Brice. "If she experiences any vomiting, fainting, shortness of breath, rapid heart rate or anything out of the ordinary, call me and take her straight to the hospital."

"I will." Brice's stomach churned. Twice in as many days, he could've lost her. Boarding up the cabin with Cassie and him snug inside seemed like an insanely good idea.

As Doc left, Brice's mother stepped forward with a cold bottle of water.

"Thank you, Mrs. Walker." Cassie drank nearly half the bottle before she stopped, recapped it and scooted off Brice's lap.

He balled his hands against his jeans-clad thighs to keep from pulling her back.

"How did this happen, Cassie?" Brice's mother joined his father on the love seat.

"My brakes failed and I skidded against the embankment." Cassie picked at the frayed edges of the scarf in her hands. "A rockslide buried my car."

Brice's mother gasped, his father cursed beneath his breath and Brice tried to blot out Cassie's words so the images of what could've happened wouldn't ravage his mind.

"Why didn't you call me?"

Guilt heated Cassie's already flushed skin. She had called Brice, three times. The sound of his voice would've made her feel better. He would've made everything better. Or at least tried to. That's why she'd hung up each time before the first ring. She needed to get through this setback on her own.

"Rafe is a mechanic who owns a tow truck." She didn't meet Brice's gaze. "You have family and…other obligations. I didn't want to be a bother."

Brice's strong, gentle hands clasped her face. "I'm never too busy for you. I should be your first call. Always."

"The car can't be salvaged." The tightness in Cassie's throat had nothing to do with the bruises on her neck. The burning constriction spread into her chest and threatened to break her in two. She forced her mind off how much she wanted to fling herself into his arms and allow him to take care of everything.

"Forget the damn car, baby. You could've been killed." The lines in his brow deepened and the color drained from his face. Until now, Cassie had never noticed the faint spider-string scar along the bridge of his nose, curving below the apple of his cheek to fade into the stubble along his jaw.

Of course, he'd never looked so pale and worried. Last night, his face had flushed when she told him about Victoria's attack. He'd been upset but not afraid. Now his eyes held a definite fear that squeezed her heart.

He cared. He actually cared about her.

For how long? A week, a month, maybe two? Then what?

He brushed his mouth across her lips, the barest contact, yet the sizzle penetrated her core with the power to weaken not only her knees but also the stubborn streak in her spine.

She glanced at his parents. Abigail's drawn features and turned-down mouth and Gavin's icy eyes set in a stoic face shored Cassie's resolve not to allow Brice's misguided affection to override her common sense and wreck her dreams.

The loss of her car changed her plans somewhat, but they still did not and could not include Brice.

"I appreciate everyone's concern, but I'd like to clean up before my shift starts."

"Doc said you needed rest. I'm taking you home."

"No. I need to work." Cassie pushed him away. "I've decided to withdraw from my classes for a year. If I save every penny, I should be able to afford a used car by next summer. Then I'll reenroll and finish my last semester."

Squaring her shoulders, she looked at Brice's mother. "Mrs. Walker, I would appreciate the opportunity to work additional hours. I can cover Natalie's shifts whenever she calls in. I'll even work in housekeeping or the kitchen."

"No." Brice glared at his mother before he turned to Cassie. "You will finish the semester and graduate on time. Whether you go on your own volition or bound and gagged makes no difference to me."

"Then the matter is settled." A dismissive air swirled amid the audible click of Abigail's heels as she stood with her husband.

"Brice is right, Cassie." An inscrutable expression darkened Gavin Walker's features. "No work for the next few days, and don't make any rash decisions. When you've rested, you may discover less drastic opportunities."

After the Walkers left, Cassie cut her eyes at Brice. "You have no say in my choices."

Brice's dark brows slashed over stormy eyes. "We'll discuss this later."

He should've had the sense to stop. Oh, no, he had to keep talking.

"Regardless, you will be in class on Monday if I have to hog-tie you and carry you to class."

"Don't boss me." Cassie pocketed her hands beneath her arms.

"Here we go," he muttered.

"I didn't appreciate that eye roll when you were a wolf, and I like it even less now."

"This morning, you refused to miss one day of class because after the first it would be too easy to skip the next and the next, until you eventually stopped going," Brice argued.

How dare he use her words against her!

"This is different," Cassie declared, although the fear he was right gripped her stomach.

"How?"

"I'm not playing hooky. I don't have a car to get to class."

"I can fix that." Brice's sincerity would've given a less independent woman pause to consider his offer.

"No!" Accepting his charity would undermine her independence. She had to make it on her own.

"So, you're a quitter." An unmistakable challenge glittered in his eyes.

"I am not."

"Glad to hear it, Sunshine. No mate of mine is allowed to quit when things don't go her way." He cradled the back of her neck, inching his face closer. Closer. Until his mouth hovered over the bow of her lips.

The accident, the aftermath and the arguing left her no strength to turn aside.

Lacking the intensity and urgency of yesterday's kiss, the whisper softness of his mouth was a gentle persuasion that wrapped her in Brice's warmth and comfort. Cassie wanted to curl into him and bask in his strength.

Oh, she was in trouble. So much trouble. Brice had been her first in many things. First crush, first kiss, first to make it to third base. She couldn't allow him to be the first to break her heart. Or her spirit.

He wasn't the type of man to hurt her intentionally. Still, when his life returned to normal, he would realize she wasn't his caliber. His initial reaction of tossing her aside had been the truest. Everything since was nothing more than a fantasy.

# Chapter 31

*I have plans for the future and you're not in them.*

The absoluteness of Cassie's words on their first night together slashed through Brice's heart to shred the most vulnerable part of his being, mostly because she used the sentiment as a shield to block the mate-bond.

Had he come home too late after all?

Tonight, the buzz inside Taylor's grated Brice's nerves. The music sucked, the food sucked and all the people laughing and having a good time sucked.

He clinked his glass at the bartender.

"Want something stronger than an RC this time?"

Brice shook his head. He didn't want to add to Cassie's agitation by returning home smelling like beer.

Following her accident, he'd taken her to the cabin, hoping some peace and quiet would settle them both. It had the opposite effect. She couldn't relax, her mind fixated on one course of action, and nothing he said steered her away from withdrawing from her classes.

Deep in his soul, he knew quitting now would become a fatal blow to her tightly held dreams. Whether or not he agreed with her plans to leave the Walker's Run Resort for bigger and better opportunities *after graduation*, he desperately wanted her to graduate, on time, because all her hope rode on that singular accomplishment.

His offer to help blew up in his face. Everything escalated from there until he realized Cassie's inability to accept his assistance wasn't a simple matter of pride. Far deeper and darker than he had experience to probe, she held fast to the belief that accepting help from anyone, for any reason, would cripple her ability to stand on her own two feet. She couldn't understand no one became a success in isolation.

Wisely he chose not to argue the point. Since nothing he said or offered to do de-escalated her rising hysteria, Brice simply walked out, climbed into his metallic blue Maserati—delivered this morning, along with all his personal effects from his Atlanta penthouse—and drove like a demon to see Rafe.

"It was bad, Walker," his friend said when he'd offered Brice a drink before guzzling a half-empty bottle of bourbon. "If Red hadn't climbed out of the car when she did—" Brice's knees still felt weak, and his stomach staggered thinking about it.

Brice cradled his head. The throb in his temples matched the tortuous beat of his heart. Agony spread through his body, amplifying the constant pain in his leg.

"How the hell did you find me, Adam?" His scent preceded the soft squeak of his shoes.

"Your car is hard to miss." Adam cautiously sat on the stool next to Brice. "If you're able to single out my scent above this crowd, then your nose must be working again."

Shrugging, Brice raised his glass and downed half of his drink. He didn't feel like talking, and when Adam decided to say his piece, he would.

It didn't take long.

"I shouldn't have kept you from Walker's Run. I failed to understand your connection to this place."

"I left of my own accord." Brice bore some responsibility in that misguided venture. "I can't blame you for the years I lost. You didn't steal them. I gave them up without a fight."

"Only because you trusted me." Adam reached toward Brice's shoulder, then curled his fingers and dropped his hand. "I was wrong to breach that trust. Our relationship will never be the same, but I want to be a part of your life, Brice."

"Is that why you fired Victoria and banished her from your territory?"

Adam looked surprised.

"Dad told me."

"Victoria violated one of our fundamental tenets when she

attacked Cassie. I don't want my reputation or my pack tainted by her recklessness." Adam finger-waved at the bartender. "Sadly, I did have ambitions for you and Victoria as a couple."

"You've known Victoria since she was a baby. Her parents will be devastated." Brice rested his right ankle on his left knee and pressed his thumb into the tight calf, rubbing deep, small circles into the muscle to ease the spasm. "Your decision couldn't have been easy."

"I did what was right for you, my firm and my pack. The Woelfesenat is aware of the incident. Philip saw the marks on Cassie this morning."

Brice's blood thinned into icy streams. The Woelfesenat had zero tolerance for acts of aggression against humans. Their reactionary responses were swift and often fatal.

Brice's heart seemed to skip every other beat. He was the reason Victoria had attacked Cassie. And if Cassie found out about the severity of wolfan justice, she would be appalled. "I'm not saying Victoria doesn't deserve some form of punishment, but as Victoria's Alpha, you have to convince Philip not to pursue the full extent of the law."

"Philip isn't rash. He'll come up with a viable solution before her case is formally brought before the council." Adam laid a hand on Brice's shoulder. "I expect he'll seek your input since you're acting as Cassie's guardian."

"Our relationship is a bit more complicated." Rolling up his sleeve, Brice turned his arm so his uncle could see.

"Is that a bite?" Adam fingered the bruise.

The wound would fade soon, although Brice had used his cell phone to take a picture so he could keep the memory close. "Cassie gave it to me. At Walker's Pointe."

"Does your father know?"

"He knows I've chosen her, and he doesn't approve. Neither does Mom." Nor Cassie, it seemed, since she was blocking the mate-bond. "He's willing to lift the Christmas ultimatum if I agree to find someone more suitable. God, how many times does he want to screw me over?"

"Gavin loves you, Brice. I made a mistake when I took you from him. He needs you and you need him. More than you'll ever understand."

"My father wants an heir, Adam. Same as you." Brice's entire world had been spinning out of control long before the day he stepped into a steel trap. He was so damn sick of being stuck in an endless tornado, tossed here, there and everywhere by people who were supposed to care about him but didn't give a fuck about what they were doing to him.

Brice tested his leg before he stood. "He doesn't need me. No one does." Including Cassie, who had a daily mantra of reminding him how much she didn't need him.

Maybe it was time to stop stalling and accept the Woelfe-senat's offer, after all.

# Chapter 32

The sweet smell of late-blooming honeysuckle perfumed the evening breeze tickling Cassie's skin. The buzz of insects vibrated in the stillness of night, and the twinkle of fireflies winked through the trees. The serenity did nothing to calm her turmoil.

Stretched out on a large flat boulder at the edge of the stream, she stared at the stars.

Big Dipper, Little Dipper, Orion—none offered wisdom or comfort about what lay ahead.

Cassie's college financial aid advisor had arranged for her to live in campus housing and had assigned her a job in the work-study program so she wouldn't have to withdraw from her classes. She should have been ecstatic, not worried about resigning from a job she intended to leave anyway, and she certainly shouldn't have been nervous about what Brice would say. He didn't want her to quit. Now she would be able to finish. He should be pleased with the news.

Deep down, she knew he wouldn't be thrilled at all. Neither was she, really.

In the span of a week, she'd grown used to his company. Especially at night, because his presence soothed the lonely ache in her heart. Even when they argued.

As she numbered the Pleiades, a faint plop splashed the water in the distance. She sat up, watching a dark blob ebbing toward her. The shadowy figure leaped from the current and landed on the embankment.

"Brice?" She swung a heavy, square flashlight in the direction of the sound and bit back a relieved sigh as a black wolf shook, slinging peals of water from his fur in every direction.

He cocked his head and stared for several suspended heartbeats. She turned off the flashlight and set it aside.

In a blink, Brice the man rose naked, haloed in a silvery sheen.

Cassie sucked her bottom lip between her teeth watching him stalk toward her. Since the night he'd found her in the hospital parking lot, Brice had stopped prancing around the cabin naked, and she missed how comfortable he'd been for her to see him.

*Stupid roommate rules!*

She could only blame herself.

"What are you doing out here?" Brice ran his hand through his dark, damp hair. His eyes searched her face as if she were a huge mystery.

Cassie believed herself too boring to captivate his attention for long. Brice, however, being all that he was, mesmerized her so completely that Cassie knew he'd enchant her forever.

"I needed to clear my head." She slid off the rock.

Brice closed the slight distance to tower over her. Tall, broad and masculine. On instinct to protect her personal space, Cassie placed her hand on his chest and then wondered why. Brice didn't care much for boundaries, except to test them. Over the last few days, he'd certainly pushed hers to the limits, and then some.

Trailing down his scarred flesh to his belly button, her fingertips tingled from the soft buzz of electricity. Eyes nearly hooded, he sucked in a breath.

"Does it hurt?"

"No." His raw, needy sigh scraped her skin. "Your touch always feels damn good."

Cassie lowered her face to hide a smile. "I meant when you change forms."

"A current travels down my spine and into my nerves, but it isn't painful."

"One second you're a beautiful wolf." Cassie allowed him to lift her chin.

"The next, I'm a man." He touched his lips to her mouth, a sweet brush of tenderness that made her ache for more.

More of life. More of love. More of everything.

If she had died today, what would she regret? Aside from being dead, that is.

Not earning her degree would suck, but what caused her stomach to fist and roll were the missed opportunities with Brice. She couldn't afford to fall in love with him. Yet somewhere deep inside, Cassie realized her biggest mistake in life or death would be to allow him to drift out of her life without grabbing on to one consequential moment.

She cupped his neck, pulling him forward and sealing her mouth to his. Taking the hint, he angled his body into hers, nudging her back until she was sandwiched between him and the boulder. He deepened the kiss, holding her face with both hands. The length of each finger heated her flesh, holding her steady as he nipped her lower lip without breaking the skin. Then his tongue soothed the momentary sting.

A chaotic flutter swept through her belly, and further down, a clenching need sprung to life. Of their own accord, her hips moved against him in a slow grind that only intensified the need. A deep, ragged moan rose from Cassie's core.

Brice stilled. He lifted his head, turning on that fierce gaze that bore into her soul.

She'd seen this look. Every night when she climbed into bed, every morning when she awoke to his smile. And every time he kissed her, touched her. Only tonight, caution tempered the desire in his eyes.

Had she waited too long?

"Cas." He pivoted away. "I can't play the hot and cold game tonight. Go back to the cabin before I get carried away."

"Quit telling me what to do," Cassie replied sharply. "I don't want to leave. I don't want you to stop."

Her declaration dangled between them. Cassie's heart demanded that he believe her. He had every reason to turn her down. She'd been such a ninny to discourage his interest, belittle his feelings. If he walked off, leaving her cold and wanting, it would be what she deserved.

"Do you understand what you're saying?" he asked in a deep, husky voice that quickened her pulse.

"Yes."

He turned back to her, slowly.

"And I know what I want." She didn't want to fight the pull between them, not anymore. She wanted to explore the desire he'd awakened. Wanted to seize the moment before it was too late.

In a moment of boldness, she drew a single finger across the tip of his penis and down the faint ridge of the underside of his shaft. He shuddered, eyes half closing.

Encouraged, she wrapped her hand around as much of him as she could, squeezing gently and leisurely stroking up and down his length, stopping only to gather moisture from his arousal to smooth the glide.

"You're killing me," he whispered raggedly.

His vulnerability shot a feeling of feminine power through her veins. She sank to her knees and ran her tongue across his slit. His taste surprised her—warm, slightly salty and deliciously male. Sucking the mushroom tip into her mouth, she stroked the length of his shaft.

Twining his fingers in her hair, he lifted his hips ever so slightly in soft thrusts. Groans of pleasure fell from his parted lips and fed her arousal. The deeper and more guttural the sounds he made, the wetter she became.

"Enough!" he growled.

The force of his command sent a shiver down her spine. Wondering if she'd done something wrong, she looked up. The feral hunger in his eyes wiped away her fear.

He lifted her to her feet, hauled her against his body and claimed her mouth. Hard, hot and huge, his erection dug into her abdomen, an insistent distraction. All she could focus on was how it would feel thrusting inside her.

Brice's hands disappeared beneath the baseball jersey he'd given her to wear to bed. He touched his way up her stomach with possessive urgency. His long, nimble fingers imprinted trails of heat along her ribs, shortening her breaths. Instead of moving upward to her breasts, his palms slid to her back, rubbing small circles in the muscles along her spine, pressing her so tightly against him that she felt as if their bodies would merge.

Her nipples tightened into points so sensitive every rub and scratch of her shirt reverberated in her sex. Heat smoldered in her pelvis. Her body felt uncomfortably hot. She wanted to peel out of her clothes and feel Brice's slick skin against her bare body.

As if reading her mind, Brice whipped the nightshirt over her head and dropped it on the ground. He leaned back, staring, as if memorizing every line, every curve, every imperfection.

"God, you're beautiful."

She heard sincere desperation in his hoarse voice.

He traced along the curve of her breasts, over the fleshy peaks, and strummed her nipples, pulling something between a groan of pleasure and primal yowl from her throat. His own growl answered—fierce, possessive, demanding.

His hands dropped to her ass, kneading the globes in a slow grind instead of the place she really wanted him to stroke. He lowered his face, dotting kisses in the valley between her breasts. His stubbled cheeks brushed against the tender sides. He licked her taut nipple before sucking the peak in his warm, delicious mouth. An electric heat zipped through Cassie's body, buzzing her head to toe with a crescendoing thrill converging on her sex.

Gasping, she anchored her fingers in the dark waves of Brice's hair and pressed her hips into him, craving the feel of his body, his strength, his very essence.

His hands took on an urgency, palming a path from her midriff down her belly. He cupped her mound and, through the damp cotton panties, teased her folds. Tension coiled in her body, drawing in every muscle almost to the point of pain.

"I want you. So much it hurts. But if this isn't what you

want, tell me now." Pure desperation and restraint rasped his voice. "Once I taste you, there's no turning back."

How many times had he told her that she was his?

Right now, she was. Utterly and completely.

"I want you, Brice. More than anything. Right here. Right now."

The triumphant curl of his smile sent a flutter of caution through Cassie's mind. "Promise me one thing." She stroked the scratchy stubble along his jaw.

"Anything." Holding her hand against his cheek, he kissed her palm.

"No biting."

Brice flinched, and his breathing faltered. Cassie hated the hurt she sensed. He believed her to be his true mate. However, she wouldn't trust their futures to a misguided fantasy. One day, he'd thank her for keeping him from making the biggest mistake of their lives. His bite would not only bind them together in an unbreakable union but also create a very big risk for an unplanned pregnancy.

Gazing upward, Brice seemed to search the heavens for something. Patience, perhaps. Or maybe he was simply contemplating if Cassie was worth all the aggravation.

"I promise. No biting." His thumb traced the bow of her lip. *"Tonight."*

"Thank you." She stretched her neck as Brice nuzzled and kissed his favorite spot behind her ear. He was a man of his word, so she let go of any fears of becoming pregnant and repeating her mother's life.

Instead, Cassie gave herself to the sensation of soft, hot kisses at the hollow of her throat and the delicate tease of Brice's fingers along her upper thighs and pelvis. Her body shuddered, alert to every sweep of his hand and lick of his tongue.

Expectancy charged the night air. She could almost hear the crackle.

He knelt before her and kissed her stomach, then pressed

his face against her skin and breathed in her scent. He moved his nose lower and lower until he reached her mound.

The anticipation was nearly unbearable. Every touch, every kiss, every time he breathed against her skin, sizzling currents of need and want shocked her core. Her sex clenched in a maddening frenzy to be filled.

"Brice," she whimpered, embarrassed to be so wantonly needy.

Hooking his thumbs inside the waistband of her panties, he inched them down her legs until she wished he'd rip the damn things off. She'd never felt so aware of her body. It was as if Brice had flayed her skin, laid bare her nerves and plugged them into a light socket. By the time she stepped out of her panties, she was panting.

"Wh-what are you doing?"

"Pleasuring you." His tongue slid along her folds and her body melted. Brice's hands clasped her ass, steadying her while his mouth devoured her sex.

Cassie shivered. An indescribable pressure rose inside her core. Her hips rocked in a rhythmic dance to match Brice's lavish licks along her sex with maddening precision.

Cassie knotted her fingers in his hair. More, she wanted—needed—more.

"Oh, God," she gasped as his warm, wet tongue speared inside her. The undulations of pleasure he unleashed were so strong, so intense, so incredibly primal that she cried out in an unintelligible language.

She closed her eyes, giving in to the excruciating bliss. The orgasmic force shattered every cell in her body. It must have, because her entire being came undone. If not for Brice's strong arms and muscular body anchoring her, she would've simply drifted into oblivion.

"You okay, Sunshine?" Brice swept damp tendrils from her face.

"Mmm," was all Cassie could mumble. Beyond delighted, her entire body whirred.

Brice stood, his hands still supporting her unsteady legs. "You are amazing."

"So are you." She laved her tongue over the scars at the base of his neck and moved up and over his chin to capture his lips. He tasted of salt, raw masculinity and her.

The control he'd shown moments before evaporated. His hands, his mouth, his rock-hard body crushed her against the boulder. Possessive. Demanding. Needful.

Invigorated by his touch, she felt heat course through her again.

Lifting her leg against his hip, Brice thrust inside her. Pain ripped through her sex. Cassie cried out, digging her nails into his back as her whole body tensed.

Brice stilled. His expression darkened to confusion and then…regret?

He started to pull away.

"Don't." The sultriness of her voice came from a dormant place he'd awakened. "I want this." She clasped his face in her hands. "I want this with you."

He didn't look convinced. "Cas, you should've told me this was your first time."

"Why does it matter?"

"I would've done this right. Champagne. Candles. Rose petals scattered across a nice, soft bed."

"I don't drink, so the champagne would be wasted." She laced her fingers behind his neck and wrapped one leg and then the other around his waist, using the boulder at her back as leverage. "I wouldn't want to stain the sheets, so I would've vacuumed the rose petals from the bed. And candles can't compare to the moon and stars above us." She nipped his lower lip. "I can't imagine a more perfect time or place than right here, right now. With you."

Brice smiled that heart-stopping, soul-tingling smile and kissed her. Slowly, deeply until she was lost in the sensation of his mouth, his skin, his very presence.

When he moved, the rhythm was slow, unhurried. She

arched to welcome each thrust, clenching to hold him deep inside.

Cassie had read about how the experience would feel. Even Imogene had explained the mechanics of intercourse.

Despite all that, Cassie wasn't prepared for the rush of emotion. To experience Brice so profoundly, she could only describe the sensation as a union of their essences. Sharing breaths, sharing bodies, sharing souls.

Soon a sinful pressure built inside her at the crux where they joined. He thrust harder, faster, deeper, lost in the moment.

She was lost, too. Lost in the strength and passion of this man, pouring his all into her, bringing her to the highest pinnacle of ecstasy until she splintered. In that rapturous moment, Brice slipped further inside Cassie's heart. To the most tender, most vulnerable, most untouched part. And opened her to the very thing that would break her.

*Love.*

Imogene had warned her to stay away from him. In fact, when Cassie had told her about finding Brice's hospital room, her mother had insisted that Cassie keep away from all men or suffer her fate. Cassie knew good advice when she heard it, but Brice made her mother's wisdom difficult to heed.

Eyes hooded, he stilled. Cassie simply stared, knowing that no man would touch her as deeply or completely as Brice Walker.

Bold assertions for a freshly deflowered virgin. Yet she knew it to be true because she would never give her heart to another man. It had foolishly bared its fragility to the one whose ultimate rejection would smash it into irreparable pieces. If she allowed it.

She wouldn't wallow in self-pity, though. She would be grateful for what they shared.

Brice rubbed his nose against her cheek. "No regrets?"

"Absolutely none," she said, pulling herself back into the moment of experiencing something spectacular. "How could

I regret making love for the first time, with you, under the stars, next to this beautiful river? It was all so natural. Nothing orchestrated. Nothing fancy. Just simple and—"

"Fucking amazing." The excited hitch in his breathing and his wide-eyed delight said Brice didn't have any regrets, either.

Yet.

# Chapter 33

Brice had known human desire. Knew the wolfan lust a full moon provoked. But he didn't know *this*—a want so sharp it stabbed his heart. An excruciating need to fill and be filled that wrenched his soul.

He smiled at the soft streams of sunlight streaked across the face of his sleeping beauty. Coppery eyelashes dusted her delicate cheeks. Masses of curls sprawled over the pillow, and her small hand lay tucked beneath her chin.

All night he'd fought the urge to claim her during each exquisite coupling. Never had he wanted a woman so intensely, so frequently, that he sought the experience again and again and again until they fell into an exhausted sleep.

Cassie had responded to his every touch and at the precipice of each orgasmic triumph, her soul beckoned his. Still, he'd held back claiming her because she opened herself to him only sexually. She wasn't ready for a mateship. Her will was too ingrained to trust her heart to him.

He'd taken all that she had offered and was grateful.

Last night, he'd teetered on the edge of giving up. This morning, he was thankful not to have had the opportunity to do so.

Cassie's eyelids fluttered open on a sigh.

Brice's face ached from the broad smile he proudly wore when she looked at him.

"Morning, Sunshine." The musky scent from their night of coupling filled his lungs, filtered through his body and nestled deep in his core.

She didn't turn away from him embarrassed or scurry from the bed. Instead, she returned his smile and his greeting with a husky, "Morning."

Her skin glowed and his ego grew, knowing he had pleased

her well. He looked forward to repeating the performance once they made it through today.

"What time is it?" Cassie yawned.

"Time to get dressed." The past few days he'd avoided dwelling on his grandmother's death. Now the inevitableness of his final goodbyes had come.

"You'll get through this." Cassie slid her arms around his neck.

Their bodies melded in a tender embrace. Though tapped out and fully sated, he tingled from the contact. He loved the feel of her against him. She was soft and delicate, while he was hard and scarred.

He nipped her ear, smelling his scent on her skin.

*Mine!*

"I'll jump in the shower first." She nudged him.

"We could shower together."

"Not a good idea." She kissed his cheek, and Brice allowed her to roll out of his arms.

Cassie pulled on his baseball jersey.

"I've seen you naked," he teased.

"I'm not as accustomed to prancing around in the nude as you are."

"You can practice. I won't complain." Propping on his elbows, Brice waggled his eyebrows.

"Next time." Her eyes didn't smile when she did.

Brice felt a pinch in his chest. "Cas?" he called out as she strode down the hallway. "Is something wrong?"

"Just a little sad," she answered, closing the bathroom door.

Brice pulled on cutoff sweats, more out of recent habit than anything else, and padded barefoot into the kitchen. The coffee in the carafe of the automatic maker had grown tepid, so he warmed it in the microwave and considered making breakfast. However, if Cassie's dread of the coming task was similar to his, neither could stomach eating.

The red blinking light on the answering machine caught his attention. Brice's finger hovered over the Play button. The message probably wasn't for him. Anyone needing to reach him would call his cell.

If the message was for Cassie, Brice didn't want to pry, though he did wonder who had called. She claimed not to have friends. Yet Hannah had expressed concern for her, and Shane had nearly challenged him over her well-being.

Jealousy ruffled Brice's mettle. How close was Cassie to the pack outsider? Did Shane want something more? Had Brice's sudden appearance interrupted something between them?

Brice rolled his shoulders. Cassie was *his* mate. Not Shane's or anyone else's.

Of course, Brice could just play the message. What would be the harm in that?

The pad of his index finger rested on the silver button.

Embarking on a committed relationship meant showing Cassie respect. He didn't need to manage every little detail of her life. She wouldn't appreciate his interference and frankly, he didn't want that kind of mateship. He wanted one built on trust.

Careful to avoid the guilty disapproval of her reflection, Cassie dried her hair. She ached for more than one night of Brice's lovemaking, and if she wasn't careful, she just might lull herself into believing it was possible.

But one more night would lead to another. And another and another until she forgot that Brice wasn't her Prince Charming. Then, when his real princess appeared, he'd turn Cassie out without any further consideration.

Still, she was thankful Brice hadn't heard the message her new roommates had left. While he showered, Cassie called them back. So excited about meeting her, Cassie's roommates wanted her to come today. After explaining that she had a prior commitment, Cassie agreed to move in tomorrow.

In the morning, she'd explain to Brice her plans to finish

the semester in campus housing. He wouldn't be happy, but it was for the best.

Taking a deep breath for courage, she viewed her reflection long enough to apply face powder and lip gloss. She grimaced at the bruises on her neck. Instead of miraculously fading, like she'd prayed, they'd turned darker and uglier. She dusted a light coat of powder over them. Unfortunately, the makeup failed as an effective camouflage.

In the midst of yesterday's turmoil, she'd forgotten to wash the dirty, sweaty, faded scarf. In its present condition, that scrap would be more noticeable than the bruises, and Cassie didn't want to attract unwanted attention at Margaret's memorial. Maybe if she sat in the back, no one would notice her or the hideous marks.

Brice strode into the bedroom, wearing a towel around his hips and a serious frown on his face.

"You know—" she pointed at his groin "—I've seen you naked."

That brought a flicker of life to his lips. His unhurried gaze traveled over her. One brow shot up. "You're wearing that?"

"Something wrong with my dress?" Cassie pulled at the fabric, checking for stains or holes she might have missed.

Brice's puzzled expression was almost comical. "It's yellow. Don't people wear black to a funeral?"

"Margaret loved bright, happy colors." Cassie smoothed the waist of her simple summer dress. "I'm wearing this for her."

"You're amazing, Sunshine." Brice hugged her, and Cassie smelled her cherry-scented body wash on his skin.

He kissed the top of her head and Cassie felt the vibration of it in the soles of her feet, which were planted solidly on the floor. She checked to be sure, because she had the sensation of floating on air.

"Come with me." Brice led her into Margaret's bedroom.

They navigated around the boxes his uncle had delivered from Brice's penthouse and walked over to one of the four rolling garment racks. Cassie's mouth fell open. She'd seen this many clothes only inside a department store.

"You should wear black," she said in a gentle tone when he picked out a dark blue suit. "People have certain expectations of you."

"I don't care." He opened a rectangular box that contained at least three dozen silk handkerchiefs. He selected one the exact shade of Cassie's dress. "Perfect."

His broad smile faltered as his gaze fell to the hand Cassie held against her throat. He shuffled around the boxes to Margaret's dresser.

"What are you looking for?" Cassie watched him open and close drawers.

"These." He pulled out a fistful of scarves. "I didn't remember them yesterday. You know my brain doesn't function well until I've had my first cup of coffee."

He dumped the colorful neckwear across the bed. "You don't need to be ashamed of those bruises, Cas. But if you're more comfortable with them covered, maybe one of these will help."

Cassie sorted through the collection. "I didn't know Margaret had these."

"She used to wear them to church when I was a little boy." Brice scratched his head. "I hope they're still in fashion."

Cassie picked two that would complement her dress without drawing attention to her: a white gauze scarf with a feather-weight viscose texture and a silky one with a peach abstract pattern.

"I like this one." Brice fingered the vibrant indigo flowers on a pale blue pashmina.

"It's lovely." Cassie worked it gingerly around her throat. "No one will mind if I borrow it?"

"They're yours now." The vividness of his gaze dimmed. "Granny would've wanted you to have them."

Cassie's chest ached. She'd lost so much in the span of week. The trailer—her home for ten years. Her car. Soon, her job. And most of all, the woman to whom Cassie owed so much.

Margaret Walker was gone, and she'd left a big hole in Cassie's heart. Brice's kindness made the hole bigger. Cassie needed to plug the breach before she lost any more of herself.

Thank God Brice hadn't suggested driving his horrifyingly expensive car. He helped her out of the truck.

"You are so beautiful, Sunshine." He kissed her, soft and sweet.

Cassie tasted the longing. Hers? His? She couldn't tell.

He drew back. His hesitant eyes reflected a vulnerability that she doubted anyone else would notice.

She took his hand, wanting to be strong because Brice needed her to be. "You're as handsome as sin, Mr. Walker."

Tucking her arm beneath his, they walked inside the church. The greeter directed them to the area off to the side, where Brice's parents and a few other people were gathered.

"You should be with your family," Cassie said. "I'll meet you after the service."

"We'll sit together." Brice's tightened his hold on her arm. "Granny considered you family. She wouldn't want you to sit alone, and neither do I." Grief wore through his ruggedly handsome face. His full mouth, devoid of a smile, pulled tight from the stress.

"Oh, all right." Cassie swallowed the sting in her throat and offered Brice an encouraging smile. "Do you want to stand with your parents to greet the guests?"

Brice shook his head. His eyes gravitated to the table at the front of the sanctuary, where a rainbow spray of wildflowers rested behind a silver urn. The natural fluidity of Brice's movements faltered and his limp became more pronounced the closer they came to the first pew. She stroked his arm and offered soft reassurances while ignoring the increased whisperings as they passed each row.

When they sat down, both breathed again. Brice slid his

arm over her shoulders and tipped his head to hers. He closed his eyes and swallowed.

Maybe he was counting. Or maybe he was trying not to throw up, which is what Cassie wanted to do.

Brice stood as his parents approached. Not knowing what the proper etiquette was, Cassie stood, too.

Stiff-armed, Brice hugged his mother, whose strained, pale face and red, swollen eyes were a harsh contrast to her usual elegance. He shook his father's hand, though neither spoke.

"I'm very sorry for your loss," Cassie said softly over the grapefruit-sized lump in her throat.

Abigail Walker stared at Cassie's extended hand. Maybe it wasn't appropriate to handshake at a funeral. She was just about to drop her hand when Brice's mother accepted the greeting.

"Thank you, Cassie." Abigail Walker sat down without meeting Cassie's gaze.

The angles in Gavin's face appeared sharper than Cassie had ever seen them, so she found it difficult to gauge his reaction to her presence. She offered her heartfelt condolences. No matter his opinion of her, Cassie knew how it felt to lose a mother.

Gavin enclosed her hand in his two large palms. "Thank you for coming," he said in a gruff voice.

Brice squeezed her elbow, extracting her from his father's grip. Cassie returned to her seat, and Brice left no space between them.

Cassie laced her fingers through his and tried to return the strength she'd siphoned from him over the week. She prayed his common sense would return, too. Then he would see how out of place she was in his world.

# Chapter 34

People spilled from the resort dining room, lingered in the lobby and sauntered in and out of the lounge for drinks. Nearly everyone in Maico had joined the Walkers and their covert wolfy friends for Margaret's memorial reception.

Cassie tried to look inconspicuous, sitting alone at the table Brice had ushered her to when she refused to join him and his parents as they mingled with their guests. It was hard enough to make it through the service, feeling the heat of everyone's stares at the back of her head. She wouldn't fake-smile and chitchat as if she hadn't noticed.

The conglomerate smells from the buffet of Margaret's favorite foods—fried chicken, country-fried steak, green beans, mashed potatoes and gravy, and fresh-baked biscuits—saturated the air. Ordinarily Cassie loved the scent of good old-fashioned country cooking. Right now, her nerves made her so jittery that her stomach rebelled against the heavy odors.

She took a tiny sip of iced tea. Unfortunately, the cold drink did nothing to settle her queasiness.

"Miss Albright?"

Cassie gazed up at the elderly gentleman with a short crop of precisely cut silvery strands. Suitably dressed for mourning, he wore an expensive-looking black suit, crisp black shirt and thin black tie. His rich, dark eyebrows slashed over deep-set eyes.

"Hello, Mr. Krussen."

"Would you mind if I joined you?" He didn't wait for an answer. He simply pulled the chair next to her away from the table where Brice had deposited her and sat. "Thank you for your recommendation of Mabel's Diner. The food was tasty, and the ambiance adequately reflected Maico's local color."

"I'm glad the restaurant was to your liking," she said politely without engaging further conversation. Her nerves were still raw from the gawks, finger pointing and loud whispers she'd endured at the memorial service.

"Brice seems quite fond of you." A neutral smile he must rely on often slid too easily into place.

Already on edge, her body painfully tensed for The Talk. She'd expected it, sooner or later, from any number of "well-meaning" people; however, coming from a member of the imperious wolfy council, it seemed a little over the top.

She remained quiet, watching a room filled with people Margaret had touched over her lifetime. People who respected and loved her dearly. People who grieved her loss, missing her terribly.

Cassie's heart constricted with an aching pain. She would never garner the acceptance and adoration Margaret had achieved. Brice couldn't see it, but Cassie could, and she didn't need anyone to point out her shortcomings.

"I was quite disturbed to learn of your attack." Michael's gaze lingered on the delicate scarf around Cassie's neck. "Rest assured, Victoria will be punished for the assault."

"It was a personal catfight, and no one else needs to nose into our private business. I wasn't seriously hurt, and she learned I don't take kindly to bullies." Cassie emphasized the latter, taking some measure of pleasure in the flicker of his understanding of her true meaning. "The matter is settled."

Amusement tinged the corners of his diplomatic smile. "I'll inform the council of your position when we convene for Victoria's hearing."

"Please do." Cassie sipped her drink.

"I like your frankness, so I'll be direct." His hand rested on her arm, the warmth of his palm lost to the cold, impersonal touch. "I've observed your interactions with Brice over the past couple of days. It's evident you care for him, so it's prudent for you to understand that his attachment to you threatens his future. You need to let him go."

"Brice and I are friends. Close friends." She could admit

to that. "Our paths lie in different directions to attempt anything more."

"What a relief." Michael's smile turned genuine. "I feared he would make you his mate so he could, quite literally, watch over you as Margaret had asked."

Michael's words slammed into her with unexpected tidal-wave force. She struggled to breathe.

Her one perfect night with Brice had been nothing more than a cheap fabrication. The pain in her chest, throbbing and unrelenting, exploded into a shattering numbness.

Her dignity shriveled. Brice only wanted her because his grandmother had turned Cassie into his charity case. All the talk about mate-bonds was nothing but a bunch of hooey.

Good thing she never believed him.

Cassie's hand trembled, and she had to be careful not to spill tea down her face while taking a drink. The cold wetness shocked her dry mouth, driving an icy resolve into the pit of her stomach.

Resigning from her position at Walker's Run Resort and moving to the college campus was absolutely the right choice for her to make.

"Excuse me, Mr. Krussen. It's been a long week, and I'm utterly worn-out."

"Of course." He stood, offering a gentlemanly hand to help her stand.

She hurried to the employees' restroom and leaned against the counter. A single, silent sob rocked her body.

Someone knocked and the restroom door squeaked open.

"Cas?" Brice's soft tone washed over her. "Baby, what's wrong?"

"Exhausted," she said, too drained to pretend otherwise.

He netted her in his strong arms. Cassie rested her cheek against his chest, his heart beating a comforting drum despite the treachery hidden within.

Wishing she'd never learned the truth, Cassie turned her

face into the fabric of his blue button-down shirt. It smelled fresh, clean and just like him.

"Let's go." His long, warm fingers laced through hers.

"No." The pretense had gone on long enough. She wanted a break from it. From him. "I need some fresh air. I'm going home. Alone."

The disappointment on his face crunched the pieces of her splintered heart. "I'm not staying without you."

"Your family needs you. Your people need to see you."

"They need to see us."

"There is no *us*."

"Cas." Brice reached for her, and she leaned away. He dropped his hand, but his eyes held a plea she forced herself to ignore.

"I don't belong. Not at your table. Not in your home. And not in your life."

"I thought you accepted the bond between us."

"Lust," she said flatly. "That's all it is."

"What about last night?" Brice's voice dropped to a whisper.

"Sex. Nothing more," Cassie lied. The first she remembered telling. She hated lies. One followed another until it became hard to tell the truth.

She'd just taken one giant step toward becoming her mother.

Brice flinched. His lips parted. "You don't mean that."

"I do." The second lie tumbled from her lips. "I'm grateful you were my first, but it was just sex. It didn't mean anything to me."

Brice's features darkened, the light in his eyes extinguished. When he spoke, his voice sounded cold and bitter. "Last night might have meant nothing to you, but it meant everything in the world to me."

She met his gaze, ready to confess that she'd lied. The hardness in his face and the pure disgust in his eyes declared a retraction was too late. The poison had already settled into Brice's heart to destroy his faith in her.

His name evaporated from her traitorous tongue. Because she couldn't give voice to her regret and stop him, Brice stormed out.

Cassie's heart froze in her chest, where even the faintest beat would break her open.

She was doing the right thing, Cassie reminded herself. She wasn't right for him. He needed a strong, respectable lady wolf by his side. Not a scrawny scrap of a human who had a streak of bad luck that ran the length of the Tennessee River.

Cassie's throat burned. No matter how hard she swallowed, she couldn't dislodge the corrosive lump. She stumbled out of the restroom and down the hallway toward the lobby.

Someone called her name, though the person sounded far, far away.

"You need to sit down." Shane looked as ethereal as his voice. "You're about to faint." His face contorted in a weird scrunch. He pushed her into the employee break room and forced her to sit.

Awareness crept back into her mind. Cassie shook her head. "I'm fine."

"You don't look fine." Shane's mouth pressed into a hard frown. "What the hell happened between you and Brice?"

"Nothing of consequence." Another lie.

"Would you mind if I asked a favor?" Cassie stared at the floor so it would be easier for him to say no if he didn't want to get involved.

"We're friends, Cassie. You can ask me anything."

"I need a ride to the college in the morning. I'm moving into the campus apartments."

Shane spat curses out of the side of his mouth. "Did the prick kick you out?"

"No." Although given the way Brice stalked off, he might. "Since I have no car, I had to choose between work and graduation."

"Wait a sec." Shane squeezed Cassie's arm. "Brice doesn't want you leave?"

"We didn't make it that far into the discussion." Cassie touched her hair, trying to be casual about the incident.

It seemed to take forever for Shane to respond. "What time should I pick you up?"

"Is seven too early?" The weight on Cassie's shoulders became heavier. The knots in her stomach twisted tighter and multiplied.

"I can make seven." He tilted his head. A wry smile crept across his lips. "Promise me something."

"What?"

"Hang out with me at the library or in the rec room or even at your new place from time to time. Deal?"

Cassie nodded, because the pressure in her chest had caved in her throat.

# Chapter 35

Gulping for each breath, Brice tore through the woods. No matter how hard or fast he wolf-ran, Brice couldn't escape the sharp claw of pain shredding his heart.

Cassie couldn't have meant what she said about their coupling. Yet when he'd looked deep into her eyes, he saw the power of her conviction.

It had to be the stress of the last few days. Cassie was weary and overwhelmed, and he'd asked too much of her. She had wanted to return to the cabin after the memorial service, but he insisted that she attend the reception because he needed her soothing presence. He hadn't thought about what she needed.

Fear threaded through his turbulent thoughts.

He'd fucked up.

Again.

His first big mistake cost Mason his life. This one would cost Brice everything.

Every muscle in his body burned as he pushed past his endurance. If he had a fucking heart attack like Granny had, so be it.

Landmarks blurred in his peripheral vision. Brice had no idea where he was headed until his nails slid into soft moss and stopped him from sailing over the cliff.

As the adrenaline surge ebbed, the roar faded from his ears. His vision cleared, his breathing eased, but the pain in his heart remained. Strength gone, Brice the man flopped to the ground in the very spot where he had confessed to Cassie that she was his true mate. Had it been only a few days ago?

It felt more like a lifetime.

The sun shrank behind the trees, retracting its warmth and leaving Brice as cold on the outside as he was on the in-side. The calling he'd felt for Walker's Run dwindled to negligible pulse. His eyelids slid lower and lower as darkness encroached, and he prayed to the heavens that this day had simply been a bad dream.

"Brice?" A warm, gentle hand squeezed his shoulder. A hand too large to belong to Cassie.

Brice forced open one eye.

Crouched low, Gavin Walker peered at Brice's face. "Son, are you hurt?"

Instead of answering the question, Brice simply sat up. "What are you doing here?"

"Rafe raised an alarm. He kept the sentinels at bay until I reached the sentry gate. He insisted I should come the rest of the way alone."

Brice glanced at the tree line and saw the red wolf shrink into the darkness. "Go home, Dad. I don't need you." Brice would rather talk to Rafe. He, more than anyone, would understand Brice's pain.

"Maybe not." Gavin's voice cracked. "But I need you."

"You never even wanted me." Brice's usual fury failed to erupt. Now that the physical pain of Cassie's rejection had subsided, nothing but a hollow clang clamored inside him. "You only need me now because Mason is dead."

Gavin shook his head and walked stiffly to the cliff's edge.

"You were only a week old when I brought you to Walker's Pointe." Gavin's eyelids slid shut. His head tilted back, and the faintest smile breezed across his lips.

"As soon as I stepped in this very spot, you opened your eyes and reached your hands out to gather the territory into your tiny fingers. Then you threw back your head and howled. A happy little howl that I can still hear."

"Is that why you decided not to throw me over the cliff?"

When Gavin whipped around, there was no disgust or disapproval in his eyes. Only sorrow and pain.

Brice lowered his gaze.

"If I ever find out who put that lie in that hard head of yours, I'll kill them," Gavin snarled.

Truthfully, Brice couldn't remember. Maybe as a child, his impressionable imagination had manufactured the detail as an explanation for the missed birthdays, overlooked accomplishments and general indifference.

None of it seemed to matter now.

He couldn't change the past, and since his happily mated future had crashed and burned before his eyes, he had only one option left.

Brice picked up the blanket his father had left on the ground, wrapped it around his shoulders and stood. "I've been offered an apprenticeship with the Woelfesenat. I'm going to accept."

"Like hell you are." Anger rolling off him in waves, Gavin stood nose to nose with Brice. "You never thought much of me as your father, but I am, and I will not allow you to separate from Walker's Run."

He grabbed Brice's jaw. "I know that look. Your eyes would flash that same defiance whenever you spouted that nonsense, *Always the Alpha, never my father.* Well, let me tell you something. As Alpha, I would kick your ass out of the territory for turning your back on us for political notoriety. But as your *father,* the only way you'll join the Woelfesenat is over my dead carcass!"

Gavin forcefully released him. Brice stumbled backward, muffling a grunt of pain as he stepped too hard on his right leg.

Concern flashed in his father's eyes, and Brice knew the shove had been unintentional. He straightened.

"I can't stay in Walker's Run." Not without Cassie.

"How miserable were you in Atlanta, believing you'd lost your family, your friends? Your entire pack?"

Pretty damn miserable, if that was any measure.

Gavin's scrutiny bore into Brice. "I thought so. Now imagine the agony of that loss magnified across the span of your lifetime."

Brice's mind raced with blurred memories, his consciousness honing in only on the restlessness, isolation and loneliness. The burden on his spirit became heavier and heavier until he sank to his knees beneath the weight.

"You are the true heir to Walker's Run." Gavin's hand rested on Brice's head. "Mason's path was the Woelfesenat, not yours. Leaving will destroy your spirit."

Hadn't Tristan tried to tell him as much?

"Did Mason abdicate the Alphaship when I was born?" Brice looked at his father, ready to listen.

"Yes." Gavin squatted in front of Brice. "Walker's Run never gripped him the way it does me, or you. Your destiny is, and has always been, to lead this pack. Your brother gave his life to protect you because he loved you and believed in you. Don't waste his gift."

"This is unbelievable." Brice massaged the furrows in his forehead. How many times could his world turn upside down?

"Easy, son." Gavin touched Brice's shoulder. "No one expects you to take over right away. There's time to build your family." He paused. "Do you still believe Cassie is your true mate?"

"Yes." Brice wove his fingers through his hair. "I know you don't think she's an acceptable choice, but she is my choice."

"Only a true mate is acceptable to a Walker, son. I wanted to be sure you hadn't chosen her out of convenience."

"Cassie is many things. Convenient isn't one of them." A harsh laugh broke in Brice's chest. "I feel her in my soul. I'm anxious when we're apart and at utter peace when we're together. Except when she doesn't listen to me, and then I'm all out of sorts."

"Having a bonded mate isn't an easy road, but I wouldn't trade the journey for anything in the world." Gavin chuckled, but he looked as tired and worn-out as Brice felt. "When you reach my age, I'm sure you'll feel the same."

"I won't get the chance, Dad. Too many things have gone wrong. Cassie rejected the mate-bond. I'm losing her." Brice rubbed the throb in his calf. Her fingers did a much better job than his to dispel the pain. His heart squinched at the thought that he would never again feel her touch.

"You haven't lost Cassie until she goes somewhere she can't come back from." Gavin reached down and helped Brice stand. "Tonight you rest. Tomorrow you win back your mate."

A shiver rippled through Brice's being. With Cassie, things were never that simple.

# Chapter 36

At 6:55 a.m., Cassie placed the cell phone on the kitchen counter next to the pancakes she'd wrapped in aluminum foil for Brice to eat later.

He'd called last night. First on the landline, asking her to pick up the phone. When she didn't, he called the cell and left a message she replayed all night long.

Stupid, really. He hadn't professed undying love, only said that he would stay with his parents unless she invited him to come home. He also confessed that he missed her.

Her heart latched onto those words because she missed him, too.

Throughout the lonely night, she rewrote her goodbye letter a dozen times before settling on something nonpersonal. Giving Brice an indication of how bad she felt might encourage him to seek her out. To bring her back.

Under no circumstances could that happen. One day her future self would thank her for the sacrifice.

*Yeah, right.*

Twenty minutes later, Shane hadn't arrived. Cassie wiped down the counters for a third time. She wanted to be gone before Brice came home. Neither of them could afford for her to change her mind. A high probability if he intervened.

An engine hummed outside and then subsided. Cassie ushered Shane inside before he had a chance to knock.

"Sorry, I overslept." Sleepy-eyed, he wore wrinkled cargo shorts and a shirt turned wrong side out.

"It won't take long to load up." She led him into the living room, where her meager belongings were stacked.

"Is that it?" Shane scratched his mussed hair.

"Yep, everything I own."

A strange expression crossed Shane's face, though he said

nothing. He grabbed the boxes and headed outside. Cassie followed, toting her suitcases.

Shane piled the items in the truck bed while she went inside to collect her purse and comforter bag. She glanced around the cabin that, in a few short days, had become a real home. Heartsick, she closed the front door and locked it.

She climbed into Shane's truck and buckled her seat belt.

Shane shuffled through his backpack. "Damn. I forgot the library books due today."

"We can pick them up on the way." Cassie ignored her sour stomach. "Oh, I almost forgot. Can we make a quick stop at the resort? I need to hand in some paperwork."

"No problem." Shane backed out of the driveway. "It's on the way."

Neither spoke as he drove down the winding mountain road and pulled into a parking spot close to the entrance.

Before Cassie climbed out of the truck, Shane touched her arm. "Are you sure this is what you want?"

"I need to do this," she replied, because she honestly didn't want to do it at all.

Thankfully Hannah and Natalie were busy behind the guest services counter. Cassie hurried to Abigail Walker's dark office and laid her resignation letter and house key on the desk. She felt a twinge of regret as she waved to Hannah instead of personally saying goodbye.

"Let's go." Cassie hopped into the truck and closed her eyes as Shane pulled out of the parking lot.

She'd expected to leave someday. But now that someday was here, Cassie didn't want to go. Of course, having no future at the Walker's Run Resort, she had made the best choice possible.

Shane parked in front of an old U-shaped brick building that stood three stories high.

"Want to come up?" He shut off the engine. "It might take me a while to find the books."

Cassie followed him up the concrete stairs to the third floor, fourth door. He looked over his shoulder, grinning.

"Ignore the mess."

She stepped inside. Clothes littered the couch, and an open cereal box sat on the glass coffee table. Shane moved through the room, shuffled through some books on the floor and moved to the kitchen before he disappeared into the bedroom.

Cassie perched on the arm of a worn recliner. A gaming console and television filled the tabletop entertainment center. A baseball bat and glove were propped in the far corner. Candid pictures of Shane and his friends decorated the walls.

From the look on his face in the photos, Shane was genuinely happy. And he should have been, because he fit in.

"Got 'em." He emerged from the bedroom waving two books. "Thank God. I didn't want to pay another fine."

"How many have you lost?" Cassie trailed behind him.

"Four, but Zach borrowed two, so technically he lost those."

The door banged open. Shane stopped short, and Cassie plowed into his back.

"Two for one." Vincent Hadler towered in the doorway. "My lucky day."

Shane dropped the books. "Get out," he shouted in a vicious tone Cassie had never heard him use.

"You need a lesson in manners." The older man slid his leering gaze from Shane to Cassie. "So do you."

"You're the one who needs to learn manners," Cassie said, forcing her voice to remain steady.

"You won't keep that sass for long, babe." Hadler's sneer scraped her nerves.

Cassie rubbed her arms to soothe the sting.

"You won't lay a paw on her." Shane stepped ahead to shield Cassie.

Hadler flicked his open hand toward Shane's face, causing him to wince. Hadler laughed. A cold, spiteful laugh that slithered down Cassie's spine and coiled into the pit of her stomach.

Shane's head snapped up, his face twisted in an ugly snarl. Thrusting his shoulder into Hadler's chest, he slammed the bulkier man into the door frame.

"Run," Shane yelled at Cassie, but the two men blocked her exit.

Hadler rammed his fist into Shane's side. Shane doubled over, gasping. Hands clasped, Hadler hammered Shane's back until he dropped on one knee.

Cassie snatched the library books off the floor. The first one skimmed Hadler's shoulder as he lunged for Shane. The second landed with a solid smack against Hadler's ear.

Bellowing, he turned and stalked toward Cassie.

Now she understood why Vincent Hadler gave her the creeps. He was crazy dangerous and mad-dog mean.

"Cassie!" Shane grabbed Hadler's waist. "Run!"

Heart thundering, she raced toward the open door. As she reached the threshold, her head jerked violently.

"You aren't going anywhere." Hadler's fingers corkscrewed through Cassie's hair. He hauled her back inside the apartment and kicked the door closed. "Yet."

Shane pushed to his feet. Blood oozed from a jagged cut at the edge of his mouth. "Let her go."

"She owes me a dance and my balls an apology." Hadler pulled her close and yanked her hair so that her head tilted backward to touch his chest. He leaned down, running his nose along the curve of her jaw, then licked her ear. "I intend to collect."

Disgusted, Cassie refrained from kicking her heel into his shin, afraid he'd snap her neck.

"Leave her the fuck alone before I snatch that cocky smile off your face and shove it up your ass." Shane stepped forward, his hands clenched. Gone was the carefree young man Cassie had known. If someone could drop dead from a look, this Shane McQuarrie would definitely be a killer.

"Don't be stupid, *boy*. This fight ain't about you." Hadler released Cassie's hair, snaking his hand up her stomach to squeeze her breast. "Walker took something from me. Now I'm going to take something from him."

"You're insane." Cassie slammed her sneakered foot down on Hadler's ankle.

He cried out, loosening his grip. Cassie wrenched free. Shane charged, and the two men crashed to the floor.

Cassie bolted into the bedroom and locked the door to the sound of shattering glass. She rushed to the window. There was no ledge or balcony to climb. Just a straight drop from the third floor to the graveled ground. Her heart pounded, ready to make the jump with or without the rest of her.

The door splintered open.

"Come along nice and quiet," Vincent Hadler panted, sweat-streaked and bloody from the nasty cuts on his face and arms. "Or Shane dies."

Brice froze in the kitchen. He couldn't think. Couldn't breathe. Couldn't speak.

Not that Cassie would hear him if he did.

Shane's scent lingered in the cabin, so they couldn't have been gone long.

The handwritten note slipped from Brice's cold, stiff fingers. A snarl, so deep, so vicious, so ridiculously primal erupted from his chest and thawed his nerves.

Heading out the door, he shouted into his cell phone. "Where is Shane's den?"

"Chatuge View apartments, number twenty," Gavin answered. "What's wrong?"

"He took Cassie." Brice climbed into his Maserati and spun out of the driveway.

Cassie had left him. Packed her things and left.

The raging fire in his heart flared to such an intensity that he feared his chest might spontaneously combust. He had to make this right. Make Cassie understand how much he needed her. Walker's Run coursed through his blood, but Cassidy Albright inhabited his soul.

Turning sharply into the apartment complex parking lot, the wheels squealed on the dusty asphalt. Tristan paused at the outdoor stairs.

Brice slammed to a stop beside Shane's vehicle. Cassie's suitcases were visible in the truck bed.

Tristan loped over, concern shadowing his smile. "You here to see me?"

"Shane," Brice answered through gritted teeth.

"Me, too. I'm responding to a 911 call from a neighbor who reported a disturbance in his apartment."

"Dammit! He has Cassie." Brice darted up the stairs three at a time.

On the third floor landing, Tristan shoved past Brice and planted himself in front of Shane's door. "I'm here on official business. Wait outside until I say it's okay for you to come in."

"I'm not leaving without Cassie."

"I know." Tristan rang the doorbell. "I'll make sure Shane doesn't do anything stupid."

Nothing moved inside the apartment. "Shane, open up. It's Tristan."

"For chrissakes." Brice shoved open the door. The stench of sour milk nearly curdled his stomach.

"Cassie?" Brice yelled, weaving around the overturned recliner. Glass littered the carpet. Something or someone had smashed the coffee table.

"Brice." Tristan yanked him by the collar. "Go outside or I'll drag you out and handcuff you to the rail."

"Tristan," Brice growled.

"Until I know different, this is a sheriff's office matter. Now go." Tristan's hand landed squarely on Brice's chest. "The longer you stand there and glare at me, the longer it will take for me to clear the scene. Do you understand?"

Though it nearly killed him to do so, Brice backed out of the apartment. He had no idea how long he stood outside, because his thoughts ran rampant with the images of what he'd seen in Shane's living room and the fact that Cassie hadn't answered when he called. She would have if she were there and in any condition to respond.

Brice's heart drilled his chest. The high-velocity vibration nearly drowned out Tristan's all clear.

Brice sprinted inside. Cassie wasn't in the bedroom, bathroom or closet. He dashed into the kitchen where Shane, sprawled on the floor, moaned. Tristan helped him sit up. The pup's right eye had swollen shut. He bled from his nose, mouth, a large gash at his temple and various minor cuts on his body. He'd taken a beating but had no apparent life-threatening injuries.

"Where is Cassie?" Squatting, Brice grabbed the young man by the shirt.

Shane's glassy eyes were vacant, and he had trouble focusing.

"Give him a second." Tristan gripped Brice's shoulder. "Someone knocked him cold."

"Cassie?" Shane's bloodied mouth twisted. He pushed against Tristan in a discombobulated effort to stand.

"Dammit! Where is she?" Brice clutched Shane's arm, helping to steady him.

"Hadler," Shane said, thick and slow.

A tremor rocked Brice's soul. Vincent Hadler had a reputation for cruelty, among other unmentionable things.

"Where did he take her?" Tristan asked calmly, when Brice wanted to shake the answer out of Shane. Every second they lost waiting for his response was another second Cassie faced mortal danger. Alone.

"An abandoned house on the northwest side of the territory." Shane's tongue flicked the jagged cut on his bottom lip, and his mouth crumpled in a painful grimace. "Hadler said you'd remember it from five years ago."

"The old MacGregor place?" Brice clawed at the tension tightening around his neck. Only a handful of people knew the location of the rogue attack. Hadler shouldn't have been one of them.

"I tried to stop him." Shane spat blood on the kitchen's stone-patterned linoleum floor. "He's baiting you for a challenge, Brice."

"He's got one." Brice spun on his feet to leave.

"Whoa." Tristan blocked his path. "I can't let you go off half-cocked. You have a duty to this pack."

"My duty is to Cassie." Brice shook off Tristan's restraining hand. "She's my mate."

"It's not just you he wants." Shane's glacial eyes suddenly looked decades older than the pup's actual years. "Hadler wants the pack."

"That's never going to happen." Brice gave Tristan a commanding look. "Call my dad, then get Shane checked out at the clinic."

"You can't go after Hadler alone." Tristan refused to step aside.

"I'm not." Brice bouldered him out of the way, pulled the cell phone from his hip pocket and headed to the car.

"I need you," Brice said when the call was answered. "Be ready."

# Chapter 37

Cassie's fingers ached from clutching the passenger door armrest. Her heart's hard, steady beat kept her from a dead faint.

*Please let Shane be okay*, Cassie prayed, even though her prayers often went unanswered.

"You aren't allowed to hurt me." She feigned bravado.

"Who's gonna stop me?" Vincent Hadler's coarse laughter caused the bile in Cassie's stomach to spew into her throat. Apparently, Wahyan laws against harming humans didn't matter if no one was around to enforce them.

She needed to figure a way out of this mess on her own. Shane might not wake up in time to tell someone what happened, if he woke up at all. And after yesterday's argument and the note she'd left, Brice wouldn't waste his time on her ever again.

Until she'd met him, Cassie had absolute confidence in her ability to take care of herself. His arrival had sucked her into a dangerous new world where her survival skills were sorely lacking.

"What are you going to do me?" The scenery whirred past the car window in nondescript shapes and colors. Drab. Boring. Nothing worth notice. Same as her life.

"Whatever I want." The filthy grime in his voice slicked her skin. His gaze drifted from the road to the rise and fall of Cassie's chest from her quickened breaths. His tongue darted between his lips to gloss his lecherous smile. "Maybe I'll make that Walker boy watch us before I kill him."

Cassie's spine stiffened, tightening her stomach and increasing her urge to hurl. "Brice won't come. He doesn't care about me."

If he actually wanted Cassie to be part of his life, he wouldn't have walked away from her. Brice Walker was the type of man who fought for what he wanted. Yesterday, he hadn't even tried.

She couldn't blame him, though. She'd caused him nothing but trouble since he'd shown up naked in her bedroom. Correction, *his* bedroom.

"Oh, he'll come." Hadler eased off the gas pedal, and every muscle in Cassie's body clenched. "You see, humans act based on their emotions—" he turned off the highway "—which makes your kind unpredictable. Wahyas act on instinct. He'll come because I took something that belongs to him."

"I'm not some*thing*. I'm some*one*." Cassie readied herself. "And I don't belong to anyone."

"I'm about to change that, *Sunshine*. Walker owes me. You and his pack are his retribution."

The car jostled over deep potholes in the washed-out road. Through the thick nest of trees, Cassie glimpsed a farmhouse. While Hadler's attention focused on not driving them into a ravine, she shoved open the car door and jumped.

She slammed into a ditch, pain searing her shoulder. Seconds later, the car careened to a stop.

Cassie rolled to her feet and ran for her life. The soft soil beneath her sneakers grabbed at her feet, and the muscles in her legs strained to propel her forward.

In one week, Cassie had ended up right where she started. Being chased by a wolfman.

*"I'm coming, Cas. Do whatever you can to stay safe. I will find you. I promise."*

Cassie shook Brice's imagined voice from her mind. This wasn't the time to succumb to delusions. She wove through a thicket of trees. Sapling limbs snagged bits of her hair, yanking strands from her scalp. Unforgiving branches and leaves scratched her arms as she protected her face. Sweat and blood trickled down her skin. She had a hard time catching her breath.

Up ahead she saw the farmhouse, run-down and abandoned. The place she ran to for safety didn't look safe at all.

Stopping, she swallowed the bitter frustration that in the

dead of nowhere, no one but Vincent Hadler would hear her scream.

Cassie smashed face-first into the dirt. Air gushed from her lungs in a sharp, agonizing *oomph*. The heavy paws digging into her shoulders turned into thickset hands.

"I don't do foreplay." Hadler flipped Cassie onto her back. He forced open her mouth with a bruising kiss and rubbed his sweaty, naked body against her.

Repulsed, Cassie bit his tongue.

"Bitch!" He slapped her face.

She tasted the vileness of his blood.

"Do that again and I'll—"

Cassie rammed her palm up his nose. Hadler howled, bloodcurdling and fierce. The moment he fell off her, Cassie sprang to her feet in an all-out run. If she could make it back to the car—

She slammed to the ground again. This time, her hands braced the fall.

"Before this day is through, I'll see that wild streak tamed." Hadler the man tugged at her snug jeans.

"Get off me." Cassie grabbed a broken tree branch and whacked him upside the head. The blow stunned him long enough for her to wiggle out from beneath his weight.

On her feet and running, Cassie heard Hadler the wolf gaining ground. Fear should've powered her momentum. Instead, her body lumbered in slow motion, except for her heart, which beat so fast that the thumps blended into a continuous thrum.

The third time Hadler tackled her, Cassie's strength failed. Even though her brain screamed for her to get up, she simply couldn't move. Cruel laughter slithered along her skin, its venom poisoning her last bit of hope.

Suddenly a black blur streaked over her head and knocked Vincent Hadler from her back.

Before she could breathe easy, piercing crystal-blue eyes peered at her down the snout of a russet-colored wolf.

"Rafe?" Cassie's voice trembled.

He sat on his haunches and shifted into his human form. "Let's go, Red." He helped her stand.

"We can't leave Brice." Cassie clutched Rafe's arm until her legs stopped wobbling.

"I promised to get you out of here. And that's exactly what I'm going to do."

Cassie glanced at the gray and black wolves circling each other. Spittle glistened on their bared teeth. Their growls crescendoed.

Panic squeezed her heart. "Please, Rafe. You have to help him."

"I am." Rafe's steely eyes narrowed. His pupils tightened into vertical slivers. "By doing exactly what he asked. So, unless you want me to knock you out and carry you to the Jeep, *run!*"

Brice wouldn't say that he relaxed the moment Cassie bolted out of the woods with Rafe snapping at her heels, but he definitely found it easier to concentrate. Instead of sidestepping the gray wolf's latest advance, Brice returned the charge.

Surprised, Hadler retreated.

*"Scared?"* Brice taunted the older male.

*"I ain't afraid of you."* Hadler pointed his grizzled muzzle at Brice.

*"You should be. You stole my mate."*

*"She ain't yours no more."* Hadler's laughter clanged in Brice's mind as he fled deep into the forest.

White-hot and blistering, pure fury pulsed through Brice's veins. Instinct demanded that he charge blindly after the gray wolf. Reasoning cautioned against the impulse.

Hadler hadn't accomplished what he implied. Once Brice had connected with Cassie through the mate-bond, he sensed everything she experienced. If Hadler had made good on his boast, the ethereal link between Brice and Cassie would've been broken.

His mind unfettered by the taunt, Brice focused on where his paws landed during the nearly two-mile chase through the thicket. The old, nagging ache in his leg became a constant reminder that if he hadn't stepped into that trap years ago, Mason wouldn't have died. Cassie would've been safe. And so would the pack.

Following Hadler over a fallen tree, Brice's front paws absorbed the impact of the jump before his hind feet touched down.

Hadler whipped around. *"Remember this place?"*

Digging his nails into the muck, Brice slammed to a stop. *"I'm not likely to forget it."* His life had gone awry in this cove.

*"We have that, and the taste of Sunshine, in common,"* Hadler sneered.

Brice's tendons pulled and stretched at the restraint it took to keep from lunging prematurely. *"You and I have nothing in common."*

*"Maybe you need your memory rattled."* The gray wolf hunkered down.

Braced for the full-body slam, Brice felt the impact reverberate along every nerve. Toppling, their vicious snarls followed them down.

Brice's teeth sank into Hadler's furry flesh. Blood pooled in Brice's mouth, bitter and rancid.

Yelping, Hadler thrashed until he jarred hard enough to break free. Brice scraped his tongue against his teeth. God, he wanted to throw up.

Thick ribbons of drool dangled from the corners of Hadler's twisted mouth. His obsidian eyes gleamed with maniacal arrogance as he slammed Brice's right side.

The ache in Brice's leg turned into a fiery throb; the flames scalded all the way up his hip. Silencing the scream of pain searing his throat, Brice chomped Hadler's exposed ear, even as Hadler's teeth slashed across Brice's shoulder.

Locked in a deadly waltz, they snapped and bit any vulnerable spot to gain dominance. Soon the air became saturated with the coppery smell of blood and the pungency of wolfan male sweat.

Dark, terrifying memories invaded Brice's vision, followed by a disoriented sense of eerie familiarity. His gut wrenched.

*"Kill them all,"* Mason demanded. So clear and lifelike that Brice jerked his head to look behind him, allowing Hadler to escape.

Angered by the figment of his imagination, Brice stalked a semicircle around the aged pine Hadler used for cover. Brice's shoulder burned. Blood stung his left eye from the gash above his brow, and his right hind leg trembled from the sharp, shooting pain.

An arid breeze ruffled his fur. Brice's muzzle tingled and twitched, and the sensation of hot pokers singeing his nostrils caused his nose to run. He snorted several times to clear his nasal passages.

The pervasive wind continued to tease and torment his olfactory sense until, just as quickly as it had started, the stinging in his nose stopped. His next full breath drew in a repugnant musk. The fuzzy part of his memory erupted in singular clarity. Next came a primal fury.

After the attack, when asked how many rogues he'd seen, Brice answered four because that's how many bodies were found. In truth, he couldn't remember. Not as a man, anyway.

His wolf knew, though. The wolf had always known. The rogues numbered five.

From the pit of his stomach rose a heart-stopping, nerve-numbing howl.

*"Took you long enough to remember."* Hadler's cruel, telepathic laughter shredded Brice's conscience.

*"You murdered my brother."* Brice's body shook from the surge of primitive hormones and the fight to keep the primal rush from pushing him to the feral edge. *"Stole my mate. And dare to take my pack?"*

*"That about sums it up."* The gray wolf eased from behind the tree, a toothy grin plastered on his snout.

*"Was that your plan from the beginning? To seize control of Walker's Run?"* Brice crouched, ready to spring.

*"I didn't give a shit about your pathetic pack. I had a job to do."* Hadler snorted. *"But you went and made it personal."*

"I made it personal? You son of a bitch. You killed my brother!"

"Mason was the job, nothing more. But you got involved and slaughtered my packmates. So I'm goin' to do the same to yours. Starting with that tasty little redhead."

"You'll have to go through me."

"I intend to." The gray wolf barreled into Brice's hindquarter. Excruciating pain speared down his right hip and leg and strangled his breath.

Hadler plowed into him again. Brice tried to block the pain from his thoughts. He needed air. Lots of air. No matter how much he gulped, he couldn't find enough air to fill his lungs.

Sharp teeth pierced the soft spot close to his jugular. Not a kill bite, but a taunting one. Brice buckled from the pressure.

*"I'm disappointed,"* Hadler sneered, locking his jaw. *"I expected more of a fight."*

Brice's struggle to dislodge Hadler was fruitless. Lightheaded and losing strength, Brice focused his thoughts on the spot where his brother had died.

*I'm sorry, Mace.* Brice's heart tightened. *I've failed you, and everyone else, again.*

The warmth of a hand grazed Brice's shoulder. Mason's voice whispered the same words he'd said when Brice had stepped in the steel trap.

*Hold on, little brother. Today isn't your day to die.*

A howl sounded on the ridge and a lone, golden wolf charged down the slope.

*Mason?*

It wasn't possible.

*"I'll see you dead if it's the last thing I do."* The golden wolf plowed into the gray and knocked Brice free.

By the time Brice caught his breath and scrambled to his paws, the young wolf had engaged the older in a death quarrel. Brice hesitated to join. Two against one wasn't a fair fight. He wouldn't succumb to the despicable tactic Hadler used against Mason.

*"Oh, I'll be the last thing you see, but I'll be far from dead."* The gray latched onto to the golden's shoulder and drove him into a tree. Unconscious, the injured wolf crumpled into a heap in his human form.

Hadler rounded on Brice. Bloody spittle dribbled from his sneering muzzle. *"The same goes for you."*

Five years ago, Brice swore he'd never kill again. Today he would break that promise. He launched into Hadler, ripping through fur and flesh.

Hadler's yelps fell on unsympathetic ears. This wolfan had killed Mason, kidnapped Cassie and threatened Brice's family and friends. No matter what happened to Brice, Vincent Hadler would not leave this cove alive.

Hadler threw his weight into Brice's bad leg, forcing a momentary retreat. Wild-eyed and panting heavily, the gray wolf glared at Brice.

*"I had you dead before that piece of shit interfered."* Hadler tipped his head toward the young man beginning to stir.

*"Maybe. Maybe not. But I'm right here, you son of a bitch. Come and get me."*

Snarling, Hadler dived through the air. His legs stretched in a pointed formation.

Brice waited until the last possible moment to rear on his hind legs to catch the gray wolf by the neck. Brice's teeth pierced muscles and cartilage. He tasted dirt and hair and the nauseating tang of blood. With one hard jerk, he ripped open the gray wolf's throat.

Vincent Hadler the man flopped to the ground. Brice felt no pride or elation at what he'd done, only relief that Hadler would never threaten anyone again. He was also grateful that Cassie hadn't witnessed the brutality.

Vincent Hadler's other victim shifted into his wolfan form and charged. Brice backed out of his path. Instead of goring Hadler's throat to share in the kill as Brice expected, the golden wolf eviscerated the man's genitals.

Sympathy for the abuse Shane must've suffered at Hadler's cruel, lascivious hands twisted Brice's heart.

Vincent Hadler's horrified expression was the one he took to the grave. His last breath drowned in a gurgling wheeze.

Brice shifted and laid a gentle hand on the golden wolf's scruff. "Easy, pup. He won't hurt you or anyone else again."

The young wolf's entire body trembled. A second later, Shane drew a shaky breath. "I had to be sure."

Brice glanced over the bruises darkening Shane's skin. Some were from the fight at the apartment, though the discoloration over his ribs probably came from Hadler slamming him into the tree trunk. "Tristan should've taken you to the clinic."

"I didn't need Doc." Shane wiped the blood from his face on his arm. "I needed to finish this."

"I appreciate your help, Shane. You gave me time to get my second wind."

"You would've found a way to beat him. I just needed to be a part of it, you know?" Shane turned quickly, the contents of his stomach emptying on the ground.

"Easy does it." Brice kept his hand on Shane's shoulder.

A series of howls broke through the woods. Most prevalent was the Alpha's call. A sense of déjà vu swept over Brice. Only Shane wasn't Mason. And Brice was far from dying.

Physically, anyway. His heart and soul continued to teeter on shaky ground. How would he ever convince Cassie to accept him after all this?

Wiping his mouth, Shane shot a glance at Hadler's mutilated corpse. "I'd rather not wait around to explain that."

"No one in Walker's Run will judge you for what Hadler did to you."

Shane remained quiet, his gaze lowered.

"Think you can make it out to the road?" Brice asked.

"Yeah, I'm okay."

"Good." Brice shifted into his wolf, howled his response to the wolf calls and turned his muzzle to Shane, who also shifted. *"Let's get the fuck out of here."*

# Chapter 38

Cassie flicked the nearest air vent closed. It was too hot to sit inside the Jeep without running the air conditioner and too cold with the stream blowing directly on her.

Although aggravated, Cassie didn't try to escape her vehicular prison. She had nowhere to go until she knew Brice was safe. At least he wasn't facing Vincent Hadler alone now.

Shane arrived as she and wolfy Rafe reached the Jeep. Shane turned wolf—his clothes disintegrating during the shift—and darted into the woods. Thankfully Rafe didn't try to stop him. He simply shoved her inside the Jeep, yanked his clothes off the seat, and set up guard like a rottweiler.

Barefooted, dressed in a pair of jeans and an unbuttoned shirt, he patrolled the perimeter of the Jeep, his arms crossed high over his chest. No one made it past Rafe to question her.

Not even Gavin Walker, who had arrived with Tristan and Mr. Coots. There might have been some teeth bared during the growl fest, but she wasn't one hundred percent sure, because Dr. Habersham stepped in and blocked her view.

Clutching Brice's clothes, Cassie breathed in his scent. Clean and woodsy. Cassie hugged herself, remembering the way he made her feel safe and secure.

Her eyes burned, and a hot lump of gratitude formed in her throat. Brice had come for her. Maybe there was something to this mate-bond thing after all. Maybe she could become a part of his life. But could she ever be a part of *them*?

She studied the throng of Wahyas. Once the Walkers and their entourage arrived, a series of loud bays commenced until answered by a single, crisp, clear howl that Cassie instinctively recognized as Brice. Utter relief made her lightheaded.

The jubilant cheers had since subsided. The minutes dragged, and Cassie spotted a definite restlessness among the wolf people. Their jerky head nods and squinted glances in her direction were hard to miss. If Brice didn't make an appearance soon, Cassie wondered if they would turn on her.

She immediately regretted her thoughts. The Walkers, Shane, Hannah and Tristan were nice, decent people who wouldn't hurt her or anyone else. She might've included Rafe, but he had threatened to knock her out, and the way people backed away from him whenever he snapped at them for getting too close—well, he might be a little more dangerous than she ever imagined.

A hush spread through the crowd. Cassie leaned against the window and peered in the direction they had turned. Her heartbeat marked the passing of each second until two wolves emerged.

"Brice!" Cassie absconded from the Jeep in total disregard of Rafe's orders to stay put.

The throng of people split, giving her a clear path as she ran. A golden wolf edged away from the black. By the time Cassie reached him, Brice had changed into his human form.

He scooped her into his arms and swung her in circles, holding her so tight that she couldn't breathe. She didn't care that he was dirty, sweaty and bloody, or that she might pass out from lack of oxygen. He was alive. That's all that mattered.

"You're safe, baby," he crooned in her ear. "Hadler won't hurt you or anyone else again."

"He's dead, isn't he?" She sucked in her breath.

"Yes." Brice set Cassie on her feet. "I had to put him down to keep everyone safe. You understand that, don't you?"

"I want to." Cassie clung to Brice. The powerful beat of his heart thumped a reassuring rhythm. "But I can't handle anything else. I'm at my limit."

"Trust me to handle what you can't." His fingers sifted through her hair before his thumbs hooked beneath her jaw, tilting her face to his. "When you feel the urge to run, run to me, not away."

His lips brushed her mouth in a kiss that electrified her

body. She wanted to trust him, to believe the bond he claimed existed between them was real. In time, maybe she'd overcome the hesitation to put all her faith in someone other than herself.

Rafe handed Brice his pants. He dressed, answering his father's questions. A few times Brice nodded toward Shane, wrapped in a saddle blanket Tristan had given him.

A black car bearing the Walker's Run logo bounced to a stop. The crowd's excitement escalated from a mosquito hum to a full-blown roar. Anticipation built as Booker Reynolds, Adam Foster, Philip Bartolomew and Michael Krussen exited the vehicle.

"It appears we're too late." Michael's stern gaze targeted Brice. "Of all people, I would've expected a better handling of the situation from you."

"Some things can't be negotiated," Brice replied. "Protecting my mate, my family and my friends, among them."

"Unless I'm mistaken, you haven't claimed a mate." Booker's upper lip lifted in a derisive curl.

"I claimed him," Cassie said over her thundering heart. Normally she didn't make her private affairs public. However, now it seemed prudent.

Brice lifted his arm to show everyone the faded bruise from Cassie's bite.

"Your mark is meaningless." Booker looked down his long, slender nose at Cassie.

"Not to me." The harsh lines around Brice's eyes and mouth faded in the brightness of his smile when he looked at her.

Cassie relaxed, knowing she'd said the right thing.

"You are out of control. You killed a man who posed no threat to you." Booker's nostrils flared, pulling back his lips to expose his canines. "We were leaving this afternoon."

"Vincent Hadler wasn't going anywhere." A chill rose from Cassie's clenched stomach. "He wanted to take over Walker's Run. He said the pack and I were his retribution."

"For what?" Philip asked over the crowd's murmurs.

"I killed Hadler's packmates." Brice's crisp, clear voice silenced the whisperings. "Because they killed Mason."

Cassie's breath caught in her throat. For a split second, time was suspended as if a black hole imploded, sucking sound and oxygen, thought and reason into a glass vacuum. No one moved, not even a blink.

Then everything rushed forward with the speed of an Amtrak making up for lost time. The vibration of two dozen voices yelling at once gloved Cassie's skin with the eeriness of walking into a hundred spiderwebs. She rubbed her arms, but the sensation bore into her muscles and anchored in her bones.

Cassie glanced at Brice. His clamped jaw stretched his skin in such a way that it sharpened his facial features. He resembled a marble carving of an avenging angel. She sensed the violence in him and his restraint.

Yes, he had an animalistic side, but Brice also had compassion and intelligence. For that, Cassie was grateful. If Brice and his kind turned into vicious animals to handle every problem, Cassie would never be comfortable living among them.

Wait—was she actually considering a life with him?

Her stomach rolled in a loop-the-loop. The fun kind, like the thrill of flying upside down on a roller coaster. Only this wasn't the time to be heady.

Vincent Hadler was dead.

Now that everyone knew who had murdered Mason Walker, Cassie hoped Brice would let go of the past. Although from the way he ground his teeth, he had quite a bit more to say before he could.

"Hadler said someone hired them to kill Mason." Brice turned to his father. "They were tracking us all along. It wasn't my fault. I'm not the reason Mason died."

"I never thought you were, son." The sternness in Gavin Walker's face softened. "No one did."

Brice's breath escaped in a rush. Even as apparent peace settled between father and son, discontent bobbed among the crowd.

"Booker." Abigail Walker's voice wavered, and Gavin laced his fingers through hers.

The sweet gesture of unity broke open Cassie's heart. Sick of self-imposed isolation, she craved the comfort of family and friends.

Brice kissed the crown of her head, and his warmth spread through her, down to the soles of her feet. Still, she wondered how much of his affection stemmed from the promise he'd made to Margaret.

Vows were solemn to Brice. Would he ever see her as more than an obligation to fulfill? How would she ever know the truth?

"Did you know Vincent had attacked my sons?"

"Abigail." Although Booker's arms opened in a supplicant manner, his cold, beady eyes ruined the effect. "Brice accuses a wolfan unable to defend his honor. It's understandable that you want to believe him, but Brice has been under significant stress. His accusation isn't credible."

"Do you have proof?" Michael addressed Brice.

"I finally recognized Hadler's true scent, and he was more than happy to brag. That's all the proof I needed." Brice exuded so much confidence that Cassie believed anyone who doubted him would have to be crazy.

"Forgive me." Booker dramatically waved his hand over his heart. "I require something more substantial than hearsay and your fluctuating sense of smell."

Brice's unconcerned shrug reflected the crowd's attitude. It appeared all stood behind him one hundred percent.

"I accept Brice's word." Philip's authoritative reply eased some of Cassie's apprehension. "The council would not have offered him an apprenticeship if we had any doubts about his credibility or integrity."

"Apprenticeship?" Cassie's question drowned in the crowd's collective gasp. Apparently Brice had kept this news from everyone. Was he planning to leave just when she was warming to the idea of staying?

"This is an outrage," Booker bellowed above the bustle. "The council cannot be tainted by wolfans with impure bloodlines."

"The council is aware of your elitist position, Booker. However, we do not share it," Philip snapped. "On every task presented, Brice demonstrated the aptitude and temperament the council seeks."

"As did Brice's brother," Michael added. "Since we now know that his death wasn't a matter of circumstance, I must ask, Booker, was Vincent Hadler operating on your order when he killed Mason Walker?"

Unless the morning sun had wreaked havoc on Cassie's eyes, the bronze color in Booker's face lightened about three shades. A faint grimace flickered across his standard bland expression.

"Booker." Abigail walked to him and smacked him hard across the face. An angry splotch of red stained his cheek. "You son of a bitch. How could you do this to me?"

Cassie expected Booker Reynolds to deny involvement, to sweet-talk Abigail Walker and make people believe there had been a grave misunderstanding.

"You were mine," Booker's unrepentant voice thundered.

"I was never yours." Abigail's pronouncement muffled Booker's echo.

An eerie stillness engulfed the entire area. No gasps or whispers emanated from the crowd. No birds chirped. No bugs hummed. No cars rumbled on the road. No planes trekked across the sky. The wind suddenly fell into oblivion.

Cassie dragged her gaze from them to Brice. Like the others', his eyes were transfixed on his mother and her oldest friend.

"Brice," Cassie whispered, uneasy in the heightening tension. "Stop this before it gets out of hand."

"You would've been mine, Abigail. Should have been mine." Booker's face turned a deep cranberry. The veins at his temples bulged, as did those in his neck. He pointed a long, spindly finger at Gavin. "That half-breed stole you from me, defiled you with his seed, and there was nothing I could do to save you." Indignant and proud, Booker tugged at his coat lapel. "However, I won't allow his abomination to desecrate the sacredness of the Woelfesenat."

"Mason and Brice are not abominations. They are my children. I conceived them. Carried them. Birthed them. Nursed them at my breast. They are mine, Booker. You are the one who stole from me!" Her last word rolled into a growl. She sprang into the air as a sleek black wolf.

Booker Reynolds's startled eyes bugged and his faced paled as all the color spewed out of the gaping hole where his neck had been.

A deafening scream ricocheted around Cassie. Her burning throat steamed the air she swallowed. No longer could she feel Brice's strength or the warmth of his body. The sunlight failed, casting shadows everywhere. Her heart banged in her head but couldn't silence the roaring vortex that sucked the crowd, the woods and everything in between into a frenzied whirlpool of dark chaos.

# Chapter 39

Fucking hell breaking loose was nothing compared to a pack of Wahyas hell-bent on vengeance. Grateful Cassie fainted before the frenzy exploded into insanity, Brice swung her over his shoulder and rushed behind Rafe, who cleared a path to the Jeep.

No one in the pack would hurt Cassie. On that Brice would stake his life. However, if she saw the frenzy of wolves descending on Booker Reynolds's remains, she would never get the savagery out of her mind.

It was bad enough for her to witness the first strike. Brice hadn't anticipated such an immediate reaction from his mother. Of course, he hadn't expected Reynolds to confess, either. A call for a formal hearing in front of a fully seated Woelfesenat would've been more logical.

Too late for that now. Philip and Michael would have to sort out the mess in the coming days.

No wolfan would deny Abigail Walker her right to a mother's justice, so the inquiry would be a simple formality. One Brice intended to keep Cassie out of. An interrogation, no matter how delicately conducted, was still an interrogation.

Cassie said she'd reached her limit. This could break her.

Rafe helped them inside the Jeep. After turning the vehicle around, he drove over the bumpy trail slower than a blind man on a Sunday. However, once they reached the highway, he chunked caution into the ditch. They made the twenty-minute drive to the turn to the Walker's Run Resort in less than ten. Only when they passed the resort did he slow down again.

They meandered past the rentals and snailed the hairpin curve. The closer they came to the cabin, the more Brice's gut knotted. Rafe pulled to an easy stop in the driveway. Brice bounded up the steps with Cassie in his arms and headed straight to his room to lay her on the bed. Her face contorted as she took deep, staccato breaths. Her eyelids twitched open, and the fear in her eyes broke Brice's heart.

"I'm not going to hurt you," he insisted softly.

"Animals." Cassie's head bobbed in a tight, controlled shake. "You're a bunch of wild animals pretending to be human. There's nothing civil about you."

"What you saw was barbaric." Brice perched on the edge of the bed to take the weight off his throbbing leg. "But that only happens in extreme circumstances."

"It seems to me that it happens a lot." Cassie's accusatory gaze landed on his scarred throat. "Normal people don't rip out someone's throat."

"*Normal* is relative to species. We do what we have to do to protect those we love. Wahyas have their own justice, and today it was served." In his spirit, Brice felt Cassie falling away from him with the speed a runaway freight elevator.

"When I moved out the first time, I shouldn't have stopped in the hospital parking lot. I should've kept driving." She looked at him with large, defeated eyes. "You're never going to let me leave, are you? You're going to keep me here because of what I saw, because of what I know."

"You aren't a liability, Cas. You're my mate." Brice's heart climbed into his throat.

"Don't say that." She clasped her hands over her ears. "I don't want to be a part of this. Just leave me alone."

Brice reached for Cassie, wanting to calm her with his touch. She scurried to the far corner of the bed. Clamped in a flat seam, her lips whitened. The porcelain tone of her skin turned ashy.

There would be no reasoning with her today. Perhaps not any day. Fear spread through her spirit, attacking the tendrils of the mate-bond. The infection fed into Brice, but he refused to let it take hold. Each beat of his heart shouted "I love you" through the mate-bond.

The psychic declaration might've swayed a she-wolf. Cassie, however, drew her knees to her chin and buried her head beneath her arms. A total lockout.

Numb, Brice stood and walked to the door. "I'll have Doc come by to check on you."

"I've had my fill of wolves today. Thanks," she answered without lifting her head.

"Doc is human, Cas. You might feel better if you talked to him."

"I don't need a doctor. Want me to feel better? Then leave me the hell alone. I want my life back to the way it was before I learned about *werewolves*."

"As you wish." Brice backed out of the room. Pain banded around his chest, squeezing his heart until he felt it would burst. He wanted Cassie, needed her in his life.

At the moment, she required the opposite.

Air shredded his lungs. He staggered through the empty living room. The cabin that had always been his sanctuary closed in on him, stifling and stagnant. He had to get out.

Nearing the kitchen, he heard a metronomic squeak outside. Brice walked out onto the back porch. Rafe rocked in the porch swing. His inquisitive gaze swept Brice's face.

The squeak stopped.

"Sorry, man." Rafe was probably the only person who understood the utter desolation consuming Brice.

Unable to form words, Brice plopped next to him.

"So what are you going to do to fix this, Walker?"

"Exactly what she asked me to do. Leave her alone."


"Brice?" Cassie called, groggy from the sedative Doctor Habersham had given her despite her vehement protest.

Had she truly gone nuclear with her meltdown? Or had it happened in one of her endless nightmares?

"Brice?" Cassie regretted the awful things she'd said in her moment of sheer panic. "Are you here?"

Only silence answered. She shuffled out of bed and into the living room. The cold realization that she was all alone settled in the marrow of her bones. Shivering did nothing to dispel the hopeless feeling.

On the kitchen counter, she found a cell phone, a set of keys and a carefully folded note. Fear snaked around her heart like a python, ever so slowly squeezing the life out of her. She realized then how callous it had been to leave a note for Brice.

Her hands shook opening the letter.

My dearest Cassie,
I'll never regret the night I found you asleep in my bed. Nor can I forget how your touch warms my soul. You are my reason for living, but I cannot bear to be the cause of your fear.

I understand you need time to process all that has happened. Time to finish college and realize your dreams. I want to give you all the time you need, so I've agreed to work with the Woelfesenat on a peace-keeping project in Romania.

Please take care of the cabin in my absence. You know how much it means to me. The car in the driveway is from Rafe. It belonged to Lexi. It's good for him to let go of her things, so please don't give it back.

I will be close in spirit, Sunshine. Trust in me and in the bond that brought us together. I will return to you when I can. In the meantime, I leave you with these written words in the hope that one day you will want to hear them from my lips.
I love you with all my heart,
Brice.

A tidal wave of grief surged in Cassie's chest, crushing her in sorrow and regret. She'd been stupid. Selfish. Unyielding and cruel. Still, Brice professed his love.

A burning pain exploded in her heart, propelling agonizing shrapnel up her throat, into her head and behind her eyes. Her knees refused to hold her upright. She sank to the cold tile floor, wishing for a hole to swallow her whole.

For the first time since she was seven, Cassie cried.

# *Chapter 40*

A firm knock at the front door dragged Cassie from the lingering effects of the unwanted sedative and crying herself into exhaustion.

"Brice!" She jumped up and ran to the door. A stampeding rumble vibrated in her chest.

"Oh, Cassie!" Hannah reached for her. "I've been so worried."

Instinctively Cassie stepped backward.

Hannah came to an abrupt stop. "Are you all right?"

Dear, sweet Hannah. Loving mother. Kind coworker. *Savage wolf.*

Would Cassie ever be able to look at these people and not see them as a bunch of wild animals?

For Brice's sake, she had to try. She took a steadying breath.

"Physically, I'm okay." She motioned for Hannah to come inside. "The rest I'm not so sure about."

Hannah squeezed Cassie's hand. "You look terrible."

"Thanks." Cassie's forced laugh sounded strangled, and tears blurred her eyes. One by one they trickled down her face.

Hannah gave her a mother bear hug. "Now, now," she cooed. "Everything's going to be just fine. We're good people, Cassie. Everyone's worried sick about you."

"Hello, Cassie." Abigail Walker appeared in the doorway. "Forgive me for involving Hannah. I wasn't certain you'd open the door for me, and I need to speak to you. May I come in?"

An involuntary tremor coursed through Cassie's limbs. Hannah linked her arm around Cassie's waist.

Cassie appreciated the support. "Of course, Mrs. Walker."

"Call me Abby. There's no need to be formal." Sadness shadowed her smile.

"I need it to be this way." Too much had happened in too

short a time. In order to restore order in her life, Cassie needed some things to remain constant. "At least for now."

Abby made her way into the living room. "As you wish."

Cassie's breath stuck to her lungs. Brice had said that, too. The moment she saw him, Cassie intended to take back everything she'd said about wanting him to leave her alone. That had been a bald-faced lie. She was through with lies. From this point forward, she vowed to speak only the truth or not at all.

"I'll call you later," Hannah said.

"You're leaving me alone with her?" Cassie whispered.

"You'll be fine." Hannah smiled and closed the door behind her.

Abigail Walker sat politely on the couch. She looked delicate in cream-colored slacks and an emerald silk blouse, with not a hair on her head out of place. Nothing about her appearance suggested that hours ago, she had ripped out a man's throat with her bare teeth.

"Where's Brice?" Before listening to whatever Abigail Walker wanted to say, Cassie needed to make things right with Brice.

"On a plane to Romania with Philip," Abigail said softly.

"He's gone? Already?" Cassie edged over to the love seat and sat down, her hands limp in her lap. "I said awful things. I didn't mean them. I wanted to tell him… I wanted him to know—" Cassie couldn't push out the words, not when Brice couldn't hear them or see how much she meant them. "He said he loved me."

"Then he does, Cassie." Abigail looked tired and weathered, and her mouth trembled with a tentative smile. "Brice doesn't say things he doesn't mean."

"When will he come home?" Cassie wondered if the disassociated feeling of her body had anything to do with not being able to breathe. She longed to be tucked against Brice's chest. His embrace grounded her and kept her from drifting into nothingness.

"No one knows, and we won't be able to communicate

with him until he returns." Abigail rose gracefully and joined Cassie on the smaller couch. "I know that you were frightened by what happened this morning. What I did to Booker was something I had to do. One day, when you are a mother, I hope you'll understand and forgive me."

Abby unfolded the paper she pulled from her pocket and handed Cassie's resignation letter to her. "I believe you were under duress when you wrote this. Take some time. Be sure of what you want."

For the first time in a very long while, Cassie had no plan of action. Her heart hurt too much for her brain to figure out her next step. She had a place to live, a car and apparently her old job. She also had three new roommates waiting eagerly to welcome her and a new job on the college campus. "I don't know what to do."

Abigail smoothed back the tangled curls that curtained Cassie's face. "You are irreplaceable to the resort and to my family, Cassie. I know this acknowledgment comes late. It is nonetheless true."

Cassie traced her thumbnail over the lines in her palm. "You're only saying that because you believe Brice will come back for me. He won't. I know he won't because I can't feel him anymore."

"You're both hurting." Abigail's gaze searched Cassie's face. "When your emotions settle, you'll feel him, hear him again."

"How can you be sure?"

"Because I know my son." Abigail patted Cassie's leg. "Brice won't give up. He loves you."

"What if he made a mistake? What if everything between us is a fluke?"

"It isn't." Abigail's eyes crinkled. "When Gavin found Brice and Mason after they were attacked, neither of them was breathing. Doc put them on life support but didn't give us any hope that either would survive.

"Before Brice left, he told us what you did when he was

in the hospital, and we finally understood why we didn't lose him along with Mason.

"Your presence touched Brice. You gave him hope, helped him fight to live. Through that terrible time, the two of you forged a bond. One so strongly rooted that it survived five years of separation before you even had a chance to know each other truly. Your bond will continue to thrive if you don't shut him out.

"I know the things you've learned over the last week are difficult to process," Abigail said gently. "Try to put that aside for now and just allow yourself to believe in Brice, because he has put all his faith in you."

The ache in Cassie's heart became a numbing throb. No matter how much she wanted to believe, a lifetime of broken promises had taught her not to get her hopes up. Something always came along to smash them to smithereens.

"Can I get you something to drink, Mr. Bartolomew?" The leggy flight attendant flashed a too-white smile.

"Scotch with a lemon wedge and two ice cubes." Philip opened his briefcase.

"Mr. Walker?" She stooped next to Brice, thrusting her ample chest forward in his face.

"Water." Disinterested, Brice turned his attention outside the window of the Woelfesenat's private jet and focused on the dark blue waters of the Atlantic Ocean. Thousands of miles now separated him from Cassie. As much as it had nearly killed him to leave, he believed she needed time and space to work through her doubts and fears. He only wished that he would've had time to explain fully their connection through the mate-bond and the fact that she wouldn't truly be alone.

"It's been a horrendous week, Brice. How about something stronger?" The locks on Philip's briefcase snapped closed.

"Cassie doesn't like it when I drink."

"She isn't here to complain."

"She's always here, Philip." Brice tapped his chest.

Philip chuckled. "Fetch our drinks, Penny. And tell Anthony to start our supper."

"I'm not hungry," Brice grumbled.

"He will be by the time supper is served."

Brice not only heard the censure in Philip's voice but also sensed the councilman's ire. Unless sick or dying, wolfans didn't turn up their noses at food.

"Yes, Mr. Bartolomew." Penny's footsteps receded.

A thick file landed in Brice's lap. Irritated, he swung his gaze at Philip.

"Background information." Philip adjusted his seat to a slight recline.

Brice smacked the folder on the small table between them. "I told you earlier, I'll have time to read this in the car once we arrive in Bucharest."

"I know," Philip answered in a more gracious tone than Brice had given him. "I thought you could use the distraction."

"You thought wrong." Leaning against the headrest, Brice closed his eyes and counted.

Mason had taught him to count when angry. He'd said it would give him time to think rationally before responding.

Though Brice wasn't angry, the rote calmed him, for a short while, anyway. This had to be the millionth time he'd counted since he left Cassie.

He called to her through the mate-bond. Nothing stirred in his soul except a hollow clang.

The small village where he and Philip would headquarter for the negotiations lacked modern conveniences such as phones and internet. His only connection to Cassie would be the mate-bond. He didn't want to consider what would happen if she didn't respond eventually.

"It doesn't do any good to brood."

"I'm not." Brice snapped open his eyes. "I'm tired and frustrated and why the hell are you smiling like that?"

"Like what?" Philip feigned innocence.

"A hyena smoking weed." Brice dropped his growl at Penny's approach.

She set Philip's drink on the table and handed Brice a chilled bottle of designer water.

"I can work out that tension." Penny drew her fingers across Brice's shoulders. "To help you relax."

"Penny is an excellent masseuse." Philip winked. "She has very talented hands, among other things."

Brice caught her wrist before it drifted farther down his chest. "I don't want to relax."

"Are you sure I can't change your mind?" She puckered her lips in a suggestive pout.

"I doubt Mr. Walker will need anything further, Penny." Philip reached for his drink. "Except supper, of course."

"Very well." She gave Brice a lingering look.

Brice unscrewed the cap on the green teardrop bottle and downed the contents in one chug.

"Gulping isn't good for your digestion." Philip sipped his Scotch.

"You sound like my grandmother." Brice scanned the jet cabin for a garbage can. Not finding one, he tossed the bottle into the empty seat across the aisle.

"Margaret was a wise woman." Sadness dimmed Philip's eyes. "Your grandfather was one of my closest friends. Yet I envied him because of how much she loved him."

"You were in love with my grandmother?"

"No. I've never been in love. Never cared to be, except around them. They made it seem so amazing." Philip sighed. "You asked why I smiled. It's because watching you yearn for Cassie brings back memories of Nathan mooning over Margaret. You don't look a damn thing like him, but you sure got a whopping dose of his personality."

"Why is that so funny?" Brice frowned at Philip's laughter.

"You've allowed a human female to knot you up, same as he did."

"Make your point, Philip."

"I wasn't a believer in the mate-bond until I saw it thrive between your grandparents. Nothing in this world or beyond could've torn them apart."

"So I've heard."

"The same with your parents. And you and Cassie."

"Things are different for us. She doesn't believe in the bond, Philip. After everything that's happened, I'm not sure that she will trust me enough to let me in." Brice rubbed the ache in his chest that had persisted since Cassie's rejection.

"You worry too much. The bond is what it is. It doesn't wax or wane with the moon. It is a constant like the sun. Is it any wonder that you call her Sunshine?"

"I call her Sunshine because she makes me feel warm and alive. Now that we're apart, I feel like crap. When we arrive in Bucharest, you'll have my full attention. But for the time being, Philip, leave me the fuck alone."

# *Chapter 41*

Cassie sat on the edge of her chair and worried the tassel of the honor cord worn over her graduation gown.

She'd done it. She'd finally done it.

In a matter of minutes, Cassie would finally clutch that hard-earned degree in her hands.

The moment wasn't as fulfilling as she had imagined.

At least she wasn't alone. Somewhere in the building sat Hannah and Shane. Friends whom Cassie hadn't realized were friends until a couple of months ago.

Squinting over a blob of faceless people, she searched for Brice, although he'd sent no word that he would come. She simply hoped.

The man next to her stood, and Cassie followed him to the area where the cum laude graduates waited for their names to be called. Moments later, she clicked her low heels across the stage to receive the fruit of her labors and sacrifices. Accepting the chancellor's congratulatory handshake, Cassie wondered if what she'd gained was worth the loss.

*I'm so proud of you, Sunshine.*

*Brice?* Her lethargic heart cartwheeled. *I knew you'd come! Where are you?*

Cassie smiled at the photographer, dying for Brice's answer.

*I'm always with you.*

She walked away, smile still plastered to her face and disappointment clawing in her chest. She wanted him to be here physically. Not just in her head.

There were times she dreamed of his touch, of his loving her, and the dreams were so real that when she awoke her lips were swollen, her muscles were sore, and her skin tingled; but her heart always broke to discover the experience had been only her imagination.

Cassie returned to her seat and unfolded the note she had tucked in her sleeve. She smoothed the edges, frayed from the countless times she'd opened and reread her favorite part, *I love you.*

She loved him, too. Over the past three months, Cassie had realized that her efforts to escape the life her mother had given her had come to the same end. No roots, no ties. No worthwhile relationships to enrich her life.

In the short time Cassie had spent with Brice, there had been good and bad moments. And she would still rather have all those than none at all.

When the graduates stood one last time as a class, shouts went up along with a flurry of graduation caps. Then it was over.

Thank God for Hannah and Shane's noses. They found her before the convergence of people swept her away.

"Congratulations!" Hannah squeezed her. "I'm so happy for you. I know how hard you worked."

"I can hardly believe it." Cassie stared at the certificate holder that in two weeks' time would bear the official document validating her accomplishment.

Shane hugged her. "For someone who just got her degree, you don't look all that impressed."

"For a long time, I thought this was the most important thing in my life." Cassie smiled. "Things aren't important. People are, and you are two of my favorites."

"Woo-hoo!" Shane twirled her in a tight circle. "It's time to celebrate."

Shane and Hannah whisked Cassie off to a surprise party at the resort. She drifted through the crowd of coworkers and more than a few pack members. They offered her congratulations, hugged her neck and kissed her cheeks. For all its pizazz, the party seemed surreal.

Slipping into the sanctuary of the employee break room,

she sat at the round table where she and Brice had once shared a lunch. Had it been only three months? It seemed like a lifetime.

Maybe it was. She certainly wasn't the same woman Brice had startled from her bed.

"Skipping out of your own party?" Gavin Walker's soft voice lilted through the quiet room.

Cassie lifted her head from her hands. "I needed some downtime."

"I expect today has been bittersweet. I'm sure you're missing your mother, and mine."

Cassie bit back her tears. "And Brice."

Gavin sat in the seat across from her. "I hoped the party would fill some of the void."

"I don't know most of these people." She cringed at the strain in her voice. "Why are they here?"

"For you," he said.

"Why?"

"Because Brice loves you."

"I didn't let him claim me before he left. A lot may have happened since he's been gone. He may have found someone else."

"I know my son, Cassie." Gavin patted her hand with a gracious smile. "Nothing could change his mind or his heart where you are concerned."

"I'd feel better if he would tell me that in a card or letter. It's been three months and not a peep. What if something's happened to him?"

"Relax, hon. The Woelfesenat would've informed us if Brice became ill or had been hurt. Put your mind at ease. He'll be home soon."

"And if he isn't? Brice said that he had to claim a mate by Christmas or you'd banish him from Walker's Run."

"He told you about that?" Gavin swiped his hand over an embarrassed grin. "Brice and I were at odds when he came home. I said some things that I shouldn't have because I was desperate to keep him here. I would never turn him out. Walker's Run is a part of his soul, just like you are."

"Thanks, Mr. Walker." Cassie stood to hug him.

Gavin embraced her warmly. "I've always wanted a daughter," he whispered in her ear. "So I wouldn't mind if you called me Dad from time to time."

"Let's not get ahead of ourselves," Cassie said as her heart pinched. "I'm not mated or married to your son."

"Brice declared his intention, so the rest is just icing on the cake." Gavin tucked her arm beneath his, twitching his nose. "Speaking of cake, let's go cut yours."

Cassie wiped the steam from the bathroom mirror, ignoring the water seeping from her eyes. Brice had missed her graduation and her party. And the cherry pie she baked this morning was still on the counter, untouched.

She'd been so sure that he would show up tonight. It hurt that he hadn't. Without a way to communicate with him, she had a hard time fending off the doubts.

Cassie lifted Brice's jersey from the hook on the back door and slipped it over her head. The soft fabric against her skin always made her feel close to him.

She closed her eyes and hugged herself. "Brice, when are you coming home? I need you."

After several minutes of silence, Cassie stepped out of the bathroom and walked down the hallway to the bedroom. Climbing into bed, she heard a noise in the kitchen.

A tiny starburst of hope erupted in her chest. Squelching it, she tiptoed into the kitchen, baseball bat in hand—just in case—and flipped on the light.

"Brice?" Cassie's voice faltered.

There he stood, his arm shielding his eyes.

"Oh, God. I'm sorry." She dropped the bat and reached for the switch.

His hand closed over hers before she doused the light. She wanted to hug him, kiss him, but wasn't sure what he wanted.

"I see you found the pie." She nodded at the half-eaten dessert on the counter.

"I couldn't resist."

Finally. His voice—not the one stored in her memory, but his real voice—bathed her ears.

She didn't allow herself to luxuriate in the hum of his Southern baritone. It was too soon to fall back into old patterns. She needed to know if anything had changed for him in the months he'd been away.

She grabbed the coffeepot and went to the sink to fill the carafe to have something to do with her hands. "Everyone will be glad you're home."

"What about you, Cas?" He slipped behind her, shut off the water and took the glass pot from her shaky hands. His presence wrapped around her in a gentle persuasion, coaxing her down from the peak of her anxiety. "Are you glad I'm home?"

"Of course." Trying to express the deluge of feelings would turn her into blathering idiot. "Why wouldn't I be?"

"You weren't too happy with me or my kind when I left." His cheek brushed against her hair. The sweet familiarity broke open the ache she had carried in her chest since the day he'd left.

His strong arms circled her waist. "I missed you."

"I missed you, too." Missed him so much she thought she might die from the heartbreak. Those first few hours and days, when she felt completely and utterly abandoned, were the worst she'd ever known. Then one day a profound sense of Brice had electrified her being. Inexplicably, she had felt his relief, then pure, unadulterated joy. He passed one thought before the connection faded. *I love you.*

At the time, she hadn't known if the moment was real or imagined. She still didn't know.

The tenderness in the whisper-soft kisses he planted along the curve of her neck was a salve to the rawness she'd lived with for the last few months. But she didn't want simply to cover it up, pretend it wasn't there anymore until it festered into a poison that infected her body, mind and soul. "You left me." The words burned her throat. "You promised never to do that."

She might not have believed him at the time he made the oath, but she remembered it every single day he was gone.

His warm sigh scraped her skin, and her body responded with sweeping masses of chill bumps. He gave her enough room to turn in his arms, but he didn't step away. Brice's brow wrinkled beneath a tumble of hair. His eyes peered at her, sharp, guarded. "I said I wouldn't leave you to fend for yourself, and I didn't. I made sure you had a home and reliable transportation."

"And the promotion your mother offered me?" Cassie fingered the edge of his cable-knit sweater.

"I'm not involved in the resort's management, Sunshine. My mother wouldn't put someone in a position if she didn't have every confidence of success. Not even if I asked for a favor. Whatever she offered, you earned. But if you aren't happy with the additional responsibilities or aren't getting the experience you wanted, we can look for other alternatives. I want you to be happy, Cas."

"Even after what I said to you?" She couldn't look at him for an answer. Already teetering on the edge, if she lifted her gaze from her feet she just might fall.

"Did you mean it?"

"No." Cassie pressed her cheek against his chest. The horrible, shameful things she'd fired at him had come from fear and confusion.

Brice held her, tight and secure, and her fears of falling into oblivion subsided in the safety of his arms. "Baby, you were frightened and overwhelmed. Probably in a state of shock, as well."

"Then why did you leave?"

"You needed time to sift through your feelings, time to learn to trust yourself and to trust me."

"Do you still feel the same for me?" She held her breath, knowing her entire world rested on his response.

"No."

Cassie's stomach dropped to the floor, yet everything she'd eaten seemed to rise in her throat. She struggled to break free of Brice's hold before she threw up.

"Easy, Cas." Brice gently pushed up her chin, but she wouldn't open her eyes. "What I feel for you grew stronger every day we were apart."

His words soothed Cassie's tumultuous stomach. His long fingers curled around her hand and he placed it over his heart, beating a strong, steady promise. "Didn't you sense me? Hear me? Feel me, whenever I thought about you?"

"I thought it was my imagination." Brice's mother had tried to answer Cassie's questions about the phenomenon. The explanations fell short, not because of any lack in Abby's attempts to encourage her. What Cassie had needed, wanted, was Brice's assurance.

"The mate-bond kept us connected." He kissed her knuckles. "It will always keep us connected."

A thrill replaced the ache in her chest. "I heard your voice in my head at my graduation."

Brice gifted her with a devilish smile. "You were the most beautiful graduate I've ever seen."

"You were actually there? Not in my head?"

"I wouldn't miss one of the most important days of your life. And I have no intention of missing any of them, ever."

Emotion nearly overwhelmed her. Even though she didn't see him at the ceremony, to know he watched and supported her as she accepted her degree almost made up for the months of separation. "Why didn't you come to me after the ceremony or at the party?"

"Today was all about you. If someone had seen me, we wouldn't have had a moment's peace, and the magnitude of your accomplishment would've been lost in the chaos." Hands on her hips, he drew her close, brushing a light kiss over her mouth. A tease, a test, a temptation.

She had one last doubt to extinguish before giving in.

"The full moon," she began.

"Rises tomorrow night." He wound her hair around his finger, rubbed the strands against his cheek.

"You've been gone for three."

His gaze locked onto hers. Those blue and green eyes clear and true.

"I understand you needed a partner during the full moons, but I need to know if there were any other times." She dropped her head. "I don't want to wonder."

"There hasn't been anyone but you, Cas." He paused until she looked back at him. "I swear."

"I thought you had to have sex during a full moon."

"If you had completely closed yourself to me, I would've gone berserk because I want you. No one else can give me what you do, and when I finally reached you through the mate-bond and you let me in, that opened a whole new level of intimacy for us. Those nights you thought of me touching you, loving you, those weren't dreams, baby. That was our mate-bond, and what we shared is real as it gets." He reached into his jeans pocket and pulled out a velvet box.

"I love you, Cassidy Albright." Down on one knee, he flipped opened the cover to reveal an exquisite solitaire diamond in a platinum setting. "Will you be my mate? Through good times and bad? From now until we are no more?"

Cassie cried. Not the wrenching sobs that had raked her soul when Brice left, but giant tears of happiness. She'd have been a fool to say anything but "Yes."

Brice slipped the ring on her finger. "We'll have a ceremony, as big or small as you want. Whenever you want, wherever you want, but tonight, I'm going to make you mine."

He stood, picking her up. Cassie wrapped her legs around his hips and kissed him, pouring every ounce of her heart and soul into him.

He carried her into the master bedroom, never breaking contact with her lips until he lowered her to the great big heirloom bed.

"What about the taboo?" she asked.

"The old bedding is gone. I bought a new mattress set, and Rafe helped me get it here while you were at the party." Kicking off his shoes and socks, he shucked out of his sweater. "This one is all ours, baby."

He lifted the hem of her nightshirt, inching it up slowly over her abdomen. He kissed the slight curve of her stomach, laving a path to her belly button, then blew a warm breath over the moist trail. Chills burst forth on her skin while a liquid heat formed in her sex.

He rubbed his softly stubbled jaw across her midriff. The ticklish sweep of his whiskers awakened places recently neglected, except in her dreams.

She wanted his hands, his mouth, his skin. Here, there and everywhere. All at once.

"We don't have to go slow," she insisted.

"This is the first time I've made love to you, in person, in months. I'm going to savor every minute." He traced his mouth up her breastbone, kissing, then licking the valley between her breasts.

Her nipples tightened in tight, pointy buds, straining for attention. He focused his concentration on nipping the curve beneath her breasts while his hands teased her with feather-light strokes between her inner thighs, coming close to her apex but never quite reaching it.

"Oh, God," she groaned every time his fingers caressed the crease of her hip drawing down toward her mound. Each caress shot electrified ribbons of desire straight to her core.

He scraped his teeth across her nipple, flicked his tongue against the pinnacle, then sucked the achy bud into his warm, wet mouth at the same time he slid his fingers over her mound. A flood of creamy desire rushed her sex and dampened her panties. The friction of the wet material against her swollen folds was stimulating and frustrating.

"Take them off. Now!"

She heard a soft, sucking plop as he dragged his mouth from her breast. "Sorry, Sunshine. You're going to have to wait." Then he devoured her other breast.

The weight of his hand pressed against her mound, only to disappear when she began rocking her hips.

Turnabout was fair play, so she reached between their bodies, sliding her hand down his chest to the button on his jeans, and continued downward to the hard ridge pressing against the zipper. She ran her hand up and down the length, gently squeezing at random intervals.

Brice's breathing hitched. Something guttural vibrated in his throat, causing her sex to clench. Her clit ached. Her swollen folds throbbed. All the tension in her body bunched between her thighs.

Brice's lips skimmed the curve of her neck. His tongue danced in the hollow of her throat. She grabbed his face, pulled him to her mouth and fastened on his lips in an urgent, demanding kiss. She delved into his mouth, chasing his tongue, sweeping the inside of his cheeks, tasting a hint of cherries everywhere she explored.

Her short nails scraped down his chest. She tugged at the button on his jeans until it finally opened. She slid the zipper down, separating the teeth one at a time. She slipped her hand inside, loving the warm, velvety feel of hard, sleek maleness against her palm. Everything feminine in her electrified. Her sex became wetter, the clenching fiercer.

Growling a curse, Brice pushed away, shoved down his jeans.

Her breath caught in her throat at the sight of him, standing at the edge of the bed, rigid with desire for her. After all she'd put him through, he wanted her. Needed her. Loved her.

She loved him, too. Always had, she supposed.

"I'm revoking rule number one," she said. "Prance around the house naked all you want. I promise never to complain."

A stellar grin broke across Brice's face. "I'm not going to be the only one naked." He pounced on the bed and whipped off her nightshirt.

"Not complaining." She lifted her hips, allowing him to slide off her panties.

"Mine!" he growled, staring at her sex while tracing his fingertip along her seam and brushing her clit.

She groaned, aching for him to fill her completely.

"Get on your knees."

She did as he wanted, rolling onto all fours in the middle of the mattress. Her nipples pinched tighter and her sex throbbed in anticipation as she felt Brice move behind her.

He brushed aside her hair to caress the nape of her neck with his lips. One hand burned against her hip. The other slid down her stomach and cupped her mound. His long fingers curled, and the first tease of her folds caused her to buck from sheer lightning.

He entered her from behind, pushing slowly, sinking deeper and deeper until buried to the hilt with his sack pressed into her folds. The incredible sensation of joining with him again in the flesh nearly overwhelmed her. He'd never lost hope in their bond, and she was humbled by the fortitude of his faith in her.

He began thrusting gently and strummed her clit with matching strokes. She clenched, holding him deep inside each time he filled her. This was how he loved her, patient, caring and true.

The hand on her hip dug deep into her muscle. His thrusts came harder, faster, until a frenzy consumed them, driving them further and further over the edge. Her muscles tightened, pulling more and more tension into her sex.

The moment of her climax, she felt a sharp pinch from Brice's bite. His presence surrounded her body, infiltrated her mind and imprinted on her soul.

Her entire body trembled as a new eruption of indescribable pleasure exploded from her core, storming her senses from every possible direction. She didn't fear drowning in the pulsing flood because Brice was there with her. He would always be with her. She'd never have to face anything alone ever again.

His teeth remained clamped at the juncture of her neck and shoulder until the last wave of their orgasms subsided. Collapsing, Brice pulled her into the curve of his body, holding her close like a coveted treasure.

In unison, their pants slowed to deep, even breaths and their heartbeats returned to a normal, steady rhythm. After a few minutes, the roar of the tide subsided in her mind.

"I love you, Sunshine," he whispered in her ear.

Knowing he truly did, she murmured back, "I love you, too. *Benji.*"

Brice grinned easily. "Guess I need to work harder to convince you that I'm not a scruffy little dog."

Cassie laughed as he guided her hand to a very convincing part of his anatomy.

\* \* \* \* \*